A.A. Gill was born in Edinburgh in 1954, and studied at the Slade School of Art. He is the restaurant and television critic for *The Sunday Times*, for whom he also writes a weekly opinion piece, and he provides a regular cookery column for *Tatler*. Voted Critic of the Year 1997 in the British Press Awards, A.A. Gill has two children and lives in London. *Sap Rising* is his first novel, his second novel, *Starcrossed*, is also published by Black Swan, and he is also the author of *The Ivy Cookbook*.

D1392124

Also by A.A. Gill
STARCROSSED
and published by Black Swan

SAP RISING

A.A. Gill

BLACK SWAN

SAP RISING
A BLACK SWAN BOOK : 0 552 99679 3

Originally published in Great Britain by Doubleday,
a division of Transworld Publishers

PRINTING HISTORY
Doubleday edition published 1996
Black Swan edition published 1997

5 7 9 10 8 6

Black Swan Books are published by Transworld Publishers,
61–63 Uxbridge Road, London W5 5SA,
a division of The Random House Group Ltd,
in Australia by Random House Australia (Pty) Ltd,
20 Alfred Street, Milsons Point, Sydney, NSW 2061, Australia,
in New Zealand by Random House New Zealand Ltd,
18 Poland Road, Glenfield, Auckland 10, New Zealand
and in South Africa by Random House (Pty) Ltd,
Endulini, 5a Jubilee Road, Parktown 2193, South Africa.

Printed and bound in Great Britain by
Cox & Wyman Ltd, Reading, Berkshire.

For Flora and Hector

Chapter One

If you were a pigeon you could fuck forty times a day. It is something to be borne in mind when you are filling out the form for reincarnation. You'd also be able to fling yourself off the roof more than once. If you were a pigeon living in, say, Sussex, you might decide one morning to get away from the dreary grind of rape and silage and go and visit the city. Sample the crust and cake pots, take in the sights.

If you were a pigeon, one of the sights you would undoubtedly ache to take in would be Buchan Gardens. You might give the wife a quick hump as dawn broke, and set off up the A21. Over Royal Tunbridge Wells, past East Grinstead, over the M25, through Orpington, Sidcup, Bromley and Bexley and hit the river at about Greenwich. Seeing England roll away on every side, it will all look much the same as it has always done to thousands of generations of pigeons. To a pigeon, the tarmac and concrete tapeworms ferrying moulded shower attachments, plastic dog shit, lentils, humming risk assessors and women in love with riding instructors are just as natural as chine and fen. The land rises and falls as it always has.

Anyway, you've got to Greenwich; turn left, with the sun behind you and follow the Thames up to Vauxhall Bridge, then cross to the north bank over Pimlico and Belgravia, on to Knightsbridge and now glide for a couple of minutes. Beneath you and to your left is an odd forgotten corner of the new city, a quiet slice of London that isn't really anywhere; like the back of the cutlery drawer. All round is clatter and clamour, but here the old fish-knives and apostle spoons lie and mottle.

At its centre is Buchan Gardens. One and a half acres of immaculate, placid green. The garden is a neat oblong enclosed with black, bellicosely spiked railings. On three sides it is overlooked by a continuous five-storey creamy cliff of town houses. Their doors are porticoed and brassed, their windows long and elegant, their fronts pilastered and encarped. The fourth side of the square is occupied by St Bertha's, an unremarkable brick Victorian church that might be styled 'timid Gothic'.

The high classical buildings on each side make the garden look like a neat English Shangri-La, a secret place. Inside, wide gravel paths crunch like a railway hotel breakfast and the view is serenely splendid. Captive Nature weeps and tessellates, cantilevers and indentates in a glaucous glaverous curd, wrapping the garden in gorgeous shifting layers of camouflage. The paths are wide enough to accommodate a brace of Household Cavalry kettle drummers thumping abreast. They march past the very finest, the fittest, the most fecund, early rising, clean living examples of the husbandman's art. Hidden in this herbaceous border is a brick potting shed, like a South Coast gun emplacement. This, and four tank-trap benches, dedicated to fallen and forgotten square dwellers, are the only man-made things in the garden.

If you turn your back on the plants, you face the lawn. What a lawn, striped and ironed like an obsessive colour-sergeant's honeymoon pyjamas. In the middle stands a London plane tree.

It is arguably the finest plane tree in the entire city, and in a city blasé with impressive plane trees it may well be the finest plane tree on the continent. In the world. In fact, if they have plane trees on Alpha Centuri it's a fair bet that none of them could shake a twig at the one in Buchan Gardens. To a pigeon this is a once-in-a-lifetime tree, a tree to bore the gang about during the chilly November days in the stubble. Not, I may say, for its aesthetic arboreal value, but because this leviathan is the most exclusive pigeon brothel anywhere this side of the Bois de Boulogne. Its well-appointed branches are just hotching with feathered totty, all amazing specimens; no street-walking, feral birds here, with manky backsides and arthritic toes, no scrawny rock-doves looking for a quick bill and coo. These chicks are all prime woodies – pilgrim, stunning birds with pouting breasts and downy tummies, beady-eyed squabs who can do things with a flick of a quill that would drive any cock mad with desire.

You've glided long enough. Come on down, relax, find yourself a pigeon hole, exchange regurgitated brioche with a chick who is just dying for it, ruffle some feathers.

From behind the potting shed Angel Tenby shaded his eyes and watched the pigeon descend. The white bars of its wings caught the early morning sun. With his other hand he continued to rub his penis in that slow rhythmic way that true countrymen go about familiar tasks. He was vaguely remembering Brunt, the old gardener, who taught him almost everything he knew about earthy things. Brunt had forgotten more than most men knew about gardening and wanking.

'Young Angel, slow down,' he'd said in his soft, West Country burr, when he had found the fourteen-year-old shaking a quickie off the wrist behind the roller. 'Slow down, find Nature's rhythm. Now, to start with, get a proper grip. You don't want to squeeze the life out of him. Here, let me show you. There you are; firm but gentle. Look after him and he'll serve you all your life. Would you care for a go on my old thing?' and he flipped a vast gnarled knob out of his ancient mossy moleskins with just a touch of pride.

9

'Oh! What a beauty,' Angel had whispered. 'Can I really have a go?'

'Of course you can, boy. Don't expect a little chap like you is going to do much damage to it. It has been out every day, come rain or shine, for near on fifty years now. That's it, get a grip, gentle but firm. Two hands to start, and feel Nature's rhythm.'

There and then, Angel had decided that he would do anything to own a pizzle like this behemoth. And he would devote his life to country practices. He'd knelt and learnt at old Brunt's knee for seven years. Many is the rainy afternoon they had sat together in the Melon House, talking over earthy matters. Brunt sucking on a dottle-gurgling churchwarden, Angel chewing a purple Victoria. Together, gently but firmly, catching Nature's rhythms.

Angel now sat with his back against the warm ivy-cladding of the shed, his legs stretched out in the dappled sunlight. He was hidden from accidental view by a large stack of decaying grass cuttings. He breathed in the odour of hay and petrol, of bone and blood and hoof, of tarred twine and slug pellets, and the peculiar sweet perfume of his own crotch. He listened to the priapic pigeons in the branches above, and looked down at his penis – a real countryman's tool. The handle fitted with snug familiarity into his palm, the tool remembering the craftsman's grasp. Now, after all these years' use, it had grown to be quite like old Brunt's: huge, gnarled and bent with use, burnished a glossy teak colour, friendly to the hand. It had indeed served him well. The foreskin was a bit loose – perhaps it didn't have quite the rigidity it once did – but Angel wouldn't have swapped it for anyone's, not his tool, they would bury him with it. With a twinge of pride he felt the semen thickly rise like bubbling tapioca. With a practised movement he pulled a packet of delphinium seeds from his waistcoat pocket, held it open with finger and thumb, and, with a nonchalant flick, splashed two thick globs of jissom neatly inside.

'Never waste your juices,' old Brunt had said; 'they're Nature's bounty and the gardener's friend. Spunk into a seed packet, or a tray of seedlings, anoint a tomato or nourish a marrow, but never waste it boy, it's the syrup of life. Adam was the first gardener and before Eve seduced him with his own Russet, he'd mulched Eden and so it's been with countrymen ever since.'

Old Brunt had been assiduous about not wasting any of his functions. He'd crapped in the strawberry beds, casually wiping himself with the frost-hardened straw, he'd saved his pee in jars, buckets, old coffee pots, and, on occasion, when no other receptacle was available, in Angel's Thermos. He'd kept it all in an ancient watering-can, till it was viscous and cloudy and smelt like a tannery. Then he would carefully bathe the asparagus with it. Brunt even spat with accuracy and care. When he died, Angel had taken his ashes and forked them into an ailing wisteria that clung to the west front of the Big House. Within two years the creeper had blocked out every window on three floors. Come summer its pendulous flowers had been unbelievable. Spectacular buboes hung livid and purple, a monstrous haemorrhoid. It had hummed like a turbine with a million insects and twitched like a warm cadaver.

Angel was an old-fashioned gardener. He was almost of the garden; solitary and smelly, he worshipped nature without sentimentality or favour. Everything about him seemed hard and strong; his joints bulged like a coppiced poplar and his long fingers were as tough and supple as birch hurdles. He could have been anywhere between twenty-five and sixty.

He never ventured beyond the railings of the garden, spending his days wanking into seed packets and eating earth. He was not a gardener who had grand landscaping plans; he had no wish to create, just to be part of it all. He understood the futility of trying to harness nature. Rather Angel was a verger in a wild church, sweeping leaves and tending the dying; vowing that he had less power than thistledown.

'Try lifting that paving-stone,' he once said to Charles Godwin, the Garden Committee president. 'No, don't bother, you'll just put your back out and I'll have to call an ambulance. But this bit of fluff, this aimless seed, will lift and break that slab in a season, and it won't even notice. That peony in your

11

window that you're so fond of, it would root in your brain pan and sprout down your nose, just as happy as in that chinky pot. You may love it but it thinks no more of you than a car park does of Tennyson. People who talk about the delicate balance of nature have never tried to wrestle privet.'

It wasn't that Angel despised people, it was that he was simply uninterested in them. They were soft and riddled with doubt and pomposity. Angel didn't understand why all human life wasn't run like a vegetable garden, why cripples weren't simply pulled up and thrown onto the compost, why the old and infirm weren't ploughed under or left to be strangled by the young and vigorous.

Angel's greatest joy was knowing that he would die and be buried. Once he found a corpse in a ditch. It had only been there for six months, and already it was 50 per cent vegetable.

'You couldn't tell where the man started and the briar and the dog rose and the bladderwort stopped. It was wonderful, I sat beside it a long time and just breathed deep of the odour and let the Dame have her way. And then I had a bit of a wank, because I wanted to leave something of myself there, a sort of sacrament to the wonder of it all. The police said it was a young boy who had been abused and murdered on his paper round. I said at least he was being treated proper now. They kept me in a cell for a weekend and made me jerk off into a jar. "Don't you go and waste that," I said. "That rubber plant looks a bit like it needs some attention."'

Angel remembered these things languidly as he sat post-coitally in the warm sunlight.

'Tenby, Tenby?' a frail reed sung uncertainly across the lawn. Angel swore under his breath. Struggling to his feet, he folded his penis back into his fly, and walked slowly round the shed. He stepped onto the gravel path, carefully wiping a gobbet of semen onto an azalea, and watched a dapper man walk with fast, neat little steps across the lawn towards him. As the figure got to the plane tree, two dozen pigeons clattered out of the foliage and circled the square.

'Tenby, good news I bring,' the man called in an exaggerated staccato, a voice like a bishop's catamite at a gymkhana. This precise, polished little figure jarred with the discreet greens and greys of the square. He was utterly, glaringly, incontestably bogus.

'You've got dengue fever,' muttered Angel under his breath. 'Morning, Your Grace,' he said out loud.

The man who now stood in front of him, beaming his best servant's smile, was Lord Vernon of Barnstaple, quite probably the most easily and remorselessly mocked adult male outside sheltered accommodation. It wasn't just that he encompassed that blissful brace of ridicule – covert homosexuality and overt snobbery – it was that he was an object lesson in how to get it – all of it – wrong. He was like one of those picture quizzes in teenage girls' magazines where you have to spot the deliberate mistakes. Idle men at his club used to take it in turns to list the carefully considered solecisms as he stood beaming and hearty at the bar. The Cabochon dress cuff-links worn with a business suit. The four inches of shot cuff and cutaway collar a different colour from the shirt. The fob chain dangling from the lapel. The indiscreet handkerchiefs; one cascading from his sleeve with more initials on it than an American Army corp, and the other gaudily frothing from his breast pocket. The tidemark where his foundation had been inexpertly smudged into his weak chin.

Vernon of Barnstaple had given more pleasure to more people as an unconscious object of ridicule than he ever had in a lifetime of dedicated public service as a Conservative politician, and latterly as the chairman of various fey quangos.

'Fine tidings, Tenby. This morning I received a missive from the Principessa's secretary telling me that she will be able to grace our little soirée *dans le jardin* after all. Now, I've come to tell you first because I know it will excite you, and there must be a million things you want to do to the gardens so that they appear at their very finest.'

Tenby slowly looked at the square over Vernon's shoulder. He noted the neat beds, the lawn like hand-knotted Axminster, the raked gravel paths, the sunlight playing over the utter perfection of it all, and grunted. This was not quite the reaction that the old poof had wanted.

'You do know that the Principessa's gardens at Villa Santa Donatella are quite beyond anything.' He pronounced the Italian like a sixteen-year-old ordering spaghetti for his girlfriend. 'I have never had the privilege of viewing them myself but I have a marvellous book. We can't compete for their sheer grandeur, of course, but we can perhaps show our humble patch of greensward to its best advantage.'

'Have you told the Committee you're planning a party?' said Angel.

'Not yet – thought I'd tell you first. We only have a week you know. I don't envisage any problems in that department,' Vernon replied testily.

'If you say so. I'd better have a word with Charles, though.' Angel peremptorily finished the conversation by spitting into a rhododendron, and turning back to his shed.

'Really!' muttered Vernon. The glow that had bathed his morning when the engraved and escutcheoned card from Florence had revealed its good news over the wheatmeal toast, fat-free spread and thin-cut marmalade had dimmed. He had wondered for a moment, while he carefully put scented, cedar-wood shoe-trees into his monogrammed slippers, whether to bring it to show Tenby but had decided against. He didn't want it sullied by rough hands. It was now safely propped up on his cluttered mantel beside last year's invitation to a royal garden party and a stiffy for a £120-a-seat charity ball in a discothèque.

Vernon made his way back to his flat. He thought crossly about Tenby. The man always managed to make him feel uncomfortable, wrong-footed. He, on the other hand, was always charming, never overfamiliar, never patronizing. Vernon prided himself on what he called his common touch, honed, he thought, by years of canvassing his horrible pooterish constituency, a stucco nest of seaside landladies and penny-arcade millionaires on the Lincolnshire coast. How was it that this mere gardener, this peasant with questionable personal habits, always managed to make him feel like a prep-school boy being interviewed by the headmaster? Vernon assumed that was what he felt like. In fact his only connection with prep schools had been entirely pederastic.

The reason he felt discomfited was that Vernon the noble lord, for all the artifice of Jermyn Street and Savile Row, was quite plainly as common as pimples in a youth club. And it was equally obvious that Angel's blood was as blue as an early Picasso, despite the camouflage of mulch, moleskin and the lengthened vowels. Angel was the second son of an ancient earl. Vernon was a man who had assiduously dedicated his life to reinventing himself. So many years had been spent playing make-believe in other people's dressing-up boxes that when he had heard Angel's surname – a name that he knew well, whose coat of arms he could expatiate on, whose Latin motto he could translate, whose ancestral home he'd paid £5 to wander jealously around – he couldn't, wouldn't, connect it with the man who toiled beneath his swagged window. The truth would have struck a horrible blow to the very core of Vernon's jealous, insecure courtier soul.

Lord Vernon of Barnstaple, life peer and closet homosexual, was driven by a high-octane mixture of insecurity and shame. It had driven him a long way, from humble, horrible beginnings as the son of a housemaid in North Wales. Iris nurtured him with suffocating regret and bitterness. He, in return, treated her with contempt and deep embarrassment. His first taste of the humiliation that was to drive him to fame, riches, power and ridicule was having by far and away the smallest penis in the bath after rugby – a game that still made him shrivel and shudder.

He joined the Young Conservatives because the Scoutmaster who first gently took his virginity was a member. Vernon fell deeply in love with the Scoutmaster and was devastated when the man married a Welsh Nationalist librarian from Pontypridd. His big break came at a party conference when, at the age of nineteen, as one of only a handful of paid-up party members from the Valleys, he spoke for a motion that said 'The Union of the United Kingdom is the Greatest and Most Successful National Federation in History and Should be Celebrated with a National Holiday'. He finished his rather squeaky, singsong speech with the ringing phrase, 'What this country needs is a little less Celtic fringe and a little more short back and shires'. Being a particularly dull conference, the phrase was taken up by the press, and photographs of the small, shallow Welshman with a severe short back and shires filled the front pages. At the same time Vernon also came to the notice of a whip of Monday Club persuasion, who took him on as a researcher and catamite. He lost two hopeless Welsh selection boards and his accent, and that might have been that. The whip was retired to the Lords for allegedly entertaining rent-boys and Vernon found himself without a job or prospects.

In desperation he called the Arts Minister, a man he had met at party functions twice, and manually assisted with a bodily function once. Grudgingly, the minister asked him to come down for the weekend. He had no intention of picking up the whip's cast-offs. Stackpole was a revelation to Vernon. To a seasoned country house *aficionado*, it was not a house that merited more than a passing glance. For Vernon, whose architectural and social education had been limited to Welsh parlours and brutalist committee rooms, Stackpole was an imitation of Heaven. As he was shown into the hall with its Ashanti spears, portraits of pre-pubescent midshipmen, and frayed maps of bits of the estate that were now Bovis culs-de-sac, he felt a welling of envy and self-pity that was almost physical. It was a revelation that was as profound and permanent as the conversion of a saint. This smell of ancient dust, this dull gleam of fading gilt, this vision, this sense of yellow age, would be Vernon's Eldorado, his Grail, his best of all possible worlds.

By the end of the first Stackpole dinner he realized that the key to the future was the minister's wife. He used the one undoubted talent he had inherited from his mother, he was ingratiating and servile. The minister's wife, realizing that she had propelled her husband to the edge of his envelope, decided, on a whim, to start again with Vernon. It amused her, like training a gun dog. She was particularly entertained by the fact that he was such unprepossessing raw material. It made the challenge more exciting. After this weekend Vernon's career in politics and snobbery took off.

Vernon strutted back across the lawn and wondered idly whether to serve Pimms or champagne, or Pimms and champagne, and whether, if Angel were the last man in the world, lust would overcome taste.

Their brief meeting had been watched with depressed interest from the front ground floor window of No. 27 by a naked man who stood partially concealed behind a huge teak and ormolu writing-desk. 'God, that man's about as ridiculous as a man can be without wearing a red nose and having custard poured down his trousers,' the nude said over his shoulder to a sofa. 'I wonder why he's bothering poor Angel?' Charles Godwin picked up his cup of coffee and took a gulp, made a face, and considered the garden. It was looking particularly ravishing; simple yet stately; ordered yet organic; the bedding plants given room to flourish, each in its allotted space, complementing its neighbour; all served to make a uniform harmonious picture. If ever a shrub got above itself, or a lowly ground cover suffered, the fair but firm Angel was on hand to prune and relocate. Never passing judgement, never blaming, just doing what was right for the individual and in the best interests of the whole. Charles settled into a reverie on the 'Enlightened Political Paternalism of Urban Gardening'. Here were plants from the four corners of the globe, maples from Japan, rhododendrons from the high Himalayas, alpines from the precarious scree of Switzerland and heather from the peat hags of Caithness. All living leaf by stem happily together; individuals without a common language but bound with a common purpose. The trick was in choice and breeding. It needed a God-like hand to pick out the weeds. A weed, after all, is just a flower in the wrong place. Nothing in the garden in Buchan Square found itself in the wrong place, nothing was chosen at random. There was nothing random about beauty. Beauty could only flourish under strict discipline and order, administered by a benign, impartial omnipotent hand. All flourished under the dappling munificence of the plane tree – mighty and ancient – a true king, apart yet central, lofty but integral.

Charles's gaze drifted from the garden to the railings and on to the pavement. It was like turning a page of Rousseau and finding that it had been bound with Nietzsche. Ugly aggressive man jockeying for *Lebensraum*. The stinking crumpled tarmac painted with garish yellow dos and don'ts in guttural morse. The paving-stones furnished with hard smooth poles barking orders and shouting times like static drill sergeants. Green nature obliterated under a slick shit-mired plain. Cars aggressively parked, feet on the kerb, backsides provocatively skewed into the street, alpha baboons. Cars – men's alter egos – claiming territory. A little Morris Minor blocked in, bumper to bumper, by a killer Mercedes and a metallic armoured Audi. Might making right. How horrible, how crass. Charles's philosophical slow pan moved back through the window to the room he stood in.

It was quite something. One would hardly ever see so much clutter in one space outside an auction house or a BBC Dickens adaptation. Furniture, fixtures and fittings stood and hung from every vertical and horizontal plane. Someone had once said that it looked like a Ruritanian dentist's waiting-room or a conservation breeding area for occasional tables. That was less than fair. All the individual pieces were good, some were exceptional, but together they suffered. They seemed to nudge each other for attention, detracting, whispering polite 'excuse mes'. The whole was a free-for-all. A charming Davenport containing sombre nineteenth-century first editions sprouted a Tang horse, a lamp made out of a ginger pot with a toffee-tasselled silk shade like a pagoda, and four leather-tooled frames containing stupendously ugly Victorian women, one in the embrace of a defunct tiger. It was as if the bookcase's own understated charm and cerebral contents were not enough when compared with its neighbour: an outrageous gesso carved Italian table with a mosaic marble top and the bronze head of a gladiator, two

18

cut-glass candelabra, a pair of Meissen shepherdesses, thirteen Russian enamelled pillboxes and a French oval clock held aloft by Old Father Time, three cherubs and an unlikely classical ruin. The room looked as if it had been invited to sit down and eat furniture and had well and truly overindulged itself.

Charles sighed. His possessions swamped and stifled him. Other people stood on top of their possessions; their things raised them up. Charles just felt weighed down by his. He disappeared underneath them. How he wished he could be rid of them! Unfortunately, Charles was an animist. It was the closest thought he had to a religion. He believed – sometimes as strong as faith, he knew – that the furniture and the paintings, his things, had souls. Souls and memories. They knew him as intimately as he knew them. They reclined and judged him – not always kindly. He in turn placated them, curried favour by talking to them and spending more than he should keeping them happy, polished and screwed together in their endless, bad-tempered old age.

Charles caught sight of his pale long body in a circular Edwardian glass. The smoky mirror distorted him. Not much of a hero, he thought miserably. Probably one of the least inspiring things the mirror had ever reflected. Not brave enough or wayward enough to be interesting. He knew that few people who met him ever remembered him. If Charles had disappeared it would have been the most riveting thing he had ever done.

His body was in its late thirties and had been most of his life. He had blondish thinning hair, and was tall and slightly stooped, as if the air were a sagging Elizabethan lintel. He had a thin mouth that he unconsciously pursed most of the time. This tic, combined with his permanently knotted brow, gave him the look of a man with diarrhoea who thinks he is about to fart.

Two characteristics that redeemed this otherwise forgettable form were a pair of the deepest blue eyes that never blinked and the most beautiful hands in the world. Only women ever noticed Charles's hands. They were pale and etiolated with perfectly cut and polished nails. Naked of all adornment, they continually moved, they fluttered and stroked ceaselessly like hungry insects. They touched lightly, padded endlessly. His hands had a junkie's appetite for sensation; blindly they felt the surface of everything, skating along a marble tabletop, then darting to fondle a leather button. Stroking his cheek before running devil-may-care through his hair. When everything at arm's length had been fingered, they sat restlessly in his lap, playing lasciviously with one another.

There was a third thing about Charles that may or may not be important. He had sensationally elegant genitalia. One hears so much about size these days that perhaps it is worth spending a moment to discuss aesthetics. The first thing you would notice about Charles's meat and two veg was their perfect proportion; as if designed by an ancient Greek using a mathematical formula of beauty, they were like a gazebo set in a Capability Brown landscape. The penis was a delicate pale sienna, sporting a smooth foreskin that swelled as aerodynamically as the wheel arch of a Ferrari. When erect, the whole edifice cantilevered with the elegant curve of a Viennese art nouveau figure. Beneath this Corinthian cock, adding weight and *gravitas,* was a smooth, taut opulent scrotum that might be an evening purse or a guinea pouch of the softest kidskin. It held two perfect oval testicles, the left hanging a touch lower than the right in a manner to show the ensemble at its best advantage. The whole was framed in a riot of Hellenistic, antique gold curls. It all looked simply stunning.

Charles rarely used his cock to do much more than relieve the pressure on his bladder. Like taking a rare and fabulous Hispano Suiza out for a ride, the penis is a wonderful idea, but in practice inconvenient, slow and noisy, and Charles was always worried that it might break down halfway.

It was not just his genitalia that had fantastically good taste, Charles was overwhelmed by good taste. He was buried under tertiary terminal good taste. He couldn't drop a shopping bag without the contents arranging themselves in a pleasing still life. Taste was Charles's disease. In a car-boot sale the only good piece would cleave to him like an unwanted sick puppy. There was no effort in his eye, just an innate gift. In a right world where people with big hearts would become social workers, those with a sense of justice, policemen, and men with weak stomachs, chefs, Charles would be a curator. His eye put to service on behalf of the nation's heritage, he would summon up a golden age of municipal beauty.

Morosely he watched himself in the mirror and listened to the room creak and mutter.

The Davenport whispered to the Chinese Chippendale, 'Who does he think he is? What's he ever done to deserve me? He's not worthy to oil my hinges. I belonged to a mad venal count. Now *he* was a man, he knew the worth of furniture. He once bent an imperial grenadier over me and buggered him so violently that there are still teeth marks in my finials. That was a man who knew what a commode was for.'

'Quite,' replied the chair. 'What does this grey little mannequin, with his twittering fingers, know about living up to his furniture? When I was young and living in a palace, children would play on me, fit to break my back. Once a general who had sacked a hundred towns, leaving nothing but ashes and split hymens behind him, drank so much hock that he pissed himself through my satin cushions. I have been the last stick standing in a game of musical chairs where a grand duchess and a serene highness fought to push their bottoms onto me. Once a footman cut his throat and bled to death with his head in my lap. Those were the days when it was worth being a chair. People knew the worth of furniture.'

'He has taste, though, this chap,' said a rosewood and ivory coffee-table from Fez. 'He found me in the Stygian gloom of a junk shop, buried under a G-plan room divider and a marbled melamine headboard with attached occasional tables.'

'He does have an eye, but does he have a life?' interrupted an arch secretaire.

Charles shuddered and shook his head to silence the voices, and turned his gaze again to the garden. What a contrast. How great was Nature. How clever was Angel.

He was jerked from his day-dream by his realization that Lord Vernon had changed direction and was now mincing purposefully towards his window. Charles imitated a lamp stand in the hope that he might physically as well as metaphorically merge into the room.

'What ho, Charles,' the phony voice called through the open window. 'I bring a missive from o'er the Rubicon. How *very* nice to see you.'

Charles smiled weakly, and, following Vernon's gaze, remembered, with a start, that he was naked.

Chapter Two

'I am so pleased you could all come at such short notice,' said Charles, carefully threading his way between a boule commode and Khedival silk ottoman with quattrocento Venetian tapestry cushions. He placed the lacquer tray with the Genoese silver coffee pot and a porphyry plate of biscuits safely onto a Bangalore antelope-hide pouffe. 'Help yourself to the Bourbons everyone. They forget nothing and learn nothing.'

He bit his lip and swore silently. Why did he say such camp twinky things, for Christ's sake? He knew that most of the Garden Committee suspected him of being a turd-burglar already, living alone in this temple to creamy good taste. Bon Bon Velute had said, 'My, it's lucky you don't have children,' as if it were a prediction, when she first visited the flat.

The Garden Committee sat on various bits of antique loveliness, their knees clasped, their elbows glued to their sides, their heads slowly swivelling from side to side like a coachload of pensioners passing a particularly sumptuous road accident. The first ten minutes of every meeting were inevitably taken up by one of them finding some previously undiscovered geegaw and cooing over it. They would make Charles tell them where it came from and how much it was worth. He hated discussing his things in front of them. It was like doctors talking about their patients in geriatric wards. It seemed so rude, so uncaring. He could sense the room sucking its teeth with disapproval. Celeste Kotzen's eyes lit up at the sight of an Egyptian mummified ibis that was lurking behind a copse of Georgian treen, but Charles swiftly opened the meeting before she had a chance to enquire.

'Shall we start, Bon Bon? Will you read the minutes of the previous?'

'Minutes of the Buchan Gardens Garden Committee – 28 June. Present were Charles Godwin, President; Celeste Kotzen; Bryony Mullins; Dr Spindle; Stephen Marle; and Bon Bon Velute, Secretary. Apologies from Colin Royster. Colin is much better, by the way. I saw him last week – the bandages will be off any day and the smell should subside.'

The Garden Committee was a soft pastel collection. A glance would have told you that they were middle class. Their residence in Buchan Gardens placed them squarely at the smug end of comfortable. To an outsider, to a man herding the middle classes into a cattle truck, there would have been little that differentiated them, but, like Protestant sects, it wasn't the great orthodoxy that they held in common but their minute differences that each of them polished like amulets against their neighbour's evil eye.

Bon Bon Velute felt the most vulnerable. She knew that she hadn't been born to live in Buchan Gardens and she knew that the others knew. A short, childish-looking thirty-five-year-old, she had married the semi-retired rock star, Belman. He had been attracted to the narrow-shouldered fifteen-year-old by her long blond hair and huge breasts. In deference to his tastes and as a proof of the efficacy of their long and essentially happy marriage, she still wore as much of her bosom outside her clothes as possible and her hair in an adolescent fringe. Bon Bon had never worked although she called herself an ex-model, her left breast having appeared on one of Belman's record sleeves with 'Mother's Ruin' and a syringe tattooed above the nipple. She joined the Garden Committee because she had that working-class urban belief that anything green and clipped is posh.

Celeste Kotzen was not English at all, or middle class. She was Hungarian and aristocratic. Her parents had brought her to London as an infant during the Budapest uprising of '56. After St Mary's, Wantage and a stint in a West End gallery, she had ended up sounding as English as church bells and whips on buttocks. If you saw Celeste the words that would probably spring to mind by free association would be trim, svelte, brittle and bitch. She had a neat angular face, with lips that were slightly too thin, a nose that was slightly too long and dark eyes that might have been borrowed from a semi-vegetarian shark. She was married to a man whom no-one had ever met and who left the house before dawn and arrived back after dark. Celeste was referred to as Countess Dracula in and around the square. She had a taste for perpendicular sex with large young men, preferably in hats. She had joined the Garden Committee because she felt the garden added at least £5,000 to the value of her house, and Celeste had never quite shaken off the immigrant's belief in the essential goodness of bricks and mortar.

Stephen Marle was universally loathed and he knew it and worked hard at it. He could have been any one of those supporting villains that Shakespeare always did so well in the histories. He was soft and unctuously handsome, with thick blond hair and thick blond teeth. He worked, a little, as a freelance architectural historian and critic, but most of his time was spent as a professional boyfriend. Some, no, truth to tell, all the members of the square referred to him as 'that disgusting little rent-boy'. This was a cruel judgement. Stephen had given up actually charging by the hour some years ago and he had only started because his childhood hadn't been everything it might. To Stephen's eternal fury it hadn't been cosmopolitan, titled and wealthy. It had, in fact, been cruelly ordinary, with a single parent of each sex, a sister and a dog called Polly. Stephen blamed most of the unhappiness of his life on the bitter fate that had inflicted quiet love and middle-class comfort on his formative years. He had joined the Garden Committee because Lord Vernon told him to, and, in general, he did what Vernon told him to because that's what Vernon paid for.

Nobody ever enquired of what Dr Spindle was a doctor. Charles hoped it wasn't medicine. If at some unfortunate time a person had to call 'Is there a doctor in the house?' on Charles's behalf, Dr Spindle was definitely not whom he wished to see parting the crowd. The doctor's defining characteristic was his smell. It was a pervasive, sweet-savoury damp, animal with vegetable connections smell. A pervasive odour that always waddled a couple of steps behind its owner, like a fat dog. The doctor looked like an old photograph. He was monochrome and gritty, his features were imprecise, and you felt that they might come off on your fingers. He suffered from all the freedoms that old bachelors revel in. The freedom never to wash more than a quarter of his body at a time; the freedom to wear the same clothes for a month; the freedom to eat slimy tinned ham and processed peas every day; the freedom to have conversations without end or point; and the freedom to hum the 'Dambusters' March' over and over again. He had joined the Garden Committee because he had some very interesting and, although he said it himself, ground-breaking theories on horticulture, and because he was a pedantic old bore and pedantic old bores are drawn to captive groups who meet regularly.

Bryony Mullins was a handsome woman without frills. Her face had been eroded and polished by thirty African summers and twenty-two Scottish autumns and sixty-eight Wiltshire winters and a similar number of springs improvidently thrown to the rest of the world. Her grey hair was cut for expedience rather than style and her clothes, mostly tweed and leather, followed its sartorial lead. The first time she had stepped into Charles's flat, she had shaken his hand like a groom tossing off an impotent stallion and boomed, 'Quick, point me at the crapper. I've got a chocolate teddy's arm that's fit to split me from arse bone to piss flaps. If I hold on a moment longer I'll be buggered and fucked all at once.' Charles had simply gaped and pointed.

There is no point in my introducing you to Colin Royster as he is dying.

'Minutes of the previous dum-ti-dum-ti-dum,' read Bon Bon. 'Matters Arising dee-di-dee-di-dee. Number one – general discussion on the wording of the new sign for the East Gate regarding correct usage of fewer or less as regards groups of accompanied minors. Dr Spindle said he would contact the Pronunciation Department of the World Service on behalf of the Committee.'

'No joy yet, I'm afraid,' chipped in the doctor. 'Should hear in a few days – or less than that. Sorry, my little joke.'

'Proposal to purchase new hoe owing to perishing of shaft of old. General discussion ensued. Celeste said she might have a spare one in the country. Bryony opined that an adze might be more suitable and a longer-lasting tool. I, Mrs Bon Bon Velute, suggested that a new handle might be the answer. A spirited discussion ensued as to which wood would be most suitable for said handle. No firm decision was reached. Dr Spindle was deputed to look into the wood *vis-à-vis* durability, cost and splinters. And Bryony said she would try to get her hands on an adze anyway.'

'Jury's still out on the wood,' said the doctor, 'although ironwood from Botswana is definitely looking promising.'

'I tried Peter Jones for an adze but they don't stock the buggers so I'm going to put in a call to Oxfam,' added Bryony.

'In the meantime,' continued Bon Bon, 'the President was asked to tell Tenby to make do with his other tools. The Committee unanimously agreed to leave the reseeding of the bald patch around the plane tree in the capable hands of the President and Tenby.'

'All done,' chipped in Charles. 'Angel and I spread our seed on the barren ground last Wednesday,' and then he swore at himself again and tried to frown in a butch way.

'The garden account for the month stands at £12.52 debit, leaving a running total of £24.38 credit in the current account and £543.00 in the contingency deposit account. In Any Other Business Stephen Marle said that the Committee might like to consider purchasing some sort of practical yet attractive uniform or livery for the gardener, because, whereas the garden looked splendid, the gardener was something of an eyesore. The President said he would give it some thought. There being no other business Mrs Velute proposed a vote of thanks to the President which was carried unanimously.'

Bon Bon put down her pad and smiled at the room. Reading the minutes was something she took great care over. She looked expectantly at Charles. It was at this juncture that he usually said, 'Very nicely put, Bon Bon', and made her feel like the girl who won the prose recital prize at school back in Brize Norton.

Before he could open his mouth Bryony Mullins broke in. 'Let's get the screaming fuck on with it,' she snorted. 'Are we going to let that semen-dribbling, wet fart of a queer peer have his orgy in our garden, and play daisy chains with his loose-sphinctered bum-chums, while a lot of sandpaper-snatched fag-hags spike the sodding grass with their white peep-toed stilettos?'

Stephen Marle winced, as if a blow were threatened to his midriff. Bon Bon didn't bother to write anything down. Bryony's swearing was accepted as a sort of disease by those who knew her. If she had said 'damm' or 'bloody hell' a lot then somebody might have taken her aside and said '*pas devant*' or something, but cursing on such a grand baroque scale seemed unconfrontable.

'I must concur with Bryony,' said the doctor. 'The garden rules are quite specific – no organized public gatherings of any sort shall be permitted. I'm surprised that Vernon should even have mooted the project.'

'I must say I think you're being somewhat unreasonable,' interjected Marle. 'These are merely rules not Holy Writ. They are there for the good governance and smooth running of the garden. I don't think we can really object to a man of Lord Barnstaple's standing showing a few friends round and offering them a glass of champagne. I think it would be unconscionably rude of the Committee to make an issue of it, leaving aside the fact that the purpose of the soirée is entirely in the public good.

As I am sure you are aware, the Principessa's art collection may well find a home in this country if she is courted in the right manner. And as the Prince of Wales is coming, I really think it behoves us to bend to Lord Barnstaple's request.' The moment he said it, Marle knew that this final phrase was a mistake. He opened his mouth as if to swallow the offending words again, but Bryony grabbed them like a terrier.

'You can bend for the shite-gobbler all you want, Marle. I think the rest of us will keep our botties to the wall and our backs ramrod straight. I for one won't have that dirt-box truffle hunter expecting us to simply swallow it on the nod because some mulatto whore who fucked her septuagenarian husband to death has inherited a couple of smutty etchings and wants to use them to meet the cunty Prince of Wales.'

'I'd quite like to see the Principessa,' Bon Bon said quietly. 'They say she's very beautiful. Belman played for her thirtieth birthday in Monaco – he said she was really something.'

'We must bear in mind the precedent,' said the doctor. 'If we allow Vernon to use the garden for a party, however decorous and worthy, we really don't have a leg to stand on when the next Tom, Dick or Harry asks. Before we know where we are we will be having pop concerts. Sorry, nothing personal intended, Bon Bon.'

'Well frankly, I don't care much one way or the other,' said Celeste. 'We're going to be away that day, and anyhow, I suggest we leave it up to Charles. You've spoken to him once already, haven't you? What do you think?'

'Well.' Charles hesitated. 'He caught me at something of a disadvantage and I was noncommittal. I said that I would have to consult with all of you first. My initial feeling was that we should decline, but Vernon was very persuasive and said that he had already sent out the stiffies and to dish at this juncture might cause some sort of diplomatic incident, and frankly I'm wavering.'

'Sodding cheek of the man,' spluttered Bryony. 'Railroading you with his filthy politician's tricks. You're too nice you know.' The members of the Committee nodded in agreement.

'It is, of course, entirely down to you Charles,' said Marle.

'Yes,' said Charles unhappily.

At this juncture it might help to explain briefly how the governance of the garden was achieved. Angel Tenby was, in effect, the secretariat, the civil service. He was responsible for the impartial day-to-day running of the garden, and was expected, unquestioningly, to put into effect the Committee's decrees. In practice, like all civil servants, he picked and chose, doing what suited and finding circumlocutory ways of avoiding the rest. The Committee was the executive, the people's representative. They worked with and amended the huge volume of law that had been handed down from committee to committee since time immemorial. It was made up of an undetermined number of square dwellers and it was self-appointing. Members sat for as long as they could stand it. At their head was the President. The President's power was absolute. The book of statutes ran to several hundred pages and included such arcane laws as 'Perambulators shall be conveyed in a clockwise direction at speeds including but not exceeding 3 m.p.h. – sub section: all perambulators must contain an infant' (this last amendment had been added when a tramp, finding the gates unlocked, had parked a vastly overloaded, odoriferous grey pushchair onto the lawn). However, Rule 57 boldly stated that the President shall take any action that he deems in the best interests of the garden, and that the President's decision may overrule all singular or some rules laid down by statute. In reality the President could do whatever he liked. This worked admirably so long as he did nothing.

The election of the President was as arcane and Machiavellian as the election of a Pope. Charles still didn't really understand how the lifetime appointment had fallen to him. The obvious choice had been Vernon, who had served vocally and assiduously on the Committee for five years and, when the previous incumbent had slipped slowly into dementia, had taken over the running of the garden. However, he was not liked by the Committee and they had baulked at handing him the whip and reins of power, though no-one could be induced to stand against him. Just as they thought that the position was lost, and just as Vernon counted it won, a removal van had stopped outside No. 27. Actually, a whole fleet of removal pantechnicons had blocked the entire square and gingerly proceeded to decant Charles's things. In many a window curious faces examined the treasures as they were paraded by brown-coated minions. Each new arrival brought forth little sighs of avarice and wonder. After an hour of this antiques roadshow, Bryony made three brief telephone calls and Celeste was deputed to approach Charles, who lingered on the pavement imploring the hirelings to be careful.

'Good morning.' Charles had turned and seen an elegant, brittle, immaculately accessorized lady who had been forty for almost five years. For a brief moment he thought she had been unpacked by one of the brown-coated men.

'I am Celeste Kotzen, your new neighbour. Welcome!' Then she paused and said, 'You are going to live here, aren't you?'

'Yes. Hello. I'm Charles Godwin and this is my furniture,' said Charles, unnecessarily pointing.

'You don't mind my asking, but do you have a job?' Celeste smiled at him disarmingly.

'Oh well, I er actually, no, well yes, sort of. I teach bridge a bit.'

'Oh good,' said Celeste.

'You don't play bridge, do you?' said Charles.

'Oh no, I can't stand it.'

'Oh good,' said Charles, 'neither can I.'

'I know this is a bit forward, and you must think me terribly pushy, but would you mind awfully being President of the Garden Committee?'

'Well, I don't know anything about gardening.'

'Oh, that doesn't matter, we've got a man for that. It's just that we need a President, rather badly. It doesn't involve much, just a couple of meetings a year. Basically it runs itself.'

'Well, I'm not sure,' said Charles as he watched a pagoda of Chinese Chippendale chairs rock precariously past.

'It would be a good way of getting to know everybody,' said Celeste winningly.

'Oh well, OK then, yes. Thank you.' Charles leapt past her in time to catch an alabaster saint who was rolling towards a second martyrdom.

From his balcony across the square, Vernon of Barnstaple watched the caravan disembark its opulent cargo with buttock-clenching envy, and buttock clenching was not something he practised often. 'Inheritance,' he muttered over and over like a mantra. 'Inheritance.' A vile chemical cocktail, more powerful than adrenalin, flowed through his veins. It made his palms damp and his eyes prickle. As Celeste turned and walked away, giving a thumbs-up in the direction of Bryony's flat, he felt also the cold chill of Nemesis.

Charles quite enjoyed being President of the Garden Committee. It was a nicely pointless job. The decisions that had to be made were of such monumental trivia that they managed to consume vast amounts of energy and time, and as most of Charles's life was spent in attempting to neatly dispose of time and energy it suited him very well. The end result was so obviously blameless and worthwhile. The garden was so obviously a 'good thing' in a world where there were very few things that were undeniably, unarguably good.

Now that the formal business was finished, they got down to gossiping. Bryony, Bon Bon, Mrs Kotzen and the doctor started to speculate on the relationship between the middle-aged couple in the ground floor flat at No. 28.

'What that woman needs', said Bryony, 'is to be bent over her precious Jacobean sideboard by a dozen Trinidadian limbo dancers and rogered without ceasing until the spunk spurts from her ears and she sees visions.'

'It's an interesting theory,' said the doctor, trying to visualize it.

Mrs Kotzen was obliquely trying to question Charles on his love life when there was the sound of a key in the door and a small, ravishingly beautiful oriental girl, apparently wearing nothing more than a transparent housecoat, entered and stood in the middle of the room and surveyed the Committee with silent timeless oriental loathing.

The Committee swivelled and regarded her back.

'Ah, Lily, is it eleven already?' said Charles, his eyes drifting across the faces of the five clocks that syncopated mechanically in his room, and all pointed ornately to quarter past. 'Heavens, um, Lily Ng, the Garden Committee.' Charles pronounced the surname correctly, as the Chinese would pronounce it, as in the sound of a man with advanced piles negotiating constipation, nnnnnnnnggggggggg.

'Hello, Lily Ng,' said Lily, using the anglo approximation of her surname, 'Ing'. Charles's hands fluttered foolishly. 'I come to do, Charles, you go and dig garden now.'

The Committee took half a second to digest this order, and, as a man, shot to its feet. All of them had been taught from the earliest age that servants' orders must be obeyed instantly and without cavil. Everything stopped for the staff. It could be the first morning of your honeymoon, but if the maid knocked to turn down the bed you disengaged with alacrity and took a gondola until she had finished. Cleanliness was next to Godliness, and staff were the Almighty's representatives on earth, regardless of race, creed, colour or sex. In any other occupation Lily would have been roundly patronized by the Committee, but her exalted position as a 'daily' raised her above all that, raised her to the highest caste it is possible to attain in England, a servant, the untouchables.

'Yes, yes, quite so,' said Mrs Kotzen. 'Mustn't sit here jabbering when there is real work to be done.'

The Committee filed out. Bryony grabbed Charles by the lapel. 'Now remember, dear, you're not to bend over. Get some lead in that winkie of yours. Don't let that cock swallower turn you round. Stand firm and tell him where he can shove his fucking soirée, stiffy and all. Wouldn't even touch the sides – isn't that right, Marle?' she said maliciously. Stephen pulled a face and sidled past.

Charles closed the door on them and turned to Lily.

Chapter Three

'Now, Lily, do you think you could start on the dusting in here, I've bought you a new feather thingy. And then you could do the ironing, I know you don't like it but I can't send any more shirts to the dry-cleaners – they break all the buttons. And if there is any more time after that the bathroom needs . . .'

'Oh c'mon, Joe, let me show you a good time,' interrupted Lily in a singsong voice. She put one small hand on her little hip and pouted.

'Oh, Lily, please don't start all that again. Really, I'd far rather you did the dusting,' said Charles, with a fearful expression.

'You shy, Big Boy. I do you good and proper, very long slow jig-a-jig.'

'Lily, please, I must insist, the dusting.'

'I suck you big time, all the way, no spitting, deep throat.' She took a step forward and tweaked her nipple through the thin cotton of her housecoat, at the same time shoving two crimson-tipped fingers into her heart-shaped crimson mouth and making a slurping, sucking noise, pretending to swallow something huge and knobbly.

Charles took an involuntary step backwards, and his calf hit the Cyrenian coffee-table. The Royal Worcester jumped; a forgetful Bourbon slid to the floor. 'Lily, you're not to do this. You are my daily.'

'Daily, nightly, make it worth your while, Joe,' giggled Lily, making a grab for his groin.

Desperately Charles sidestepped and made a dash for the kitchen. 'I'm going to get the feather thingy, and you're going to dust.'

'Whatever you say, Joe. But I don't think so.'

Charles had found Lily Ng, like everything else in his life, by accident. He had been in Mr Patel's buying a paper. In front of him had been Bridie Cork, Bon Bon's housekeeper. She was an unpleasant woman, quick to make judgements and quicker to voice them. Clutching a copy of *The Lady* and the *New Musical Express*, she said, 'I noticed you've got another illiterate looking for skivvying work in the window, Mr Patel.'

'A Chinese girl came in last week, little thing, didn't look like she could lift a broom, wore sunglasses. She only paid for a week so it comes out today,' replied the shopkeeper.

'Chinese, well she would be. Illegal and under age, I'll be bound, they come from the four corners, don't they, to take jobs, Mr Patel? As if there weren't any local girls who'd give their eye-teeth for a job. Look at what she's charging though, £4 an hour. You wouldn't get a white woman to work for that, would you Mr Patel?'

Mr Patel busied himself in the box of rubber bands, paper-clips, ink-pads, old receipts, broken sweets and squashed packets of Regal that newsagents all keep to avoid talking to their customers.

'No, that you wouldn't, Mr Patel. Do you know why they can afford to charge so little, Mr Patel? Because they steal; they steal and they sleep five to a bed and they eat indecent bits of animals, Mr Patel. No morality, these foreigners, and they're lazy. They may be able to build stereos and such that you need a degree in engineering to find Jim Reeves on, but they don't know how to polish a brass finger-plate. The Chinese are the worst, you know. Up all hours, murdering each other, with tongs. They should be sent back. Live and let live, is what I say and they should live with their own. Why only last week . . .'

Charles shuffled uncomfortably and coughed.

Mrs Cork turned and looked him up and down. 'In a hurry are you Mr Godwin? Ever so sorry, thought you were a gentleman of pleasure.'

'If you don't mind, Mrs Cork, I'd just like to pay for the *Telegraph*.' She stood aside theatrically. 'Thank you. I couldn't help overhearing – you reminded me, I need a cleaner. Mr Patel, would you be so good as to give me that card.' Mr Patel leant across and pulled it out of the window. He caught Charles's blue eye with his own watery brown one, a hooded blank look, as emotionless as an owl.

'Are you going back home to Ireland for Easter, Mrs?' the old Indian said, without a trace of irony. The housekeeper pursed her lips like a razor-slash and breathed out noisily through her nose. 'Chance would be a fine thing. Some of us have to work all a Christian God's hours. Put this on account, if you'd be so good,' she mimicked Charles, gave the shop a critical once over and bustled out.

Charles bought his paper in silence. As he turned to leave, Mr Patel pulled a small paper bag from under the counter. 'Humbug, Mr Godwin?'

'Don't mind if I do, Mr Patel,' Charles smiled and caught the brown eye again; it remained inscrutable.

How Lily came to be a small card floating in a newsagent's window is a hard and sad story. She was half Chinese and half Vietnamese. Her father had been a third generation Mandarin, living just outside Saigon; her mother was Vietnamese. Her father worked as a school inspector throughout the wars, and when all the children had been drafted into the Army, or the schools were too dangerous to attend, the Americans had paid him to inspect empty classrooms. Lily's mother was a hairdresser, specializing in the ornate wigs of the classical theatre. When the war closed down the theatres she had done the hair for strippers and hostesses.

After the war her family's grasp on life was tenuous. Her father was sent to be re-educated in the paddy fields, and her mother was forbidden to work because she had married a Chinese. They all nearly starved.

Through a mixture of luck, connections and selling everything they owned, Lily's father got them on to a leaky fishing boat that set sail in the middle of the night, with the rudder lashed to a course set straight ahead. After two weeks at sea a British gun boat picked them up. Lily's first memories were of a camp in Hong Kong: the wire and the rain; the gangs and the charcoal fires; the impassive Gurkhas who patrolled the filthy alleys between the huts; the laughter and the plans; the raging inflation of intrigue and rumour.

After a year her brother was born, and a year after that there was an opportunity for her mother to take the infant to Canada. It meant splitting the family, but the little boy was ailing, and with an infinite sadness and stoicism they had all gone to have their photograph taken as a family for the last time. It was a snap of failure. Lily was five, she sat on her mother's knee, the woman's hands tight around her waist. She wriggled and looked straight, impassively, at the camera. The next day was the last time she had seen her mother, waving from the back of an army truck.

Six months later Lily and her father were on a flight to London. He had vague plans of reaching Toronto, but they ended up in a Chinese chippie in Kilburn. Then they lived in a two-roomed flat in a council block in Camden Town where their neighbours were Greek, Bengali, Nigerian, Persian, Senegalese, Croatian and drunk.

Lily went to the local school where she suffered – not from the other children, she was popular enough, ran fast and fought her corner. It was the teachers, with their liberal enlightenment, who assumed that Lily, being oriental, would be cleverer than the rest, that she would pick everything up effortlessly, because that was the thing about orientals, wasn't it? They worked hard and adapted. In fact, Lily wasn't very clever, and she had no aptitude for school work. When she had mastered enough of the language to feel confident she stayed away and hung out in the chip shop cleaning tables, mopping vomit. Her father benignly ignored her, squirrelling money for the promise of Canada, and writing beautiful empty letters to his son.

Lily was no trouble. She didn't do drugs, she didn't sleep around, she was quiet and respectful. The truth was that by the time she was fourteen she hadn't the slightest idea who she was, or how she should behave. She didn't mind Camden, but it was no more home than Hong Kong had been. She didn't have her father's fatalistic obsession with Canada. She didn't plan; she had no views on the future. She did, though, have a desperate secret passion for the country of her birth. She asked her father to tell her about Vietnam but he just said, 'Forget it Lily, it was a good place, then a bad place, then no place at all. It's gone now. I don't have any memories. Canada is the place.' But it wasn't for Lily. She wanted to be someone, something. She wanted to be Vietnamese. And not knowing left a hole at her feet. She cast no shadow here. She began to watch films about Vietnam. She watched with rapt attention all the syrupy Wagnerian angst that Hollywood wrung from the war that had finished before her birth. She watched them as if they were training manuals on how to be a Vietnamese girl and, slowly, she became a hard little street child. She relearnt the singsong whiny accent; she absorbed the patois, the slangy language of cheap sex in American tempo. She practised the walk and the moody languor; she wore sunglasses and searched the North London street markets for skimpy tat and Suzy Wong dresses. With no mother to show her how to be a woman, Lily invented one for herself out of *The Deer Hunter*, *Apocalypse Now*, *Platoon*, *Full Metal Jacket*, *The Green Berets* and a host of lousy, mawkish gung-ho television dramas.

Lily liked the person she became. She felt polished and hard, like jade. She felt slinky and sheer, like satin sheets. Smart and complete; airtight. Her father watched the metamorphosis as a sort of cartoon flashback and said nothing. It would all be sorted out in Canada.

Lily hadn't planned on having sex with Charles – it had just seemed easier than doing his cleaning. She might have acted like a red-light good-time girl, but she had, up until then, been rather miserly with her Teflon sexuality, and had certainly never done it for money. Once with a boy from school, just to open the account and have something to talk about, twice with a whip-thin cook at the take-away leaning against the Fanta crates, and a sort of maybe once with an American student who had picked her up after a matinee performance of *Platoon* and kept saying 'this is just too weird'.

She had wrapped herself in her sunglasses and her hardest personality and gone to Buchan Gardens. Charles's flat horrified her; all those things, all that clutter. She had always lived in spartan, minimal scrupulous rooms. She knew everything she and her father owned, and she could have packed it up and carried it on her back anywhere within ten minutes. How could one man accumulate so much that was pointless and untidy?

Charles had also had second thoughts about what was, after all, merely a gesture to put down that ridiculous Irish woman. Charles didn't let people into his life or loose on his things readily, and the sight of this blankly beautiful oriental girl standing on his doorstep in her tiny skirt and high heels, with one hip thrust almost to the point of dislocation, chewing gum as if her teeth were trying to escape, hadn't reassured him at all. But she had slunk past him into his hall and said, 'OK. Show me the ropes Big Boy,' and they toured the flat; Charles rattling warnings, directions, instructions; Lily chewing, deaf and appalled. The first day Lily worked like a vegetarian in an abattoir. She had picked up her money and was out of there, swearing that she would never go back. Charles silently promised that he would call her later in the week and ask her not to return. But the next Wednesday, there she was, and he let her in.

The sex happened by accident. Lily was looking for an ironing-board, and she walked into the bathroom. Charles was shaving, wearing only a towel. It reminded Lily of something she had seen in a TV film: a captain shaving in some brothel in 'Nam, the dog-tags flecked with foam, the old-fashioned razor, the heat and sweat, 'Country Joe and the Fish' on soundtrack, and, instead of turning round, she had said, 'Hey Joe, let me do that,' and she had slid between a speechless Charles and the basin and taken the razor from his hand and shaved him very slowly, very neatly. Charles had watched his own stupefied face in her sunglasses as she ran the razor down his cheek and whispered, 'It's one, two, three, what are we fighting for? Don't ask me, I don't give damn, next stop is Vietnam.' When she had finished, she gently tugged the towel from his waist and dabbed his face. Then, putting both hands on his shoulders, she had lifted herself onto the rim of the basin, hoisting her knees up to her hips. She spat the gum out. 'Kissing tongues is extra, Soldier Boy,' she said.

Lily liked fucking Charles, or at least she liked the business of seducing Charles. It was fun and it made her feel Vietnamese. It made her feel at home.

Charles hated being seduced by such an awful tasteless cliché. He hated the fact that he rather enjoyed fucking the 'daily' even more. Each time Lily left he swore it was the last, that the next time she would hoover or she would go. And occasionally he would get his way; he would be out when she came, and Lily would morosely shift dust, but mostly Lily got her money the easy way, the Hollywood way.

'Lily, here's the feather thingy.' Charles came back into the room holding a long multi-coloured feathery stick like a parrot kebab. He held it at arm's length. Lily was rummaging in her bag.

'Lily what are you doing?'

'Just putting some atmosphere on the stereo, Joe.'

'Well keep it down.'

'It's our tune, baby. "Miss Saigon".'

'It's not our tune, we don't have a tune. It's only a tune in the most liberal sense of the word. Look Lily, this has got to stop, I mean it. Listen to me – you're here to clean the flat and do the ironing. I know that in the past we've sometimes been, well, sometimes been sidetracked, but it's got to stop.'

'Oh, Soldier, you going to beat me with your stick? You going to abuse me, Soldier? You like to tickle my pussy with your parrot?'

'Lily, please, don't. I'm putting the feather thingy down now and I'm going out. I want you to dust.'

Lily smiled and made a naughty boy clucking noise and darted between Charles and the door.

'Lily, please.'

Lily shrugged in a fluid serpentine movement and the thin housecoat fell to her ankles. She was naked from her glasses to her stilettos. She put both her hands behind her head and aimed her body at Charles, and as bodies go it went.

Lily's body was as close to belonging to a little boy as it's possible to be and still join the Brownies. It was slim to the point of emaciation, delicate and supple; her legs were long and bony, only meeting each other briefly at the calf and the knee. Her hips jutted and her breasts looked like the end of ice-cream cones, with long tensile nipples. Her tummy curved adolescently down to a bald man's nape of pubic hair, which inefficiently fringed her slotted pudenda. All together, she looked heart-stoppingly frail and young, until you got to her face, with its broad, bow-shaped painted lips and black glasses, high cheeks and neat geometric hair.

The whole image raised strong and contradictory feelings in Charles. He wanted to wrap her in a blanket and alternately ravish her and read her *Black Beauty*. He also quite seriously wanted her to do the dusting. 'Oh Lord,' he said faintly.

'You long cock want a coat of varnish,' laughed Lily, taking a large step sideways and pushing forward her vagina and inserting a finger. 'Mmmm,' she moaned theatrically, extracting her finger and licking it. 'Mmmm. You turn pussy to honey, Joe. You wanna taste?'

'Oh Lord, oh hell,' said Charles despairingly.

Lily inserted the finger again and turned her hand as if winding a large mechanical toy. 'Mmmm,' she said, holding her finger up to her snub little nose. 'Cunty smell good.'

She darted round the coffee-table. With an involuntary shriek, Charles leapt backwards and sat heavily on the arm of the chesterfield. He scrabbled over the back of the chair. Lily's outstretched hand nearly grabbed the seat of his trousers. 'Don't fight it, Joe. It good.' She advanced round the furniture. 'It smell good, sweet and sour prawn ball. You eat all up.'

'Aaagh,' said Charles, sliding along the wall, tripping over pouffes, occasional tables and a Macedonian funeral urn.

'You like little Chinese take-away? You want sixty-nine to go, Joe?'

She delicately stalked him. The room was not designed for swift movement. Charles noticed, in his haste to escape, that the furniture impeded him more than it did Lily. He definitely heard the bookcase snigger as the library steps barked his shins. Lily lightly bounced and slid over it all like a child shrimping in rock pools. They made two swift circuits of the room with Lily laughing and cooing obscenities and Charles swearing and exclaiming in a girlie way. Finally, in a neat move that owed something to his prep-school rugby fives, Charles feinted back, grabbed Lily by her upper arms, and pushed her on to the sofa, and then leapt over the coffee-table and made it to the door. His fingers were just on the handle, when a quite different stern voice barked behind him, 'Joe, touch that door and the lady buys the farm. I mean it, Joe.'

Charles turned and looked back over his shoulder. Lily was standing in the fireplace, her little breasts heaving up and down, a sheen of perspiration glowing on her thighs. The glasses had slid down her nose and her exquisite black eyes shone. In her right hand, above her head, she held a Meissen shepherdess.

'Lily, you wouldn't!'

'You feel lucky, Soldier?'

'Lily put that down this instant,' said Charles, trying to match the ferocity in her voice.

'You wanna see the broad in one piece again you get your sorry frame over here,' she snapped back.

43

'Lily,' said Charles, losing his resolve. 'Lily, please be careful, you have no idea what that's worth.' The shepherdess smiled inanely and clutched her petticoats. Lily pretended to drop it.

'Now,' she said.

'Lily, please, I'm coming,' capitulated Charles.

'Maybe, maybe not. You been a bad, Joe,' chided Lily, back in her singsong voice.

Charles did as he was told. In front of her, he reached out tentatively to take the ornament. 'Not so fast, Joe.' Lily put her free hand on his chest and pushed. 'On your knees.' Charles groaned and sank to the floor. His head came to just below her chest. He looked up imploringly, a nipple brushed his forehead. 'On all fours,' she whispered. Silently, he put his palms on the soft silk of the Isfahan prayer-mat. Lily gently took hold of a handful of hair and pulled his head back. Pushing her hips forward she slid her vagina down his face till, snugly, damply, her lips kissed his.

'You eat me, Joe. You eat me good or the white bitch gets it.' Charles gently ate, like someone tasting hot onion soup with Gruyère and *croûtons*. Lily's grip on his hair became fiercer. She pushed her pubis hard against the bridge of his nose till it ached and he had to breathe through the side of his mouth, making a noise like an asthmatic pug.

'Oh you so good, Joe, you very hungry. I taste good?' Lily tasted of sea shells and folded linen; of warm bread and silver polish. Charles felt light and free. Her knees slowly buckled and she turned him on his back, like a circus act turning a performing horse. Letting go of his hair, she knelt over his face and reached down to undo his trousers. Rocking her pelvis backwards and forwards, Charles's nose bobbed in and out of her little crimped bottom.

'Oh boy, oh boy, Joe. What we got here?' Lily pulled his cock out of the nest of underpants, flannel and shirt-tails. 'What we got here? You been doing exercise with weights, Joe? He got bigger. I think this time he choke me good and dead. I not putting this inside me. No way, Joe. Him too *beaucoup*; too *beaucoup* a long way.' She held Charles's elegant cock with the finger and thumb of both hands and slowly slid it between her lips. Charles was amazed at the heat. He felt the tip of his cock jar on the roof of her mouth and then go on. Lily gagged and came up coughing and laughing. 'Oh Joe, you push gum down my throat. I swallow, I forget. We jig-a-jig now.' Swivelling round, Lily managed with a bit of fiddling and a few tense instructions to push the cock inside her. Charles was again aware of the heat and the almost painful tightness. His face was slick and flushed; he looked up. Lily sat over him, her feet flat on the floor, bent slightly forward, one hand on his chest for balance. With a start, he saw that she was still holding the shepherdess, who was still holding her petticoats.

'You don't move, Joe, you stay stiff. I gonna come first. Then we see about what we do for you.' Lily started to rock back and forth, her brow knitted in concentration, her lips parted, breathing in sharp gasps; the see-sawing grew stronger, faster. Charles closed his eyes and wallowed. He was amazed that he could feel nothing but the wet sliding grip on his cock and light pressure on his chest. She seemed to have no physical presence at all. With an aspirant explosion, 'sheeee', and a ripple of giggles, Lily grabbed an orgasm.

She sat for a moment, head bowed, and then slid off. 'OK, Soldier, I all yours. How do you want it?'

'Lily, oh, just don't stop.'

'What you want? You want blow-job, come in my mouth, make me choke? You want jig-a-jig? Take me standing up, sitting down, from behind? You want do it in dirty boy's hole; I pretend I your buddy at school? What you want?'

'Oh I don't know, I can't think; oh dear, I'm not very good. Well, why don't you choose. I'll have whatever you're having.'

'Come on Big Boy, you say what you want. You want tie me up, piss on me, jerk off in my shoe while I swear at you? Come on, Soldier, give an order.'

'Lily, you're impossible. OK, why don't you, um, suck it a bit more, just to stop you saying all these revolting things.'

'OK, Joe. One extra special blow-job coming up and going

down.' Lily went to work with a cool skill, bobbing noisily. Her little hands squeezed and stroked, teased and pried. Charles lay on his back with his arm crooked over his eyes, concentrating, and slowly the tension grew in the pit of him, like a rubber band being wound round and round. He felt the semen bubble and spume at the base of his cock. His breath came in long shuddering gasps. His tense thighs shook and then, just as it felt it would snap, the tension was released, the band unwound, stammering jets of sperm. Lily's neck arched, her nails dug into his chest and she pursed her lips, bracing her back. Charles sighed and it was finished.

Lily looked up and took off her sunglasses. There was a placid look of triumph on her face. Then she smiled a smile of such innocent charm and leant across to her handbag and pulled out a piece of gum. Lying in the crook of his arm, she unwrapped it and tore it in half. They lay in silence for a few minutes listening to the muted traffic and their own rhythmic chewing.

'I like working for you, Charles,' said Lily softly.

Charles sighed. 'Why do you talk in that ghastly way, Lily? It isn't really you.'

Lily sat up and put on her glasses. Thrusting her face close to his she said in her singsong voice, 'Oh yeah, Joe. And who am I, huh? I just a little Vietnamese girl, another blow-job, another dollar,' and she got up, stepped into her dress and shoes. 'You got my money, Joe?' she said, preening in front of the mirror, combing her hair with her fingers and snapping her gum. Two minutes later she was standing in the door, hard and sharp and silky. 'See you next week, Joe. Be a good boy.'

'Lily, next time I want you to clean, I mean it.'

'Yeah, sure, Joe,' she said, and bending down she picked something off the floor. 'Here, catch.' The shepherdess arced across the room. Charles fell across the sofa, just catching it as the door closed.

He sat naked and shivering in the suffocating room. The furniture gossiped. He listened to it wheezing and creaking, whispering each to the next, disapproving. For a long time he sat and stared at the fireplace, blank and miserable. He felt desperate, bleak, alone and pointless. He tried to recall the weightless relief of orgasm, but all he could remember was the ridiculous noise he had made. With a flash of anger and self-loathing, he pulled back the hand that held the ridiculous shepherdess and flung it at the grate, but his fingers wouldn't let go. He put her down gently on the side-table, and then turned her a little so that she looked out of the window. Why hadn't he let Lily smash the bloody thing? Then he could have gone and he wouldn't feel so bloody awful and the ironing would have been done. Charles's willy dribbled coldly onto his thigh. He got up, pulled on his trousers, picked up the feather thingy and started dusting.

Directly opposite Charles's flat, on the other side of the square, on the third floor, Lord Vernon of Barnstaple was on his hands and knees on a carpet that was very similar to Charles's, but had, in fact, come from the fabled East via Barker's bargain basement. From the waist up he was wearing a Bengal striped shirt with a white collar and a none-too-discreet coronet and gothic VB embroidered on the chest. Over that he had a yellow cashmere-rich cardigan, and a slightly skew-whiff Old Carthusian tie. From the waist down he sported a straining pair of 1950s ladies knickers. Vernon's face was red, his eyes bulged, and the veins on his neck stood out.

Behind him knelt Stephen Marle, dressed in a similar conservative casual fashion above the waist, but without the imperial underwear. His corduroy trousers were already at half-mast. He was trying, none too elegantly, to pull the knickers down.

'I think you've put on some weight – the waistband's caught in a fold in your tum tum. I bet Arthur didn't have this problem getting them off Marilyn.' Marle giggled. 'Try breathing in. There.' The knickers concertinaed like a collapsed tent at Vernon's knees.

'What on earth are you doing now? Just get on with it. I'm getting cramp,' said Vernon petulantly.

'Look, Miss Impatient, I'm just trying to get a bit of an erection. If his Lordship wants to get fucked, his Lordship will either have to wait for the band to stand or deign to give me a hand.'

'Oh come round here.'

Marle shuffled round to face Vernon, with his limp little penis held between finger and thumb like an injury for matron. Vernon put his hand into his mouth and extracted his five front teeth. His lips collapsed inwards, making him look remarkably like his own aged mother.

'Chritht,' he muttered, 'have you wathed thith? Come on, thtick it in.'

Stephen popped his little cock into Vernon's mouth. 'Oh, Vera Vacuum,' giggled Marle as Vernon sucked like a child trying to unblock a milk-shake straw.

'There, that thould be enough,' said Vernon, pushing the semi-tumescent cock out of his mouth with his tongue. 'Now get round the back and thumb it up.'

Marle shuffled back on his knees. 'Now dear, where does it hurt? Oh yes, just here, I can see it's a little tender. Never mind, just a dab of ointment. Now this might feel a teensy bit cold.' Marle dabbed at Vernon's winking sphincta.

'Oooh, what are you uthing?'

'We ran out of KY after your little soirée at the weekend, and you forgot to get any more – I put it on the list – so we're making do with Brylcreem.'

'Oh God,' said Vernon, 'thith ith tho undignified; a peer of the realm having hith arthe anointed like an RAF thergeant at the barberth.'

'Don't be such a Connie Complainer, you're lucky to be getting poked at all at teatime on a Wednesday. Don't wriggle. Oh no, slipped out. Righty ho, into the burrow, mousy. There we are, slipped in a treat. I expect Your Majesty can feel the benefit.' Stephen rested his hands on Vernon's fleshy hips, and started to pump slowly. 'Talking of the RAF, did I ever tell you about that cottage outside Biggin Hill. There was this simply vast aircraftman second class. I said, "Lord, if this is second class, you'd need a shoehorn to go first." He was famous with all the girls – they used to call him doodle-bug because he whistled and left a large hole when he came.'

'Oh, thut up,' said Vernon irritably.

'I think this Brylcreem's rather nice – at least I'll have manageable pubes. Would sir like a centre parting?'

'Tell me about the Garden Committee. Are they going to be difficult about the Printhipetha?'

'Oh, they're all wind and no turd. I shouldn't worry about them. It's Godwin who holds the key, and I can't make him out. He's either remedially stupid or incredibly bored. Do you think he's one of us? If you ask me he's sexless. He's just in love with all that old tat he collects.'

'There you thow your innate lack of tathte and breeding, Thtephen. That tat is a very fine collection. I've got the meathure of friend Charleth: he ith lonely and he doethn't want to give offenthe. I think if I offer him an invitation and bully him, he'll come round. Look, have I got my backthide in the air entirely for your benefit, or do you think you could deign to reach round and toth me off? You are tho thelfith.'

'Pardon me, Miss Manners,' Marle reached round and began vigorously wanking Barnstaple. 'If you get much fatter you'll need an extension.'

Melbourne, their Lhasa apso, waddled into the room, wagging its stained and ragged tail. He trotted over to the odd couple, sniffing, and then wriggled under Vernon's tummy and tried to lick the end of his shuffling cock.

'Thoo, thoo,' shouted Barnstaple. 'Mellie – blanket.' Melbourne sneezed loudly, covering the cock and the hand with fetid spit, and then ambled to the sofa where he lay with his head resting sideways on his paws regarding the couple.

'Eergh,' said Marle. 'Ooh, I think my time's up, here we go. Ooh yes, *je suis arrivée monsieur*. My.' He ground his hips and Vernon's buttocks juddered. 'Ooh yes, that's better. What a relief. Now come along Tail End Charlie – don't lag behind.' He slapped Vernon's bottom and shuffled until his hand was a blur.

'Oooh, oooh,' panted Vernon, 'quicker, quicker.'

'I've only got one pair of hands, dear. Quicker! Pick up Paul Daniels if you want sleight of hand.'

'Oooh yeth, I'm coming,' Vernon's voice, in extremis, had a definite Welsh lilt to it. 'Now, now quick. No,' he screamed, 'not into my bloomerth. Oh, be careful. Oooh, aaagh, no not on the carpet either.'

'Into what then,' shouted back Marle.

'Into your hand, you idiot. Oh itth too late. Oh look at that. Go and get a J cloth, it thtainth. You know Printheth Margaret thtood jutht there.'

'Well, lucky she'd gone before you arrived.'

'Don't be fathetiouth. What'th that blethed dog chewing?'

Marle went and retrieved something from Melbourne's jaws. 'Your teeth, Your Majesty.' He handed the mangled and sticky plastic and wire to Vernon, and made as dignified an exit as a man can with his trousers round his ankles.

'You beatht,' said Vernon with feeling, and sat heavily on the carpet.

After a couple of moments he felt a dampness seep through the cotton. 'Oh thit, I've got thpunk on Norma Jean's knickers.'

By one of those strange acts of synchronicity that we read so much about these days, and that used to be called coincidence until coincidence became passé as an anecdotal device, everyone who had been at the Garden Committee meeting had sex of some sort that afternoon.

Bon Bon languished in her kidney-shaped bath with her husband, Belman, who shaved her armpits, legs and pubic stubble. He had developed a penchant for very young girls in his touring years and had a horror of body hair. He himself, of course, was covered like a moulting chimpanzee from shoulder to ankle in coarse curls. Bon Bon thought the mild fear and discomfort of having a stoned rock legend with a shaky hand negotiate her little folded places with a straight razor a small price to pay for keeping her husband at home.

Mrs Kotzen spread herself decorously over the imported maple island breakfast bar and work station in the middle of her architect-designed, walk-through basement kitchen cum dining area and was rigorously and silently serviced by the muscular and pimply boy who delivered her groceries. She tipped him a pound and a Bath Oliver with home-made tapenade.

Bryony squatted on her sturdy cast-iron and horsehair bed, which was covered in zebra skin. She wielded in one hand an eye-wateringly ferocious, anatomically correct black dildo, and held in the other a creased and smeared photograph of Paul Robeson in *Sanders of the River*. She barked offensive orders. 'Come on you black stud – fuck me till I fart. Don't slack you nigger rapist. Harder, you filthy great buggering ebony spunk wagon.' The vibrator hummed and hammered like a channel-tunnel excavator on overtime. Bryony came with a basso profundo stuttered exclamation. 'Fuck fuck fuck fuck fuck fuck fuck fuck fuck fuck.'

Whether what the doctor had could be classified as sex is debatable. It would certainly have got him arrested if he had done it in public. He wandered about his tiny basement bachelor flat, opening and closing drawers, unscrewing jars and sniffing the contents, losing and finding various spectacles and humming the 'Dambusters' March'. All the while he had his hand thrust deep into the pocket of his soiled and fraying trousers. Actually, the pocket bit had been cut out. His hand comfortingly massaged his smelly penis and pendulous scrotum. This wasn't so much sex as habit. The doctor had long ago ceased to notice what he did with his hands. Finally, he sat down to listen to the weather forecast. 'Tyne, Dogger, German Bight' – a thin spasm of slimy precipitation tweaked its way down his thigh to be absorbed by the stiff cavalry twill.

There was something in the air, some wind-borne pheromone wafting out of the garden.

Chapter Four

When Charles had finished the ironing he went and sat at the table in the window looking over the square. He ate a cheese sandwich and an apple. He couldn't shake the terrible sense of loss and gloom. He distractedly picked up a pack of cards and started dealing bridge hands, bidding in his head. One pair, uh – pass; two spades, pass; three no trumps, pass; four hearts, no bid. He played the hands without moving a card, then swept them altogether, shuffled and dealt again. Pass, two hearts, no bid.

He looked out at the evening light falling on the garden, the pigeons coming in to roost in the plane tree. A thin trail of smoke rose into the still air, a bright flame just visible through the hedge, a point of light and warmth in the darkling forest. Charles suddenly felt an almost unbearable sense of loss. He got up, went to the Chippendale bureau that doubled as his limited drinks cupboard, and took out a bottle of Scotch. Pulling on his tweed shooting coat, he walked across the silent road to the garden gate. The air was cool and smelt of burning wood. Angel was singing.

Charles approached the fire across the lawn. The grass felt spongy under his feet. The garden seemed vast and echoing, as outside often does when you spend too long in a room. Charles breathed deeply and walked silently. He wanted to surprise Angel who was crouching over the fire with his back to him. When Charles reached the massive plane tree he stopped and listened. The tree murmured and rustled above him. In the distance the traffic hissed. Angel was humming 'Jerusalem' and conducting with a smoking stick. The evening smoothed out the noises so that they melded into a sort of natural tone. At the bottom of it all Charles could hear his blood beat.

'What are you lurking under that tree for?' shouted Angel without turning round. 'Pretending to be Natty Bumppo?'

Charles smiled and strode into the ring of firelight. 'May I avail myself of the comfort of your camp-fire, Chingachgook?'

'Sit down, you daft bugger.'

'How did you know it was me? And I'm very impressed that you know about Natty Bumppo.'

'Ah, the long Caribbean, Hawkeye, Leatherstocking, Deerslayer. I've read more than seed packets and sunsets, you patronizing old sod. And I could sense you by the smell of sex and failure.'

'I think Deerslayer was the name of his rifle actually. Here, I've brought you a peace offering.' Charles put the whisky down between them.

'Fire-water. You're welcome to a baked potato and a sausage for that.' Angel unscrewed the cap, pressed it between finger and thumb, and threw it on the fire.

Charles felt absurdly grateful for this small, unconsidered gesture. The need for company was intense, and tearfully pitiful. Angel took a long pull, put a hard hand on Charles's shoulder, and squeezed. There was recognition and understanding in the gesture; the hug of ivy on oak. Charles sipped and pulled a face and passed the bottle back. Angel took another gulp and got up. 'I'll get you a stick.'

'Why do I want a stick?'

'Don't be daft,' said Angel from the shadows. 'A man sitting with a fire has got to have a stick. No-one can sit in front of a fire without wanting to poke it, to rearrange it, to help it. A fire is every man's oldest friend; fires belong to us. You watch a woman with a fire. She'll stand back and look and hug herself. She looks at it the way she looks at a naked man: she's fascinated and frightened. But a man, now, he'll kick it and prod it. Men and fire, they know each other.'

'You're a weird bloke, Angel. Where do you get all this stuff from? You don't see a woman from one month to the next, except Bryony, and she's hardly typical of the gender.'

'Now that's where you are wrong. I see more from the outside looking in than you do from the inside looking out. You'd be surprised at what I see from this garden. Why just today, I watched a man chased round his own drawing-room by his cleaner and given a good seeing to on the carpet.'

'Angel, you've been spying on me!'

'I just happened to be up that plane tree this afternoon, and I just happened to have a grandstand view through your window.'

'That's too embarrassing.'

'In fact, Charles,' said Angel with a throaty, whisky laugh, 'I seem to find something to do in that plane tree most Wednesdays and Mondays. She's a supple lass that little Lily, and she's got the measure of you.'

'This is so humiliating. It's bad enough that my cleaner won't clean, but putting on a free show for the gardener to wank over is too awful.'

'Yep, I'm up there with the pigeons, beating the meat.'

'I ought to charge.'

'I'll tell you what. I'll give you some excellent grass. This year's crop is just coming up behind the shelter. It's good stuff – I've been nurturing it with the proceeds of your little sex show.'

Charles took a swig of the bottle and pushed the side of Angel's woolly head gently with the flat of his hand. 'You filthy old vegetable pervert.'

Angel reached into his pocket, took out a worn silver tobacco tin and started rolling a joint. 'Put the sausages on sticks,' he said.

They subsided into a gentle silence, passing the bottle and the joint back and forth, mesmerized by the fire, watching the sausages spit and bubble, and ruminatively poking at the embers. A siren hee-hawed distantly. Charles dragged his eyes away from the fire. It was quite dark now; the garden looked different. It had thrown off the comfortable pinstriped symmetry of polite formality and it was revealed as somewhere wild, mysterious, a place of an older nature. The thin white light of the moon and the pools of yellow street lamps were like an X-ray, revealing something less benign. The fluted shadows flickered. The firelight swarmed across the lawn and jumped up the huge plane tree's psoriasised trunk like firedogs. The back of Charles's neck prickled. He turned to look over his shoulder, aware that he was no longer the President of the Garden Committee but a tweedy interloper, clinging to the comfort of a ring of bright light and company. He felt things that an off-licence of whisky and a whole squat of grass couldn't have made him say out loud.

Angel coughed. 'Don't fret, Charles. It's only Nature. You see her for what she is in the dark. The dark reveals as much as it hides. You don't see what you know, you see something else, something ancient. I love it, I love this place when it's black, when the shadows strip away the culture, when the garden is not being respectable. Here, grab the bangers – I'm hungry enough to eat your head.'

They ate sausages and potatoes, with knobs of butter that Angel had buried in oilskin under the forsythia. 'Charles, would you do me a favour?'

'Anything,' said Charles, stoned and expansive. He was absurdly pleased to be asked. He wanted to give something to Angel, to be of service to him.

Charles's need for friendship was like a vacuum, like a leech's heated cup sucking in comfort from company, sticky and hot. He had a tearful, barely contained need for affection and recognition, but he could no more speak this loss than he could ask a stranger for friendship. For Charles, culture had become the great metaphor. The feelings he wouldn't claim could be attributed to art, to literature, to music, to opera, TV commercials, photographs retinized in fanned magazines. Charles could weep bulbous tears over pictures on a wall or a song in the air, but he couldn't cry for himself. Now, sitting in the darkness, he imagined himself as Hawkeye in the Sea of Wood at the very Northern Plain of the chilly Age of Reason. He saw himself as a Pathfinder in the great stillness of the wilderness that stretched all the way across from the New World to the Industrial Revolution; the deadened, silent shadowed forest of eighteenth-century romance. And Angel was his Mohican, the man who heard the tree fall, who noted the snapped, sappy twig's message. He really wanted to bind this man of the forest to him by obligation, to make them blood brothers. Charles imagined waking in the morning to find the smoking embers and an empty place beside him, the tobacco tin and the oilskin bag gone, and just moccasin prints in the dewy grass, disappearing into the permanent dusk of the wood. Charles feared being left in this whispering darkness more than anything.

'Anything, just ask for it.'

'Would you get Lily to give you a blow-job in that leather armchair facing the window – on the floor I keep missing bits, and that chair would be just perfect from my point of view.'

Charles laughed, and the laughter was like changing channels. 'Oh, shut up. I'm never going to fuck her again. From now on she's doing the ironing, and you can toss yourself off to that.'

Angel made a face and laughed with him. 'Talking of wankers, that ridiculous poof Vernon came to see me,' he said, flicking the roach into the flames.

'Yes, me too. Was it about his blessed party?'

Angel snorted. 'I don't care for the man, as you know, and I don't want to do him any favours, but if it's tricky for you and the Committee I don't mind him having his party, as long as he doesn't want me to hand round the canapés.'

'Don't you really mind all those people with their stilettos in the lawn, the drunks in the flower-bed? The garden's looking so lovely, it's all so fragile.'

'Fragile? Fragile! Don't be mad, it's Nature, man, the toughest thing in the universe. You could invite the Sealed Knot to recreate the Siege of Newark, a rave, and a vintage tractor festival into the garden and Nature wouldn't miss a beat. She couldn't care less, simply couldn't care less.'

Charles was shocked. He turned and stared at Angel. 'But all your work, all the time and trouble, the years it takes to get the lawn looking like a bowling green, all the plants you've bedded – in more ways than one – all that love and nurturing. How can you say you don't care – it doesn't care?'

'Charles, listen. I care about growing things, I just don't care how they grow. I keep this garden looking regimented because it's what you and the Committee want. You want a garden, you need a gardener. I'm a gardener because I love Nature, but, frankly, it could be thistles and hogweed as well as roses and geraniums. If it were left to me, I'd just let it go. Nature is most beautiful when she does her own make-up. I just want to be part of it.'

'But Angel, this garden has been like this for years. It was here before you were born, and it'll be here after you're dead. I know you love the permanence of things – the way the seasons come and go, and yet this space remains sort of timeless.'

'Bollocks. Nosebleeds and bollocks,' said Angel angrily, rolling another joint. 'You really don't understand. This place isn't timeless, this square is a mere blink in time. Everything man makes is just sandcastles; absurd hubris to think that any of this is important or for ever. What's one cocktail party to that plane tree, or that heather's thousand thousand seeds?'

'Oh,' said Charles quietly. He didn't want to argue, to spoil the closeness. 'I just thought that when you look at the square, the garden and the houses, it's difficult to imagine it any other way.'

There was a long silence. The bottle passed. 'I can,' Angel said finally. 'Don't laugh, but I know about this patch of land. I know what it used to be like. When you dig a place, when you listen to it, watch it, it tells you what it was. The story of this land is locked into every grain of earth, every leaf and branch. It all remembers.'

'And it's told you?'

'I've heard it, no, I've assimilated it. I suppose I'm part of it – we all are. Look into the embers, watch the fire. The wood we're burning is from the beech tree in the corner, I've been tidying it up. It's a hundred and fifty years old, its roots grow down twenty or thirty feet, its leeched nourishment from the bowels of this square for a century and a half. The story of this place is in the wood and now it's told in the flames.'

Charles hugged his knees and rested his head. His nervous fingers distractedly played with the prodding stick. He stared at the fire, a green twig hissed and cracked.

'The first man who ever settled in this place', said Angel softly, 'was on the run. A generation before the Romans came, Gurdfrith, also known as Gurdfrith the Smith, had been apprenticed to a blacksmith, but had cut the first two fingers off his left hand, his sinister hand, sharpening an adze.'

'What a coincidence. Bryony is trying to get you an adze.'

'Don't interrupt. Losing his fingers put Gurdfrith out of a job. He became a tramp, wandering the Thames Basin and the Downs, stealing a bit, doing the odd day's work.

'One day he came across a girl and a dog, herding pigs, the rough red-coated long-snouted pigs that foraged in the oak woods on the chalk downs outside Guildford. He passed her by, and then doubled back, and waited in a holly grove. She was singing to the pigs. He could hear the silvery, lilting voice as he crouched in the bracken, the holly scratching his back. The pigs started when they saw him. The girl stopped singing, and said something to the dog. Gurdfrith took two long steps and grabbed her from behind. She cried out, a shrill explosion of breath. The pigs squealed, the dog skulked into the shrub. Gurdfrith pulled her to the ground, ripping at her smock dress, pushing her face into the chalky mud of the track with his bird-claw hand. He pushed the back of her neck hard. Her delicate, rhythmically blue tattooed arms flayed. The man whimpered with lust and fear, his breath coming in gasps. He roughly pushed his good hand between her legs and pulled her bottom up. He struggled with his trousers and fumbled with himself. He wanted it to be fast because of the terror and the squealing of pigs, and the howling of the dog and the fear – but all that just made it take longer. The rape went into a muddy slow motion, muscles twisted and jerked in spasms, his jaw clenched. When Gurdfrith's thighs were sticky with blood and mud and semen' – Angel coughed and spat into the fire. The phlegm bubbled and hissed – 'he slowly let go the raptor grip, his tendons knotted and ached, his knees locked, his calves cramped, and the little girl slowly slid sideways, like a toy boat sinking into a millpond. She lay quite still, her face down, her battered arse skewed and gaping in the chill clammy mud.

'Gurdfrith looked up, twitching with panic. Everything was still and sullen. Just the distant soaring cry of a rook. He knelt for a moment panting in the circle of pigs, who regarded him with hard, knowing liverish yellow eyes. He pushed the girl's shoulder; she turned on her back. Her face was white with chalk mud, one eye screwed closed and puffy. Her lip and cheek were smeared with blood. Her jaw unjointed, gaping in a drunk's yell – it was tightly packed with pale goo and grass, and vicious chips of flint. Gurdfrith started to scoop murk from her mouth with his claw – it slopped down her chin. A small tooth stuck through her lip.

'A gust of wind rustled the hair on the pigs' backs and clattered the holly trees. Gurdfrith stumbled to his feet and murderously kicked the little body. Right, left, right, left into the cover of the curved bracken. The little girl rolled over and over down a small incline and sank beneath the khaki waves.

'Turning back, the man noticed a glint on the road, a small gold torque, Celtic design, inscribed with runes. The face of a man-god arrayed on one pommel, and a girl with her hands to her face weeping on the other. The pigs watched him pick it up.

'Gurdfrith remembered the last word the girl had spoken was to the dog. He called the name. Loqui came whimpering, slithering on her belly, her tail whipping the bloody mud, then rolled on her back and spread her legs, offering her pouty submissive sex in a disgusting bestial simile.

'The man turned his head, called her name again and, wiping his hands on his cloak, strode fast into the sea of bracken, north, into the wind. The dog and the pigs followed at a distance in hurrying silence.

'Gurdfrith and the pigs and the bitch lurcher continued north, forded the river and, after a month, stopped here. He felt safe, this was not a place people came to; it was marshy, difficult ground, with wiry grass and thin stunted clumps of oak and ash, little beeches, and thickets of hawthorn. Gurdfrith stopped here because he was exhausted, and there was a beck that ran down to the Thames. It's still here, it runs under the church hall – it's always damp in there. Anyway, Gurdfrith built a little bothy out of sods and birch wicker. He built a sty and scraped an existence.'

'God, Angel, what a dreadful story.'

'It's not a story, it's history. Didn't you see it in the fire?'

'Well, I saw it in my mind's eye,' said Charles, uncomfortably. He saw nothing but flames in the fire. The fact that his imagination was permanently laid up in the dry dock of the rational here and now had always irked him. He was moored, apologetically, to the eerie fantasies of others. 'You certainly made it live for me though. What happened next?'

'I'll tell you next time you have a spare bottle. Bed now, I think.'

He walked unsteadily with Charles to the gate. 'After Gurdfrith and his pigs, I don't reckon Vernon and his arse-lickers are going to make much difference to the garden.' He looked up at the moon.

'No, I don't expect they will,' Charles yawned.

Charles lay in bed and listened to the furniture creak and cough. A blackbird started to sing outside. A thin band of bright silver shone across his pillow. He lay and slept dreamlessly.

Chapter Five

'Principessa, Principessa, Principessa. Salutations, salutations, salutations. Welcome, welcome, welcome.'

Vernon spread his hands like a man about to be frisked at an airport. If it hadn't been for the sober intervention of his ears his grin would have cut the top of his head off.

'Sir Barn-Stable. How nice,' replied the Principessa.

Sophia Consuela zu Hint und Sodder; Countess of Polk und Kunst; Keeper of the Demi Postern; Protector of the Puce Friars; Hereditary Arbiter of the Holy Roman Court of Byzantine Fecundity; and Frequent Flyers' Platinum Card holder. Née Chelsea Bistow, late of Fort Lauderdale, she was an imposing woman. In her clear plastic peep-toe stilettos and precipitously piled, rose-gold striped chignon she towered over Vernon. Her features were what an unkind viewer, or a prospective mother-in-law, might call obvious. Her eyes were big and brown with a double layer of spiny lashes, like a poisonous fish. Her nose was tilted and pointed with oddly triangular nostrils. Her lips were stuffed like an overnight bag with bum fat and collagen. The face was faultlessly scrimmed and all-weather proofed – no skimping here, the full three coats. Her breasts were the finest you could buy, her hips were generous, her bottom a shelf where a tired man might rest his weary head, her legs were, well . . .

Vernon thought the last time he had seen something that looked like this it had been on a turntable in the window at Hamleys. Inwardly, he screamed with camp laughter, he hissed and snorted. 'How ridiculous, how cheap, how common, you absurd little tart. You look like an East End drag act. God, heterosexuals are disgusting – fancy putting your willy anywhere near that fishy plastic spunk sponge. Fancy wasting one of the grandest titles in Europe on that twat on springs.'

Outwardly though, his face was a picture of rapt awe with just a touch of cringing deference and a varnish of avuncular camaraderie.

The Principessa appropriately arranged the muscles that still had sensation in her face, and leant forward to plant the merest smear of scabbed maroon lipstick on a vibrating cheek. The hot musk of Akimbo rose from the gorge of her cleavage and mixed rakishly with Old Flannel Shag that lingered on Vernon's peristaltic wattle.

The arrival of the Principessa's Mercedes had brought the tortured conversation in the garden to a halt. Everyone had turned and watched the chauffeur leap to the passenger door like a Butlin's magician with a big finale. They saw, with studied metropolitan disinterest, the unfolding of the long legs and the flashed inch of garter. The rest of the Principessa was followed by a tall man, the colour of a well-kept salad bowl, who might have been a bull-fighter's boyfriend.

Vernon had been over the other side of the garden, lovingly adjusting a waiter's tie, as the car had pulled up. With some sixth sense he had gleaned that nobility was present. Turning mid-Windsor, he mimsily galloped across the lawn, body-swerving in and out of the two or three hundred guests who had found that they had nothing better to do on an overcast

June Wednesday than drink free champagne and support the social ladder.

Vernon erupted through the crowd just as the Principessa stepped past the flunky on the gate. 'Let me introduce you to some important people,' he said. Stephen Marle, who had been hovering, produced a gleaming smile and wiped his hands on the side of his trousers.

Vernon took the Principessa's elbow. Ignoring Marle he said, 'May I present Girton Bister, Minister for Overseas Development, Privy Councillor, collector of vintage Morris Oxfords and pretty women, and one of the most accomplished anecdotalists in the House – Her Serene Highness the Principessa zu Hint und Sodder.'

Vernon took a step back and flashed his palms in a gesture of munificence as if he had just introduced the Queen of Sheba to Solomon. Bister was not a man a practised Hollywood agent would have thought of casting as Solomon. He was fat and bald and thyroidal; his nose looked like a cockroach's double garage. He fixed the lady with a smoked-oyster eye, obvious interest and some distress. His Adam's apple bobbed frantically and his lips parted to reveal the best part of a prawn vol-au-vent. His hand waved up and down as if patting a small invisible boy and, finally, the House's most accomplished anecdotalist managed a gurgling hawk which projected a gob of gannets' breakfast, with commendable velocity and accuracy, into the lolling uplands of the Principessa's cleavage. It hung for a moment and then slithered, skittishly, down a crevasse. The breasts juddered as their owner let out the merest sigh of polite revulsion.

A camera whirred and flashed, and a small man in a grubby linen jacket and Old Carthusian tie bobbed up between the minister and his lunch.

'Your Highness, Frinton Birthright, London *Evening Standard*. Might I have a word?' Frinton gave a terrifying smile, revealing a mouthful of khaki teeth that seemed to have been carelessly inserted upside down.

'Of course, I'd be charmed. I always have time for the

gentlemen of the press,' she said, with as much saccharin as she could muster.

'Is it true that you plan on giving your husband's art collection to the nation?'

'We are, at the moment, considering a permanent home for our collection, yes, but there are many possibilities. Sir Barn-Stable is offering us his professional advice.'

'When you say "we", Your Highness, does that mean your husband has regained consciousness?'

It was a truth understood by the world's gossip columns that the Prince had come to true love late in life, after three, or some had it four, false starts up the aisle. In his seventy-eighth year, when you might have thought Cupid would have found better things to do, a dart had found its mark at a discothèque in Gstaad. What Chelsea had been doing there was a question of much speculation. Some said she was working the tables with a tray; some said she was working them without a tray, or indeed underwear. All agreed she worked very hard on the old man.

Within a week they were engaged, within a month they were married, and within a month and a week the strain of the cherub's quarrel had proved too much for the frail prince, and he had succumbed to a stroke of such Teutonic thoroughness that if he had been a mere mister he would have left hospital in a body bag. But he wasn't, and princes can't go and die willy-nilly; their deaths have to be planned, arrangements have to be made.

The trust that looked after Hint und Sodder's temporal interests moved with unaccustomed alacrity. They hired a battalion of doctors to have His Highness connected to every bit of puffing, beating, draining, throbbing medical equipment in Zurich. His new bride and sole heir was slightly slower off the mark. She hired a phalanx of lawyers and issued a barrage of writs in an attempt to allow the old man to meet his illustrious ancestors, or, as she put it, to leave the final decision to the great physician and judge in the sky.

For a year the doctors and lawyers met daily in the private wing of the Joseph Princip Memorial Hospital, whose only patient lay in mute air-conditioned decrepitude. A stalemate in every sense. After a while the Principessa found the state of affairs wasn't too bad. She was both kept and free, but the situation was messy and she didn't like mess.

The doctors insisted there was no reason that her husband should not now outlive her, thereby leaving his estate to his cousins. Her lawyers said that it was a shame there hadn't been issue, and the Principessa's eyes had lit up.

One night she was discovered by a nurse pumping her husband's cock with one hand while holding a styrofoam cup in the other. After that, the doctors had fitted a catheter with a galvanized clamp attached to an alarm onto the patrician organ of generation. Undeterred, the game girl had directed her lawyers to subpoena her husband's testicles. The case for who owned a vegetable's sperm was slowly making legal precedence in the High Courts of eight countries. 'A man's spunk belongs to his wife, or the marriage vows mean nothing,' the Principessa had once memorably said to a speechless papal nuncio.

Now she said, 'My husband is much improved. I sit with him regularly and we read Goethe and Schiller together.'

'Very touching, remarkable devotion,' said Frinton, insincerely. 'But do you have any comment on the athletic and candid photographs that have been published in certain continental magazines this month?'

The pictures had been taken by an enterprising paparazzo at a private hacienda in Mexico. The Principessa was fuzzily naked, disporting herself libidinously with a papaya and a man who may or may not have been the salad bowl. It was difficult to tell because in the snaps his face was entirely encased in her buttocks.

'I have not deigned to view the rag, but my maid tells me they were of her and the gardener. To a common eye we look kind of similar from a thousand yards.'

'I think that's probably enough now,' said Vernon, hastily interrupting. 'There are a lot of people to meet.'

'This way, love,' shouted a photographer. 'Best front forward, that's it. Smile, chin up, shoulders back, deep breath, wet your lips – not you Vernon.'

The Principessa and Barnstaple both snapped into their professional Madame Tussaud's 'How I Wish To Be Remembered' poses and were bathed in the momentary brilliance of fame. Behind them Stephen Marle gave posterity his 'haughty profile with cigarette'.

'Cankered arse-holes,' muttered Bryony, 'cankered arse-holes and scrofulous cunts,' she repeated, louder, through her kitchen window at the not-celebrities; the column-inch fillers; the marginal politicians. The various secretaries and filing clerks who called themselves personal assistants from a dozen deadly arts quangos. The thinning, cynical, single, debs' eunuchs with old school ties and concertinaed socks, who had been sold from promotional party list to party list all their lives. She swore at the assorted social kapok-function stuffers; the middle-class unemployed; the freelance serial liege-men who flapped around the trestle-tables that stood in as a bar underneath the great aloof plane tree in the centre of the garden.

Bryony took a gulp of Black Russian tea laced with dark rum from her favourite tin mug, and shoved her hand deep into the pocket of a Selous Scouts private's greatcoat that did service as a dressing-gown. Finding the stub of a Senior Service, she stuck it in her mouth and lit it from the asthmatic gas stove, filling the already fetid room with a smell of singed hair.

She lifted the huge pair of Zeiss gunnery range-finder's binoculars that hung round her neck and inspected the revellers minutely.

'Cheap fucking nose job. More fucking cellulite than a sumo wrestlers' reunion. Fuck, that repellent human cuspidor from *Newsnight* has brought his mistress. Fuck, she's a mangy dog.'

Dropping the glasses, Bryony turned to a daguerreotype of Lord Roberts who hung swagged with clotted yellowing fly-papers over the zinc-netted game larder. 'It's worse than we thought, Bobs. That bogus sewer probe has turned our little Arcadia into a designer refugee camp. It's fucking intolerable. The man has walked all over the Committee, he's rubbing our faces in society's used nappies. Action is called for. Something must be done.'

She drained the cup, shuddered, and reached for the Zulu assegai that lived beside the sink in case of emergencies.

'*Impondo zankomo*,' she growled, impressively but incomprehensibly, and turned with a rolling jog along the corridor that sported the serried calcified horns and fangs of Africa. Moving with the grace and power of an impi on a mission, Bryony sung the battle hymn of Shaka's imperial guard, stabbing a wart-hog behind the ear with a hissing '*Usuthu*' as she turned into her bedroom. The hog looked askance but said nothing – it was not the first time.

Across the road, Charles was also viewing the garden with distaste. He was struggling with a right-hand cuff-link.

'I really won't be long,' he told the footman's chair, 'just a quick turn around the garden. God, they're an unattractive crowd. There's that girl who used to read the weather, or maybe she's the "Call Me Old-Fashioned" columnist on the *Mail*. I wonder where Angel is?'

The chair said nothing, just gave the coffee-table a knowing look.

Charles quizzed himself in the glass, and the glass quizzed him back. Blue single-breasted suit, cream shirt, foulard tie, discreet links, polished black calf shoes.

'Overdressed,' said the mirror.

'Yes,' said Charles. 'I'm not good at this sort of thing.'

'Not good at anything, really,' replied the mirror.

'Except children's games,' laughed the folded card-table.

'I'll only be a minute, just put in an appearance. Let Vernon patronize me, and then back for the afternoon movie.'

The charcoal-grey double-breasted suit on the gate didn't ask Charles for his invitation. If he hadn't been invited, he quite plainly wasn't any sort of troublemaker.

Charles began to make his way, as nonchalantly as possible, towards the drinks table. It took him some time. He was continually blocked by pinstriped backs. It was like a maze where the walls kept rearranging themselves. Using his shoulder as an ineffectual ice-breaker, rhythmically repeating 'excuse-mes' like a sonar, Charles made it to the bar.

Men in front of him confidently called for plural drinks. Finally, a hurried steward served him a wineglass full of water. Charles hung on to the corner of the table feeling that peculiar self-inflicted shy hysteria of being unnecessary in a crowd. The feeling that's a mixture of self-pity and self-disgust; the sense that everyone else had been given a script except you; the panic of being lost in a funfair, the prolonged moment when you turn and realize that your mother is not beside you. Being a single man at a cocktail party where you know no-one and no-one wants to know you is a unique misery that reaches right back to the locked room of dark childish horrors. He took a sip of water.

The barman returned and said, 'Something else, mate?'

'Oh, um, er yes, um, another glass of water, thanks,' said Charles.

The second glass gave him just enough confidence to move back into the crowd. A man holding one glass is in need of rescuing; a man holding two is on a mission. The coven understood and parted.

If this had been a room Charles would have made for the bookcase. Bookcases were his friends, he could talk to bookcases. He invariably spent most of his time at parties scrutinizing spines, both calf and flannel. He had read the first ten pages of almost everything that Jeffrey Archer had ever written at other people's soirées; it hadn't endeared him to either. Now he made his crab-like way to the garden's vegetable equivalent – the flower-bed. He walked along the familiar border, trying to look like Gertrude Jekyll, engrossed. He had inspected a dozen yards when behind him a familiar booming nasal carillon called.

'Charles, how kind, how kind.'

'Hello Vernon. Good to see you. A good turn out – nice people.'

'Yes, I think we can safely say we have skimmed society's churn and anointed our greensward with the cream. Now who haven't you met? The Principessa, I'm afraid, is being lectured by Stephen about his "Palladio Visionary Blueprint for Bovis".'

Vernon had sucked all the cachet and photo opportunities he

could from his guest of honour and had left the boring common little tart for his jackal, Marle, to pick clean.

'Let's find you a fellow soul.'

'No, really,' said Charles desperately, like a child who has been told to play with the bigger boys. 'I'm happy just watching. I've, er, um, got to be . . .'

'Nonsense. There are some very useful people here,' said Vernon conspiratorially, and he linked arms and mincingly towed Charles towards the serried ranks of the useful. Pausing for a moment, he stood on tiptoe and bobbed his nose like a foxhound who has temporarily lost the scent.

'Ah yes,' he said, and steamed forward to a navy-blue silk back which he tapped, as if he were a best man knocking on a brothel door.

'Iona, can I drag you away? There is someone you simply must meet.' The back turned to reveal an impressive front.

'Iona Wallace, art historian and a rising star with the gavel, divine of antiquities at Gandolfs and, I need hardly add, one of the most sought-after and peerlessly beautiful girls in London – Charles Godwin. How shall I describe you, Charles? Card player, collector, gentleman of leisure? Perhaps just a dear, dear neighbour and the man we have to thank for the glory that surrounds us.' Having done his dutiful damage Vernon sniffed the air, and, spying someone even more useful over Charles's shoulder, steamed off, leaving the pair bobbing in his wake.

Charles offered his hand, but found that it contained a glass. He hurriedly tried to grab it with his other hand but found, too late, that that too contained a glass. His desperate hands, keen to hold something new, now released both, and tipped a stream of fizzy water down the front of his trousers.

'Oh hell,' said Charles.

'Oh dear,' said Miss Wallace coolly, 'you've wet yourself.'

Charles's hands ran frantically in and out of his pockets, the right one emerging from his breast pocket with a white handkerchief which he daubed violently on his groin, and then, remembering its manners, extending itself again to Iona.

'Thank you. I already have a handkerchief,' she said.

'Sorry,' said Charles, firmly sending both his hands to their respective pockets in disgrace. He looked at his shoes and frowned.

'Let's start again,' said Iona. 'I'm Iona Wallace. I work at Gandolfs, the auctioneers.' There was a pause. 'You're Charles . . . ?'

'Sorry. Godwin,' said Charles.

'Why are you here?'

'I live here.'

'With Vernon?'

'Yes, uh, no. In the square, not with, sort of under, and opposite. Very opposite, about as opposite as you can get. Directly opposite. We're only just friends – well more acquaintances really,' he tailed off unconvincingly.

'Right. And what do you do?'

Oh hell, oh fiery pit, oh nemesis. This was the question Charles dreaded. He knew that every time he met another human being they would ask it and he would be found wanting, and he would never ever have an answer. Not having an answer would firmly place him in the box marked 'Not Needed on Voyage' and it would send him into the hold of self-loathing and despair. He approached the question at a run.

'Do . . .' his foot hit the bar, he dropped the baton. 'I er, er nothing, er I mean I do nothing, well, not exactly nothing, just not anything, really. Not what you'd call much of anything. I . . .'

'Vernon said you were responsible for the garden.'

'I'm President of the Committee, silly really.'

'Do you know a lot about gardens?'

Charles caught the slight tone of boredom in her voice.

'No, no nothing, well very little. I like flowers, of course.'

'Of course. So do I. Perhaps I should be a president.'

Charles felt a chill of despair with his crippled conversation, his remedial social skills, and fury at this bloody girl who was bored and making fun of him. This bloody auctioneer, this furniture pimp, this chattel dealer. A woman who could take other people's things, their loved ones, rip them from their natural environment, tear them from their friends, split up pairs, ruthlessly single out the whole from the chipped, the sturdy from the rickety, and, like a concentration camp gauleiter, practise a rough vegetable-and-mineral eugenics and then hold these poor dumb things up to cruel scrutiny. This chit who could sell a hundred years of polish and love and care and shout numbers over them; bang her life-and-death hammer over them. This home wrecker. Charles's brain crashed through the gears.

'Yes, well. By the way, you can't be one of the most peerlessly beautiful women in London,' Charles heard himself blurt petulantly.

'Oh? Can't I?'

'No.' *Charles* – the sentient, sweet, thoughtful, polite human Charles shrieked inwardly, and retreated to the small black deep Anderson shelter in the back of his head. 'No, of course you can't. Vernon said you were one of the most peerlessly beautiful women. It's a tautology. Peerless is an absolute. You can't be "one of the peerless". You can't have a peerless breast, for instance.'

'Aaargh!' whined the inner Charles. 'Where did breast come from?'

Automatic Charles ground on regardless. 'Because there is always another breast beside it – well, presumably, unless you're an Amazon with a mastectomy. Now, you could have peerless breasts, plural, taking them as a matched pair, but then, of course, being an auctioneer you'd probably split them up and call them unique, which would also be a tautology but bloody typical. You'd say a "unique breast, one of a pair," and sell it to someone who already had dozens of breasts and didn't really love any of them; someone who had chests full of breasts and employed someone else to polish them and who would just show them off to impress people and say, "Look at my new breast. I've quite a collection, you know," which might seem a bit apropos of nothing but what I mean is it's, er, it's not a thing, um, grammatical.' Charles's hands shuffled miserably.

'Well, leaving aside my tits, that's two of us who aren't peerless,' said Iona, with a velvety softness.

'What?'

71

'Well, you've got Lord Vernon of Barnstaple. I'm sure he's quite enough peer for a lonely misogynist garden president.'

All through this cocktail banter from small-talk hell Charles had been staring rigidly at his toecaps. The last remark jerked his head up and he furiously confronted Iona's face for the first time. The shock of what he saw flung the inner Charles out of his sub-cranial manhole and squashed his nose against the window.

Beauty is an intangible quality. Beauty, pretty, handsome, sexy, all live in the same place, wear each other's clothes, speak the same language, but they're subtly different. Ninety-nine men in a hundred would have no trouble ticking the box marked beautiful next to Iona's picture, but how beautiful? And if that beauty involved more pretty than handsome and whether it was sexy would probably have divided them. Charles's committee was in no doubt about what it saw.

Iona was ravishing; she was absolutely, exactly Charles's thing. If he had been sat down with Scotland Yard's Identikit and asked to compile a wanted poster for someone he could sin with on a regular recidivist basis, the image he could come up with would have got Iona arrested within an hour.

It was a long oval face with an elegant wide jaw; high cheek-bones; a strong straight Athenian nose; heavily lashed, cool amused eyes; a wide mouth and topped off with a broad forehead and floppy fringe of blond hair. It was rather a sensitive, haughty, masculine face. It was a face that could have played Orlando or Sebastian without benefit of the stick-on moustache. It was a face that might have led the first eleven in a fag's pash fantasy. It was a face that, given the endless possibilities of arrangement, was not altogether unlike Charles's own; a passing stranger might have thought the pair related. Iona was erotically, egocentrically very very Charles indeed, and, if he had never opened his mouth or offered her a damp handkerchief Charles would, could, might have been very Iona.

She, too, now saw him properly for the first time and it compounded her irritation; this childishly shy, gauche poof. Why were all the passable possible men either walking wounded, socially inverted, or mono-erotic mutual masturbators, or, as in Charles's case, patently all three? Charles and Iona, who in altered circumstances would have found so much in common, so much to admire, regarded each other from behind battened hatches. But that's cocktail parties for you. Ships that pass in the early evening all too often lay mines and vanish making smoke.

But before Charles could say 'Good Lord, is that the time?' and bolt for home, or Iona could catch the eye of an imaginary friend and excuse herself, there was an explosive bellowing commotion from the gate.

They turned to see an extraordinary figure leaping from foot to foot, berating the charcoal suit. At first sight this character appeared to be an animated haystack or a piece of macramé that had come seriously adrift. From shoulder to calf it wore a huge circular raffia or straw cape. Its arms and legs rattled with brass and bone bangles and it waved a large black truncheon in one hand and the sort of patent leather handbag favoured by Princess Margaret in the other. Its head was a four-foot-high black tribal mask carved in a fearful expression of post-colonial rage with rows of human teeth set in the gaping mouth and fringed with mangy bits of fur, feathers and cowrie shells. It was the very embodiment of the phlegmy rasping omnisexual incandescent voice that rose and cawed from its maw over the stunned and inquisitive hush.

'I won't tell you again,' it shouted. 'Stand aside you scrotum-faced pile of sheep's dags, or I'll shove this dildo so far up your puckered shitter that your colon will prolapse like a slimy gibbon's tail and you'll be able to crap in the can and stand in the corridor at the same time.'

'Oh Lord, Bryony,' said Charles.

'Bryony; that ethnic Hallowe'en compost heap is a Bryony?' said Iona, and she threw back her head and laughed.

Charles registered that, tautology or no, Iona was even more incomparably, uniquely, peerless when she laughed.

'I'm sorry. Will you excuse me? I'd better go and, um, help,' he said, and his hand, furtively disobeying orders, crept out and gently touched her arm.

'Look here, Wurzel, I'm not telling you again. This is a private party to which you are uninvited. It's not fancy dress,' said the flunky, holding his clipboard defensively.

'If you think I'd deign to join in this malevolent gavotte of the damned; this play-pen of procurers, perverts, pimps, prostitutes, paedophiles and . . .' the mask was momentarily lost for 'p's 'these plop plop poos then you're even more syphilitically gormless than you look. I'm going for a walk.' And she took two steps forward, waving the handbag and jabbing the ebony cock. The flunky fell back and looked around for back-up. It came in the form of Vernon, who broke through the now dense semicircle of bovinely curious guests.

'I'll handle this.' The maestro of the quango unctuously walked towards Bryony, a little fat PE teacher going to sort out a playground ruck.

'You're not going to fucking handle me, you contagious little spunk repository,' growled the mask. 'Tell your lickspittle to let me past.' The cock jabbed menacingly towards the guests. 'And while you're at it tell that roll of human lavatory paper, that collection of spavined grotesques, that legion of the damned, to fuck off back to their matt-black, chrome and frothy coffee holes.'

A titter rolled across the company. There is nothing the urban urbane like better than being collectively insulted. It comfortingly confirms their own beliefs.

Vernon turned to face them. 'I'm sorry,' he began. Then he saw Charles hovering. 'Ah, Charles, would you be so good as to have a quiet word with poor Bryony here?'

'Yes, Charles,' echoed the haystack. 'You have a fucking word, as fucking loud as you like. Tell this git colony to form up in twos and fuck off quick time to someone else's garden.'

Charles looked miserably from Vernon to the haystack. 'Oh dear.' He felt the expectant gaze of several hundred eyes on him. 'Oh Lord. Bryony, why are you dressed up like that?'

'These', came the hoarse reply, 'are the magic ceremonial

robes of the grand shaman and medicine man of the Central African Ngomi people, and I'm wearing them in a fucking act of solidarity. One day the Ngomi woke up to find cunty Belgians all over their lawn. This is the Ngomi's ebony knob of potency. Fuck with them and you get fucked right back, with knobs on. And this is my handbag because the robe doesn't have any fucking pockets and I've got nowhere else to keep my cunty latch keys and bits and bobs. Now Charles, are you on the side of the indigenous people or the invaders?'

'Oh dear,' said Charles, who could see Iona staring at him with a bemused smug look.

'It must be obvious to you all', said Vernon, holding up his hand, sensing that the situation was getting out of control, 'that this lady is in need of her medication. We all know her in the square and love her. We care deeply, but, as you can see, sometimes she needs protecting from herself. Now, if a couple of the serving staff would help the door person to guide her firmly but lovingly back to sheltered accommodation, I would be most grateful.'

'Fucking mad, am I?' bellowed Bryony. '*Usuthu!*' And holding the dildo low like a Marseilles knife fighter she lunged at Vernon's back.

Entirely coincidentally, at precisely the same time, the flunky decided that the auguries were auspicious to earn his wage and he in turn leapt at the haystack's rear. His aim was to secure it in a bear hug and then await orders. However, his aim was somewhat behind his intent, and he misjudged the position of the body in the straw and grabbed, instead, an armful of musty African savannah.

Feeling the tug from behind, Bryony swung the handbag in a high vicious semicircle. The reticule, containing latch keys, bits and bobs and a Victorian cast-iron kettle stand, just in case, caught the chap with some force on the point of the chin. But being a professional, a veteran of Stringfellows and a dozen Royal Variety Performances, even as consciousness hissed and bubbled down his nostrils, he maintained his grip. Poleaxed, he hit the deck, dragging the shaman's cape with him.

It caught Bryony just below the knees. She staggered and fell, her outstretched penile arm searching desperately for Vernon's fleshly puckered erogenous zone. But for the want of an inch or two it might have found its mark. Instead, it slid between his legs, and the full thirteen inches right up to the bangled fist emerged, like a dirty conjuror's tick, to greet the glitterati. Just as she in turn bit the turf, Bryony, with a wing-half's desperate effort for touch, wrenched the heavy dong priapically skyward, mashing a carelessly lolling testicle onto pubic bone.

Vernon's face, which up until that moment had reposed in adipose calm, was miraculously galvanized into an intense expression. The look a mime might make if asked to do a child sucking hot porridge up a straw whilst watching group sex. The *Evening Standard*'s photographer gunned the motor drive, firing film from the hip.

There was a moment's divine stillness, a brief second when all the combatants and witnesses were caught in a waxen tableau vivant. An image that would be graven on retinas and pain memories. It was a moment that would pay for dinners until they lost the teeth to consume them. Slowly, like a stunned heifer, Vernon slid to his knees, tenderly grasping the ebony organ. His forehead thudded on the cool grass.

'Ooooohhhh shit,' he hissed, with a theatrical Welsh whisper.

'Fuck,' gurgled the winded Bryony.

At the top of the square an ambulance hee-hawed.

The party leapt into pandemonium. A great guffaw of glee rang across the garden. The pigeons in the plane tree clattered out in an hysterical fly-past.

Charles and Stephen Marle got to the tangle of figures on the grass simultaneously. Marle grasped Vernon's shoulders and crying, 'Baby, my poor baby,' turned him on his side where he lay in a foetal position holding the only unwelcome cock of his life.

Charles attended to Bryony. He helped her first to sit and then, steadily gulping air, to rise. She viciously wrenched the dildo from Vernon's hands, provoking a weak scream as the solid, exuberantly carved glans grated the already deeply impressed bollock.

'Bitch,' yelled Marle. 'Oh my poor baby, baby. My little lordling.' He tried to undo Vernon's flies, at the same time kissing the peer's furrowed brow.

Bryony staggered back, her head swaying from side to side under the weight of the votive Ascot-sized head-dress. She stretched out her arms for balance, still grasping the handbag. Bereft of the Ngomi's magic cape she now stood naked except for the bangles that rattled to her elbow.

Bryony had never, even in her youth, been blessed with a body that had elicited wolf-whistles or libidinous thoughts from strangers. Some bodies are ball gowns, hers was overalls. Comfortable, hard-working, low maintenance, hot wash with plenty of room for growth. It may not have been beautiful, this ravaged, memorially white figure with its flapping breasts and poached-egg nipples; sagging cretonne tummy; mousy, mangy pubic bush which crept down her thigh to meet the meandering knotted varicose veins; this body may not have been built for sin, but with its creased joints and gnarled digits, the moles, spots and scars of a lifetime's use, it riveted, appalled and endeared. This was the most shockingly, nudely naked person that the crowd, blasé to unclothed girls, exposed breasts and buttocks, flat tummies and waxed pudenda had ever seen. It was awe-inspiring.

Bryony swayed unsteadily, her gesture unconsciously imitating a crucifix and a gladiator's valedictory salute. The glossy *louche* layabouts were agog. They broke into spontaneous applause.

Bryony saw none of it. She peered through her tiny eye-holes fighting for breath, aware that her nose had taken a whacking. She also dimly perceived, due to the coolness wafting about her parts, that she probably wasn't wearing much and that, possibly, she'd overdone the rum in her tea.

'Fuck off you cunts,' she shouted, covering herself as best she could with her handbag.

The sirens became insistent. An ambulance slid to a halt at the gate. Two joyfully Day-Glo men, one tall and gangly, the other squat and bandy, leapt from the cab and sprinted into the garden.

'Stay calm, stay calm. If the person next to you is bleeding, apply pressure. If they're unconscious, don't move them. Take deep breaths,' said the tall one. Then, 'Bloody 'ell. We were told a woman collapsed. Right, this is very important. I need to know what drugs or substances you've all been abusing. You, quickly but calmly, what the 'ell are they all on?' he said to Charles.

'Drugs. Oh no. I don't think they're serving drugs. I don't think there are any drugs involved,' said Charles. 'Although, of course, I couldn't be sure. Um, it's not, no, there's been an accident. Er, Lord Vernon, er, slipped and er, damaged his tummy.'

Vernon sat up, pushing away Marle, who had been attempting to fan air into the peer's silk boxer shorts. 'Not me you halfwit. Take her. Strap her down. Knock her out. Inject her with bubonic plague. Take her and lock her up. She's mad, mad, raving.' He began to cry. 'And she's ruined my party.'

'There, there, baby lordling,' Marle cooed.

'Well, we'll get you in a minute, sir. Stay calm and breathe through your nose. Now what's this?' The ambulanceman pointed to the flunky who was snoring gently on the pillow of straw.

'Leave him,' sobbed Vernon, batting Marle away again. 'He's paid for. Take the harridan. Why won't anyone listen to me?'

'OK. Madam, are you injured?' the tall ambulanceman turned to Bryony, taking care to look the mask in the eyes. 'Would you like to be examined by a female paramedic social worker trained in rape counselling?'

'Don't be fucking disgusting, young man,' said the mask. 'I'm a trained bloody nurse. There is nothing wrong with me, as you can see.'

'Yes,' said the ambulanceman doubtfully, letting his gaze wander for a moment. 'Right, Des, a hundred mill of Valium and an ice-pack for the castrated poof and let's get sleeping beauty here into the meat wagon.'

As the short one said, 'Right you are, Trev,' a high-pitched yelp came from the crowd, 'Cooee, Charles, over here.'

The Principessa burst through the ranks. She moved with a strange undulating gait. She was trying to run and curtsy at the same time. At the curb a modest black Daimler had pulled up in front of the ambulance. Peering from the rear window was a familiar, bemused and uneasy face.

'Your Majesty,' said Vernon struggling to his feet, kneeing Marle in the face as he did so, 'Welcome, welcome, welcome.' He flung his arms wide and his trousers fell to his ankles. A small acorn-like penis and a huge swollen testicle gaily wobbled through the vent of his underpants.

The appearance of the Prince elicited an ironic moan from the audience, a salute of sorts from the tall ambulanceman and an obscene gesture from Bryony. The heir to the throne took in the spectacle with infinite sadness and appeared to say something to the driver. The car pulled away just as the Principessa got to the door handle. She was left in mid bob, a cloud of exhaust fumes and a strobe of flash-guns.

Again, like a bad Jacobite drama, a cry rang out from the wings, 'Help, help, come quickly.'

A small distraught woman with red eyes and an apron ran to the gate. 'Please come now,' she said to the ambulancemen, 'I called an hour ago. Why are you down here? She's up there.'

The ambulancemen looked at each other and then at the little woman.

'It's Mona Corinth. I think she's dead.'

The name hit the party like a swarm of bees. The ambulancemen led a dash for the gates.

Charles was elbowed aside by the *Evening Standard* photographer and Birthright. 'Why me, why does it always happen to me?'

'What are you complaining about,' said the reporter, 'this is two front-page stories. It's a Sunday supplement; it's a fucking serialization.'

'I know, I know,' said the paparazzo, 'but I've run out of film.'

Chapter Six

Mona Corinth was a bit special; had been a bit special. She had slipped into the past tense just as the ambulance arrived.

Mona was the square's secret treasure, its discreet trophy. Few had ever spoken more than a muted hello to the poor old lady who rather resembled an Indian Army cavalry colonel in a headscarf, but all felt proud to be her discreet neighbours. On her infrequent early morning walks, the curtains would twitch respectfully, eyes would follow her protectively. A sighting would become part of the small change of the currency of Buchan Gardens gossip. For the fifteen years she had lived in the top floor of No. 40, Miss Corinth had only ever been seen in shapeless fawn twill trousers, flat expensive Italian shoes, an ancient New England yachting windcheater, dark glasses and a 1940s headscarf with pictures of gendarmes and the Eiffel Tower on it. In fact, the only actual bits of her that the square had ever been privy to were the famously huge, turned-down mouth, the parchment-coloured cheek-bones that cantilevered like a hawk's elbows and the beautifully manicured hand that held the lead of her constant Alsatian. But still, they all knew her face intimately.

It was one of the most famous faces in the world. From the igloos of Baffin Island to the stilt huts of Manchuria, young and old could point to her photograph and say, 'Oh, Rona Corinth, oh yes.' And then they would invariably say, 'Get your eyeballs their own brassière; keep them out of mine!' – Mona's most famous line; the sentence written hurriedly, thoughtlessly, by a red-headed Jewish assistant scriptwriter who had had it said to him by one of Louis B. Mayer's receptionists, and had scribbled it into a dull scene to give Mona a close-up. Ever afterwards it was attributed to Scott Fitzgerald, who had a credit on *Twilight of the Andersons*, the most snot-searingly tearful of Miss Corinth's dozen films.

Mona Corinth had been a star; no, is a star – she lives eternal, moodily, in a polished smoky silver-grey on slow vicarage Sunday afternoons and sweaty erect late-night hotel rooms. After being the most famous actress in the world she became the most famous recluse in the world. Mona left Hollywood at the very apex of her career. Failing, in 1950, to pick up the Best Performance Oscar, she had simply dropped the keys of her untouched, unloved mansion with its collection of Lippizaner horses with the chauffeur, along with a typed note saying: 'To Whom it May Concern. Mona Corinth will make no more films, give no more interviews, and never again appear in public. You have had more than I was prepared to give.'

She had flown to Europe, and tried to settle first in Switzerland, then Tuscany, Madeira, Cape Town, Paris, but had been remorselessly driven by photographers and would-be friends to steal into the night with her faithful dresser, Lottie. Finally, they had slipped and lodged in the cul-de-sac of Buchan Gardens, where she had been gratefully ignored in the way one might ignore a seven-foot naked black man with a fourteen-inch cock and a machete on the Circle Line.

'Quick, quick,' said Lottie, breathlessly, to the gaggle of puffing party-goers as they galloped into the lobby of No.

40. She leant on the button for the lift, the door slid open. She ushered in the two ambulancemen and barred the way to Frinton Birthright, the photographer and half a dozen inquisitives.

'Only four allowed to ride in safety. Mr Godwin, please will you make up the numbers?'

Charles pushed through the crowd muttering 'excuse mes'. They ascended in silence, all looking at the ceiling as if willing the motor to pull faster.

The door opened directly into the penthouse and darkness. Lottie scuttled into it, the other three recoiled.

'Shit,' said the short bandy ambulanceman.

A thick viscous smell oozed into the lift – a smell of hot dog food, pee-soaked rubber and lily of the valley.

'Quick, this way,' Lottie called from the gloom. The ambulancemen and Charles stepped gingerly into the hall; the lift doors hissed shut. There was a thump and a crash and another 'shit'. Charles trod on something soft and giving that let out a mournful 'peee'.

At the far end of the corridor a dim lamp clicked on. Like a child's night-light covered in a rust-brown silk square, it cast a fragile, tired sheen on to the walls. Charles was uncomfortably aware that they were not alone, that they were being watched. Ida Lupino blew a kiss by Charles's ear. Ronald Colman gave him a man-to-man eye-meet. The black and white living dead climbed and choked the walls like unpruned honeysuckle. Frail occasional tables leant against a dado rail, staggering under the weight of hundreds of silver-framed matinée idols. Bela Lugosi snarled from the floor through cracked glass.

As if on cue a long muffled howl rose in the distance. It started as a thin high-pitched keening and descended through a cappella luge to an inhuman scream, finally becoming a low icy growl that seemed to emanate from all points of the compass. It gurgled and throbbed and made the hair stand up on the back of Charles's neck and his shoulder blades prickle.

'Shit. What the shit was that?' said the short ambulanceman.

'Oh no, no, Mary Mother of God. Stendhal has got to her. Come for the love of God, hurry,' shouted Lottie.

The wail began again from the top.

The three men ran down the corridor, tripping on squeaky toys and sticky bones. They followed the housekeeper round the corner. She pressed herself against a wall by the door, taking up the classic position of housekeepers in a thousand melodramas before the discovery of 'something horrible'.

'In there, I can't bear to look,' she gasped, slipping, equally comfortably, into the familiar dialogue, and slowly and unnecessarily pointing at the door handle.

The tall ambulanceman, sensing that things might be getting out of proportion, stepped forward and pushed the door. 'Stay calm. Breathe through your . . . Fu-ck-ing . . .' The corridor was suddenly flooded with light. 'Hell,' finished the bandy one.

Charles squeezed past into the room. The howl cut off to a threatening, syrupy glottal growl.

The room was extraordinary. Hanging from the ceiling was a vast crystal chandelier made for some forgotten imperial ballroom. The walls were covered in crimson watered silk, curtained with heavy grey velvet; an ornate gold dressing-table with triptych mirrors and a narcissistic hypochondriac's collection of smells, potions, powders and pills stood in a corner. Opposite him was a large oil painting of a naked Diana and assorted dryads strolling with a pack of Dobermann pinschers. All this Charles took in peripherally, along with the scatter of clothes on the Aubusson rug, the upturned tray with the spilt bowl of bortsch, the bookcase with the stacks of old magazines propped against ugly deco awards, the French *armoire* which spilt shoes and tulle, an Italian painted chest with the television on top and a Prague glass vase with waxy South African flowers.

He registered it all as if by osmosis, attention gripped by the oversize heart-shaped bed with coral pink satin sheets and heart-shaped lace pillows. The bed squatted against the far wall, hideous and lascivious, with steepling chiffon ruched and held aloft by a flying, naked bat-winged chrome maiden. Under it lay Mona Corinth in a dramatic pose of romantic death, one arm flung out to the side, the fingers curled as if they had just released life. The other hand touching her throat. The head, with its long sparse white hair, was arched back, the flying-buttress bones made more impressive by sunken cheeks and a swallowed tongue. The vast lips had been left ajar as if by a departing soul. The drooping grey eyes that did 'stoic panic and righteous pique' in unblinking reaction shots better than anyone in Beverly Hills now stared, heavy-lidded and sated, at the bolting chrome maiden above.

Mona lay on her back, a powder-blue baby-doll nightie rucked up to her armpits. Her skinny frail body was half twisted over at the hips, the top leg pushed up and crooked at the knee, as if she had toppled over in the act of hurdling, or perhaps more a pose from a cheap porn mag. Her sex and buttocks gapped and sagged, pathetically obscene now they were beyond shame.

Straddling her from behind was a large smooth-coated Alsatian, his back legs splayed, the pads spread so the claws could get a purchase on the slippery sheets. His spine was arched with determination and the hackles stood like serried exclamations on his twitching shoulders. His terrifying head faced the door, the lips curled back showing the pinky-white gums and monstrous yellow gin-trap teeth. A faint hum, almost a purr of dreadful menace slid from between the glistening dewlaps. Brown eyes watched them, amoral, unsurprised, darkly bestial.

The three men stood and tried to stare back, but one by one their eyes faltered and dropped. There are animals and animal desires man simply cannot outface.

The dog's haunches began to jerk rhythmically, the disgusting, pelvic, abdomen-tightening, manic pumping that is sniggeringly familiar from playing-fields and country weekend drawing-rooms, the laughable shocking imitation of masculine desire. The dog's thin, sticky pink cock wagged obscenely, blindly probing the corpse's backside. Jabbing and buckling, it nuzzled into the crease of her bottom and slid awkwardly down like a drunk's lipstick, till, with carnal persistence, it furrowed the pursed lips and buried itself in the old cooling cunt. The shaggy head dropped a little, the jaws parted, a long flat tongue lolled between canine teeth, little bubbles of saliva caught in its rasp.

Mona Corinth softly responded. The flat old breasts wagged at her armpits, her crushed-linen stomach undulated, her head swayed from side to side, the mouth falling open in a mockery of ecstasy.

'For the love of God stop him, stop him. The devil. The devil.' The sudden explosion from Lottie made the men jump. She pushed past them into the room and flew at the couple on the bed. Before she had taken two steps into the room the dog let out a roaring bark of such ferocity that Charles thought he could feel it like the wind on his face, smell the stinking breath of corruption. The maid stopped dead as if the noise were a solid wall, and let out a pitiful cry. The dog continued a staccato stream of rapid insults.

Lottie turned to the door, tears streaming down her apple cheeks. 'Please,' she said, 'you are men.' But because they were men and this was man's work they just gaped. With a despairing sob, Lottie grabbed the vase of flowers with both hands and flung it. It hit the back wall, showering Mona with water and gaudy, twisted fleshy petals.

The Alsatian made to lunge, neck bulging, jaws snapping with the clatter of a rifle bolt. The barking turned to a high, maddened whine and Mona's slight body turned like a sleepy lover finding a more comfortable, amenable position and slowly slithered down the satin sheets, her arm elegantly pointing the way to the floor. The lolling head followed. A ship capsizing, the body, gaining momentum, slowly sank. The hysterical priapic dog scrabbled to keep his footing, his claws rucked and snagged the fluid sheets, he yelped and bit at the mattress until his teeth ran with streamers of coral pink bunting, but he was locked, hooked, corkscrewed into his mistress and inexorably, with a scream of rending silk, he followed her. They came to rest in a heap of torn bedding, back to back: Mona with her face in the bortsch and her bottom held aloft by animal desire, the dog panting and growling, never taking its dull darkling eyes off the living humans. His flanks heaved and his legs convulsed and twitched as spasms of salt, sweet, hot DNA sinfully leapt a million years of natural selection and avidly squirmed into the decaying uterus.

The housekeeper collapsed into a small heap sobbing, her arms crossed over her head. 'Please stop the devil. My dear lady. Please, please.'

'Right,' said the tall ambulanceman in a squeaky voice, and then, 'Right,' again in his normal one. 'Des, see to the German lady, er gentle, no sudden moves. You mate, go and call the police. Tell them, tell them, oh Christ, tell them to bring a dog handler. No, tell them to bring a gun.'

Charles stared at the couple in the corner, trying to make sense of his instructions.

'Go and get the fucking police, mate.' The ambulanceman shook Charles's shoulder. 'Now!'

'Oh right.' He stepped backwards. 'Right you are.'

He turned and stumbled down the corridor, something squeaking childishly under his foot. Rin Tin Tin grinned at him from the wall. The lift doors hissed open. He stepped in and went down.

The gawping crowd in the lobby had gone. Only Birthright lounged against the wall, drawing heavily on a cigarette. 'Godwin, isn't it?' he said, blocking Charles's path with a miasma of champagne breath and smoke. 'Charles, Vernon's gardener?'

'I'm sorry, I haven't got time to um . . .' said Charles, edging past and striding on to the street.

Birthright trotted beside him. 'Mona Corinth; *the* Mona Corinth. "Take your balls out of my bra"? That Mona Corinth. She's upstairs?'

'Yes.'

'That's who the ambulance was for?'

'Yes.'

'Dead is she?'

'Yes.'

'Foul play?'

Charles gave him a look that he hoped was all disgust. They had got to the garden gate. 'I'm sorry, only square owners are allowed into the garden,' he said, and let himself in.

'Do you know if she had a boyfriend?' shouted Birthright. 'Was she having a dyke thing with that housekeeper?' Charles said nothing. 'Pity,' said Birthright, 'she was one of my favourites, *The Little Foxes*.'

'That was Bette Davis,' said Charles, before he could stop himself.

'Whoever, anyway they're all dog meat in the end. Right?' Looking at his watch he swore and sauntered off.

Charles started to shake. He felt light-headed; he wanted to cry, to be hugged, to have someone hold his head while he threw up. The garden was empty, only the flapping trestle-tables and a few discarded glasses remained of the party. He stood under the huge plane tree and listened to the pigeons coo and flatter each other. It all looked just the same – serene and dignified. Events, time, happened on it, over it, not to it. The darkest, rawest emotions of men were of less importance than a sunny day or a shower of rain.

'Are you all right?' said a quiet voice behind him.

For a moment Charles imagined that the tree cared. 'Angel, I wish you wouldn't creep up like that. Yes, no, yes, no, I'm fine. It's been a bit of a day. I've got to go and call the police.'

'They've been and gone. Vernon wanted them to arrest Bryony.'

'Did they?'

'No. They laughed and told her not to catch cold. She's in bed with a bottle of rum and that great pizzle.'

'Did you see what happened?'

'Wouldn't have missed it for anything. I gather Mona's dead?'

'God yes. I've got to get er . . . somebody.'

'I heard Stendhal calling. Was he saying goodbye to her?'

'I wouldn't put it quite like that.'

'You go home. Don't call anyone. I'll sort it out. You don't want to have to explain things to the police,' said Angel, with a knowing, reassuring smile.

'If you're sure. Is Bryony OK?'

'Singing the victory song of the Ngomi. If you're not doing

anything this evening come to the potting shed and tell me all about it.'

'Right, yes. Thanks Angel.'

'Charles is having a little confab with the garden gnome.' Marle stood at the window holding a cup of tea as if it were an angry scorpion. 'I'd love to know what they're talking about.'

'I know what they are talking about. They're talking about me. Are they laughing?'

'Difficult to say. They're both smiling.'

'Bastards. They're laughing at me. The whole of London will be laughing at me tomorrow. But they'll pay. The bloody Garden Committee, this mediocre middle-class square – it'll pay. I'll, I'll . . .'

Vernon lay on the sofa with one arm crooked over his eye. He was wearing a plum, quilted short dressing-gown with a huge crest on the breast. He was naked from the waist down, his spindly hairless legs spread as far apart as they would go. His swollen scrotum rested on a family pack of frozen *petits pois*.

'Would you like more tea, sweetie?'

'No, I wouldn't like any more bloody tea. I want vengeance. I want that horrible woman locked up or dead or crippled. I want that gardener sacked, and I want that useless, snotty, patronizing waste of space, Godwin, off the Committee.'

'Yes, when the chips were down it was the Bryony woman he went to. And you always said you had him in your pocket. Well, see where charm gets you.'

'Oh, I still can't believe what happened. I'm in shock. I can't believe the police did nothing. I'm going to speak to the Home Secretary.'

'All things considered, dear heart, it could have been worse.'

'Could have been worse? Could have been . . . Are you mad? I'm assaulted with a yard of black cock by a naked harpy out of King Solomon's Mines, in front of two hundred of the most influential gossips in London, not to mention that shit, Birthright, and his peeping Tom photographer . . .'

'And the Prince of Wales,' added Marle helpfully.

'. . . and the sodding Prince of Wales, who I inadvertently flashed, no thanks to you. And that frightful painted common whore, who is now more likely to give her husband's fucking pictures to the Sarajevo municipal library than to me.'

'Us.'

'How could it have been bloody worse, you stupid ponce?'

'Oh, have a go at me if it makes you feel better,' croaked Marle, his voice cracking. 'That's all I'm good for: to be your whipping boy. I've done nothing but look after your best interests; try and make poor squashed Mr Mousie feel better on a cool bed of Captain Bird's Eye's best, and what do I get? Abused. It's not fair, it's just not . . .'

'Oh Jesus, Stephen, stop whining. Come and give me a kiss,' said Vernon irritably.

Marle pursed his lips and wiped his eye with the back of his index finger. Giving a dramatic sigh he knelt beside Vernon. 'Say sorry.'

'Sorry.'

'Say sorry, Stephen dearest.'

'Give me strength. Sorry, Stephen dearest.'

Marle leant forward and enclosed Vernon's mouth with his own, pushing his long and prehensile tongue between the ceramic teeth. His hand ran over the taut, fat little tummy until it hovered above the 'tackle couchant', then, retracting his tongue, he slapped down hard. Vernon shrieked.

'Serves you right, you ungrateful little lordling. That'll teach you not to treat me like s.h.one.t. And it could have been worse. It could have happened to me. By the way, when your sprouts have cooled, I need the peas for dinner. You can have a frozen partridge instead and stuff the vent with your nuts.' He gave a mirthless, tinkling laugh.

The peas winged past Marle's head and burst onto an Edwardian watercolour of boys bathing off rocks in February.

Bon Bon Velute sniffed, took a mouthful of Perrier and spat it at her husband's Versace shirt. Carefully, like a child learning joined-up writing, she ironed. Sleeves first, making sure the creases ran straight, then collar, then the back, then neatly round the buttons. When she'd finished she folded it, doing up alternate buttons, starting at the first from the top, and then placed it on a gaudy pile in the basket. From the utility room, next to the first-floor kitchen, she watched Angel's and Charles's brief meeting.

She had watched the whole party from behind her ironing-board. She didn't have to iron. She had a fat Irish housekeeper and a maid who could have done it, but she knew that she'd only get up in the middle of the night and do it again – do it properly. And besides, if she didn't iron, dust, wash, mend, shop, what would she do? She had always ironed Belman's shirts. Before gigs in Midlands dancehalls she had stood in the corner of graffitied dressing-rooms pressing his one Herbie Frogg shirt while the band rolled joints and snogged other girls who didn't press shirts without bass players in them.

Bon Bon could have been down there in the garden. She had been invited, or rather Belman had been invited. 'Mr and Mrs Belman'. Bon Bon had been quite excited. She wanted to go to a party in the garden. Where they belonged. It would have been fun. It was the sort of thing she had moved here for. Nice people, witty, intellectual, polite people. 'Yes, we live up there, where you can see the ornamental bay trees and the yellow curtains. No, the whole house. Actually yes, very nice. Yes, lucky.'

She had said, 'We must go. It will be nice. Lord Barnstaple and Charles will expect us, we're their neighbours.' But he'd looked up from his helicopter magazine and said, 'You go, doll. Don't reckon I'll make it. They'll only want me to buy a ticket for something or auction my underpants. Neighbours is your thing. Get yourself a new frock.' And she had said, 'OK, doll,' and made him an egg sandwich the way he liked them, thinking that maybe he'd change his mind. But this morning he had picked up his golf clubs and thrown them into the back of the Range Rover and gone to Godalming. 'Ciao, babe. Enjoy your garden gig. Don't bid more than a grand for anything.'

She had planned to go, really she had planned to go. She had looked through her modest wardrobe, washed her long hair, put on make-up, but actually, in truth, she knew she wouldn't go. She just went through the motions. Years of standing alone in strange gardens, parks, fields, tents, halls and banqueting suites had failed to toughen her to public fun. She always felt out of place, badly dressed, aware that her breasts were too big, and her fringe too long. She didn't trust the twisted, forced things on silver salvers; she didn't like drinking and her shoes always pinched. The younger, prettier svelter girls, who didn't iron, would watch her with amusement through neater mascara. She went because of Belman, so he could be lionized and roar with new chums and get wasted and stick his hand down tight jeans and have ripped-fag-packet phone numbers slipped into his pockets, and then she could drive him home, raucous and coarse.

She'd honestly thought this might have been different. This was her backyard, her patch, her neck of the woods, but she had stood in the kitchen in her high heels and Lancôme blusher and watched the people come, and she had realized that she couldn't face it alone. She simply couldn't, not without Belman as a reason for being there.

Bon Bon looked at the garden and thought, It's only a patch of earth with flowers and trees and grass. Why is it so special? So frightening? And it wasn't just this square of green. All rural, *faux* rural, nearly rural England made her feel uneasy; a stranger. Before they'd moved to Buchan Gardens, Belman had fancied himself as a country gent and they had spent four miserable lonely years in Oxfordshire. The Cotswolds had turned their rolling backs on her. She would walk in fields and know that she was walking the wrong way. She felt conspicuous, out of place, cancerous, polluting. She looked at country magazines to see how to dress, what to say and what to think in the country, but she never got it right, and she never could place what it was she got wrong. But the country knew, the green bits knew; gates would stick and sag on her, branches would snag and clutch at her, mud and shit would suck and slurp at her feet. Bon Bon envied her neighbours with their easy familiarity. The way they could come and go with sticks and guns and dogs and horses. The land would open for them, hug them, bloom and seed for them. The country was a rhythm and a rhyme that she couldn't learn; a simple beat she had wanted to feel desperately, but kept missing. To flail nettles thoughtlessly with a birch switch, to push cows' haunches making a soft clucking noise, to look at an evening sky and close the greenhouse windows, to have a coat that didn't smell of Harvey Nichols, but it wouldn't come, it couldn't be learnt, and she had found that it couldn't be bought with love nor money.

Bon Bon took another mouthful of water and spat noisily at the crutch of a pair of boxer shorts with grinning bananas on them. She looked out at the plane tree with its circling pigeons and said out loud, 'Bloody insanitary thing. Should be cut down. It's only an unmade dining table.'

The potting shed looked like something from Grimms' fairy-tales. Slivers of yellow light snuck through the windows and under the gnarly door. A smatter of drizzle glittered in the shards and pattered on the ivy. A thin waft of smoke crept from the iron chimney and sauntered across the waxing moon.

Charles crunched up the gravel path and knocked, and without waiting for a reply pushed his way in. The potting shed never ceased to entrance him. Lit by a single hissing white storm lantern, it was a tiny square room. The old tortoise stove leant against the far wall. The shed managed to contain an extraordinary amount of stuff. There, just inside the door, was an old kitchen cupboard that had lost its doors, and now fought to hold a babel of collapsing cardboard boxes; rusty tins; ribbed poison bottles; contortions of twine; jamjars of small, crumbly metal things; newspaper parcels and screwed-up brown-paper bags. Beside it, on the earth floor, snoozed the garden's mower, with its treacly engine and green-and-gold bucket. There was a bookshelf, sagging under stacks of seed catalogues, old copies of the *Illustrated London News* and *The Field*. There was a jumble sale collection of mouldy, split-spine hardbacks: Kipling's *Puck of Pook's Hill*, with an elephant and a swastika on the back; a first edition of H.V. Morton's *In Search of England*; a collection of Blake's poetry and Wavell's

Other Men's Flowers. In the corners of the room leant stacks of poles, rakes and hoes; shovels, spades, hawthorn stakes and willow-wands; a cricket bat and stumps; a fishing rod without a reel; four walking sticks, one with a horse's-head handle; a single wooden ski; a set of chimney-sweep's brushes; and the bumper from a pre-war Riley.

Opposite the mower an ancient day bed had lost two of its ball-and-claw feet and a good deal of its horsehair stuffing. This, Charles supposed but had never asked, was where Angel slept. Around the makeshift cot were drunken towers of terracotta pots, enamelled pails and galvanized watering cans, and ranged in front of and behind the stove were wee trays of seedlings and pots of sickly or broken plants, like a vegetable hospital. Obstetrics with its trays of seeds; casualty with its splints and tape, drips and potions; a shelf of cosmetic surgery with the spring-lock secateurs and a quiet warm corner of geriatrics: old woody plants come to quorm and dry and be grafted back into the cycle of the seasons.

Fitted in, hugger-mugger with the garden flotsam, were the lost and unloved orphans of the city. A Fry's chocolate vending-machine; a heat exchanger from a fridge; a bulbous-eyed, beak-faced, stone griffin from some Gothic revival church steeple.

If you looked up, the pitched roof was ganglious and goitred with hanging things. A wooden sledge, thick with sticky cobwebs; a black ham; bags of onions and seed potatoes; bunches of drying herbs: thyme and tansy, lavender and belladonna, heather and mandrake root; a tight-lipped platoon of gin-traps; a silent clutch of rabbit snares; a festoon of starling skulls, threaded on wire through their delicate orbits; a fox's skin; a red stag's antlers, slung from a beam, its tines hung with nimble corn dollies.

All this struck Charles at a first glance, but it was only the start. The shed was an impossible game of Pelmanism. The shadows were rich with dark organic shapes, everything obscured something else; it was like the magpie's store, the shrike's larder.

'Come and sit down.' Angel stood over a black cauldron that

steamed on the pot-bellied stove. 'We've got a bit of a treat.' A thick gamey smell hung over the room, trying to elbow aside the indigenous scents of grass and oil, chemicals, paraffin, bone and hoof and Angel's own sweet decomposing nosegay. 'Over there,' he pointed to a tin bucket that held ice and four bottles of champagne. 'Courtesy of Barnstaple.'

Charles sank into one of the two cottage-loaf armchairs and unscrewed a cork, pouring champagne into two half-pint mugs. Handing one to Angel, he said, 'It's been the most extraordinary day, truly frightful.'

Angel sat down opposite him. They were so close their knees touched. He took a swig. Charles tried to go on but found that, inexplicably, he was on the verge of tears. He swallowed a mouthful of fizzy wine to push down the lump in his throat, but tears welled in his eyes and then trickled down the side of his nose. He gave a ragged sigh and his shoulders heaved. He tried to say sorry but no sound came. He just shook his head. Angel carefully put down his glass and leant forward, gently held the nape of Charles's neck in his strong hard hand, pulling the head to his shoulder. He picked up a little pot with a tiny green seedling in it and put it in Charles's fretting hands. 'You water that; it needs a bit of love.'

Charles looked at the pathetically hopeful sprite through his swimming lashes and started to laugh and choke. He wiped his long nose on his sleeve. 'You are a truly weird man, Angel, but I'm pleased. Thank you. I don't know what's the matter with me.' He straightened up and took a deep breath. 'Delayed shock I suppose. You wouldn't guess what I saw today. Not if you lived to be a thousand.'

'You saw Stendhal ploughing Mona.'

'Did the ambulancemen tell you?'

'No, I've known for a long time. They were lovers since he was a pup, oh, seven years it must be.'

'Angel, it was disgusting. It was the most hateful and awful thing I have ever seen. It was truly sinful.'

'Sinful, hateful, disgusting,' repeated Angel. 'You don't know what you're talking about, Charles. You sound like that Kotzen woman. Don't be so quick to judge. She was a sad woman, Mona; an abused, lonely woman. She had been had and pawed over by millions of men who had never met her. It may have been other women, or hankies, or banana leaves that actually mopped up, but it was meant for her and it frightened her, terrified and shocked her. So she stopped being available, stopped saying things she didn't mean in other people's words, and hoped that, in time, she could go back to being Frida Konigsberg from Pilsen. But she couldn't, because their Mona, the film Mona, went on and on, and it cut her off from everyone, and particularly from men, who, by the way, she loved.'

'OK, Angel, I grant you it can't be easy being a film star, but plenty of people manage it. And it has its compensations. And a dog! Bryony's dildo seems quite sweet and natural compared to a bloody great Alsatian.'

'Yes, some people manage. Stupid, vain people who don't know or care about truth and honesty and sycophancy, but Mona wasn't like that; she was clever and gregarious, and she came from a big family of doctors and musicians and dealers in rare books. She lost them all in the war you know, everyone who ever knew Frida. The only people left were the people who wanted to know Mona, and her reputation was bigger than all of them. That foolish puppet on the screen; she hated it. And then she found Stendhal. And by the way, I've spoken to Bryony about the ebony. It's not a kind wood; it's a hard and cruel wood. I've told her if she wants a nice penis, a penis she can come home to, who'll be constant and diligent and gentle, I'll make one for her from ash or sycamore or oak. Oak's the sort of prick you want your friends to marry.'

'But about the dog.'

'Stendhal?'

'Stendhal. Yes, I saw him, I saw him fuck this corpse. It was like Anubis or Cerberus in the pit of Hades.'

'Maybe. But that says more about the eyes you look through than what was natural. Stendhal adored Mona and she him. They lived for each other. He loved her for herself, not because of her fame or something she did or said in the dark on a screen. He loved the touch of her hands, the sound of her voice, the smell of her vagina. He adored an old, sad, lonely lady and she got a devoted, young, fit lover who would have died for her. He was her beau from the past, a link with Frida and Bohemia, and where is the sin in that? The sin is in the perception, not the commission. What you saw was the final parting of two devoted lovers. He said goodbye to her in the way they had said good night for years. That's heart-breaking, not disgusting.'

'Angel, you turn everything on its head.' Charles was interrupted by the sound of scraping at the door. Startled, he looked round, then back at Angel, who got up and flicked the catch. 'No, Angel.'

Into the room loped a large black shadow.

'Christ, Angel, get that thing out of here. Keep him away from me.' In the tiny shed Stendhal seemed huge. He sniffed the air and shook himself, then padded over to Charles's chair and sat with his head cocked. 'I thought the police took him away, I thought they were going to . . . You were going to call them.'

'No, I just whistled for him. He slipped out by the fire exit. He often used to come and see me at night. Charles, stop looking so shocked, he's only a dog.'

'I am shocked, shocked and disgusted. You can make excuses all you want, but a dog fucking a corpse is not a pretty thing. You weren't there, I was. You argue everything from Nature's high ground, but however you turn it that wasn't natural, and what you choose to ignore is our own human nature and civilization and culture. Bestiality is wrong, and necrophiliac bestiality isn't just wrong, it is deeply, fundamentally appalling.'

Stendhal leant forward and rested his muzzle on Charles's lap. The large brown eyes that had seemed so devilish that afternoon now looked up at him, trusting, innocent and beguiling. The dog's eyebrows arched, as if he were trying to understand what was being said. Charles stopped mid-sentence and stiffened. Without asking his hand furtively stroked Stendhal's head, pushing down the pricked ears. The dog gave a deep sigh and half closed his eyes. 'Oh God, I suppose I can't blame him. He is a handsome beast.'

'And he's sad. He's had a worse day than you. Come on, drink up, let's eat.' Angel took three tin plates from the shelf, wiped them with a dirty rag that hung over the mower, and slopped globular brown stew onto them. He put one on the floor for the dog and handed one to Charles. The three of them ate in silence for a bit. Stendhal picked up and dropped lumps of meat that were too hot and then wolfed the lot. Turning to the champagne bucket he lapped the water with that particularly comforting noise that dogs make when they drink. When he'd finished, he put his dripping jaw back onto Charles's knee.

'It's very good this. What is it?' said Charles, mopping his plate with a folded slice of white bread. 'I'd forgotten to eat anything today.'

'I'm glad you like it – it's a garden speciality. Potage du Buchan. Two pigeons, three starlings, a jay, a finch or two, some roots, some chard and a rat.'

'You're joking?'

'Yes, I finished all the rats last week. Open another bottle.' Again they slipped into silence, drinking and smoking, Angel occasionally rattling the stove.

'Do you know, it wasn't Mona and Stendhal that upset you today.'

'Umm, what was it then?'

'It was the pig's ear you made of chatting up that blonde bird.'

Charles started. Stendhal lifted his head expectantly. 'How on earth do you know about that?'

'I was watching. She's a beautiful girl. You made a handsome couple. I could see you making a mucking fuddle out of it. It was very funny. She was so cool; you were all bent and twisted and wet.'

'Well, I'm glad you were amused,' replied Charles, stroking Stendhal's neck. 'I don't know what it is with me, I'm just so hopeless talking to people I think I might like, except for you, of course. Oh, I made such an ass of myself, it's embarrassing just thinking about it. But I don't suppose I'll ever have to meet her again.'

'Don't be so sure. I have a feeling about you two. I think your underwear might well end up under the same sofa.'

'Thanks, Angel. I suppose you can see the future as well as the past.'

'I can see more than's in front of my eyes, and that spot where you met, that's a favourable place. Three couples have fallen in love right there.'

'You were going to tell me what happened to Gurdfrith and his pigs.'

'OK, give us another drink. Well, you remember he came here with the pigs and the dog to lie low? After a year he was joined by a woman, a travelling tumbler and cutpurse who had fallen out with her troop, and was known to the Moot and Watch of every town between Bristol and the Wash. She wove traps and caught eels in the stream, and bore Gurdfrith a child, a boy. When the boy was six she disappeared. Gurdfrith said she was still a traveller at heart, but she hadn't gone far. He had buried her there, where the pillar box is. Drunk. He was always drunk and bitter and vicious. When the boy, Godwin,' – Charles opened his mouth to say something and Angel raised his hand, continuing softly – 'Godwin – you're the fifth Godwin to live on this bit of land – when the boy was nine Gurdfrith went out one night to the pigpens. Insensibly drunk, he climbed the fence and slipped. In the morning the boy found the remains of his father. He had been almost entirely eaten by the pigs, all that was left were some bits of bone and rag, a gnawed skull and a small gold torque.'

Angel took a swig from the bottle, passed it to Charles, and sighed, as if the death were a weight off his shoulders.

'As often happens, the boy was quite different from the father. Not clever enough to be devious, he was placid and hard-working. He rebuilt the bothy with wattle and daub, just behind where we are sitting. He cleared away the stands of oak and beech and planted oats and peas, neither of which did very well. Two or three times a year he would drive the pigs to London.

'When he was fourteen, he stayed for a week and returned

with an eleven-year-old wife, the daughter of a shepherd from East Anglia. In a year they had a child, a daughter.

'About six months after she was born, Godwin was tending the pigs and their few geese, when the dog, a descendant of Loqui, started barking. Over there, where the traffic-lights are on Kensington Road, Godwin saw a group of men jogging towards the steading. Visitors were rare. From one season to the next they might not see a soul, perhaps just a travelling tinker or an itinerant holy man, never a group of twenty-five men, all armed. This was early April, the beginning of the campaigning season, the time for marauding, the season for settling scores, the cruel month. It was a bit like in the cowboy films, on the frontier, seeing Indians.

'Godwin called his wife and picked up an adze and stood there – there was nowhere to run. The men came on, moving quickly in open order. They fanned out around the plot of cultivated land and stopped, leaning on their javelins. Godwin stood, breathing heavily, head down, eyes darting back and forth under his beetled brow, his knuckles white on the smooth shaft.

'One of the soldiers jumped the stream. He was dressed in a quilted leather jerkin that came down to his thighs, a pair of baggy, checked woollen breeches, sheepskin shoes. Strapped to his back was a long, lozenge-shaped cow-hide shield with a bronze boss incised with the head of a wolf. At his waist he carried a pouch, a thin skinning knife and a yard and a half of iron sword, with a narwhal ivory grip. The blade was like a long orchid leaf. Godwin imagined the wound it would leave. Where would it come; low to the vitals? Would the pain be worse going in or coming out, a slashing blow to the head or a ham-string sweep? The warrior's head was covered with a bronze helmet that had a wide nose-guard and a mask that enclosed the top of his face. On the crest of the helmet was the skull and gaping jaw of a huge pike. His face and arms were covered in blue tattoos. He stopped four paces from Godwin.

'"Iceni?" the warrior enquired lightly.

'Godwin knew that the answer to this question could mean life or death. The Iceni were the largest and most aggressive of the loose confederation of Celtic clans that ruled England from Northumberland to the Bristol Channel. If this was a vengeance raid then the wrong answer could mean his ears on a necklace and his wife and child taken into slavery. The truth was Godwin didn't have the slightest idea what tribe he belonged to – his father had never talked about his people.

'At that moment there was a female scream followed by a masculine oath. Godwin spun round to see a man backing out of the low door of the bothy, followed by his wife, clutching the infant to her breast, with the sticking knife held out in front of her at arm's length.

'Godwin shouted "Stop", and turned back to face the warrior, his grip tightening on the adze. The tip of the orchid blade felt cold and sharp on his Adam's apple. It had come out of the man's belt faster than the eye could follow. The house-carl lowered the sword but didn't scabbard it.

'The long moment hung on a point. The house-carl smiled. "Let me introduce someone. I think you might leave that", he indicated the adze, "here."

'They approached a group of three warriors. The two on each side were the largest men Godwin had ever seen, the one in the middle was slighter and wore a long coat and a helmet with a gold raven perched on top. The warrior indicated this figure. He bent his head to Godwin's ear and whispered "This is your Queen, Iceni."

'The figure lifted off her helmet with both hands and the cloak parted and fell from her shoulders. Godwin gaped. The woman was as tall as he, and perhaps eighteen or twenty years old, with a handsome, strong face, broad brow, pale-blue eyes, a wide mouth and a solid jaw. A commanding face. Her red hair was plaited like her guards', but what really dumbfounded Godwin, what really let him know he was in the presence of greatness, were her breasts. Truly majestic breasts. Under the cloak she wore just a warrior's coarse tartan trousers and gartered boots. Above the waist she was naked, except for a finely worked silver and leather bandolier from which hung a double-headed axe. The bosoms defied gravity; meaty and huge with pale-pink nipples as hard as rose-hips. Simply as trophies they were stunning, but what made them truly splendid, truly regal, were the tattoos. The most intricate and elaborate tattoos covered every taut inch of them. A boar hunt ran up hill and down dale, a sea monster dived off an eminence, a winged horseman surveyed the view from a peak, the most elaborate patterns curled and wove hither and yon, strange birds nested in crevices, wolves and foxes lurked, a hare dashed across a sloping plain. Godwin was transfixed.

'Godwin jerked his eyes up to meet the clear gaze of the Queen.

' "How nice to meet you," she said, in an unlikely, high-pitched, rather tonelessly precise voice. "How charming. Did you plant these peas yourself?"

'Godwin nodded.

' "Have you been in pigs long?"

' "All my life."

' "How quaint. And this is your wife and child?" She motioned limply in the direction of the bothy where Godwin's family were standing. "Charming. Swineherd, have you ever done martial service?"

'Godwin shook his head.

' "You look like a strong man. If you choose to do your duty to your people and join my army, you will return victorious and weighed down with booty, a fat Roman slave to clean, and a . . ." she tailed off.

'Godwin, with a peasant's fatality, said, "Thank you, Your Highness. I'm honoured."

' "We leave in ten minutes," said the warrior. "Say your farewells."

'Godwin hurriedly explained matters to his wife, who shrugged. He kissed his child, who cried, and ten minutes later he found himself bringing up the rear of the royal party with the adze over his shoulder and the dog herding twenty-six pigs and twelve geese.

'It ended badly, of course. The pigs and the geese and finally the dog were all eaten, and Godwin died on the end of a pilliam, swinging his adze, outside Winchester. The skirmish had been rather a success for the Iceni. Godwin was one of only three English fatalities. He lay on the victorious field, in the warm blood and the summer-scented grass, with the larks singing and the bees buzzing in the clover. He watched the little white clouds maunder across the perfect blue sky.

'A pair of magnificent breasts cast a shadow across his face. The Queen looked down and said, "Oh look, the swine fellow has gone and got himself killed – we'd have been better off with another goose." The sound of the house-carls laughing and the warrior saying, "Very droll, Your Majesty," was the last thing Godwin heard.

'His wife survived the campaign season and the hard winter that followed. When Godwin hadn't returned by February, and the bacon and the dried peas were exhausted, she packed a small bundle, strapped the child to her back, and walked north-east to her people in the Fens.

'The first tentative beginnings of this square fell derelict. The wort and the bramble broke down the furrows of the pea beds. The roof collapsed in the bothy. Nature smothered out the small scars and scratches that were the sum total of five human lives spent here.'

'That's a great story,' said Charles after a few moments. 'Do you really think Boudicca was here?' He regretted the crass literal question as soon as he had said it. Of course Boudicca hadn't been here, but then, of course, she had. He would always associate Boudicca with this place now. It would be a fact – he would just never be able to say it in passing to anyone else: 'By the way, Boudicca stopped in the garden, just in front of the forsythia.'

Chapter Seven

The one place in the entire world that Charles believed and wished he would never have to visit again was Mona Corinth's bedroom, so it was with an irritating, irrational feeling that the Fates were playing fast and loose with his life that he found himself shooting a sky-blue double poplin cuff, waiting for the lift back up to the film star's penthouse.

Mona's death brought great pleasure to the square. The possibilities for bathos and impromptu eulogizing were plundered profligately. Mr Patel's shop became positively festive with small knots of women excitedly sucking their teeth and interrupting each other with ever more preposterous and lurid details of the star's physically and metaphorically shrouded life. Mrs Cork was prompted to reminisce that the camaraderie was just like the Blitz. Not, of course, that she could remember the Blitz, having been conceived to the sound of the all-clear underneath a 'Careless Talk Costs Lives' poster down the dark end of Aldgate East station. As her mother had ruefully pointed out some months later, it should have said, 'Careless Sweet Talk Makes Lives', and bloody inconvenient ones at that.

A number of film crews descended on the square and then left again. There was only so much footage to be got out of an entertainment correspondent standing outside an unremarkable front door saying, 'Behind this unremarkable front door, Mona Corinth, Hollywood's greatest and most glamorous enigma, spent the last decade of her life.' Mrs Kotzen offered coffee and chocolate Olivers to a crew from NBC, and a lager and a shag to their 'best boy'.

A couple of hacks from Sunday tabloids did a lacklustre door-to-door trying to pad out the cuttings job of 'Lonely Mona. The lustful love secret she took to her grave.' Thankfully, the secret didn't involve doing it doggy fashion, but was merely a double page of photographs of every dead male film star she had ever met with a large question mark beside them. 'Did she or didn't she? Perhaps only her faithful companion, Stan, the Rin Tin Tin lookalike knows, and he's not saying,' neither was anyone else.

Vernon spent an uneasy week waiting for his humiliating party to become public, but apart from a single paragraph in Londoner's Diary that referred to him as 'sociable and artistic', which Marle correctly and helpfully deciphered as meaning 'queer snob', the story was buried under Mona.

Her funeral, like her life, was utterly private. Only Lottie and a priest were at Putney Crematorium to shed a tear and say a prayer on behalf of a grieving world.

And that would have been that, had it not been for the strange sense of humour that the Fates appear to enjoy.

First Vernon on his way to lunch with a ballet-dancer and a countess bumped into Trevor Burton, the newly ensconced vicar of St Bertha's. Trev, keen to get to know his parishioners, bounded up, offered five, and said 'Hi'. Vernon, mindful of his self-elected position as Lord of the Manor, offered in return a limp four and a curt 'How do you do?' After the niceties, the talk turned to the newly departed. Trev thought that some sort of memorial service would be in order. The fact that Mona had never set foot in his church and had been Roman Catholic by conviction didn't bother him in the slightest. The service, he mused, might be more of a free-form celebration thing. Perhaps, and this was only thinking out loud, perhaps it should involve multi-ethnic children acting out scenes from her films, and perhaps the pop star, Belman, whom he understood was a neighbour, might be induced to play a number or two. It would, Trev smiled, be a way not only of saying 'Ciao' to a friend but also of introducing a lot of new faces to the many entirely laid-back and non-judgemental 'work, rest and pray' modules that he was planning to introduce to the parish.

Vernon, whose taste in liturgical ceremony ran more along the incense, guilt and Viennese choirboy lines, maintained a fixed and glacial smirk of noncommitted interest. Saying only that he thought the various points raised should be considered in depth, taking into consideration all opinion both popular and expert, and that he personally would report back with considered findings at a date that was mutually convenient – in brief, 'Leave it with me, Vicar' – but unfortunately at the present moment in time he was late for a luncheon with Christophe Bolakof and Lady Trinny Bannister-Verge-Pomp. Stepping into a passing taxi, Vernon mentally screwed the idea into a tight ball and was about to chuck it to the Piccadilly traffic when a small germ of a plan knocked respectfully on the back of his head. He unscrewed it again. Maybe there was some mileage to be had from a Mona Corinth Memorial Service. He would run it past Trinny Pomp.

The second of Fate's fortune-cookie japes came a few days later by first-class post. Charles was having a late, rather self-indulgent, breakfast of Coco pops, double cream, hot chocolate, two eggs, three sausages, bacon and bread, all fried in goose fat, followed by toast, Normandy butter and Bachelor's jam – made with wild strawberries and sugar lumps, macerated in *frais* eau-de-vie. He was rereading *England, Their England* for the umpteenth time, using the jam spoon to hold down the pages. He noticed that the last time he had read it he had been eating marmalade.

The door opened and Lily sauntered in. She was wearing her usual wraparound shades, a pair of tight pedal-pusher slacks, little pink ballet shoes and a child's T-shirt that gave up three inches above her navel. It had 'Suck!' written above her perky little bosom.

'Ho, Joe. You miss me?' she said, and went straight to the gramophone and put on the Doors' 'Riders on the Storm'. She had 'Swallow!' written across her slight shoulder-blades.

'Morning, Lily. Turn it down.'

Lily ignored the instruction and came up behind him, wrapping her arms around his neck and pushing a hand down the front of his dressing-gown and tweaking a nipple. Charles squirmed.

'Hoover, Lily.'

'Oh, Joe, you hoover Lily.'

Charles smelt the fruity double-delicious double-bubble on her breath.

'Why you eating off picnic things, Joe?' The table was laid with bright primary plastic plates, mugs and bowls. Charles sighed awkwardly.

'The Sèvres is in disgrace. It kept making jokes. You wouldn't understand.'

'You one weird loony tune soldier.'

'Hoover, Lily.'

'Yeah, yeah. I go. We do it later. Here's your post.' She dropped half a dozen envelopes into the butter, bit his ear and shimmied off to look for the vacuum cleaner.

Charles went back to his book.

A moment later Lily came back. 'My bag full, you change.'

'I changed it last week, Lily. It can't be full – you never use it.'

'It no work. You come and look. Poke around in his bottom.'

'Start with the dusting then. Let me finish breakfast.'

Lily started walking round the room like a bored child, picking objects up, blowing on them and putting them down again, jigging in time to the music. Charles tried to concentrate on

107

his book but couldn't. He picked up the mail. The jam spoon slid to the floor. Lily darted.

'I get it, Joe.'

'Lily, no,' Charles shouted with weary anticipation, but she had already scooted under the table after the spoon, and her thin insistent fingers were sliding up his thighs. 'Lily.' There was an unequal struggle as Charles tried to grab and hold her hands, but she bit him behind the knee and he gave up. With a tinkling giggle of triumph she inspected his cock and, sticking her gum onto the leg of a horrified chair, popped it into her mouth and took two long practised pulls and then pushed it out again.

'Phew, Joe. When this last see water? You taste like a fishmonger's bus pass. I know.' She picked up the jam spoon and smeared it along his stiffening cock. 'Yum, much better. Strawberry popsicle, my favourite.'

Charles tried to ignore her and opened his letters. Gas, press release from the International Bridge Federation, a postcard from his mother in Biarritz. His stomach began to constrict, he felt the familiar tubes and veins tingle and vibrate. Lily dexterously shuffled her fingers like a butcher filling sausage skins. She licked an index finger and pushed it into his bottom.

The last letter jerked out of its envelope. He read it with slow wandering concentration. '*Phibbs and Partners*', said the serious letterhead. '*Dear Mr Godwin, I am instructed . . .*' Charles's knee began to shake '*. . . to ask you to please call on this office . . .*' His loins felt like yards of oily uncoiling rope. Lily's fingernail probed his prostate, her tongue flickered, her hand pumped, her head bobbed – it was like the engine room of a ship down there, full steam ahead. '*. . . this office at your earliest . . .*' Charles's hand gripped the arm of his chair, his nostrils flared. Lily made a farting slurping noise '*. . . this office at your earliest convenience on a matter concerning the estate . . .*' Charles reached the point of no return. All the muscles that could tense, knotted. The thick orgasm hurtled and slid round corners deep in his bowel. '*. . . concerning the estate of the late Mona Corinth . . .*' 'Aaagh.' Peristaltic jissom flew like mercury up a jam thermometer '*. . . the late Mona Corinth . . .*' Mona flickered on the screen of

108

Charles's eyelids; the big lips, the knowing eyes, the jutting breasts. 'Aah Mona.' The shot cut to the long white hair, the sunken cheeks, the flapping breasts, crudely gaping pudenda. 'Aah.' Charles's buttocks heaved the glutinous shot overboard. Lily lived up to her T-shirt.

'Oh boy, where you get it all from is what I want to know, Joe? I keep emptying the bag, but Joe, your balls work nights.'

Charles sank back into the chair, his eyes screwed tightly shut, his face a contortion of guilty disgust and warm languid electric relief. A small hand emerged from between his legs, holding a teaspoon.

'More jam please, Joe.'

Charles took it and stuck it in the jam pot and then, as an afterthought, dabbed the bottom in the mustard and handed it back. There was a satisfying thud as Lily's head hit the bottom of the table.

'Oh you fuck pig, Joe.' She scrabbled out and stood in front of him. 'Funny joke, Joe, you bastard.' She wiped her mouth and pulled down her T-shirt. 'OK, I go now. I take fifteen dollars from your wallet in the bedroom.'

'Lily, you've only been here five minutes. What about the cleaning?'

'Oh no, Joe. You've been done *beaucoup*. See you next week. Ah, nearly forgot.' Bending down, Lily retrieved her gum and put it in her mouth and swung her hips to the door, pausing to admire herself in the mirror and flick her fringe. 'By the way, Joe, who Mona? She the wifey you left back Stateside?' Pleased with this touch of authenticity, Lily popped her gum and left.

Mr Jocelyn 'Call Me Josh' Draper was not what Charles had been expecting. Phibbs and Partners was a crowded nursery-glossed converted house in a gritty tramp-rich square in the city. Charles waited in a room set aside for waiting that also housed a girl with an estuary cheese-grater accent who answered a telephone and allowed people who couldn't get to the room in person to wait in the comfort of their own homes.

A small boyish man with long blond hair, beige khaki trousers and a cowboy shirt put his head round the door. 'Hi, Mr Godwin. Good to see you. Step this way.' He led Charles up four flights of stairs, passing occasional men in mildewed worsted, carrying armfuls of files trailing pink ribbon. Josh's office was a small attic room, with a leather sofa, two beanbags and an Indonesian rice bin turned into a coffee-table. The walls advertised old films and Seventies pop groups. Josh threw himself into a Labrador bed with a satisfying crunch and motioned to the sofa, where Charles sat gingerly, making a loud farting noise as he nervously crossed his legs and tried to recline.

'I'm not quite what you expected,' said Josh. 'I am a real lawyer though. Phibbs handles a lot of music and show business work and that's my area. Generally, my clients don't appreciate all that partner's desk, watch-chain and sherry decanter shtick. They feel more relaxed with me.' He waved his palms like Al Jolson.

'Yes, I can see they would,' said Charles uncomfortably, whilst thinking if he were, by some fatal cruel jest, reincarnated as a shrieking juvenile hip-grinder with a platinum album he'd want a lawyer who looked like Enoch Powell's dad. And the thought of handing his affairs over to a bloke who obviously had a Saturday job in a record shop was the last thing he'd want to do.

'OK, business,' said Josh. 'Now I think I've got to the bottom of our confusion on the phone.'

'Ah,' said Charles.

'As I said, you definitely are the person named as executor of Miss Corinth's estate.' He pulled out a grey file from under a scatter of music magazines and copies of *Variety*. 'In fact, you and Phibbs are the sole executors. Her will is really amazingly straightforward; everything was left to her companion, Lottie. There are a couple of small bequests: two thousand pounds to the German Shepherd Breeders' Association for an Under-Five Dog Challenge Cup; one thousand pounds to the Czech State Opera for a scholarship; and here I think is the point of confusion, one hundred pounds to a Mr Otto Zittmeyer to plant a linden in his garden. Now I've done a bit of calling around and Mr Zittmeyer is an eighty-five-year-old retired publicist residing in the Closing

Credits Nursing Home in Bosky Chines, California. I didn't manage to speak to friend Otto personally, but Matron told me he had been a close friend of Miss Corinth's. I think that *he* was supposed to be the executor and *you* were supposed to get the tree. I didn't actually process this document and I gather Miss Corinth didn't come in in person – it was all done by mail. You and friend Otto's name got typographically transposed. It doesn't look as if Miss C checked it before signing; a common problem with artists.'

'Yes, I see,' said Charles. 'Well, I er, it's simple then. I swap with this Zittmeyer chap.'

'Seems simple, seems simple, Charles, but I'm afraid it's rather complicated. Probate law is a bloody minefield, thank God, ha ha. Charles, you and I may think it's obvious, but I'm afraid changing a will is akin to resuscitating the dead, which, of course, would be one brilliant way of null and voiding a will.'

'You're saying there is nothing I can do?'

'Nooo, I'm not saying that. I'm definitely not saying that – I'm a lawyer, ha, ha. I am saying that it would be difficult. We could make an application to Probate Court and in about seven years we might get a judgement that might go in your favour, and it might cost you approximately 50 Gs. And then you'd get your hundred-quid tree.'

'I see.'

'Between you and me, Charles, I don't get the impression that friend Otto is altogether up to being an executor. He is pretty much PG rated and in the final reel, if you see what I mean.'

'I think I see.'

'Best thing is to stay stum. There is nothing much to do: just oversee the disposal of the chattels. We've already arranged for a valuation. Cheque goes to the companion, bosh, bosh. That's it; after that it's just handing over the Mona Corinth Memorial Doggy Bowl to an Alsatian once a year, and, naturally, there's a drink in it for you, reasonable expenses, etc. Seems best all round. OK?'

'Well, I . . .'

'Yes, I know. You have all sorts of questions. Shona will be at your command, and please don't hesitate.' Josh hoisted himself from his nest. 'Right. Great. Let's see you to the door. God, dying is the pits, I can't tell you some of the wills I have to get together. Makes remembrance of things past seem positively Proustian. For instance, there is this incredibly famous old rocker I deal with. He's got a family in Penzance, boy at Millfield, couple of girls, dogs, horses, the lot; terrified of pegging it because, the thing is, his other, legal, missus doesn't know anything about them. His last testament is a riot. The funeral's going to be hysterical. He's got a twenty-page script, real sob stuff, loads of *mea culpa* to be read out from the pulpit, with musical interludes. I just can't wait.'

As they got to the front door, Josh handed Charles a bunch of keys. 'You know where to go. I'm told there is a safe in the bedroom, behind Diana, if that means anything to you, and the code's 38-24-36, easy to remember – just think of her in *The Pan-Handle Princess*. God, wasn't she something?'

'Yes,' said Charles. 'She was something.'

The lift doors opened on to the Corridor of a Thousand Stars. It smelt, faintly, of pine disinfectant, like the passing perfume in a hotel lobby or an ancient memory of a European forest that had been wiped away. Charles waited for the atmosphere of the last week to hit him, but it had gone; the place contained nothing but things. He slowly went from room to room, drawing back the curtains, opening windows, letting in the grey air. He was unsure what it was he was actually supposed to do. Starting in the kitchen he went through drawers and cupboards. The kitchen had obviously been solely Lottie's domain, the cheap green fitted cupboards blinked under a dodgy neon light. There were two rows of neat tinned soup, processed pork and minute amounts of dried goods packed and labelled in plastic bags; an old cloth hung crisp and parched over the tap in the sink. The cupboards underneath had the sort of utensils that you see on trestles in church halls: toothless bread knives and twisted mashers. It was a frugal, hungry room, clean and cracked and worn out. Across the hall the dining-room and living-room ran into each other. A Gothic black oak sideboard bore a long-unused canteen of German silver with an elaborate crest of a pelican with a bleeding heart. There were silver condiment sets and candelabra tarnished blue-black, a ripped cardboard box of placement-card holders in silver gilt shaped like miniature movie cameras.

The living-room had stopped living long before Mona's death. There was a pastel, chipped, petrified grandeur about it; opulent French chairs sagged, unable to rise to their fluted feet. A treasure hunter's map of ancient watery stains overlaid the fading Aubusson carpet, the floral-papered walls had difficulty making it all the way up to the ceiling. Charles's hand wandered over the surfaces, feeling the sticky residue of idling lives. The mantel was a careless queue of small objects, from an existence that didn't expect company. A roll of Sellotape sat beside a small Roman bronze of a three-legged headless horse. A little stack of tokens torn off cereal packets, a cheap wind-up alarm clock with a hiking Mickey Mouse pointing to time stopped, an onyx obelisk, some paper-clips, a curling Polaroid of Mona and Stendhal on a sofa; four burning bright forest eyes.

Charles felt the great weight of empty hours. He tried to shrug it off and went across the hall to Mona's bedroom. It had changed. Physically it was the same but totally different. There was no trace of the breath of the last time he had been here; the floor was clear, the vase was empty, the cupboards closed, the bottles and medicine had been cleared away. Charles imagined a heartbroken Lottie, padding around with a bin-liner, disposing of the detritus of her friend's life: the rattle of pills that were past curing, the letters, the curdling milk; throwing away the bits and pieces that were evidence of life. He imagined her picking up Stendhal's bowl and noisome toys. The distaste, the distress. Making that hellish bed for the last time, turning down the corners on a legend. Charles walked over to the picture of the eugenically pristine Diana and lifted it off the wall. There was the safe. He turned the dial and pulled the heavy door open. It was a big safe, fitted into a brick-duct chimney-breast. Here, Lottie had not been able to edit judiciously. Nothing had

113

been moved for a long time. There were old black boxes from defunct court jewellers, piles of scripts and photograph albums. A tin money box, a Sainsbury's bag. He began to lift the contents onto the bed.

On his third trip his hands slipped, and photographs and letters spilled onto the counterpane. The Eiffel Tower and a small snowstorm in a glass dome padded onto the bed and swirled. This, Charles thought, is how Mona's biopic would start. The artfully disarranged images, the author's nod to *Citizen Kane*, cue to a flashback. He panned over the images; smudgy faces and heavy tailoring. A hideous sparkling necklace fell out of its pale-blue velvet couch. His excited hands picked it up. It couldn't be real, the stones were too bright, too grotesque, it must have been a prop for some movie. He could imagine a white-gloved hand lifting it to the moonlight, cut to the powdered *décolletage*, a hand putting them around an arched neck, a kiss on a shoulder, a briefly stroked cheek, a smile exchanged in a mirror, soaring violins.

'Lucky I got here before you got to the underwear!'

Charles leapt from the bed and spun towards the door. Iona Wallace leant against the jamb, arms folded, cool as a close-up.

'God you frightened me,' he said. Then realizing that his ridiculously histrionic hands were holding the jewels up to his own neck, flushed hastily and pushed them into his pocket. 'What on earth are you doing here? How did you get in?'

'Valuing for Gandolphs. Through the door. You been poking around long?'

'I'm the executor, Charles Godwin.'

'I know, we met, I haven't forgotten. You had a lot to say about my breasts.'

Charles shuddered. 'Yes, I'm sorry. I've just opened the safe.'

'Find anything interesting?' Iona moved towards the bed. She looked wonderfully fresh and elegant in a short blood-coloured suit, black polo-neck and patent loafers. Charles noticed, for the second time, how easily she wore her beauty; how

114

smoothly the sex appeal flowed, and it made him uncomfortable, defensive.

'I don't know yet, there's lots of photos and scripts and letters, some costume jewellery, nothing of much value.'

'I'll be the judge of that. You'd be amazed at what Hollywood ephemera goes for these days.'

Iona sat on the bed with her legs crossed, her skirt concertinaed high. She pushed a length of blond hair behind her ear and picked up a bundle of letters. Charles sat down gingerly with his knees together and started putting the photographs into a neat pile.

'Lawks, listen to this. "I can't stop thinking of your perfect breasts with those something nipples. I remember those creamy globes, and my manhood buried between them, his purple hat disappearing and reappearing and . . ." Christ, where's the next page?'

'I don't think you should be reading that.'

'Oh, here it is ". . . I can't wait to part your beautiful fig with my manly staff, to plough you with the seed of life." Oh please. "To taste the dew from the hidden bud of your desire, to sup at the forbidden well, to lie atop my dearest love. I can't wait for the morrow when again I will clasp you to me, to see from the script that you leave me for another. But I know that is make-believe and that after our fond farewell you will be naked in my caravan and I will come to you as a man." Bloody hell, who wrote this? "Until then, My Love, My Bohemian Princess, adieu. Sleepless, your knight awaits the dawn." Signed D.K. D.K? D.K? Who the bloody hell was D.K?'

'Danny Kaye.'

'Danny Kaye? No don't be ridiculous. It couldn't be. She couldn't. Not with . . .'

'They starred together in *You Can't Kid A Kidder*, about a goatherd who gets mistaken for a prince and falls in love with a princess who's engaged to a wicked . . .'

'I get the picture. Oh no, I can't bear it. Can you imagine him in bed? All those noises and faces and all that inchworm inchworm stuff. It's too horrible. There's a PS "I couldn't wait for the folded silken purse so I sealed this letter with the sticky nectar of my loins." Eeeugh, Jesus.' Iona dropped the letter. 'Danny Kaye's spunk, and I touched it. Fifty-year-old jissom. I'm going to be sick.'

Despite himself, Charles started to laugh. Iona pulled her head back, caught his eye with her own and held it for three falls and a submission. She stared for an extra moment to make sure he was bound motionless, and then she opened her mouth and let him have it. She laughed back, full on. It hit Charles with a brutal lightness, full in the face, and trickled down his chin. It ran in liquid musical rivulets through the ravines of his ears and filled his head with cool, gushing foaming happiness. It felt like a white spray down his neck and his spine tingled. Iona laughed easily, accurately, devastatingly. Like an intravenous shot of the most marvellous drug in the world. The moment it stopped Charles wanted another hit, immediately, instantly. For the first time he understood why girls always put a sense of humour at the top of the list of things they find attractive in men. They don't want to elbow aside Brad Pitt to get to Bob Monkhouse. Girls don't particularly like jokes; they really don't want to know the one about the Essex girl and the blind chimney-sweep. But they know, or they sense, or they are born with an instinct that tells them that men are at their most defenceless, men are puppies, men will do anything, face any danger or indignity, spend the rent, risk the job, hock the future, simply to make girls laugh. Girlie laughter, the delicious needle, the fizzing cup, the beautiful, bright light barbed hook.

Charles dizzily sucked in Iona's laugh, swallowed it and felt it catch in his stomach; that unmistakable light queasy feeling, the first warning symptom of terminal desire. He picked up another letter.

' "You bitch, you utter heartless bitch . . ." '

'I beg your pardon?' giggled Iona.

'No, no, it's here. Another letter. "You bitch, you have made me wretched. How can you cast me aside with so little thought? How could you be so cruel? I love you without question. I thought you loved me. I have given up everything, left my wife and home and children. I even sacked my agent and

116

turned down *Ben Hur* to be with you. How could you, you cow, you harpy, you painted Jezebel, you temptress? Was I just good for one thing? Was I just a stepping-stone for your ambition? What about the things we planned? I am desperate; you have trashed my life. Solemnly I warn you, you must be responsible for what I now do. I am a man without hope, desperate, brokenhearted." '

'God, honestly. What a whinging cretin. Who wrote it?'

'Wait, it's nearly finished. "I have the picture of us on our blissful weekend in front of me. It was the happiest day of my life. And beside it there is *Variety*; you at that awful dinner, on the arm of Chuck. The worst night of my life. I look at them together and you know, you whore, your expression is exactly the same in both. You look at him just as you once looked at me. I shall die cursing you. Mona, Mona, my one love. Oh how I love you." Signed Clanton. Clanton? Clanton Napther. It can't be, it can't be. He was brilliant, so sexy in *The Widow's Treasure*, and he died of an overdose.'

'Oh God, you don't think this is his suicide note, I thought it was supposed to be an accident.'

'It would certainly seem to be. There's a photograph of him somewhere, I saw it.' They turned to the photographs on the bed.

Iona tipped up the plastic bag. Hundreds of glossy snaps fell in a heap. 'You know all this stuff is worth a fortune? Those letters alone. If the rest are anything like them it's worth a bloody fortune. The publicity; the Hollywood glamour; sex, stars, revelations; this is bigger than Elizabeth Hurley going down on the Pope.'

'Hold on, just a minute.' Charles fought the strong temptation to encourage Iona's excitement, but the sensible, restrained, reserved Charles raised a point of order, took control of the microphone. 'Hold on, we can't sell these, they're personal. She obviously never meant them to be made public. You couldn't really . . . couldn't really make it all, all this public, sell it. It's prurient, unkind. It's not just her, it's other people.'

'Charles,' Iona turned off the smile at the mains, 'get real. This stuff is not just worth a lot of money, it's intrinsically worthy, it's scholarship and research. It's important.'

'Oh, it's just movie stars, it's not Byron or Shakespeare,' interrupted Charles, lamely.

'Who made you civilization's censor? What we should and shouldn't know?'

'Oh, I just know it's not right. It's private, some things must be private. Our lives can't belong to whoever happens to be going through the drawers when we die.'

'Mona Corinth wasn't just anyone; this isn't just anywhere. She was a star. Hollywood is the twentieth century's equivalent of fifteenth-century Florence.'

'Oh really, Iona, that's a bit rich.'

'No, it's the truth. You can't unmake these things; you can't unfind them. You can give them to the world, or you can burn them, which would be an act of philistinism on a par with Richard Burton's wife burning his diaries. Who do you think you are?'

'I am the executor. I have to do what's in the best interests of the estate.'

'And what do you imagine that is?'

'We'll arrange with you to sell the furniture and stuff and keep these personal things and letters and photographs safe and private, I suppose.'

'Let me tell you,' Iona put her face close to his. 'The rest of the hideous broken-down worn-out stuff in this place will make about three thousand pounds on a good day, even allowing for the added interest in who it belonged to. Not much of a bequest, when you consider that you might be wilfully hiding ten times that. This is the stuff of culture Charles,' she said, softly picking up a handful of letters and photographs and letting them slip through her fingers. 'If that picture were of Christina Rossetti or Jane Austen you'd say, "Whoopee. Let's call the British Library and the TLS." '

'Actually, if that were Jane Austen, I'd probably say she's got a great pair of breasts, and William Holden is older than he looks.'

Iona had managed to spill the contents of a large manila envelope: a glossy 4 x 8 photograph of Mona and Bill Holden, sitting in an old-fashioned sort of sun lounger in a garden with a lot of sunny hibiscus. 'Crikey, Moses,' said Iona. 'Look at that.' They were both naked. Very, very naked. Mona with her legs apart, one thigh on Holden's knee. He was leaning back on his elbows and she was grasping his plantain-like penis. 'Shit, look at the size of his third man,' said Iona. Underneath, the next photograph, obviously taken on the same day, showed two men, one Holden, standing on a lawn holding two young naked girls like wheelbarrows. The girls' breasts hung hugely; they were both laughing. Mona stood beside them, wearing only a baseball hat, waving a pair of knickers like a starter's flag.

Iona shrieked with laughter. 'Do you see who that is?'

'Oh my God, who?'

'It's Laurence Olivier.'

They both started gluttonously riffling through the photographs. There were dozens; all of them erotic, some positively pornographic. Mona appeared in many with lots of different men. She was always elegant, her limbs naturally arranged themselves beautifully. Charles and Iona competed to put names to faces and bottoms. 'Oh him, you know, the cowboy.'

'Oh God, yes. And that girl, famous, with the hair. Veronica, um, Lake, yes.'

'Look at that. That's her fucking Paul Robeson.' A beautiful picture of Mona on her knees, with her chest pressed to the ground, her arms stretched out grasping the earth, and behind her, his cock half buried, the great communist baritone. Black muscles shone and strained, his neck corded, eyes glared white, big black hands lifted her hips; he was about to let his people go.

'Look at the handkerchief, they are playing Othello and Desdemona. God that's sexy,' said Iona. Then, snatching a picture to her bosom, 'Here's one for you, this is definitely one for you.'

'Show me,' Charles laughed.

She turned the photograph round and sniggered and held it under her chin. It was a portrait of Gary Cooper looking High

Noonish. He was wearing a gun belt, a pair of cowboy boots and an erection. His knees were bent and he held his palms out in the classic gunfighter's pose. Charles handed the microphone back to his other solitary self.

'Why should that be for me?' he said coldly.

'Well,' Iona, trimming, said, 'I thought he was what you'd fancy. You know, he's sort of cute, a handsome dude, big.' She laughed, trying to lower the barometer.

'And why should I like him?'

'Oh, Charles, I don't know. Perhaps you go for more Victor McLaglen types or George Sanders. It wasn't meant to be rude. I know gays don't all go for the same sort of men us girls do.'

Charles's mouth opened and closed like a fish.

'Jolly good thing really, I don't think I could compete.' She tried a half-hearted little laugh again. 'You, what I mean is, I'm sure Barnstaple's, you know, Barnstaple's very attractive, in a sort of gay way, if that's what . . . Oh God, I've put my foot in it. I'm so sorry. Sorry.' Then feeling her balance going, she added, 'Don't be so sensitive.'

Charles approached meltdown, his klaxons blared, his thoughts ran along gantries, his hands raced to his head and ran shrieking and hallooing through his hair. 'I'm not a homosexual, and if I was a homosexual, which I repeat I'm not, I wouldn't be homosexual with Vernon. I don't particularly like being a heterosexual with Vernon.' Charles came to the end of his breath, his mouth clamped shut, and he searched for something pithy and funny and conciliatory to say, but decided on dignified silence.

'Oh Charles, I just assumed, you know, the way you do. Um, Vernon introduced you as "my dear friend", wink, wink, and there was all that bosom stuff. Well, you know, I just assumed, honestly, really. Have you never been queer?'

Charles shook his head.

'Sure? Not bi?'

Shook his head again.

'Really. Oh well. Now there's a thing.' She gave him full beam; teeth, eyes, floppy fringe, the works. 'Well um, where are you taking me to lunch then?' and she drenched him in vintage, *premier cru*, chateau-bottled laughter. The hook tugged hard. Charles felt three hundred contradictory things at once. It wasn't one whole big thing yet, but it was beginning to set around the edges. He picked a passing thought.

'I'm not going to change my mind about all this,' he said, waving eloquently at the bed.

'Of course you're not.' Iona jumped up and pulled him to his feet, snaking her arm through his. 'I feel like Italian,' she said.

As Charles pulled the door shut the glass dome rolled off the bed and thudded onto the carpet, and started hesitantly to tinkle the theme from *Jules et Jim*. The final mechanical memory of a turn of an absent hand, the notes plinked into the empty room, serenading the naked and the dead.

Chapter Eight

'Good God.' Charles looked across the drizzling square at St Bertha's. 'My God, who on earth are all these people?' A dense, packed, pac-a-macked and polythene-hatted crowd stood two or three deep outside the church, a stream of taxis and black hire cars queued, a couple of film crews lurked on the pavement, and every time someone stepped out a camera or two flashed. 'Christ Almighty,' said Charles again. The sofa groaned.

A large Mercedes tipped a couple onto the pavement and the crowd leant forward. A tall girl in precipitous heels inelegantly tugged and straightened the hem of her very short skirt, grabbed the arm of her fat companion, and tottered towards the door. Another fat man, neat in a dark three-piece pinstripe, stepped forward with an outstretched hand. Charles saw that it was Vernon. He watched the hand first minutely shake the girl's and then the fat man's, and then manoeuvre elbows and shoulders so that the three of them formed a tableau for the cameras, the lord to the fore. Then, with little semaphore waves and prods, he ushered them into the church, like an overweight Border collie.

Vernon had thought circuitously, obliquely, laterally and panoramically about Mona Corinth's memorial service. The hypothesis of an inkling of a possible plan had emerged. Maybe, just maybe, there could be a way of manipulating this event for gain. Some leverage on the garden, some delicate soupçon of revenge to be won over the Committee for the shambles of his party, and even if nothing came of it, there was always an inch or two of balming publicity. Vernon had pulled out all the stops. Actually he had pulled the stops out of Marle.

Stephen had been sent hither and yon, summoning respectable pew fillers, printing up service sheets, arranging floral tributes. He had tapped into the shadowy, po-faced, secret sect of the memorial society, a loose group of ageing cadaverous men and women, retired admirals, pensioned civil servants and bereaved wives, who knew the sight-lines and acoustics of every church in the West End. Their only payment, their particular solemn pleasure, was seeing their names on the guest lists of services in the *Telegraph*. Marle had found them an accommodating bunch. Each one passed on the numbers of others. 'Did the deceased have any legal connections?' Perhaps the mothballed Recorder of the Southern Circuit should be asked. 'Had the bereaved served in any capacity during the war?' 'And without offence, on which side?' 'Would medals be in order?' The memorial society knew its place at death's door.

Vernon himself had managed a couple of meetings with the Rev Trev, who had shown himself to be an ideally stupid and malleable man with a great, soft opaque vision of the hand-waving and joyous free-form swaying that might be gained from the Heaven-sent blessing of Mona's lonely death. Vernon sat in the front pew and craned and twisted his fat neck as far as it would reach in its detachable collar. It was a good turn out. He smiled. He could still whistle up a decent crowd. There, directly behind him, were two theatrical knights, the Minister for the Arts, four MPs from the film and broadcasting sub-committee and a short bearded English child actor turned director, who

123

hadn't made a film for twenty years but was still a favourite at awards ceremonies. He had come with an ugly wife who had been famous in the Fifties for starring in a long-running children's television series of *Dick Turpin*.

But Vernon's real *coup* had been the coincidence, fortuitous, that one of Mona's early light comedies, *Pretty Maids All In A Row*, was being remade at Pinewood by Bubba Yukon, the absurd American producer, who was now trying to compose a profound grimace of reverence on his porcine face at Vernon's elbow. Bubba had immediately seen the publicity possibilities in Mona's memorial service and had loudly proclaimed the fact that as a mark of respect *Complete Betties on Death Row* would, at extraordinary expense, stop filming for a day so that Padua Pocket, the Hollywood star who was recreating Mona's role, could pay her respects to the old-time star who had, again by fortuitous coincidence, been her childhood heroine and mentor. Padua sat on Vernon's right, luscious as a wet dream, bored as a night in a Grimsby youth hostel, holding down the rim of her skirt as if it were an elastic band that might shoot back up her jacket.

Charles met Mrs Kotzen as he sidled in. She looked neat and hygienic in navy blue. 'I must say I'm very impressed, Charles. It really is a very good turn out. I think our life peer has been on the blower. Oh can you imagine how Mona would have hated it?'

'Yes,' said Charles, 'she would.'

'I hardly recognize anyone. The home contingent seems to be sitting over there, right at the back.' The Garden Committee crouched in a huddle beside the font, Bryony sporting a Tyrolean mountain guide's hat with a large black eagle's feather. The organ started playing the theme from *The Big Country*, a film Mona hadn't been in.

Bon Bon waved at them from the choir. They sat beside her.

'Isn't it moving?' she whispered. 'Who'd have thought she had so many friends. Might I introduce Mr Jocelyn Draper, Belman's solicitor. Mrs Kotzen and Charles Godwin.'

Josh, dressed in a five-button donkey jacket and bright floral tie, leant over Bon Bon and shook hands. 'Yes, we've met. Phibbs are dealing with Miss Corinth's probate.'

'Oh, here comes Belman.' Bon Bon gave a nervous giggle.

Out of the apse shuffled her husband with the vicar. They were an arresting pair. The congregation fell into a strained if not altogether respectful silence. The vicar was wearing a cassock apparently made out of a long tie-dyed T-shirt. On the front was a childishly appliquéd brown fist holding a rainbow. The word 'Yes' was picked out in large sequins. His training shoes and jeans peeped out from underneath. Belman was more conventionally dressed to his calling, sporting a tightly waisted jacket constructed out of dyed pea-green python skin and a pair of tight black jeans tucked into crimson alligator cowboy boots. Bon Bon had insisted that he wore a tie, and he had compromised on a leather bootlace with a silver Harley-Davidson toggle.

The vicar turned to face the altar, showing that the back of his cassock clearly, and not inappropriately, had 'Jesus', with an exclamation mark, stuck onto it with more sequins. 'Hi, bro,' he said to the Cross, and offered a high five and a 'V' sign for peace. Turning back to the congregation he beamed hugely and said, 'Hi, to you too. Woooh.'

His voice ricocheted out of a dozen speakers, strategically attached to pillars for the hard of praying. 'Isn't life great? I can't hear you.' He theatrically cupped his palm to an ear. 'Isn't life just the best thing?' The congregation shuffled and coughed. 'Yeah, life. You can't beat it. Today we are here to celebrate life; Mona's life! Your life! My life! The life after death! The life ever-ready! Ever-loving! Everlasting! Let us make Mona's death life-affirming. Let's say yes to life! Hello God! I'm here! Let's party! OK? OK. Wow! To start us off on the right note, a big loud joyous glad-to-be-alive note, our own resident living legend, Belman. Now before Belman leads us into the first hymn, I reckon some of you won't have been in church for some time.' The Rev laughed. 'It's OK! It's OK! You may have forgotten the tune, that's OK! The words are on the sheet. Let's shout them out! Now, to make it a bit more exciting, I want all of you on my left to sing the first line of the chorus, and you lot on my right, the second. OK?! It's sort of like an echo effect, you'll pick it up. OK! Belman, hit it!'

And hit Belman did. He bent his knees and bowed his head, so that his long hair fell in a curtain. He windmilled his arm by way of a run-up, and gave the strings an almighty clout. A noise that might have effectively woken the cremated thudded and howled round the church. The congregation was flung to its feet. Charles picked up his sheet. Hymn one – 'Free Love'. Words by the Rev Trev, music by Pinkie Dunn. After the opening trump of a chord, the actual tune was a bit of an anticlimax. Belman picked it out with a plectrum and much vibrato. It had a familiar motif: half playground skipping rhyme, half Andrew Lloyd-Webber. Raggedly, the congregation approached the first line.

> I have a love that's free,
> I have a love that's true,
> I have a love that's hard,
> I have a big love for you.
> It's a love that comes inside me,
> It's a love that makes me sing,
> And brother, sister, on your knees,
> Let me pop it in.
> (Chorus)
> If you don't want my love, go to hell,
> If you don't want my love, go to hell,
> Go to hell, go to hell, go to hell, go to hell,
> Go to hell, go to hell, go to hell.

At the first 'Go to hell' the vicar leapt to his left and waved his arm at the congregation, like an Abenazaar on ecstasy; at the second he scooted to the right and did the same. The audience stared back with chronic embarrassment, the vicar's flat voice bellowing in their ears. Charles, sitting in the choir, and technically *hors de combat*, being neither left nor right, watched their faces. Vernon's eyes bulged with discomfort. Padua, beside him, rocked to the beat like an autistic child at a disco. By the time the fourth verse came to a rousing crescendo, the congregation had decided it was having nothing to do with this hymn, and they watched the manic vicar and the oblivious Belman with blank horror. All except for Bryony, whose stentorian bark howitzered from the back singing 'Go to hell' with great feeling, for both sides.

As the last notes seeped into the rafters, the vicar theatrically wiped his brow. 'Wow. Well that's better! That's blown away a few cobwebs. Bet Mona and the Big Man are both snapping their fingers now. Let's have a little moment of meditation, of personal stocktaking. A little silent interaction with friend Jesus.' The congregation slumped with relief onto their bottoms.

'OK. Amen. How often have we thought wouldn't it be nice if all our lives were like movies? Yeah. Wouldn't it? Well, I want to ask you, Who's shooting your movie? Who's shouting "Cut!" and "Action!" on your biopic? Is it devil ego or is it Jesus?! This church is really a movie theatre. We have wafers instead of popcorn, we have wine instead of Diet Coke, but this is where you show the rushes of your life to the great producer! How do your rushes look? Are they in focus? When it comes time for the Holy Spirit to edit your epic will it be family viewing or will it get an over-eighteen certificate?! Have you overspent your budget?'

Trev warmed to his theme. No possible celluloid simile was left unexploited: distribution, marketing, post-production, dubbing, subtitles. He hopped up and down the aisles, miming panning shots, close-ups, using his hands as a viewfinder. 'Are you God's best boy?! Are you Christ's grip?! Does God get billing above your title?! Does He get credit?!'

Charles felt the congregation's embarrassment rise like steam from the pews, until the atmosphere in the church was a huge hot sticky blush. Trev swam on regardless, finally finishing standing on tiptoe and pointing a shaking hand at the roof and shouting, 'When it's a rap, when God calls "Cut!" on the last exit, like Mona, we must be able to say "Yea! Whenever you're ready, Mr Almighty!" '

There Trev paused, arms skyward, eyes to Heaven, dripping sweat, for the effect of his dynamic words to sink into the congregation, who in turn regarded him with their own silent, dark, fierce emotions. Slowly, his shoulders slumped. He walked with a weary, exaggerated humility to his seat, giving Vernon a little wink. He was pleased, he was very pleased. It had gone very well. Thank you Big Guy. The one-take vicar.

The organ started playing 'Lara's Theme' from *Dr Zhivago*, another film Mona hadn't been in. Vernon got to his feet and walked to the lectern. The congregation arranged its face appropriately.

'I remember when Mona Corinth first met me.' Vernon's jowly, polished features shone in the reflected light from the bronze eagle that held the 'Happy Tidings' large-print interdenominational Bible. He paused and scanned the audience. One fat hand tugged at a crested cuff-link. 'I remember when I first met Mona Corinth. It was here in our beautiful garden, in this square she graciously chose to make her home. It was June; I remember it precisely because the House had just risen and I had been appointed Privy Councillor and was returning from a private function at the Palace. I was strolling through the garden and had paused to see how the Princess Grace rose which I planted in memory of my dear friend, Her Serene Highness, was getting on, when a voice behind me said, in tones that were instantly familiar to any acolyte of the silver screen, "Excuse me, can I get past?" A simple enough statement that somehow, on that summer afternoon in the verdant beauty of the garden, seemed prophetic. A plea perhaps, a question rather than a request. Maybe all her life Mona Corinth had been asking "Excuse me, can I get past?" I sensed the melancholy, the fortitude that was at the heart of her powerful character. Well, on this bright afternoon, I am pleased to say, I didn't allow her egress. I barred her way for a moment and introduced myself. It was a propitious meeting, I think I can say, for both of us. Mona came to see me as something of a Father Confessor, a pair of broad shoulders, a pair of safe hands, a sympathetic ear, a man who could offer worldly advice, a humble guide.'

Charles shifted in his pew. He watched Bon Bon's dolly-fringed profile. She stared at Vernon with rapt attention. Not for the first time he was amazed at not only the man's polished brass nerve but his ability to make others admire his reflection in it.

'On that first June meeting I drew her attention to the rose and pointed out that here I was, unchaperoned, in the company of two great sensual stars, Grace Kelly and Mona Corinth. One vegetable the other animal; both immortal. She laughed at my off-the-cuff *bon mot*, that deep sensual laugh that so invigorated Saturday evenings in the dark stalls, and she said, "I should like to end up as a rose in this garden with an English lord to tend me," and we laughed together.

'Well today these sentiments are tinged with sadness. I think we can give Mona her wish, nay, I think it is beholden on us to grant her her wish. So it gives me pleasure on this sad occasion to announce the Mona Corinth Memorial Fund. Her ashes, in due course, will return to nurture the garden, but also, fittingly, I and other interested parties have set up a fund to erect a suitable statue in her memory. I am glad to say that a substantial amount has already been donated. Half of the money will be used to commission a construction by Armi Peshware, the award-winning and challenging sculptor, in whose work I know Mona took a deep interest, and the other half will be used to set up a Natural Ecology and Harmony Awareness club for young urban adolescents, overseen by the vicar here at St Bertha's. Mona, as I am sure many of you are aware, was particularly concerned with the plight of urban youth and the balance of nature. Mona's memory should grace our beautiful corner of Eden, even though she has gone to a greater Elysian Field. There are collection plates at the door, please give generously.'

Vernon looked at the spotlight above his head. 'Mona, your subtle allure will live on in our hearts and on our lawn for ever.'

'Amen!' shouted the Rev Trev.

Vernon hung his head for a moment, as if overcome with emotion, and then minced back to his seat. The service stumbled to a close with another playground hymn and a couple of free-form prayers. The Rev Trev delivered the final blessing with a flourish of bunching fists, and the congregation broke for the door as if the atmosphere in the church might be mortally contagious.

Through the press of the memorial society one figure fought the ebb. Bryony, puce and furrowed, elbowed her way towards the choir. 'Fuck off, fuck off, fuck the fuck off. Get your prick umbrella out of my snatch, you wrinkled ball-sack,' she barked at a horrified rear admiral, before shouldering him into the recently hysterectomized lap of an optometrist's widow. 'Charles,' she bellowed. 'Charles. Fuck off and die.' This to a solemn goitred genealogist who had imagined that the worst was already over. She sundered the last rank of mourners and stood blowing like a bull who has inadvertently found itself in a matador's changing-room. 'He's gone too shafting far, the fat cunt. You must call an emergency meeting – instant-fucking-ly.'

'Yes, right Bryony. Um, yes. I expect we ought to, um, discuss . . .'

'Discuss. Discuss. It's war. This calls for the fucking final solution. Tomorrow. Ten o'clock sharp. I'll arrange it, at your place. Kotzen? Bon Bon?' Bryony fixed the two women behind Charles. 'Three-line whip, understand.' They both nodded, speechless. 'Right. I'm so fucking angry I could rupture a horse. I need a rum and a wank – no, I need four rums and a tungsten front and back-bottom enema. Fuck,' she roared, and charged back into the routed memorialists.

As Charles stepped into the drizzle a hand snaked through the crook of his arm. 'Hello, Mr President.' Iona stood, wet and beautiful in a black highwayman's coat, her hair stuck in heavy blond tendrils to her neck, her face pale and dewy. The sight of her again, the look of her, caught Charles utterly by surprise. The hooks dragged like anchors in his stomach.

'Hello. I didn't see you inside.'

'No, I crept in at the back. Awful wasn't it?'

'Yes, pretty awful.'

'Well . . . you never told me about the memorial sculpture. Pretty brave to commission Peshware; she's not everyone's taste.'

'I didn't because I didn't know. That was the first I'd heard about it. The Committee is going to be pretty furious I think.'

'I should imagine. He's a bit of an operator, that Vernon.'

'Yes, a bit of an operator.'

In front of them, a huddle of photographers was listening to the American producer, Bubba Yukon, who was waving his hands. Padua Pocket stood a little way off, nervously hugging herself. The mourners scurried away in search of taxis and pubs.

An elongated Mercedes pulled up in front of the church in a cloud of sulphurous exhaust fumes. The driver jumped out and opened the back door. Bubba said something final to the paparazzi and then nodded at Padua, who took a deep breath, threw back her shoulders and walked with an exaggerated wiggle towards the car. The photographers fanned out behind her, firing short bursts of film. She got to the open door, paused, and slowly lowered her bottom onto the seat, her long legs resting on the pavement. The photographers moved in to concentrate their fire. With a studied precision, Padua lifted a stilettoed foot into the car. Her skirt slid up her thigh. Lifting her knee she shot back a small, neatly cropped runway of parted pubic hair. Fingers were rigor mortised to triggers. For a long moment motor drives hummed appreciatively. The starlet and the press flashed at each other. Then Bubba moved in, and with a brief 'That will do it, chaps,' got in beside her. The door slammed.

Iona laughed as the car pulled away. 'Don't you just love Hollywood?'

'That's dreadful,' said Charles. 'Truly shocking. At Mona's memorial service. Outside a church. It's beyond anything.'

'Oh, Charles, come off it. It's the only bit of today that Mona would have appreciated. God, it's nothing compared to her pictures. Which, rather neatly, is what I wanted to talk to you about.'

'Yes, I thought you did.' Charles felt sharply disappointed. 'Do we have to? It doesn't seem appropriate today. We've just been praying for her soul, or at least I think that's what we've been doing. Can't it wait?'

'Not for long. I've got to arrange the sale. It's an enormous amount of work.'

'OK, well why don't we make a date, um . . .'

'Hey, are you asking me for a date,' Iona said coquettishly.

Charles blushed and stammered, 'Well, you know. Another lunch perhaps?'

'What about now? Why don't you give me a drink? – I'm soaked.'

'Yes, fine. Um, where would you like to go?'

'I tell you what, Charles,' she said, as if making a great discovery, 'why don't you take me home? You live here don't you? I don't want to walk in the rain.'

'Yes, of course. Sorry, rude of me.'

Charles opened the door and let Iona go in ahead of him.

She stood in the drawing-room and gasped. The room gasped back. The ottoman whistled softly.

'Christ, Charles, this room is unbelievable. All this stuff, my God, it's like . . . I don't quite know what it's like.'

'Yes, it's impressive, isn't it?' said Charles, standing beside her. 'I hate it.'

'Oh, so do I.'

'Do you really? Do you really hate it?' Charles said excitedly. 'Honestly?'

'Absolutely. It's ghastly. I've never seen such a temple to insecurity.'

'You know, you're the first person who's ever hated my home. Everyone else comes in and adores it. Everyone simply adores it. It's like having a very glamorous mother when you're a child, your friends come to tea and all they want to do is play with her and be bewitched, and of course she goes along with it because she thinks it's nice for you, but of course it isn't, it's humiliating and ghastly.'

'Was your mother like that?'

'A bit I suppose. Here, let me take your coat. What would you like to drink?'

132

'Scotch with nothing.' Iona sat on the ottoman, which couldn't believe its luck. She was wearing the same skirt as Padua Pocket.

Charles searched for a bottle of whisky and listened to the furniture twitter excitedly. 'How on earth did he lure her back here? He must have paid her.' 'Well she's certainly got some class, I haven't been so elegantly insulted since I stayed in the count's summer house in Capri before the war, a great improvement on that chinky tart,' grunted an old German secretaire. 'She's got no knickers on, you know. My beading's gone right up her bottom,' boasted the ottoman.

'I suppose I'd be impressed with all this gear', said Iona, examining a netsuke of a chow licking its balls, 'if it wasn't my job. When you work in an auction house other people's antiques are like taking your work home.'

'I suppose it's the same for tall gynaecologists in newsagents or probation officers in the House of Commons.' He handed her a Venetian blue glass and sat opposite her on the edge of a Georgian armchair. 'Now, about Mona. I understand your points about the cultural value and not being censors and the value and everything, but frankly I think we're losing sight of the basic fact that this stuff is private and, um, actually obscene. We still have Mona's published works, if you can call films published. Her oeuvre is as she left it. She never, to our knowledge, chose to make this, her personal stuff, public; so we can be pretty certain, well we can assume that . . .'

'Why don't you get rid of it?' Iona asked sweetly.

'What, throw it away? Well, I thought of that, but my responsibility as an executor . . .'

'I don't mean Mona's things. I mean yours, all this. If you hate it, why don't you flog it?'

'Oh,' Charles slumped back in the chair, 'this stuff. Don't think I haven't thought about that too. I can't tell you how close I've come to just dropping a match into that dreadful old horsehaired nag.' He waved at her seat. The ottoman whinnied. 'But they belong to me, and, in a way, I belong to them. Owning things is a two-way street, you have responsibilities, and if I didn't have this lot, I'd have to have something else and it would all start again. We go through life and accumulate waifs and strays. You give a thing a roof and you have to care for it. There's nothing occasional about a table, a pouffe isn't just for Christmas, it's for about two hundred years.'

Iona laughed. 'I can see why auctioneers are your *bête noir*. We're Vikings, polite pillagers. Can I have another drink?'

Charles went to get the bottle.

'You're so middle class,' a Spanish candlestick grunted as he passed.

'Look, about Mona's papers,' Iona said. 'I'm not going to give up, but I've also been thinking about it, and it seems to me that your objections come down to complying with Mona's wishes, right?'

'Yes, I suppose so.'

'Well, how about if we ask her?'

'Now that's a good idea,' said Charles, putting the ivory chow precisely back. 'Why don't we have a seance, or perhaps Gandolfs has a regular medium. "Hello, could I speak to Doris in the soothsaying department, she's expecting my call." '

'If you look in the pocket of my coat you will find *Sweet Strangers*.'

'Her film? I've never seen it.'

'It's out on video. Mona plays Laura, it's supposed to be her best performance, according to the sleeve notes. Let's see if she tells us anything.'

'I think it's a bit far-fetched. I mean they're not her words, it's a script and she's playing a part.'

'Let's watch it anyway.'

'Yes, I'd love to.' Charles felt a sudden surge of joy, out of all proportion to the actual expectation of watching the forty-year-old film in the afternoon, which was, when all's said and done, what he did most afternoons anyway. 'The video's in the bedroom. We'll have to watch it on the bed.'

'You old smooth-talker, you. Bring the bottle.'

The opening credits rolled to late-Californian Rachmaninov over a shot of a heavy glass ashtray holding a cigarette with lipstick traces and a fat cigar. The smoke hung like Byzantine linen.

'Well that would make it an 18 movie today, for a start. Couldn't have smoking,' said Iona. 'Have you thought what a loss the prohibition on smoking has been to the dramatic arts. Imagine *Now Voyager* with sticks of gum.'

'And where did they get their names,' said Charles. 'Look at these people. It's like the Torah meets the Argonauts. Everyone who deals with production is Jewish and everyone who does anything arty has a made-up classical name. Look at that – Hairdo by Antigone Halo. Miss Corinth's wardrobe by Athena Troy, and then it's produced by Abraham Z. Steingelt and Mort Fink.'

The establishing shot was a large baroque house on the coast of New England. It's a stormy night. A car's headlights race. As the solid sedan turns into the drive, it picks out a name on the Gothic gateposts: Conway Breakers. Cut to elegant interior hallway. Frantic ringing of bell. A butler, pulling on a dressing-gown, opens the door. A man strides in with a gust of leaves. He shrugs off a heavy coat and hands it to the flunky. He is sleek and tall, dressed in white tie with a pencil moustache. '*I must see Laura, I must see her, you hear.*'

'*She retired an hour ago, Mr Fitzhollow.*'

'*Who is it Bostick?*' says a voice from the landing. The camera turns and tracks along the floor, then smoothly races up the curling stair. At the top, one hand on the banister, stands Mona, hard and beautiful, the big mouth darkly set, her hair perfectly sculpted, the condor eyes bleak and icy. She wears one of those bedroom confections, consisting of layers of soft net and silk with ruffles and bows. She is backlit, her figure softly outlined. '*Brad, you shouldn't be here. We agreed. You promised.*'

'Brad, we shouldn't be here,' Iona mimicked huskily, wriggling against Charles on the huge soft bed. She rubbed her feet on the ocelot counterpane. 'Don't you just love old films in the afternoon, when it's raining outside. You can just sink into them, wallow and drink Scotch.'

'*Laura, it's no good. I know it's madness, but darling I had to see you.*'

'I know it's madness, Laura. She was very beautiful, wasn't she? She hardly does anything. Every shot she makes one small move, her head, an arm, but you can't take your eyes off her.'

Charles turned and looked at Iona. Her face was very close, softly lit, hair by Antigone Halo, looking up at him, her pupils dilated, flickering reflected light. He was going to say something, perhaps, 'Darling, I had to see you,' but the words hung in the wings. They shared a breath. 'This is research, remember. Let's listen to Mona.' Charles sipped whisky and turned back to the screen. They lay in silence, Iona's head on his shoulder, Charles's fingers grazed over textures.

The story was complicated. Brad was an architect, unhappily married to Laura's sister who couldn't have children. Laura lived alone in Conway Breakers, the old family house. Brad loved her, she loved Brad, and she loved her sister. Her sister loved Conway Breakers and a terrier called Maud. Only death would get them to the final credits. Towards the end of the first reel Iona had crooked her leg over Charles's. Her hand rested lightly on his poplin chest.

Mona sat in the front of a big sedan, Brad drove. They were on a winding road behind a tractor. '*Pass him, Brad. We've got to get to the theatre, we're going to be late.*' Violins whined ominously.

Iona whispered, 'Brad, are you ever going to make a pass?'

Charles heard, but he wasn't listening and then, like a slow interpreter, the words fell into place. He looked down at her.

'What?'

'Make a pass Brad.' Her arm came up and pulled his face down to hers. Their lips touched and parted, then touched again. Iona's tongue slipped into Charles's mouth. Whisky and silver electric.

The horn blared. Mona screamed. '*Brad.*'

The hooks in Charles's stomach jerked. His insides turned to running salmon. His head exploded like time-lapse film of orchids opening.

There was a screech of brakes. '*Look out.*' A girl on a horse appeared on the other side of the road. Mona cried, Brad fought the wheel, the violins fought Rachmaninov. Iona rolled on top of Charles. His hands sprinted to her hair. The car shot off the road, the horse shied, the girl fell, the tractor driver silently shouted, teeth crashed, gears crunched. Tongues twined like fish spawning in the blackness. Silence, wheel spinning, rain on shattered glass, gossamer thread of saliva.

They kissed for a long time, kissed throughout Mona's coma, through the doctor's terse prognosis, through Brad's row with his wife, and then, as Mona, head elegantly bandaged, opened her rapturous eyes and Brad's face swam into focus above her, Iona lifted herself on her elbows and smiled her killer smile down at Charles.

'*Darling, you're here. I'm so glad you're here.*'

'You do want me, don't you?'

'Oh yes,' said Charles.

'I can't wait. I want to be naked for you.'

'I'm rather looking forward to seeing you naked.' Charles tried to sound relaxed.

'*We've been fools, Brad. Blind, stupid fools.*'

Iona stood beside the bed with her hands on her hips. 'Race you.'

Charles started undoing the buttons of his shirt, his hands tried to wriggle through his cuffs. Mona tried to sit up in bed, but fell back onto the pillows.

'I win.'

Charles looked up. Iona stood naked, arms at her sides, ankles together. The salmon leapt in his throat and fell back with a splash.

'Pretty good, huh?' She turned slowly, holding her arms out. 'I'm a terrible exhibitionist. I'm shockingly proud of my bits. Aren't these good breasts?'

'Splendid.'

'*Can I have a mirror? Am I scarred?*'

'*To me you are the most beautiful thing in the world.*'

'*Oh Brad, don't.*'

'You don't think they're too small?'

'No.'

'The nipples are good aren't they? Quite perky?'

'Yes, perfectly perky.'

'Oh hurry up. You're like those people who undo all the knots on their Christmas presents.' She bent down and grabbed a leg, ripping off socks, tugging at worsted legs. Charles shed his shirt and undid his belt. Laughing, she pulled his trousers off and knelt down and reached for the waistband of his underpants. Charles's hands, like a pair of nervous vergers, tried to usher her away.

'So exciting. Quick, let me see. Oh Brad, it's a beauty. I knew you'd have an elegant penis. It's just perfect, exactly what I always wanted.'

Iona held the cock like a piece of Meissen, turning it over and gently pulling the foreskin back to see the maker's mark. It grew in her hand. Man's one eternal, thrilling conjuring trick.

Iona leant back, let go and took hold of Charles's hands. 'Before we do this there are a couple of things we must sort out,' she said seriously.

'What?' Charles sat up, the magic draining away.

'You really do want to make love to me, don't you? You're not just saying it because you're polite, or a gentleman, or frightened?'

'No, no. I mean, yes, of course I want to.'

'Good, so do I. The next thing is, I don't go in for one-offs, one-night stands, and I won't be humped and dumped.'

'No, of course. I wouldn't dream . . .'

'So I'm going to stay the night, and we can do it twice. Being humped and humped again and then dumped isn't so bad.'

'Yes, quite. I'd love you to stay.'

'And the last thing. Don't worry about me, I mean my pleasure and orgasms and things. The first time is never the best. You just have to get it over with to have a second and a third. I don't want you doing fancy footwork to impress me. I'm already impressed. I'm sure it will be lovely. But you get on and come as fast as you like. Better out than in my granny used to say, or in than out.'

Charles leant forward and pulled her onto the bed. Iona wriggled away. 'There's one more thing. I'm sorry, I tend to talk a lot when I'm fucking, all sorts of stuff. Don't be put off, it's nerves. I just witter on about nothing, I'm terribly shy really. I know I don't seem terribly shy,' she giggled, 'but I . . .'

'I want you to come away with me,' said Brad. *'The ship leaves this evening. Darling, be on it. Come away with me.'*

Charles covered Iona's mouth. She pressed her body hard against his. His hands felt for the perfect perky nipples. He kissed her neck.

'Now, foreplay. You do like foreplay?'

'Yes.'

'You don't do it just because everyone tells you you should. I mean just because it's fashionable.'

'No. Shut up.'

'Good. Look, if there's anything you really fancy . . .'

'I fancy you. Shut up.'

'. . . you must tell me, and if there's anything you don't like. I know we'll find all this out as we go along, but do say. I like almost everything. In fact, I can't think of anything I don't like. Oh, I'm so excited.'

'Laura, I am completely happy for the first time. Look at the view, the sun going down over the Caribbean, the salt spray in our faces. I want this moment to go on for ever.'

Charles moved down Iona's body. He had that strange light feeling that you get as you step off the cliff to fall in love, like coming out of an anaesthetic, as if it were all happening to someone else. He gingerly nuzzled his face between Iona's legs. Her knees came up and she stroked the back of his head. Her vagina was neat, like a prettily folded napkin. The triangle of pubic hair was as soft as partridge breast. She tasted of a hot summer breeze on a Cornish estuary. Ozone and iodine, kelp and candyfloss.

'Oooh,' said Iona, 'I knew you would be good at this. I just knew it, I knew it. I can always tell – well nearly always,' and she chortled deep in the back of her throat.

'Better strap everything down,' said Mona's black steward, *'we're in for a rough night. Can I get you a nightcap, sir?'*

Charles *was* good at this. He was gentle and inquisitive and fastidious. He performed cunnilingus like a peckish raccoon eating stewed prunes, gently turning the stones over between his teeth. Tinker, tailor, soldier, sailor. Iona flung herself into her orgasm like a child diving into the pool on the first day of the holidays. Charles felt her vagina contract and suck at his fingers. Rich man, poor man, beggar man. Her hand tugged at his head, her pelvis bucked. Beggar man, beggar man, beggar man, thief. The whole string section went adagio and Iona burst into peals of laughter. Charles came up for air. She lay on her back, one arm over her face, breasts shaking, shoulders rocking from side to side, cackling paeans of joy.

'Wow, that was terrific. Don't look so surprised. Haven't you ever met a girl who suffered from premature exclamation before? I can't help it if I come so fast and it makes me laugh. Oh God, I'm such an easy lay. I can't ride horses because they give me hysterics, even in fairgrounds. Come here, hold me.'

'I think you've bent my teeth.'

'I'm overjoyed, it's the only bent thing about you. Kiss them better. OK, your turn. What do you fancy? Would you like a blow-job or fucking? I'm a bit of a whiz at blow-jobs and just in case you're worried, I swallow, which in this house is probably a good thing. You could glue your jaw shut looking for somewhere to spit in this room.'

'Well, either really. I'd be happy to just do anything. You know, you choose.'

'Fucking then, I'll give you a blow-job later, but I think I want you inside me right now.'

'All ashore who's going ashore.' Mona stood on the deck of the liner waving, confetti and streamers fell around her.

'Climb aboard, darling. Fingers crossed for a tight fit.' Iona fumbled and wriggled the elegant penis onto the welcome mat. 'Go for it, Mr President, I'll meet you at the end.'

He pushed into the hot darkness. Mortise and tenon, a craftsman's joint.

First fucks aren't usually very good, this one was. Like a great exhilarating sprint. Sometimes fucks are like dancing, sometimes they are like athletics. This one was a run. Not a dash, not a hundred metres, but a gently curved run; a two-twenty bend, a rattling, rhythmic, flat-out, long-strides, heart-thumping, lung-expanding, exhilarating gallop. Charles finished with a spurt, mouth gaping, lips pulled back over his teeth, eyes screwed shut. Orgasms are all about rhythm, you have to finish on the beat. He came in easy regular throbs.

When, finally, he unscrewed his eyes Iona was watching him, her mouth gently parted, an amused look on her flushed, sweat-slicked face.

'Thank you. I think this is going to be something big, very big,' she said, and kissed him.

Rachmaninov was still fighting his corner but the orchestra sounded like they were going to win. The sister and the terrier had drawn the short straw and died for the good of the film. Brad and Laura were old now. He, with unconvincing grey hair, looked about one hundred and ninety, Mona had only added six months and a couple of late nights.

'Was it worth it, Brad?'

'Oh yes my love. We're together.'

'Was it worth all the pain, the deceit, the lies, the years of longing, the agony of being apart, Brad?'

'If we had it all over again I'd do the same, but in the open, in the daylight, in the sun. To hell with them all, we've bought our hour in the evening sun.'

'But, my love, our happiness casts a long shadow.'

The violins aimed their bows and shot the fatal chords. The camera panned back and away from the couple sitting on the porch of the monstrous house, across the crashing breakers out to sea. The End. Roll credits.

Iona lay across Charles, much as she had when they'd started.

'You're crying.'

Large tears were slipping down Charles's cheeks. 'It's the film, I always cry.'

'No it's not, it's us.'

They slid into the bed. The sheets were cool and dry. Iona fitted her back into Charles's chest. She reached for his hand and placed it on her bosom. The fingers satedly traced a couple of turns round the perky nipples then slept.

Later Iona woke with a start. The room was dark and for a moment she didn't know where she was, then the warmth behind her and the stickiness between her legs brought it back. She smiled and got out of bed to pee. When she returned Charles was sitting up. He looked startled, embarrassed.

'Um, did you manage to find everything? I'd better get a guest towel. Sorry, I should . . .'

'Charles, don't go all formal and awkward on me. We've just made love. You've come inside me. We'll do it again whenever you want. Relax, trust me. I don't need guest towels.'

'I'm sorry.'

'I do want feeding though; more than life itself.'

'Oh, right. Scrambled eggs and foie gras? Brioche? Champagne and fudge ice-cream?'

'Have you been hiding something from me, Charles? Are you a professional Lothario? Do you give seminars on seduction? That's just perfect, completely divine. I'm amazed I managed to get a window in your bedroom diary.'

Charles smirked happily. The furniture was silently stunned. He came back to the bed with a large tray. 'Look what I've found.'

'I knew you were a Bluebeard. A truffle.'

He grated truffle onto the eggs. She made him close his eyes and smell her fingers and then the truffle to see if he could tell the difference. He could. But he shaved a small mound onto her pinkly puffed labia and said that they did taste remarkably good together. They watched the news and a hospital drama and Charles got his blow-job with fudge on top, and then they slept again, that heavy purple unconsciousness that is dreamlessly close to death and is only rarely caught through an urgent surfeit of life.

Chapter Nine

It was the chronic absence of oxygen that finally pulled Charles from the pit of unconsciousness. He woke to the sound of bells, and in the dazed, suffocating panic imagined that he was either being buried alive or resuscitated from a stroke. Something was pinching his nose.

'Charles, the door, the door.'

The furious staccato bell sounded familiar. 'De door.'

Iona let go. 'The door. They've been ringing for ages.'

'Christ.' Charles leapt from the bed and grabbed his dressing-gown.

'Darling,' Iona laughed, 'you look like a collapsed marquee.' A furious bladder-pumped erection prodded the madder silk into an elegant swag. 'You look like the Trooping of the Colour.'

'Oh shit.' Charles bent double. 'The bells, the bells.'

Iona buried her head in the pillows and cackled.

Bryony stood furiously on the doorstep. She was wearing black leather gauntlets, her Selous Scout greatcoat and a thunderous neoclassical expression. A bottle of rum and a bicep-knotting wank had done nothing to temper her ire.

'About frigging time.'

Behind her the rest of the Committee stood uncomfortably.

'Oh dear, have you hurt your back,' asked Bon Bon solicitously at Charles's genuflecting form.

'Don't be silly, the lad's got a stiffy. Having his morning livener weren't you, dirty boy?' said Bryony. 'Well, sorry, we need all hands on deck. No time to waste knuckle shuffling,' and she rolled like a panzer regiment into the drawing-room. The Committee and a now successfully de-tumesced Charles followed. Bon Bon got out her notebook.

'We don't need to fuck about with all that. Straight to business. How are we going to mash that Vernon's bollocks?'

'Is Stephen coming?' interrupted Mrs Kotzen.

'Made an excuse,' said Bon Bon.

'Bloody shit-pipe-sucking quisling. We're better off without him. Now, Charles, tell us what you propose to do?'

'Well,' said Charles, 'I thought that perhaps, on reflection . . .'

'You're going to go and see that little starched fart and tell him no. N-fucking-O. We're not going to put up with some vast welded turd in our garden. And then you're going to get hold of that stream of crusty discharge of a vicar and you're going to tell him that we're fucking not going to have a lot of apprentice hamburger-crazed juvenile rapists and muggers pulling up the delphiniums to smoke. That's what you're going to do, isn't it?'

'Well, um, something along those lines, yes, if we're unanimous.'

'Unanimous. Of course we're fucking unanimous.' Bryony scanned the room like an Exocet that had been stood up on a blind date.

'Well,' said Celeste Kotzen, coolly examining her fingernails, 'almost.'

Bryony locked on, her eyes laser red.

'I think', Celeste chose her words carefully, 'there just might be some merit in Vernon's scheme.'

Charles held out his hand to pre-empt Bryony launching herself across the room.

'It does seem appropriate to do something to remember Mona. She was very famous, and she did live here, and let's not forget the money,' Celeste continued defensively.

'Perhaps', Dr Spindle added, 'we could use the funds for something more appropriate, a sundial or a bird-bath.'

'Oh yes,' said Bryony, 'a bird-bath for the dickie birds, and perhaps one of those little feeding things, and a rustic shagging box. That would be nice for the animals. Why not a fucking grotto with some sodding gnomes and cunty cherubs, and a children's heavy-petting zoo?'

Bon Bon smiled uncomfortably. She wasn't quite sure whether Bryony was making a serious suggestion or joking.

'Jesus fucking Christ, Charles. Will you take a sodding stand and just tell Vernon to fuck off. We're the Committee, we decide what happens in the garden. The money and that Hollywood tit-waggler have got nothing to do with it. It's a matter of principle.' Bryony thumped an occasional table; ornaments trembled.

Everyone started talking at once. Bryony had her meagre meaty vocabulary reduced to mortared 'fucks' as the other Committee members bickered and disagreed. Charles vainly, half-heartedly, tried to umpire. But the three hobby-horses of English dissension: money, posterity and grass, ran amok. The volume rose.

'Good morning everyone.' A voice cut across the cacophony, silencing it like a conductor's baton. Iona walked into the room, rubbing her wet hair with a towel. She was wearing one of Charles's shirts and a pair of his boxer shorts. It wasn't a subtle outfit, as clichéd as a pop-record sleeve, and it poleaxed the Committee. For the first time in living memory the most exciting thing to look at in the room was animate, and they gaped as the full implication of Iona's presence sank in. So as to leave no doubt, Iona smiled back and radiated hot, post-coital sexuality like a two-bar electric heater with a broken thermostat.

'Charles,' Celeste Kotzen nudged.

'Oh sorry. Iona Wallace, the Garden Committee. Mrs Kotzen, Bon Bon Velute, Dr Spindle and Bryony Mullins.'

'Bloody delighted to meet you, dear,' said Bryony.

'I'm sorry to disturb your meeting but I couldn't help overhearing. Would you mind if I said something?' Iona sat on the arm of Charles's chair and casually draped her hand over his shoulder. 'You know this isn't really about a memorial to Mona Corinth, or modern art, or youth, or nature; it's about control and power and status. Vernon wants control; he's an empire-builder, a power-broker. If I were you I would stand against him, don't give him an inch, do everything you can to stop him. The history of this country is the struggle of people like you standing up to men like Vernon, the vested interests, the patronage brokers, the greater-good merchants. England is rotten with memorials, memorials built by men like Vernon to men like Vernon, a Maginot line of patronage and power. They tell you who has the right and the might. This fight is for the heart of the land; the planners of plans must be resisted. It's a noble struggle. It's the unwritten right of an Englishman to live in a bespoke country that's cut to fit him, that's grown up as he's grown up, to eat its greens, to sleep in cold rooms, to carry a handkerchief at all times; that's dowdy and comfortable, honey and lichen coloured, twee and winsome, reserved, twisted with neglect and eccentric obsession, patchworked with parsimony, make-do-and-mend country. You shouldn't have to live in the shadow of some fat pinstriped Trajan's Column, some satanic mill's memorial smokestack belching sulphurous vanity and ego. An Englishman's monument should be the empty tankard on a flaking window-sill, the single lost glove waving from a railing. An Englishman should depart as he arrived: guiltily, quietly, apologetically, anonymously. An Englishman's memorial is the complete absence of any sign that he was ever here.'

Iona paused and smiled and stretched out her long legs. 'Well for what it's worth, I'd tell him to shove it: his memorial. That's what I'd tell him.'

'I think I'm going to cry,' Bon Bon whispered. 'That's

everything I've ever thought about the country but never been able to say.'

'Hear, hear,' trumpeted Bryony. 'Tell him to shove his monument. Wouldn't even touch the sides.'

'Very nicely put, very nicely. I feel quite moved,' muttered the doctor, his rheumy eyes fixed on the fly of Iona's shorts.

'It all sounds suspiciously political to me,' said Celeste Kotzen tartly. 'We've never been political here, we're conservative, but if that's what you all want, then I suppose it's democratic, and I'd rather have democracy than politics.'

'Right then,' said Charles, 'we're agreed. I'll go and see Vernon and the vicar and say thanks but no thanks.'

'I feel better already. Loins girded,' said Bryony, struggling to her feet like a camel with arthritis. 'Thank you so very very much, dear.' She beamed at Iona. 'I think you're a bloody good thing. Come on the rest of you, let's leave these two to their rude ablutions.'

The Committee got up and arranged itself behind Bryony.

'There is one thing, dear, I wanted to ask you, and I'm sure I speak on behalf of the whole Committee. What's Charles like in the shagging department?'

Iona stood up and thought for a minute. 'I'm not really sure yet. I'm afraid I passed out in the middle of my fourth multiple orgasm.'

Bon Bon giggled. The doctor swallowed a gobbet of phlegm the wrong way and had a choking fit.

'Well, it just goes to show, you can never tell by appearances can you?' said Bryony.

As Charles closed the door on them he turned and Iona pressed her mouth over his. She had shrugged off his shirt and pants and she pressed her hard cool body against his, reaching down and opening the dressing-gown. They kissed like thirsty Labradors at a stream.

'Good morning, darling.' Iona led him through to the kitchen.

'You were wonderful,' said Charles. 'All that stuff about the English and cold rooms and lost gloves was terrific. Do you really believe it?'

'Sort of,' she said, filling the kettle, 'but I'm Scots so it doesn't really apply to me.'

'I know so little about you. I still can't believe this has all happened. Iona, there is so much I want to say and do, I'm so happy, and actually, I couldn't give a damn about the garden and Vernon and his memorial, I just want to go back to bed.'

'No, Charles, don't say that.' She pushed him to arm's length. 'I'm serious, you should care. The problem with you, and it's a big problem, is that you don't really care about anything. I said all that because I want you to fight, to have a quest. If you like, it's a test; if you want me you will win this adventure. I've given you my favour, now go and kill the dragon for me. I want to see what you're made of. Now, we'd better get the groundwork out of the way. I take coffee strong and black with sugar; tea with milk, no sugar; whisky straight up, you already know that; wine, red by preference; and still water not fizzy. How about you?'

'The same.'

'Well that'll be easy to remember then.'

'You're going to go, aren't you?'

'Yes. Don't look so hang dog, I've got to go to work and I've got some things to sort out.'

'When can I see you again? What about lunch, or dinner? Lunch and dinner and breakfast? Can't we go away?'

Iona laughed and pulled him to her. 'This is very exciting, I'm excited, but take it a course at a time. I'll call you later today but don't wait by the phone. Get your armour on and get out there.'

'We will go on from here, won't we? This isn't the end?'

'I told you Charles, I don't go in for one-offs.' Iona picked up her mug and walked into the bedroom.

'It's complicated,' she said, looking under the bed for her bra. 'No, it's not complicated, it's simple. There is someone else; I'm having an affair with someone else.'

Charles felt his stomach disintegrate like Sunday newspapers in a storm, his joints turned to porridge. He sat heavily on the edge of the bed, which said something dismissive in French. 'Oh,' Charles said. He said 'oh' with such self-regarding pathos that

Iona smiled, stopped and took his hand. 'Who is he? Do you love him?'

'I'm sorry, Charles. It isn't neat and easy but it's the way things are. It's the way we all are; we come with stuff. You have furniture; I've got a boyfriend. Don't look so glum; this is still exciting, I still want you. If you want me you must win me. Go on your quest, be a hero, come back covered in glory, be proud of yourself, claim your prize.'

'A moment ago I'd never been happier, now I've never felt so desperate.'

'Enjoy it, Charles. The beginning of an affair is the most excruciatingly painful and wonderful thing that can happen to a grown-up human being. The whole world fills with metaphors and similes and auguries, allegories and clocks. It's the yearning; the rarest, most potent, magic emotion there is. Love and lust are supermarket fast-feelings compared with yearning. This is the most alive you will ever feel. The rest is reading about it, watching other people do it, catching echoes of it in late symphonies, trying to remember it.' Iona stood, dressed and made-up, in the doorway, stunning and cool, her golden hair shining on the black velvet coat. 'Kiss me goodbye. I'll call you, Charles, I'll call you.'

Charles miserably got up. Iona pressed her cheek to his and whispered, 'We've made a good start. You should feel quietly confident.'

She opened the front door. A cold wind blew Charles's dressing-gown into billows.

'Iona,' he said desperately, 'I've got to know.'

She stroked his cheek. 'It was better. OK? With you bed was much better than with him. Men, you're so predictable.'

That wasn't what he'd wanted to know but he said nothing.

Iona flashed her grin and strode down the street swinging her arms. Charles stood and watched. She didn't look back.

A small slight figure walked up the road in the other direction with an exaggerated wiggle. As Lily and Iona passed they briefly turned their heads to regard each other.

'Hi, Joe,' said Lily at the door. 'Ho, it's cold enough to freeze the clip in an M16.' As always, she was wearing ridiculously few clothes: a tiny tight skirt, a little halter top and dark glasses.

'Pretty lady, Joe.' She popped her gum. 'She your Stateside sweetheart?'

'Lily.'

'I know, I know. Lily do ironing.'

'Oh sod the ironing. Lily, you give me *beaucoup* jig-a-jig, long time, chop chop?'

Lily's mouth opened then closed. She ran to the bedroom giggling.

'I tell you, Joe, these Yankee girls look good but they no good when it comes to the business. No, Joe, you need little Chinky slut to make your todger stand up and beg like marine guard.' She lay in a calendar provocative pose on the rumpled sheets. The vast bed exaggerated her immature, angular fragility.

Charles lay down and stared at the ceiling. Iona's scent curled up from the pillows.

'So, Joe,' Lily stuck her gum on the bedpost, 'that was the Mona Corinth dame, huh?'

'Yes,' said Charles, and closed his eyes.

The garden was dark and moribund like a piece of urban wasteland, a commuter roundabout, a scrap of motorway waste, a corner beside a petrol station. The wind gusted along the gravel paths, flinging leaves into corners. The plane tree's branches clacked a burst of applause, skeletons waiting impatiently for the final trump. There was no moon in the cloudy sky, the only light was the insipid pools cast by the yellow street lamps.

Charles walked gingerly across the lawn towards Angel's hut. He hunched his shoulders and sunk his chin into the collar of his tweed coat. The bottle of whisky sloshed in his pocket. The night was noisy and confused, frightening. There was no seeping gleam from the hut, no cheery smoke from the chimney. Charles knocked at the door, the noise echoed emptily.

'Angel,' he called, the voice sounding querulous. It hung in the pensive air and then scuttled away across the flower-beds.

'Angel.' His nerve evaporated into the clamorous silence and he started to walk back to the gate, fast.

He had the unpleasant feeling that he was not alone, that something was watching him, lurking, following. Out of the corner of his eye he saw a shape pass through a puddle of yellow light. It moved parallel with him, disappearing, then briefly showing dark against a patch of grey foliage. He walked faster, and when he was within twenty feet of the gate the thing turned at right-angles and leapt onto the lawn. It came towards Charles at a dead run, hurtling straight for him. He cried out. The thing's huge teeth grinned maniacally as it see-sawed noiselessly across the lawn. Despite himself, Charles turned and ran; ran with all the speed and purpose that a mild-mannered man with an eight-stone, necrophiliac Alsatian behind him can muster.

He hit the herbaceous border without breaking stride, leaf and stem enveloped him, the ground was friable and treacherous. Charles stumbled through the undergrowth. Somewhere behind him he heard Stendhal keel into vegetation. Damp twisted things plucked at him, snagged his clothes. Flat wet handfuls of green slapped his face. Bark and thorn drew blood-pipped weals on his hands and neck. Suddenly he was an interloper in another element, an uninvited foreigner in a strange land; the dark forest of fairy-tales, the tucked-up childish terror so deep it has to be dressed in gay fable and crib rhyme. 'Never step off the path', 'Stay on the road', 'Don't tarry', 'Don't wander', 'Don't stop for the flowers'. This was the other-world, the green chaos, the riot, the frail power, the beauty and the slime. The blind canopy that seeks the light but lives in shadow.

Charles flayed and fought without direction or course. The garden was far, far behind him; he punched and kicked for his life against life, blood against sap. The sap rose, something caught his arms and pinned them. A trunk loomed in front of his face. Charles gasped and tried to scream but the sound was stifled in the silence of nurseries far away.

'Charles.'

He sighed, a man drowning in plants.

'Charles, mind the peonies.'

The trunk had a face, cracked and distorted, but a face, a human face, a vaguely familiar face. The grip on his arms relaxed.

'Angel?'

'Why are you running amok in my flower-bed?'

'Oh Angel, I was . . .'

'I know, the fear. It's OK. Here, sit down. Did you bring a drink?'

Charles sank to the ground and found himself in a little dugout cave, like a soldier's foxhole. It was lined with dry sphagnum and ferns and hay. It was like a nest.

'Here, get tucked in,' said Angel.

Charles curled up at the bottom. Angel, fragrant and mossy, crouched beside him. Charles looked up at the edge of the den. It was fringed with leaves. He could see Stendhal's huge, lupine guardian head silhouetted against the sky. Suddenly it all felt very cosy, very safe, like the Indians' hide-out in *Peter Pan,* a small safe den in the blackness. He ferreted out the whisky and gave it to Angel.

'So you got hold of that Iona then.'

'How do you know?'

'Only half a bottle, and I saw her leave this morning. I told you you were in with a chance. She's a very pretty girl.'

'Oh, Angel, she's remarkable, wonderful. It was fantastic.'

'You could have left the curtains open a bit – think of your friends. So you're happy then.'

'No, I'm distraught.'

'You would be. The most beautiful, remarkable, fantastic girl in the borough spends the night, and of course you're miserable.'

'She's got a boyfriend.'

'Well, you've got Lily.'

'That's not the same. She has to make a choice. She said she'd call me, but she didn't. Angel, nobody has ever chosen me for anything. At school it was either picking me or batting first. I'd be the perfect murderer: in any line-up I'd be the last one to be fingered.'

'Are we feeling a little sorry for ourselves?' said Angel. 'Nature chose you. You've already won the greatest lottery you'll ever be in, the great million-to-one sperm race. An egg chose you over all the millions of others, all the potential Einsteins, Rothschilds, Paul Newmans. No living thing should ever think itself unlucky, we were all chosen.'

'It's not much of a comfort though, is it? I mean, Arthur Askey was chosen, the Hunchback of Notre-Dame was chosen, some bloody egg chose Vernon. Anyway, I couldn't have beaten Einstein, Rothschild and Newman: they're Jewish, my dad was C of E.'

Angel laughed and then coughed, a dry rasping hack. He lit a cigarette. In the flickering light his face was drawn, haggard, the eyes sunken and unnaturally bright. He was filthy with mud and bits of twig. His hands shook.

'Are you all right Angel? You look like death.'

'I've got a bit of a fever, flu or something.'

'You should be in bed.'

'I am. I came to wrap myself in Mother Earth. Heals everything; everything grows from the earth.'

'Or decomposes. It's more likely to kill you.'

'Then I'll have saved someone the trouble of digging a grave,' and the cough rasped at his throat again.

'I didn't see you at Mona's memorial service. Jolly sensible of you; it was abysmal, a terrible travesty. She would simply have loathed it. The only way she'd have gone was dead. But I needed to talk to you about what Vernon said because it affects you. He's set up a fund to put some modern sculpture in the garden, on the lawn, and to bring oiks in to look at the flowers.'

Angel said nothing, just nursed the bottle.

'You mustn't worry though, the Committee's dead against it. Well you can imagine, Bryony went ballistic and Iona was brilliant. She made an extraordinary speech, wearing my shirt. You should have seen her, Angel, she takes your breath away; so poised, so sexy. Anyway, you're not to worry, I'm going to tell Vernon and the vicar that it's no go; to shove their memorial and money.' Charles waited for Angel to say something but he

154

just rocked, one hand holding the bottle, the other digging distractedly in the earth. 'It's going to be all right. Don't worry, I'll deal with it.'

'You fool. You deaf, stupid fool.' Angel spat the words at Charles. 'Don't you ever listen to anything I tell you.' His eyes rolled, a sluggish bead of perspiration ran through the muck on his temple. 'Do you think I care about some sliver of iron and sour concrete? Do you think the garden cares if one hundred children run amok, or a thousand?'

The silence fell between them again, broken by the laboured sound of Angel's breathing. He swigged deep, and said softly, 'For a clever man you're very, very slow to learn. Do you know how many memorials there are in this place to forgotten men, who were to be remembered in perpetuity? Ten. The first was a small cairn to commemorate a battle that no-one bothered to name, that took place between Norman horsemen and Saxon farmers. The widows carried stones for weeks in their memory. There is a piece of broken marble over there with the timeless, immortal names of four martyrs who died for a couple of sentences in a Bible; burnt at the stake. Only their God and I know their names now. There is a Victoria Cross within five feet of where you are sitting, thrown here by a distraught widow.'

Angel breathed heavily, gulping cold damp air, his throat cackling and wheezing. 'Do you have any idea how many bones there are in this place, bodies who are their own memorial, whose very skulls are their only headstones? Hundreds. Beneath us is a family crypt with eight generations lying higgledy-piggledy in each other's ribcages, a family who believed they were more part of this place than the stones in the earth. They even called it after themselves.'

'The Buchans?'

'No, Buchan was a Victorian chancer,' Angel laughed. 'Buchan was a fat little spiv. He was the picture of that lordling of ours. He just built a couple of houses and never lived here. No, this family, who were so much part of the weft and the wend of this land, who knew every blade and rut for eight generations, their name and their memories are less than the smallest piece of gravel. Only the plane tree and I can call them.' Angel stopped and held his head, as if in great pain. The fingers of his other hand clawed at the sides of the set, scooping great fistfuls of wet slag onto his chest.

'You really should be in bed. Come back to my place. I'll make you something hot, get a doctor. Angel, please, I'm worried.'

'Understand, Charles. Listen to me. Understand.' There were tears mixed with the sweat. 'I'm growing, I'm becoming.' He stopped again. The breathing sawed in shallow draughts. 'There is no-one, nothing, here that shouldn't be here, who doesn't belong. No-one is turned away from the earth. This earth is memorial to us all.' Angel sighed. 'No, that's not true. There is someone who lies uneasy, unquiet. Nature welcomes all, she makes no judgements, asks no questions, and, although I hear her and know it, I am still human enough to mind. He was a boy, a servant. He lived here when there was just one house. A big house, red brick, a pretty house, an unhappy house. He was an ostler, good with horses; lived over the stables where the mews is. He taught the youngest daughter of this unhappy house to ride. She was fourteen. He loved her. They coupled once, over there in the corner where the laburnum is. It was the first time for them both; clumsy and funny, touching, dappled by the evening sun. She was excited, frightened. She told her maid. Her maid told her mother for money. Her father threw the ostler out after a whipping, and said if he ever saw the boy again he would kill him.' Angel was barely talking in a whisper now. Charles had to lean forward to hear. 'The boy walked for a day towards London, and then turned back, so great was the yearning.'

'What?' said Charles. 'What was that word?'

'Yearning. The yearning for the girl. It killed him. He came back and knocked at the door, demanded to see the man and marry the girl. The father hit him hard, he fell hard and cracked his skull. They carried him to the stable, laid him unconscious in a manger. Then the man walked round the garden, slowly, lovingly, an owner's love. Here, he walked here, over there, and looked at the plants; wondered at the straight box hedge; picked a sprig of lavender and rubbed it between his fingers; breathed deep; listened to the mistle-thrush in the apple tree. Then he walked back to the stable, picked the gelding knife off the wall and slit the unconscious boy's throat; cut it deep to the spine, and then told the coachman to throw the body onto the midden. I can feel the boy now, in the earth. He bothers me. Angers me. The sense of him isn't bad, it's a mixture of hope and longing, fear and excitement and sadness. It's as strong as light, and pulls as surely as gravity.'

'I know,' said Charles. 'I know.'

'Of course you do,' said Angel. 'Yes, that's why I can feel it in the earth tonight. It's you, it's sympathy. Sorry Charles, it's hard.'

'I know, the toughest lessons are the ones you can't be taught.'

'I'm tired now, I'm going to sleep. Go home. Prepare for your quest.'

'How do you know about my quest, Angel?'

'You told me.'

'I did?'

'Go to bed, Charles. Go to bed.'

Charles stood stiffly. 'Are you sure you'll be all right?'

Angel took his hand and squeezed it, his palm hot and sticky. As Charles stepped out of the den Stendhal slithered in and curled up in his place. A gust of wind blew a scurry of plane leaves over them. Charles took two steps and felt gravel under his feet. He was standing ten feet from the gate. He looked up and, with a pang as painful as a blade, thought of Iona.

Iona lay naked on her bed in her overheated room, two miles away as the pigeon flies, across the grey roofs and dun gardens of West London. She was flicking through an auction catalogue from New York; she wasn't concentrating, she was calculating.

'Have you read Gissing, *Grubb Street*?' Tony lay beside her, big and nude, fleshy and hairy; expansive.

'Yes.'

'You haven't? Really?'

'Yes.'

'What did you think?'

'I loved it, it's a great novel.'

'Think it would make a six-part drama? Helena Bonham-Carter, Joe McGann and that bloke that plays a copper in the country?'

'Horrible.'

'That good, eh? I think we'll go with it.'

'Christ, can't you leave books alone? Isn't there anyone in the Groucho who can make up a story?'

'Honey, don't knock it. You loved *Jude the Obscure*.'

'No I didn't.'

'Well someone did.'

Iona came to a pre-Raphaelite picture of a blonde knight in aluminium armour taking a flower from a medieval girl with red hair. He looked like he wanted to go to the loo and had forgotten the monkey wrench. She looked vacant. Her calculations went up a decimal point.

'What's eating you, honey?'

She dropped the catalogue and turned over. Tony was lying on his back, his thin curly hair spread on the pillow. He held a script with one hand and lazily played with himself with the other. That huge penis, thick and veined. Like a sub-normal child it lolled and dribbled and bumped into things. Iona regarded it warily. To begin with she had been impressed. It was impressive, a big cock, a family-sized, bank-holiday, stay-at-home cock, but now it was a bore, an imposition, a performance, another thing in the bed in the morning, blindly prodding. Her, Tony and it.

'Nothing's the matter,' she said.

'Come here, come here. No more work, let's fuck. Relax you, eh?' Tony dropped the script and pulled her onto him. It wasn't that he was oversexed, it was just that he used sex like Ovaltine. It was how he got to sleep. If he didn't have an orgasm he would lie awake begging, wheedling, arguing. They'd fight and have to fuck anyway. Better do it now than at three in the morning, wrung out and exhausted.

With that practised economy of habit she straddled him and took hold of the thing with both hands. Tony put his arms behind his head and smiled sleepily. Slowly, she lowered herself. The thick head nuzzled between her thighs. Tentatively Iona squatted, controlling the depth. Christ, she thought, I'm fucking a bollard. She rocked back and forth feeling like a generous kosher sandwich. Tony shifted his weight on his hips and jarred her. She snorted, closed her eyes and thought of Charles, his ravenous hands and delicate mouth.

'Tony, I slept with someone last night.'

'I knew something was the matter, I just knew it. So why are you telling me this?'

'Because I think it's important.'

'Important? It was that good, was it?' He jerked his pelvis hard.

'Ow, that hurts.'

'Was it big? Was it as big as this?' He shoved again.

'Ow. Ow. No it wasn't, it wasn't. Sorry Tony, I can't go on with this.' She got off and lay beside him.

'Oh, honey, don't stop. Look, I'm sorry, you can sleep with whoever you like; don't stop now, I'm all revved up. At least you can give me a hand-job, you owe me that.'

'Tony, I just want to be straight with you. I think this is different.'

Iona started to pump. Tony picked up the remote and flicked on the television, turning his head away from her.

'Oh yeh, harder, faster. You know I adore you. Nobody will ever love you like I do; nobody can give you such great sex. Faster.'

Iona squatted like a cold Neanderthal trying to light the stove. He came in two emetic spurts that hung, wallpaper paste in her fingers globbing fishily on his pubic hair.

Iona lay staring into the blackness, tabulating the energy, the cost, the rows, the pleading, the threats, the tears, the changed locks, the weekend segregating the bookcase, the address book, the new car, the twelve dinner parties she would have to give speeches at, the hours of telephone calls, his mother, her mother, the holiday in Greece, the regret, the guilt.

Tony snored like a child. Under the sheets the cock wept one sticky salt tear; another loser in the race of life.

'Darling, thank you for last night, it was magical.' Iona spoke to Charles in the darkness, across the crooked roofs, the muddy patches waiting for weekend sun, across the sleeping city. 'I'm sorry it's so late, I haven't had a moment. Please call me at work tomorrow. Sleep well, dream of me.'

Charles pushed the rewind button. 'Darling, thank you for last night, it was magical.'

'Charles, Charles, dear boy, dear boy, come in, come in. Stephen, Charles is here.' Vernon beamed and puffed and then beamed again. He took Charles by the hand and led him through the door of his flat. The entrance hall was doll's house Vanbrugh. A couple of Corinthian pillars held up nothing heavier than a marbled paint finish; one wall was of mirror to give an impression of size. On a pine plinth two gladiators grappled for each other's plaster genitals. An ornate German hatstand was heavily fruited with military headgear from around the world.

'How very nice to see you.' He led Charles into the drawing-room that smelt sickly of burning lavender and horse dung. 'I was just a digit away from calling you when you phoned. Sit, sit. Out of the way, Melbourne. Yes, naughty Mr Dog, we've got guests, yes we have, yes we have; best behaviour.' The bug-eyed asthmatic Lhasa apso reluctantly got off the chair and sneezed fruitily. 'Ah, Stephen, here's dear Charles. Open a bottle, dear heart.'

'Charles, you're looking very . . . fit. Sorry I couldn't make the emergency Committee meeting, but I'm sure you all managed manfully without me.' Stephen smirked and stripped the foil off a bottle of supermarket champagne, like an eager rabbi with a first-born.

'Isn't it looking wonderful?' Vernon stood in the long over-chintzed window. 'The garden really is a little treasure.

We're all so terribly indebted to you for all your work you know, Charles.'

'Well, Angel, really . . .'

'No, no. No, no. We all know how much time and effort you put into it. You should be really proud of yourself. It hasn't gone unnoticed, you know. Your name is mentioned in hallowed corridors. Anyway I expect you've come to talk about our little project.'

'Yes. As you know the Committee met and we're pretty unanimous, no we're unanimously unanimous.' Charles awkwardly plaited his fingers. 'You see the thing . . .'

'Good, good. I knew you would be. Now I've asked the vicar to join us, he should be here at any moment. Champers, super.'

Stephen handed out glasses. Charles unenthusiastically took one.

'Any nibbles, Stephen? I think we still have a tin of Madame Sukarno's cashew and dried nasturtium mix. Well, cheers. Here's to the Mona Corinth Memorial, then.'

Charles took a sour sip, felt wrong-footed, craven; drinking a toast to the thing he had come to stop. He had rehearsed this meeting a dozen times with the furniture; it had all been straightforward, not at all like this. His resolve streamed up in little bubbles and then burst.

The doorbell rang. 'Hi,' the Rev Trev bounced into the room. 'Lord Barnstaple's told me so much.' He was wearing tight black lycra leggings with a purple and orange Go-to-God-Faster stripe down the thigh and some thin, elaborately laced, sporty slippers. He carried a yellow plastic cycling helmet. 'It was great to see you at the memorial gig. Wasn't that moving?'

'Yes,' said Charles, 'very.'

'Wow, all that energy, quite something.'

'I'm sorry I wasn't able to rope you in before the service,' said Vernon smoothly. 'It must have come as a bit of a surprise, my little announcement.'

'Yes it was rather, and . . .'

'I know, I know, but I'm sure you weren't too put out. Er, it all fell together terribly fast. I can tell you, it needed some pretty

161

fancy footwork to get all the parties in line. And the service was the obvious place to make the announcement, what with the press and the great and the good. Did you see the coverage?'

'Yes,' said Charles. 'Miss Pocket managed to get a spread, in every sense of the word, over most of the tabloids the next day.'

'That's what the Church needs, more sexy good fun.' Marle murmured.

'The diaries all picked up on the Memorial,' continued Vernon, 'and I've done an interview for *Urban Cottage and Kitchen*. There is a lot of interest, Charles, a lot of interest; some of it from some very soigné circles. Film stars and youth is a very powerful mixture, Charles.'

'Sounds heaven,' interjected Marle campily.

'Look,' Charles put down his glass and stood up, 'I can't pretend there aren't reservations; more than reservations.'

'I know, I know,' Vernon patted the air.

'Let me finish. The Committee is fundamentally opposed to this statue.'

'That Bryony person was born opposed,' said Marle.

Vernon took Charles's arm. 'I understand the reservations. Heavens, no-one can ever have more than I: digging up our beautiful garden, workmen, troops of loud vulgar oiks.'

'Underprivileged young adults,' corrected Trev.

'And it's precisely because of these reservations that we want you on the Board, to oversee things. When our enthusiasm runs away with us we need a wise counsel, someone to bring us down to earth. There really is no-one else. You see, Charles, if you want to change things you've got to be involved. Let me tell you, as an old campaigner, the way to get things done is to be on the inside. This is a firm invitation, there is a seat for you at the top table.' Vernon eyed Charles beadily.

'Well, I'm flattered of course, Vernon, but . . .'

'You'll get on terribly well with the rest of the Memorial Fund Board. There is Sir Roddy Vest, you'll know his work in the theatre, of course; one of the most amusing men you'll ever meet, a one-man variety show, but behind that Garrick

Club bow-tie he has a mind as broad as the London Library. Her Grace the Duchess of Bradford, a seasoned campaigner; we've sat on dozens of things together for years. Ruben Gretel, have you met? No, well, you're really kindred spirits. Apart from being one of the most generous philanthropists since the Medici, he has a great collection of just about everything worth collecting. Then there's the vicar here, and me. So you see, it's a light, swift-moving committee, no dead wood, and, if I might say so, an élite committee, a committee's committee, but it, we, need you.'

'To be quite bluntly frank, Vernon . . .' Charles tried to make a stand.

'That's exactly what we need: bluntness, frankness. Between you and me and the Aubusson rug, this could lead to bigger things Charles. Doors are there to be opened, wheels to turn. Now are you staying for luncheon?' Vernon started to flush Charles towards the door.

'No, sorry, I can't, but before I go I want to be quite clear. The Committee has made up its mind,' Charles said in a desperate gabble.

'I'm sure they have, which is why we're talking to you, the President.'

'This is a good thing we're doing,' smiled the Rev Trev; 'a good God thing.'

'I'll send you all the bumph, fact sheets, memos, proposals, etc.,' said Vernon, opening the door, 'and you must dine at my club and meet the Board, I'll send a card. I think, really, when it comes down to it, we're in complete agreement. Good of you to come, Charles. We'll work well together.'

'Cheerio,' shouted Marle archly.

Out on the street Charles tasted the bitter gall of defeat. He'd faced the dragon and been done to a turn without ever drawing his sword. He looked up at Vernon's window. Three small pink faces looked down at him. Vernon, the dragon, waved regally.

'Po-faced little prick,' he said smiling, pouring champagne into Marle's glass. 'I think I handled that pretty well, we won't have any trouble from him.'

163

'You haven't lost any of your old magic, dear,' said Stephen.

'Is she one of us?' said the Rev Trev, sipping.

'Camp as a gang show encore, duckie,' smirked Marle, 'just won't admit it. Still keeps trying to stick it into fish paste. Oh heavens, that reminds me, the Seaman's Crusty Bake's still in the oven.'

Mrs Kotzen watched Charles walk across the square.

The delivery boy from the Italian delicatessen slouched behind her. 'OK, Madame, I'm going now.' Celeste held out a £5 note between two fingers, without looking round.

He took it. 'Thanks.' He slapped her bottom. 'Great arse. Ciao, *bellissima*,' and left whistling.

Mrs Kotzen pursed her lips and swore under her breath. Too familiar, too cocky; she'd have to find another one. And he was ugly, with heavy-lidded drooping eyes and pimples and thick lips. Big though, sixteen and already over six foot, with big bitten-sausage stub hands. Once, twice a week he'd come with a box of things she didn't need: mineral water, radicchio, tinned artichokes, vacuum-packed gnocchi, and he'd fuck her, hard, against the fridge, so that the bottles rattled. Always in the kitchen; always standing up. She didn't want him in the house, greasing up her furniture, thinking he was wanted. She'd press one heel into the small of his back, hook her nails in his greasy hair, and he'd slobber on her shoulder, and come outside, never inside, onto the Tuscan tiles. It was jabbing, hard, fast, strong, common cold fucking, and she'd give him a fiver and he'd smile his flaccid grey smile and leave whistling. It wasn't much. It wasn't passion, but it was something. Now he was getting cocky. He tried to kiss her, push her head down. It was time for someone else.

She looked out at the garden and failed to understand. What was all the fuss about? What was it the English saw in grass that eluded everyone else? The rest of Europe looked at grass and saw cheese and butter or a hotel, the English saw England. This was a country where there were volumes of philosophy in the earth and none in the people.

164

After the uprising in Hungary her parents had brought the infant Celeste to England, where her father, a journalist, had got a job with the BBC and then in films. But like so many Hungarians his real calling had been to be an Englishman. 'Hungarians make the best Englishmen in the world,' he used to say in a perfect Oxbridge–Sandhurst drawl. And he had set about making his child the perfect Englishman's daughter. It was her mother who had taught her her native language, and when on the rare occasions she dreamt, Celeste dreamt in Hungarian. She looked hard at the garden; it was nothing, bland, green with trees. It wasn't dramatic or romantic or exciting, it was just English. She appreciated it only because of the value it added to her property. Perhaps this sculpture would add more, make the square famous. Why was that not the end of it? Why weren't they all saying, 'What a good piece of fortune?' Someone dies, someone gives us money and all our houses are worth another ten grand. We can go and look at as much grass as we like, first class. At her first Committee meeting she had suggested that the residents park their cars in the garden; tarmac some of it, that would add thousands to their properties. The others had laughed, such a good joke.

However, she would oppose the statue because Vernon supported it. He was an impostor, and as one impostor she recognized another.

She heard the key turn in the latch upstairs. Her husband, bland and plain and as well-kept as an English garden, home from the office. Mrs Kotzen pulled a yard of kitchen towel off the roll beside her and wiped the sticky traces of foreigner off the Tuscan tiles by the fridge.

Chapter Ten

'Eighty-Nine, Landscape with cows, English School. One hundred? Ten, twenty, thirty, forty, fifty. With me at one hundred and fifty. All done? One hundred and fifty.' Clack, the gavel tapped a dismissive adieu to the English School of Kine. 'Lot ninety, Shepherd wooing a milkmaid in an arbour. I think I had a date with him last week, all hands and smelt of wet wool. He looks as if he's getting further with her than he did with me.' A tired titter. 'Who'll start me with two hundred?'

Iona stood on a podium with 'Gandolfs. Established 1792' on it and looked at her studiously disinterested audience. A ragged, unlovely gaggle of dealers, interior decorators, nervous newly-weds with freshly egg-shelled walls, and Italians. They sat huddled over their catalogues and Conservative daily papers, sucking ball-point pens that had pretensions to being fountain-pens, and sported a job lot of half-moon spectacles on chains. Every so often a dealer would walk across the room to examine a picture. They'd tilt their heads back at right-angles, as if they were sighting a shot down their noses, regard with a left or right of snotty contempt, and then return to their seats. Charles stood partially concealed behind a pillar at the back and watched.

The sale was a gallimaufry of spare bedroom pictures, back corridor damp-patch coverers, apprentices' trials, copyists daubs and endless leisure, amateur time-wasting. The catalogue rather grandly called it 'A Sale of Eighteenth, Nineteenth and Early Twentieth Century English and Continental Pictures'. In fact, it was a regular weekly bargain basement of forgotten art.

Charles felt a great wave of sadness and pity for these unlovely, lost souls that revolved endlessly round the dark cold world of warehouses, basements, vans and salerooms. The quick and the foxed, their backs collecting the chalk marks of the itinerant dispossessed, their frames split and chipped, dusty and flaking, many of them with dreadful untended injuries, gaping holes, painful jagged rips, horrible skin diseases, boils, scales, spots, sores, blackened bituminous cancers.

Charles watched them stacked and propped along the wall, trying to wrest some sullen dignity, tilting their faces, their best sides to the bored audience. The sense of despair and fading hope was tangible. Occasionally a small childish watercolour would weep, or a mad religious picture call out that the end was nigh. Charles thought of all the years of achievement and pleasure and joy that were collected here. The time when these pictures were strong and vibrant, full of life and conviviality; good in a room, a pleasure to sit next to; when they were fashionable and provocative, glossy and smelt of varnish and turps and money. He imagined the admiring glances, the soft compliments paid to them, the love and companionship they had given, the families they had been part of, the lives they had graced, the Christmases, the dinners, the trysts, the long years of devoted silent service in study and bedroom. This is how it ended for the unlucky ones: a desperate old age of decrepitude and senility and, finally, when their frames gave way, their stretchers collapsed and their paper crumbled and tore, some harassed specialist would say, 'Not worth the trouble and cost,' and bin it.

Charles also watched Iona. She looked like Madame Defarge's pretty daughter tapping out the condemned, a hundred an hour. She was good at it, professionally efficient but not curt. Touching up the run of lots with the odd aside, a flourish of personality to crank up the atmosphere, never holding up the proceedings. She was getting 10 or 20 per cent above estimate from a hard-nosed congregation.

The pictures were led on by a pair of aproned sansculottes; an old man with fiercely varnished thin hair and a boy, obviously fresh out of school, who held the condemned with a trepidatious respect.

They came in a steady stream. Most of them were landscapes. One after the other, they looked like a panorama of England over two hundred years; barely changing, seasons coming and going, winter sliding into spring, sunshine and snow.

Charles watched the frames flicker past like a national day-dream, a commonly agreed fantasy. This was a country that all Englishmen could point to and say, 'That's where I come from. That's my home,' and yet never find it on a map or walk through it or own it. It wasn't that the trees were not identifiable as oak, ash and elm, or that the topography was a fraud, or the colours were not nature's colours. It was a certain quietness, a torpor, a languor, a stillness that only happened in reverie; a landscape, nurtured in a collective imagination we'd never set eyes on. A place that hung on the wall like a blind window; an outside that only existed inside. Time and trouble could grub up the island, but this hookers' green, viridian, chrome yellow, ultramarine place endured inviolate; a reserve tattooed on the inner eye. Here is real England. I inhabit one place but I live here.

His thoughts were interrupted by a picture. It called out to him across the room; a clear, soft patrician voice. Iona glanced at her notes. 'Lot two hundred and fourteen, a Scottish Landscape.' She briefly glanced across at the young man who held it as if it were a waltzing duchess. 'A handsome picture.'

Oh no, no, it was more than a handsome picture. Beneath the dusty glass and reflected lights, from a distance of twenty feet, it was a stunning picture, a large late-Victorian watercolour of a loch surrounded by glowering mountains. The paint was applied with bravura, a gusto that matched the scene. There was a rare facility and reverence. This was no English Academy drudge sketching from behind rented Perthshire curtains. There was nothing in this landscape, no focal point, no hotel-lounge stag, no artful Highland cattle establishing eye contact with the middle distance, no eagles, kilts, stalking ponies, none of the theatrical Caledonia that make these pictures so accessible to the cosier South. This was a landscape without sign of man or agriculture. It was a threatening and ineffably lonely place. Having caught his attention, the painting held it.

'Who'll start us with two hundred pounds, two hundred.'

A scruffy young dealer with a donkey jacket in the front row lifted his pen.

'Two twenty.'

An Italian in a cashmere jacket, sitting with a group of loud friends who had already bought 30 per cent of the sale for their antique shops in Mantua waved his programme out of habit.

'Two forty, two sixty, two eighty.'

The two bid like tired pugilists without much stomach.

Charles looked over the shoulder of the woman in front. 'Lot two hundred and fourteen. Estimate three hundred and fifty to five hundred pounds.'

'Three hundred, three ten.'

The Italian muttered and gesticulated at his neighbour.

'Are you bidding, sir?'

He looked up at Iona, then at the picture, then back at Iona, flashed her a lot of teeth and shook his head.

'So, three ten in the front row.'

Charles's palm itched, he took a deep breath.

'Three twenty over on my left.'

Charles moved to see who the new bidder was. Leaning against the side wall was a thin, slightly stooped man, in a discreet but well-cut suit. He had a hooked bony nose and stone-washed blue eyes. He held a rolled-up catalogue.

'Three thirty, forty, fifty.'

It went to 400. The dealer in the front row got up and went over to the painting. The boy held it up. The dealer licked his finger and rubbed a smeary circle on the glass. He glanced over at the hook nose.

'Four twenty, forty, sixty, eighty, five hundred.'

The bidding went back and forth like a rally at tennis. At six hundred the dealer peered down his nose, then, without looking at Iona, he shook his head and ostentatiously flicked open an *Evening Standard*. The stooped figure leaning against the wall showed no sign of joy.

'Six hundred, six hundred, six hundred over on the wall, six hundred any advance?' Iona lifted the gavel.

The picture keened softly; Charles looked back. The wild mountain soared, the clouds drooped with menace, the loch lay taut, deep and black. An eddy of fresh frosty wind blew across the rows of seats. Charles heard the distant 'go back, go back' call of a cock grouse, smelt the faint sweetness of heather.

His hand, unable to wait, to stand the tension and the sadness, shot out of his pocket and into the air. Iona was looking over at the other side of the room.

'If you're all done then, at six hundred?' The guillotine gavel poised.

'Here.' Charles heard his own effete voice call across the loch and echo in the corries and crags. The bored women and Italians turned. Iona looked across at him without any perceptible recognition.

'Six twenty with you at the back of the room, six forty, six sixty.'

Charles realized he had been holding his breath and had to take a hurried gasp of air. It tasted faintly of rowan and harebells. The room slowly put down its pretentious pens, pushed up its spectacles, and centre-court swivelled. Charles had lost who was bidding what.

'One thousand.'

The bids went up in hundreds.

The air grew cold; the picture seemed to grow, expand out of the frame and creep like a shadow across the floor. Charles felt that he was standing alone in the blasted fastness of the Highlands, with his ridiculous finger in the air. Iona stood in her high granite pulpit intoning figures. Just the two of them in the ancient landscape.

'Two thousand eight hundred. At two thousand eight hundred pounds. Are there any more bids?' Charles waved his hand. 'The bid's with you, sir, at the back. Two thousand eight hundred pounds. All done?'

A long moment; the wind dropped, the air sparkled, one of the last utter silences on earth. Crack.

'Sold to Mr Godwin. Now, lot two hundred and fifteen. A dun mare in a field with a hayrick.'

The boy holding the 'Highlands' realized with a start that the lot had moved on and that he should be back in England. With exaggerated care and deference he laid the picture down and stared at it blankly for a brief moment.

'Who'll start me at fifty pounds?' Iona scanned the room and, for the briefest moment, she caught Charles's eye and held it with the merest impression of a smile.

Charles turned to the wall to see his adversary but the stooped man had vanished. He realized that his pulse was racing, that he was breathing through his mouth. The air was stale and dusty again, but the excitement still spumed. He felt mad and elated and fearful. It was the yearning. Charles sat heavily in a chair at the side of the room and watched his picture for the rest of the sale. Slowly his heart stopped beating its wild tattoo: 'My heart's in the Highlands, my heart is not here, my heart's in the Highlands, a chasing the deer.'

'You mad thing.' Iona was standing beside him. Charles stood up and went to kiss her. 'No, they'll think it's insider dealing. What were you thinking of. If you were trying to impress me, I'm impressed, but then I was impressed anyway.'

'It's the most wonderful painting,' said Charles, 'it just sang.'

'I haven't really seen it, I just caught a glimpse. God, that was exciting. Do you know who you were bidding against?'

'No.'

'Well, here he is.'

The stooped man elegantly sidled up to them. 'Iona, a pleasure as always.' He shook her hand.

'Ralph Pistol.' She pronounced it 'Rafe'. 'Charles Godwin.'

'Damn your eyes, Mr Godwin,' Pistol said with a silky voice, modulated never to offend. 'You and I are the only ones in this room who've got a pair that work. When did you realize what it was?'

'I didn't. I don't know. Late Victorian, watercolour, somewhere in the Highlands.'

'Aaah, I don't believe it. I've been tracking that picture for months. What made you so intent on getting it?'

'Well, it just sort of caught my eye. It wouldn't let go. It's quite plainly in a completely different league to the rest of the stuff here.'

'Quite plainly. To you and me Mr Godwin, to you and me. Just as a point of interest, how far would you have gone?'

'Oh, I was going to have it. I think I would have paid anything.'

'Good, I'm glad you said that. That makes me feel a little better. I sensed you were going to go to the mat, and I'd rather let you have it for a reasonable amount than bid you into Carey Street. Now, of course, had you been one of those ghastly Italians it would have been different. Enjoy your picture Mr Godwin, and, for your information, though I appreciate that it's completely beside the point, it's a George Stanton Ferrier and it's slightly later than you think: 1911. Iona, dear heart, warn me if Mr Godwin ever shows interest in anything else. He has an eye and he has the passion. I had it once, but . . .' he shrugged eloquently. 'Anyway, nice to meet you and well done. Here's my card. If you ever feel like parting with it I'll give you four thousand pounds cash. I have a collector, a sensationally myopic chap, but he can wait. Whenever I go cynical about this business, you know, someone like you pops out of the woodwork and I remember why I got into it in the first place. Thanks. I'm sure we'll meet again.'

'What a nice man,' said Charles.

'He's better than nice, he's probably the sharpest dealer in

Europe. You remember the Georgione that was discovered in the san of a prep school in Malvern, well that was Pistol. He'd had a verruca out when he was nine and went back twenty years later and bought it for fifty quid, then he sold it for eight million. The school suggested he should give them half, Pistol wrote a letter to *The Times* saying that considering the abject misery of his childhood eight mil was small recompense. Come on, I'll just get my coat and we can go and have tea. I'm aching to kiss you and I expect you'd like something gooey and sweet.'

On the way to Iona's office they passed the public counter, where people can bring their trusting dumb servants, the small fragile occupants of their mantel and corner cupboard. The things that have uncomplainingly served their families' nourishment, the toys that have loved them and shared their childhoods, the tools their grandparents invested with a lifetime's toil and skill.

'Iona. Could you have a look at this for me?' A rather harassed blood-filled man behind the desk was talking to a small woman in a large mac and a headscarf whose face appeared to have been hit hard, at a formative age, by a flat iron.

'Of course, David. What?'

'Madame here has brought this in.' He lifted a cottage-loaf-sized terracotta bust of a particularly vacant and sexually incontinent-looking girl. Her intricate and stylized hair had delicate rosebuds carved in it, her cupid lips were parted in a simpering leer, showing off her milk teeth. One small fruit-like breast hung over her pedestal. It had obviously been made by a craftsman with oodles of skill and absolutely no taste. 'Rather your sort of thing,' grinned David. 'Italian, my guess. Miss Wallace here is our Italian expert.'

Iona gave him a tired look.

'My Desmond got it from a dear old lady he did for', said the flat-iron woman, 'years ago. He always said it was Anne Boleyn. He was a bit of a connoisseur. And it was the dead spit of her on the telly.'

'Sorry,' said David, 'I don't follow.'

'Anne Boleyn, on the telly. *The Wives of Henry VIII.*'

'Oh right, yes.'

Iona took the bust and turned it over. 'I think David's right. It's a nice piece and I'd say Italian, probably late eighteenth century.'

'What'll you give me for it?' the flat-iron lady demanded beadily.

'Well, we don't buy objects,' said Iona, 'but if you wanted to put it into a sale then I'd expect something between seven hundred and a thousand pounds, maybe one thousand four hundred if a collector really liked it.'

'Well I never!'

'May I?' asked Charles, taking the little girl. She giggled artfully at him and said something in a foreign language with a lot of sibilance. 'Well, I don't know much about this sort of stuff, but I rather fancy it's Spanish and late nineteenth century. One of a pair; a country lass who is missing her swain.'

'What do you think it's worth?'

'Ooh, I've no idea. Do you like it?'

The flat-iron lady looked at him as if the question was impertinent and completely beside the point. 'No, I can't stand it. The little trollop's grinned at me from the dressing-table for ten years, and now my Desmond's been gathered, I want shot of the tart. She can flash her tit at someone else.'

'Well, I rather agree with you,' said Charles, 'it's hideous. I don't think it's worth ten pounds.'

'Well, who are you anyway?' she replied furiously, as if he had just taken a thousand pounds out of her bag.

'Oh heavens, I'm nobody. Really, don't take any notice of me. Iona, Miss Wallace, here is the expert.'

'I tell you what,' said Iona. 'David, why don't you send it up to Justin for a second opinion? And', she turned to Charles, 'I'll bet you it's Italian, not Spanish.'

'What'll you bet him?' said the flat-iron woman. This was obviously a subject on which she was something of an expert.

'If I'm right I'll fuck his brains out, but if he's right he can shag me into a coma.'

'Ooh my giddy God,' the woman exclaimed. 'You heard that, you're a witness.'

David's fleshy mouth hung open.

Charles hurriedly and carefully put the coquette back on the counter, and taking Iona's arm said, 'Tea, I think.'

They sat at a tiny corner table of a little Viennese-style coffee-shop run by two loud Middle-European ladies of unparalleled hideousness. They ate egg and cress and cucumber sandwiches and cakes, that, for all their profound, vaunting complexity and delicacy, tasted of granular chocolate blancmange. They kissed, once, twice, and like teenagers on exeat, found that once they had started they couldn't stop.

'So what do you think?' said Iona at last.

'Think of what?'

'Of me as an auctioneer, of course.'

'Very impressive, in a horrible sort of way. Like finding the sweet majorette next door is actually a drill sergeant in the Hitler Youth.'

'It was exciting having you there. I really wanted to jump off the podium and come and kiss you. I had this terrible urge to shout, "I'm going to sleep with that handsome man at the back."'

'Are you?'

'You bet! Well you could look a little bit excited.'

'I am.'

'You'd never guess it, Charles. You've got a face like a Methodist on the second Sunday in Lent. What happened to the longing?'

'Your boyfriend. He licked the icing off my gingerbread.'

'Oh him, that old thing. Look I'm here with you now, can't that be enough?'

'No, Iona, it can't. Well it can, but I don't want it to be. Are you in love with him? What's his name? Do you live together? Are you engaged? What do I have to do?'

'Please, let's not talk about Tony now.'

'Tony.'

'Tony. I know it's not perfect, and if you had a girlfriend

I'd probably file down the brake pads on her wheelchair, but, if it's any consolation, he's beside himself about you.'

'You told him about me?'

'Of course, I'm very honest. I may not be moral but I'm not devious. He's the one wearing the cuckold's horns and you put them there, that should make you feel better.' She stroked Charles's face and kissed his nose. 'Let's change the subject. Tell me, how's the quest going? What's happening in the garden of remembrance?'

'Oh,' said Charles, and slumped back into his chair. 'I lost the first round gracefully. I wasn't prepared, Vernon completely wrong-footed me.'

'I told you he was an operator. What happened?'

'Well, foolishly, I thought it would be straightforward. I went to see him with every intention of just saying, "The Committee has decided you can't put the memorial in our garden," and that would be that, but he was charming and blew a fog of chat and patronage over everything, offered me a seat on the Memorial Fund Board and, well it was so unexpected, and I'm ashamed to say I was flattered. I thought the best thing was just to be enigmatic and call him later, but the next day a folder of stuff arrived with plans and projections and headed notepaper, The Mona Corinth Trust, and my name was on it, along with the great and the good, and it looks as if I've agreed with everything.'

'Charles, you can't be on both sides at once.'

'I know, I know. Bryony will be incandescent when she sees it. He sent it to everyone in the square. Now I'm going to have to resign from something I never joined and it will look like pique, and enough people in the square will assume that the whole thing has the Committee's backing anyway.'

'Oh dear, Charles,' Iona smiled, 'he really has walked all over you. What are you going to do?'

'I'm not sure. I thought I might write a letter.'

'More Don Quixote than Gawain, darling. That's not the way to win Rosinante.'

'Iona, don't laugh at me. At least I tried, at least I had a go.'

'Charles,' Iona suddenly became serious, 'if you don't want to be laughed at, don't make such a feature of your own foolishness. Falling short gracefully isn't much of a life ambition.'

Charles felt a welling of anger and pricked pride, righteous self-justification. 'How do you know what I always do?' he said, 'What my life's like? I'm not much good as an intriguer. I'm not like Vernon, I don't want to be, and I wouldn't have thought you'd want me to be.'

'I don't, but I don't want you to sit out with the dinner ladies nursing your grazed good manners either, because the other boys play too rough. You're angry aren't you?'

'Yes. Are you happy? You've made fun of me and I'm angry. Satisfied?'

'Well, it's a start. Why don't you take it out on my body?' She ran her nails over his thigh under the table.

Charles paid the bill. 'Anyway Rosinante was the horse, Don Quixote's nag.'

Iona put her arm through his and nuzzled his neck. 'Oh I love it when you talk peeved trivia to me.'

They walked back to Buchan Gardens in silence. The streets of West London looked wonderful in the slanting afternoon sunlight, elegant and discreet, York stone and cream stucco with green-grey trees, mauve-grey bark; the muted colours of London in a setting light making this, for half an hour a day, a city as beautiful as any in the world. Occasional splashes of iridescent pink reflected on upper storey, mansard windows shone gold and coral like stunning brooches, thrown bolts of sky blue ran like flags from oatmeal spires. The picture utterly harmonious, genteel. The consummate style of hundreds of years of self-control, breeding and manners. Iona strode through the streets as if they had been decorated personally for her, to show her off to the best advantage. Their private atmosphere had been cool as they'd stepped into the light but, slowly, as they got closer to the square, the beauty of the place and the expectation warmed them. Ancient lights and new fire. Iona took her arm from Charles's and slipped her hand into his, warm and firm and intimate. With a mixture of joy and a sense of wasted time, Charles tried to remember when last he'd walked through streets hand in hand with a lover and couldn't. The sun's last blink shone into the west side of the garden throwing long purple shadows across the lawn.

Charles opened the door and walked into the quietly dozing flat. The heavy sensual air danced in the speckled yellow sunlight.

Iona put her fingers to her lips and led him silently to the bedroom. They stood face to face and undressed, not touching, never losing eye contact. She took his hand and led him to the corner of the room where the long Italian cheval mirror stood slightly tilted in a servile bow. They watched for a long moment, eyes dancing at the two naked strangers glowing in front of them. She put her hand on Charles's shoulder and silently, slowly, pushed him to his knees. She crooked her leg over his shoulder and pushing her pelvis forward gently covered his mouth. In the glass his hand stroked her thigh. She ran her fingers over the nape of his neck; she stared into her own half-closed eyes and smiled; a knowing, clever, scheming smile. The smile that all women have and no man ever sees.

Their lovemaking was a dance this time. Actually it was a whole dance card, a complete terpsichorean exhibition, starting with a bit of old-time: a swirling waltz, a natty foxtrot; a Latin section complete with head-twisting and rictus-grinning and, finally, a free-form disco.

When they had finished with Iona's pealing laughter the room was quiet and dark, the furniture sat in the shadows and quietly applauded. She reached out and took Charles's face between her palms and whispered. They were the first words you could have found in a dictionary that had passed between them for two hours.

'Was that as wonderful as I thought it was,' Charles replied lamely.

'Of course it was. You were there too, matey.'

'I know, I mean I just thought, well, maybe you had higher standards than I do.'

'No, what you meant was you think I'm an old nympho

who sleeps with dozens of men, and are you any good at it?'

'No, that's not what I meant exactly.'

Iona snorted and laid her head on his stomach. 'I'll tell you something though. Turn on the light. Yours is the first foreskin I've ever fucked.'

'Really?'

'Yup, all the rest were circumcized. I wasn't sure I was going to like it, but it's really sweet isn't it? So neat the way it slides backwards and forwards. Does that hurt?'

'No, it's nice.'

'I like it. It's sort of complete, the way it was supposed to be. It makes you look like a Greek bronze, only bigger, of course. Much bigger.' She giggled. 'No, I'm going to have all my sons left like this. You know Charles, I've slept with quite a lot of people and no *one*'s good at sex; couples are good at sex. Being good in bed is like being one person on a see-saw, you need someone compatible on your other end. We're good at sex together. Very, very, very good, and I think we're probably good at it because we're both deeply selfish.'

'I'm not selfish. I'm always thinking of what would be best for . . .'

'Bollocks. You go for me like Ben Gunn for a cheese-board. I like that, that's what I want. Sex is all appetite, I want to eat and be eaten by a man who's famished, not some jerk handing round his cock like it was a tray of canapés. "Are you sure you wouldn't like another mouthful, Vicar?" No, you're brilliant because you're self-obsessed and insecure. I like that in a man.' She came up and kissed him.

'You know, that's very like something Mona said.'

'Oh I completely forgot about Mona. Have you made a decision about her things? You are going to let me sell them, aren't you? Please? You will, won't you?' Iona put on a wheedling, little girlie voice and gently took his balls in her hand. 'You will let me sell them, won't you?'

'I haven't made up my mind yet,' he said. 'You wanted me to

179

be strong. Well, I'm not bowing to this kind of unprofessional pressure.'

She squeezed. 'What about this pressure?'

'Stop. I've been reading her diaries, they're all about sex. She said something about sex and appetite. She liked sex to be a huge banquet. She said it should be like crawling through a buffet with your hands tied behind your back, not served in courses by a waiter in white gloves. I'll find it.' Charles reached across the bedside table and took a small leather-bound diary off a pile of books. It had a lock and the initials M. C. in gold on the cover. 'Here. "I'd rather do sex with a man who ate peanut butter and jelly sandwiches standing up in the kitchen than a man who knows how to peel an orange with a knife and fork. I let Cary Grant have me last week; he could peel a pineapple with a plastic spoon, he's so full of bedroom etiquette. I hate myself for giving in to his endless flirtation. My bloody curiosity. He's had everyone in town and now he's had me as well. Pretty disappointing, like all the leading glamour men. He's so vain, wanting me to admire his damn legs and famous donkey cock. It is big, but, God, he doesn't know what to do with it. I've seen men cork champagne bottles with more *élan*. That's it for me, no more stars, I'm going to stick with character actors, cameramen and the odd director, if I can find one who isn't too odd." '

'I wish I'd known her,' said Iona. 'Doesn't she sound great? Now, I'm hungry. Do you want to take me to dinner or have you got another post-coital feast, just on the off chance that you might have got lucky tonight?'

'Um, smoked chicken and celeriac soup, herring roe and crispy bacon with soda bread, cold partridge with rowan jelly and rice pudding with sherried raisins? Or we could get a pizza?'

'Oh, tough decision, man.'

They sat in the dining-room. Iona wore an antique Japanese kimono, with cranes flying over it, open to the waist. She lit every candle in the room, including a huge candelabra formed out of a laocoön. They ate and Charles read bits from Mona's diary.

'You read really well. That's so nice, I love being read to; I

180

want to sit in a cottage by the sea and listen to you read Daphne du Maurier to me.'

Charles got to a list that Mona had made, obviously drunk and lonely on New Year's Eve in 1948. It was of all the men she had ever slept with, with star ratings and occasional bitter comments, like the review sections of a Hollywood magazine.

'God, she had everyone. Do you realize what that list is worth to a Sunday newspaper? Charles, you have to sell this stuff.'

'I added them up,' said Charles. 'There are a hundred and fifty men.'

'One hundred and fifty by 1948, and she was only forty. That's incredible.'

'Sad really.'

'Sad. What's sad about it? That's great. She was a handsome, famous, rich, talented lady and she had lots of sex. If that's sad, Lord make me miserable.'

'Oh come on, Iona, you can't mean that. It's a sign of terrible emptiness, loneliness, never being able to find love, constancy, fidelity for more than a couple of nights.'

'I can't believe you're saying that. I can't believe any man is still talking like that. If that were Errol Flynn's diary you'd be saying, "Yeah, well, what did he do for the weekends then?" Come on, Charles, how many people have you slept with?'

'I don't know, I've never counted.'

'Don't be so silly, all men know. They can't remember their waist size or their mother's telephone number or how many inches there are in eight, but they all know how many girls they've shafted.'

'Well, do you know? Do you keep a score?' Charles huffed back.

'No, not off the top of my head.'

'OK, let's find out.' He went to the bureau and got two bridge score pads and little pencils with tassels. 'We'll write them down.'

'Do you think this is such a good idea, Charles?' said Iona quietly.

'Yes, I want to know. I don't know anything about you. I want to know.'

'OK, first names only and no cheating.'

'Fine.'

'And no recriminations, no laughing and no cross-examining?'

'OK.'

Iona started to write and then looked up. 'What counts as a lover?'

'What do you mean? People you've had sex with.'

'Yes, but do you mean strictly penetration, because I've gone to bed with people and not actually done it but had great sex.'

'Well, um, orgasm then. If you had an orgasm that's it.'

'Oh, hold on. Stewards' enquiry here. That wipes out three-quarters of my score before I was twenty. Can I count faked orgasms?'

'No. Oh, all right, if an orgasm occurred at the time with you present.'

'So hand-jobs count?'

'Well it's a grey area.'

'You bet.'

'Well, if hand-jobs count my score doubles.'

'Use a lot of cheap hookers, do you?'

'No, boarding-school.'

Iona laughed and they both started writing, Charles with his hand round his paper like a spelling test.

'Charles, do they have to be human and conscious?'

'Iona!'

'No dogs? I'm only joking.'

'That's in very poor taste.'

Of course, Charles knew his score before he started. Fourteen. Fourteen girls who had taken him on board, eight of them for one night only, two for between three and five times and two with whom he had had season tickets and could comfortably call ex-girlfriends without fear of contradiction, and then Lily. He bumped up the total by including a couple of girls who had allowed him to stick a hand in their underpants at student parties and a girl who had painfully squeezed his cock through his trousers during a Saturday matinée of *The Graduate*. Eighteen. It was hardly Casanova. It was hardly *Walter: My Secret Life*. It wasn't even Charlie Drake. A handful of one-night stands, a couple of gropes, two girlfriends and a cleaning lady. He turned his paper over.

Iona was writing methodically. She got to the bottom of the page and started on a new one. Charles watched with a growing sense of distress. Every so often she would bite the pencil and stare into the middle distance. Her writing was neat and depressingly small. She giggled and shook her head and wrote more. She stopped, put down a name and then crossed it out. 'No cheating. We agreed. No editing,' said Charles, sharper than he had meant. 'There's no point in doing this if you're going to lie about it. Who are you crossing out?'

'Really, I wasn't cheating. I just can't sort of remember. It was in France and I went to bed with this fantastically beautiful painter and his friend sort of joined us. They were sweet. We spent the whole summer together. They were inseparable, shared everything, but I was so drunk I can't really remember if they shared me or not. I think the friend just watched.'

'That counts,' said Charles, thinly. 'Group sex counts.'

'Oh actually, hang on, I did sleep with the friend anyway. He drove me to the station and I fucked him in the back of his Deux Chevaux with my foot sticking out of those old fold-down windows. A gendarme caught us. God, it was funny. That was such a good holiday.'

Charles went to make coffee and quietly boiled in the kitchen, cursing himself for suggesting anything so humiliatingly stupid. He came back and Iona was sitting smoking and smiling.

He made to pick up her three-page list and she slapped her hand down on it. 'Fair exchange; you show me yours, I'll show you mine. Let's take them to bed, bring the bottle.'

Charles carried the wine and the coffee on a tray to the bedroom, and handed his list to Iona. She sat naked, cross-legged in front of him as he counted. The pain of retrospective jealousy became physical, every name a twisted, rusty dart in his groin: René, Alphonse, Gordon S., Gordon Mac, Gordon G., Gordon D. 'You did sterling work in the Gay Gordons, didn't you?'

'It was a popular name in my year at Edinburgh. Gordon Mac was the serious one; I only had the others because I didn't want to risk calling the wrong name out in the dark.'

As the innocent game had lowered Charles's spirits, so it had raised Iona's. Happy, funny, poignant, exciting memories flooded back and worse, she was apparently utterly uninterested in his short bedroom memorial. She held it casually, face down, unread.

'Who's this?' Charles shouted. 'We said first names, not initials, M.O.T., who's M.O.T?'

'Oh, I can't remember his name; man on train,' and she laughed.

Charles's fury and hurt burst like a cloud full of acid rain. He threw the slips of paper at her. They fluttered onto the sheet. He turned over in the bed. 'Very funny, man on train. We could all be M.I.P., men in passing; or B.O.S., bit on side; or N.O.T, nothing on television.'

'Charles,' Iona leant forward and put her arm round his neck. 'Don't be such a victim, such a childish victim. That's all in the past. It hasn't got anything to do with you, except that I suppose if you like making love to me you should thank all these other men, because I practised on them so that I could be good for you.'

'Very clever. Oh, Iona, I know I shouldn't react so stupidly but there are so many, and I want to be special.'

'Do you?'

'Yes. I hate your past. I hate there being all this time when I didn't know you.'

'You shouldn't be jealous of the past, there is nothing you can do about it.'

'I know,' said Charles miserably, 'but do you understand?'

'No, darling, frankly I don't think I do.'

There was a long pause. Iona watched Charles's finely worked profile. He should have said something conciliatory, something special, but he couldn't. Instead he said, 'There's a name missing. Tony's.'

'Oh yes, Tony.'

'We need to talk about him.'

'There's nothing to say.' Iona rested her head on Charles's chest. 'I've made my calculations, I've made a decision. It was the partridge that did it. I'm going to dump him.'

'Really?' said Charles. 'Honestly? Because of me?'

'No, because of four Gordons. Yes, because of you, but I must let him down in my own time, in my own way. Don't nag me, OK?'

'You won't fuck him again?'

'Well, you've got to have the revenge fuck, haven't you? The one with your bags in the hall, knickers round your ankles, clutching your Penguin Modern Classics Camus. Where you both cry and have the most God-Almighty orgasm and he dribbles down your leg as you wait for a taxi in the rain surrounded by Sainsbury's bags bursting with bikinis and walking shoes, and his mother's Christmas present. And you can hear him playing "Surabaya Johnny", which was your tune, top volume from an open bedroom window. Yes, I think I'll probably try and avoid that.'

'Oh, Iona, I . . .'

'Yes.'

'I've just thought of another missing name: mine.'

'You're not on it, stupid, because you're not part of my past; you're my future. And do you think you could manage to be a central part of my next half-hour? I haven't read this yet.' She looked at his list. 'You put my name on it, you bastard. God, look at this, Veronica, Sophie, Perdita, Charlotte, Fiona. Did you just work your way through a pony club? Caroline. Which one had the best body?'

'You do.'

'Of course I do. Now which bit do you like the best?'

The past fell to the floor, the Gordons lay heavily on the

Perditas, Charlottes and Fionas, who couldn't believe their luck. René, Hubert, André, Felix and Monty watched, and then, with a thud, Cary Grant and 149 film stars landed heavily on Caroline.

Chapter Eleven

' 'Oo's a bootiful boy, den? Yes, he is. 'Oo's de most bootiful boy in de whole world, den? Yes, you are, yes you are. Oh, 'oo's a likkle well-bred man, den? Yes, you are.'

Vernon walked jauntily across to the garden, holding a red leather lead as if it had an imperial borzoi or The Empress of Blandings shackled to the other end. Melbourne shuffled asthmatically after him, blinking bulbous syrupy eyes at the terrifying expanse of sunshiny outside.

Vernon unlocked the gate and bent to unhook the lead. 'Off you go little man, run and frolic.' The dog stood on the gravel and wheezed the air. Nemesis hung in the breeze. He gave Vernon a stare of stupid loathing that looked very much like adoration to the peer and trotted onto the lawn.

Vernon began to perambulate, his corpulent stomach swathed in acid-lemon cashmere set like a spinnaker. He was dressed week-end casual: bottle-green corduroy trousers, polished brogues,

Argyle yellow-and-grey socks and a jaunty Paisley cravat. Hair roguish, with just a touch of eau-de-Portugal.

It was perfect, just perfect. The garden was a blank canvas; oh, the possibilities. The Mona Corinth Memorial would be just the start. Once he had a foot in the garden, so much would follow: a sculpture park, exhibitions two or three times a year and concerts – open-air, small, select, good soloists. Then, he rubbed his fat little palms, opera. Nothing opens doors like opera, nothing brought out the tiaras and limos like dead Italians and raped peasants. Yes, an opera festival; first in a marquee, then something a bit more permanent, but always exclusive, mind, always chic and expensive and all of it his. The vicar could have his horrible yobs in on a couple of afternoons in the winter. Perhaps get in some with incurable diseases, bald heads waggling in wheelchairs, attract a Royal. Possibilities, possibilities. Vernon looked at the glory of the garden and saw miles and miles of embossed card, all of it with his gaudy coat of arms. It was going to be fabulous. That big plane tree would have to go, of course, but first things first. He'd neutered the Committee, now it was time for the odious gardener. The years spent on boards and advisory panels had taught Vernon that self-aggrandizement, like God, was in the details. See to the little people and the big people would fall into line.

'Tenby, Tenby,' he shouted.

Melbourne started fearfully and began to crap lumpy mucus and scrape his claggy, wormied bottom along the grass.

'Charles, Charles, look.' Iona was standing at the window eating bits of brioche with marmalade and drinking coffee. 'Vernon's in the garden, go and talk to him.'

'I'm not dressed,' Charles called from the kitchen, 'and neither are you. Don't stand there without any clothes on. I'm doing the eggs.'

'I'm hardly likely to turn Vernon into a ravening sex maniac, and fuck the eggs. On with the breastplate and the buckler. Slay the dragon while the damsel eats breakfast in the nude and watches.'

'Never turn your back on eggs and I refuse to face Vernon on an empty stomach.'

'Spoil sport. There's nothing a girl likes better than men fighting first thing.'

Angel was just getting into the morning short strokes when he received the call. 'Sod,' he said, depositing a thick libation of semen onto a sickly looking poppy. 'That bloody man is a spunk magnet. He must be able to smell it from three hundred yards.' He looked down at Stendhal, who lay beside him, ears pricked. 'You stay here, don't move, and no licking the poppies.' Buttoning his fly, he wiped his hand on the dog's back and walked slowly across the lawn.

'Tenby.'

'Here, Your Majesty.'

'Ah, good man, good man.' Vernon cast a wary eye over Angel's extended hand and patted him on the shoulder. 'Walk with me a moment, will you?'

Angel fell into step and Vernon grandly led him up the garden path.

'You know how much we all appreciate what you're doing here with the garden,' he said with practised ease. Angel remained silent. He knew nothing of the sort, and cared less. 'We really do. And I must say it hasn't gone unnoticed. I've had some pretty influential people ask me about you, and you've got something of a reputation you know. You're happy in your work, aren't you? Yes, I'm sure you are, but are you contented? It would seem to me that for a man of your rare talents, this little patch might be, well, limiting, not enough scope. Now, I've just had an enquiry from a lady, a person of some consequence. She needs a head gardener for her estate in the Shires. It's a wonderful place, Capability Brown park, Elizabethan knot-garden, acres of greenhouse, arboreta, nutteries, kitchen gardens, orchards, lakes, one of the great treasures of England, and I'm prepared to recommend you.'

Angel remained silent, his brow furrowed.

Vernon continued to plough. 'It really could be the making of

189

you. I expect you heard there's going to be some changes in the square and, between you and me, the Mona Corinth Memorial is only the start. There are great things afoot and, frankly, they might not be quite your thing. I'm not sure they're entirely my thing, but who are we to stand in the way of the common good? All in all, Angel, this opportunity might be heaven sent. Don't make up your mind now, think about it, but I ought to give the lady an answer soon.'

'No,' Angel bellowed.

'Now don't be hasty,' said Vernon, taken aback by his vehemence.

'No. Lie down.'

'I beg your pardon?' Vernon turned.

In the middle of the lawn the dark shadow of Stendhal was bearing down on Melbourne.

'Oh my God, Mellie, Mellie, here. Come to Daddy.'

Melbourne regarded his predicament with arse-paralysing panic. A hurtling Alsatian doesn't leave a small, sickly Lhasa apso with a lot of options, and he didn't have a lot of brains to choose between those options. When his snot-blocked nose and tear-filled eyes had confirmed that there was, on the horizon, the canine equivalent of the *Bismarck* steaming dead ahead, Melbourne, with all the cunning and natural woodcraft that was his birthright, closed his eyes and pretended to be a dead tea cosy. Then, an instant later, he lost his nerve, which left him only natural selection's two old standbys: fight or flight, which, considering the size, weight, health, armament and water displacement of Stendhal, was no choice at all. 'Run' his tiny brain screamed. Unfortunately Nature had not been generous in the running department either. Melbourne stuck his tongue out and sent urgent shots of adrenalin to his legs which took off at a rate of inches. Hearing his master's familiar voice, he headed in the opposite direction. All the horrible things that had ever happened to him in his horrible short life had been accompanied by those childish tones.

'Tenby, do you know whose dog that is?' screamed Vernon.

'He was Miss Corinth's.'

'Well, whose is he now?'

'No-one's. He lives with me.'

'Well, call it off, man.'

'Stendhal.'

There was no question of Melbourne getting away. He vaguely had plans to make it to the herbaceous border and bury himself like a chicken bone, but as plans go it wasn't really a runner. Neither was he. Stendhal, glossy and muscular in the sun, bounded with easy fluid strides, a Teutonic superdog, supple and tough, clean of wind and limb, unencumbered by an ounce of fat or morality. He ran a long parabola before making his final approach, belting across the greensward, tongue streaming, teeth gleaming. He was a fine sight unless, of course, you were a fearful, lathered Lhasa apso with agoraphobia.

Iona and Charles and a small French table watched over the poached eggs on haddock with hollandaise.

'He's a handsome dog,' said Iona.

'He's a monster,' replied Charles with feeling.

At the last moment, Melbourne tried to jink. Looking wildly over his shoulder, he caught just the briefest shadow of grey and then the earth span. Stendhal hit him broadside. With a soprano squeak the little dog shot into the air, turned a couple of times, and hit the grass, rolling over and over. Without losing power or rhythm, Stendhal caught him with his two front pads in the solar plexus. The clawed feet, with eight stones of sinew and muscle behind them, propelled at twenty-five knots, plunged and thudded into the fluffy diaphragm, forcing two small lungfuls of air, at speed, through the fretted sinuses and explosively down the bogey-blocked nostrils. There was a stream of snot and a noise like a fat boy sitting on a whoopee cushion.

It would be humane at this point to imagine that Melbourne slipped mercifully into unconsciousness, and that the frantic squealing and wriggling was no more than automatic spasms, insensate reflex quivers. Vernon consoled himself in the weeks that followed with the tearful belief that his dear companion had suffered no pain. It might also be kinder to assume that Stendhal's motives in what came after were merely energetic high jinks, exuberance that had got out of hand, and Angel certainly clung to this interpretation as explanatory balm. But truth to tell Nature is not a caring, tasteful censor, a humane liberal, and the uncomfortable fact is that Melbourne had never been more corporeally aware and Stendhal had never been anything but psychotic.

Stendhal knew what this little animated posing pouch wanted. What it wanted was a jolly good seeing to. It wanted four inches of roll-in roll-out, pale pink, pointy doggie dick. Holding Melbourne down with his front feet, he unleashed the great slippery bitch prong and, lowering his haunches, shuffled it in a series of jerks and slithers towards the erotically protesting lap-dog.

'For Christ's sake, stop him,' screamed Vernon, jogging across the lawn.

Angel caught his arm. 'Don't go too close, they aren't listening now. All they're aware of is the roar of their natures. Interfere and he'll take your throat out.'

'Their natures. Their natures,' shrieked Vernon. 'You mad, insanitary shit-bag. That filthy, common, scrap-yard thug is trying to rape Melbourne. It's nothing to do with Nature, you half-witted, stinking oaf, it's a sex crime. Stop him, pull him off, shoot him, kill him.'

Whatever Stendhal's warped instinct may have insisted, this was not Melbourne's lucky day. Lhasa apsos are furry dogs, fluffy, childishly tressed dogs, and to the unaccustomed or uncaring eye they look, in repose, much of a muchness either end. Unfortunately, in their earlier acrobatic encounter, Melbourne had been hastily caught back to front, and, equally unfortunately, Stendhal's blind cock nuzzled not a damp, grottily puckered sphincter, but a moistly quivering nostril. Unable to execute an entrance, even with half a dozen hefty pelvic stabs, it worked its way south to the gaping, rasping, harelipped mouth, and there found a more amenable, but no more welcoming entrance. Stendhal shoved his dick past the curling, spammy tongue and down the well-bred little man's throat, and proceeded with great appetite and fervour to fuck the effete mite's brains out. Desperately hawking, unable to breathe, publicly humiliated, callously violated, gagging and retching, Melbourne exerted the sort of genital stimulation that Alsations rarely experience.

'Aaaaaah,' ululated Vernon. 'Do something, you shitty, dim common sod.'

Angel stood, rooted, silent and stoical, like John Wayne watching a wagon-train massacre.

Vernon howled with exasperation. He turned and ran for the garden shed, panting, 'Rape! Rape! Help, rape!' at the top of his voice.

Tragically but understandably, in extremis, unable to breathe, his oesophagus bruised and torn, Melbourne performed the final foolish act of a profoundly foolish life. He bit. Suicidally, he exercised the one option left to him: fight. He bit with all the power left in his small, chicken-liver-and-cat-food needle teeth. Shocking pain shot from Stendhal's sticky groin to his sickly damaged synapses, causing him to ejaculate instantly and copiously into his mate-victim's lungs, and, simultaneously, it made him furious. Pain may be a sexual stimulus, but it is also painful. Lunging with the noble head, he grasped Melbourne by the hindquarters and bit back; bit until tooth met scything tooth, severing the spinal cord with a snap like a cheap cracker. Extracting his penis and leaping to all fours, he tossed the little dog into the air. Melbourne landed, for a second time, in a wet bloody heap, and with a last flickering sparkle of life, he dragged his limply twisted back legs towards the dim distant herbaceous border. Stendhal pounced again and, grabbing the small head between his ravening jaws, raced and bounded round the lawn.

Bursting out of the shed, Vernon, keening wildly, pounded after him, brandishing a rake. 'Murder, murderer.'

Angel started after Vernon, who stopped mid-stride and took a swing at him. The three of them dodged each other for two circuits.

Charles and Iona reached the gate at about the same time as Bryony.

'Judas,' she hissed at Charles. 'How many pieces of silver did you get pushed up your botty to join the other side?'

'Bryony, I can explain. It was . . .'

'Hello, dear, nice to see you. Bite his bollocks off,' Bryony cut across Charles and smiled at Iona.

Vernon came to a panting tearful halt in front of them. Angel stopped a judicious distance from the rake. Stendhal and Melbourne lay together in the middle of the lawn. Having raped and murdered the small pet, the Alsatian decided the best thing, all considered, would be to eat the evidence. Ripping a flap out of the corpse's stomach, he stuck in a long nose and pulled out silky coils of offal. The little circle stood in silence for a moment, watching.

Then a slow chugging started, like someone trying to start a cold Citroën. It emanated from Bryony. Her bosom began to wobble and then, with a gurgling cough, the engine caught. She threw back her head and bellowed great gusts of helpless laughter. Stendhal paused, chops dripping, and looked at her crashing through the gears of merriment. The sound in the heavily charged atmosphere was contagious. Iona smiled, then smirked, then snorted. She half turned, and covering her mouth, fought for embarrassed self-control. Angel looked at the two women, then at the *distrait* Vernon, and sniggered down his nose. Charles pushed a knuckle into his mouth, making a soft mewing sound.

'Oooh, bastards,' screamed Vernon. 'You bastards.' Double-handed he swung the rake over his head at Bryony, who was convulsed, holding her knees and fighting a rear-guard action for bladder control.

Angel caught the swinging rake and wrenched it from the lordly hand. Vernon staggered and fell heavily to the ground. He knelt, prone, like a guilty Muslim and pounded the grass.

'Do something, do something,' he implored Charles, who cleared his throat and said, in an unnaturally high voice, 'Um, why don't you go home, Vernon, and have a cup of sweet tea, and we'll, um, tidy up here?'

Iona snorted.

'Tea, tea! I don't want tea. I want him arrested. Call the police, the RSPCA. I want him sacked; that stinking navvy sacked, do you understand? And his murdering dog put down.'

'Oh, I don't think we should be hasty,' said Charles. 'I think it was an unfortunate accident, and, well, you know, dogs will be dogs.'

'Do as I say.' Vernon's puce tear-stained face streaked with sweat, snot and grass cuttings stared at Charles, his voice a controlled livid growl. 'Sack him now.'

Bryony stopped laughing. Iona turned as if to say something but didn't.

'No,' said Charles, calmly. 'Angel is the square's gardener, employed by the Committee. He has our full support.'

'Here here,' Bryony muttered.

'The unfortunate incident just now was an accident; no-one was really to blame, except perhaps you, for not having your dog on a lead.'

'*My* dog?' said Vernon incredulously. 'What about *his* rapist, mad, murdering dog?'

'Angel has the Committee's permission to keep a dog in the garden.'

'For vermin control purposes,' added Bryony helpfully.

'Quite. For ratting. So, we're very sorry, but least said soonest mended. And by the way, just while we're all here, will you take my name off your Board. I never agreed to sit on it, and the Committee has decided that there will be no Mona Corinth Memorial here. That's our final unanimous decision,' he added with a weak smile.

Vernon rose to his knees and pointed a melodramatic courtroom finger at Charles. 'You fool, you stupid gutless nonentity. I offer to make something out of you, out of the kindness of . . . You realize who I am, who you're dealing . . . I'll crush you and your damned Committee. Committee, ha, ha. Sad nobodies, coffee-mornings. I'll show you committees, I know more about dealing with committees than . . .' It was Vernon's turn to laugh mirthlessly. His jowls wobbled and shed clippings and damp grass as he raged. 'This is not the end, you'll regret this, Godwin.'

Stendhal trotted over, his huge muzzle clotted with gore. He leapt up and planted two rust-red paw prints on Vernon's cashmere chest and, licking his face, smeared it with streaks of blood and gelatinous mince.

'Aaah, aaah.' Vernon staggered to his feet, spitting. 'Get away, get away from me.' He spun round, kicking and punching. The dog sprang sideways, anticipating a new game. Vernon strode to the gate, Stendhal capering around him on the off chance that he might have another small pet about his person.

The five of them watched him make as dignified an exit as he could muster.

'Well done, darling,' said Iona.

'Yes, fucking well done, Charles. Horrible little dog.'

Iona took Charles's arm. 'Fancy a cup of coffee, Bryony?'

'Wouldn't say no. I think I need a swab-down in the bog.'

'You all right?' Charles asked Angel.

'Fine. I'd better go and dispose of the little rat.' But Stendhal was already seeing to it. What was left of Melbourne was scraped into a shallow cool grave in a dark corner of the garden; another nameless corpse whose body would eventually leech and seep into the common verdant riot of life. Not an entirely unmourned or unmarked grave. Vernon sobbed over the lead in his bedroom, and Stendhal cocked his leg and pissed on the patch of disturbed earth so that he could find it later if he got peckish in the night.

'Dinner at Zanuck's, the usual crowd. Sat next to John Wayne and his breath. The man's mouth smells foul, like the pit of hell, I hate to think what he eats. He spent the whole of the first course talking about his bowels, apparently he's very constipated. I told him buggery always works for me; he should get one of those Indians to bend him over a saddle. He got very on his high horse and says it's not nice for a lady to talk dirty, that here in America ladies behave like ladies, and as I am a guest in this country I should try and learn a few God-fearing manners. I got angry and asked if it's the God-fearing manners that send him down to Mexico to get laid by under-age brown girls. He's full of shit, both ends, and he can't stop being a fucking cowboy. Actors have no imagination, just typecasting. He asked me if I am a communist, nastily. I must learn to keep my mouth shut. Ended up in bed with Alan Ladd, small guys try so much harder. He tells me that he really fancied the little boy in *Shane*.'

The doorbell went and Charles put down Mona's diary.

The policeman was old to still be a constable. He had neat thinning grey hair and apologetic eyes. It was not an arresting face, which is probably why it had never been made up to sergeant.

'Mr Godwin,' he said, reading from a notebook, 'Constable Spry, Earl's Court. Might I step in and ask you a few questions?'

The furniture was agog. 'I knew he was a criminal,' said a footman's chair.

'Not a very important one,' shouted a small desk; 'they've only sent one old man. I remember when they arrested the squire, they had to send a whole squad of militia. He wouldn't go quietly; ripped one of my handles off. It still aches. And all for a dead baby.'

'I understand there was an incident this morning in the garden, sir.'

'Well, not much of an incident; a dog fight. Lord Vernon's Lhasa apso was accidentally killed.'

'A Lhasa what, Sir? I understood the animal was a Melbourne.'

'No, his name was Melbourne. He was a Lhasa apso, a Tibetan temple dog.'

'Quite a small dog, was it? Unpleasant, yappy, hairy little thing? Quite. Now, you were present?'

'Well, I arrived after, really, or at least at the end.'

'Quite. With a Miss Iona Wallace?'

'Yes, and Bryony Mullins.'

'Girlfriend, sir?'

'Heavens no, I mean Bryony isn't.'

'Quite. And the other?'

'Yes, well, I'm not really sure; a close friend.'

'Quite. Now, it's my understanding that an Angel Tenby set his dog on to this Melbourne creature and had it killed for sport or vindictiveness, and then he, not the dog, set upon Lord Vernon with a rake and abused him. Is that your recollection?'

'No, no, nothing like that. It was a fight and the little dog got killed, and Vernon got angry. He had a rake, and he tried to hit Angel and then Bryony, and Angel took the rake away, and we all went home. That's the sum of it. Did Lord Barnstaple tell you he had been attacked?'

'No, sir, the Home Secretary did, or rather the Home Secretary's Personal Private Secretary. Would you be so good as to introduce me to this Mr Tenby, and the Cabinet-worrying hound?' The old policeman spoke without a trace of humour.

Charles led him into the garden. The evening was pale, warm and still.

'This where it happened?' The policeman took off his helmet and rubbed the back of his head.

'Yes. On the lawn. Ah, here's Angel.'

The gardener walked slowly towards them, wiping his hand on his moleskin trousers, Stendhal at his heel.

'Mr Tenby, I understand there was a dog killed here today.'

'Yes.'

'By this dog here, er, Stendhal?'

'Yes.'

'Was there any other kind of incident?'

'No.'

'Perhaps involving a rake?'

'Oh, Lord Vernon got one of my rakes from the shed, I put it back.'

'Quite. Is he violent? The shepherd, not Vernon?'

'No.'

'A well-trained dog, would you say?'

Angel said nothing.

'Would you be so good as to ask him to sit, sir?'

'Sit, Stendhal, sit.' Stendhal sat instantly.

'Would you tell the dog to stay, and walk over here?'

'Stay.' Angel walked; Stendhal remained motionless.

'Now call him, sir.'

'Stendhal.'

He came, then he walked to heel, lay down and finally rolled over and played dead. Charles thought, He's just like the psycho murderers in American films, they're always as charming as sin when they're arrested for the first time. Stendhal looked up at the policeman with a very good imitation of innocence.

'Right, that's a very nicely behaved dog you've got there, Mr Tenby. Beautiful dog. Ever had any trouble with him?'

'He's a credit to the breed,' interrupted Charles.

'Quite. I like shepherds; worked with them for twenty years. Never met one that had a nasty thought in its head. Loyal, level, honest and true.' He patted Stendhal on the head. 'Now, this Lhasa apso, foreign dog; nervous was it? Excitable, prone to fits of pique?' Again said without any discernible sense of pun.

'Well,' said Charles.

'Quite. I think that's about it. Now, I'll have to make up a report and it's up to my station inspector whether or not to prosecute. I can't see a problem, but I must warn you that the Home Secretary's Personal Private Secretary doesn't call me every day. It's a very nice garden you keep here, Mr Tenby. How do you keep that lilium harlequin looking so lush? Mine never prosper.'

'Drainage and muck,' said Angel.

'Really? I've been putting lime on mine.'

'Oh no, no. You mustn't spoil them. These ones don't like lime, they're simple souls really.'

'Quite. Very interesting. That magnolia grandiflora, now, I've walked the beat in London for twenty years and I've never seen one anything like as large, and still in flower. Very impressive Mr Tenby. Would you mind if I, er . . .'

'I'd be delighted. Do you garden?'

'Allotment out in Hammersmith; never get enough time. Have you ever grown kohlrabi?'

Charles left the two of them squatting beside the herbaceous border, examining handfuls of earth, like two small boys in a sandpit. Stendhal snuffled the lawn, hoovering stray gobbets of evidence.

The light on Charles's answerphone blinked. 'Darling Gawain, will you meet me at six-thirty? Carey's Club, twenty-five Frith Street. It's a book launch, duty. Just ten mins. Toby Sills, *Over the Top. The Private Life of Lord Kitchener*. We can go out to dinner afterwards. Big kiss.'

Charles found Carey's without difficulty. The pavement outside was crowded with young men and women frantically waving at each other as if the whole side of the street were an Atlantic liner about to depart. He pushed through into a low-ceilinged, dingy room. Beside the door was a pile of books guarded by a PR lady with lipstick on her teeth. The cover of the dauntingly large hardback showed a computer-montaged photograph of a Victorian subaltern bending over and Lord Kitchener of Khartoum leap-frogging him. The field marshal was wearing his famous walrus moustache, peaked cap, leather gloves, swagger stick, brassière, stockings, suspenders and patent leather stilettos.

Charles sidled in and found a vacant patch of wall and looked around for Iona. He recognized quite a lot of the people in that fuzzy demi-famous way, where you're never quite sure if it's the chap who sells you your newspapers or who was once married to Anneka Rice. The party was a pretty exact replica of Vernon's garden do and Charles had a hollow sense of déjà vu. In front of him a girl in a black bustier and jeans with cropped white hair was crying. She appeared to be about fourteen, terribly vulnerable and small. She was deeply upset, weeping without vanity. She wiped her nose with the back of her little hand. 'You bastards, you bastards,' she sobbed, her mouth bubbling with tears and spit. Ranged in front of her three men laughed. They were big, muscular, predatory men, confidently jutting hips and groins, all angular elbows and chins. They laughed easily, carelessly.

The girl pushed the heels of her hands into her eyes. 'Oh God, shit,' she said pitifully. Then, blinking, she started to laugh with them, took a glass from one, drained it, and said, 'Oh what the hell, I can always get another one,' and then she smiled with a desperate brave sadness. Charles thought if he'd been her father the little tableau would have broken his heart.

'Charles.' Stephen Marle slid in front of him and leant one hand on the wall beside his head, blocking his view. He blew a long stream of smoke at the ceiling. 'Well, who's been a foolish boy then?'

'Hello, Stephen. I'm sorry about Melbourne.'

'You will be, His Lordship's hopping. I haven't seen him so furious since I cocked up the train times for Balmoral. Bad mistake, love. He's going to have your nuts for ear-rings. This is war. He's going to get the garden come hell or republic, duckie.'

'Well, um, I don't really see . . .'

'No you don't, you never have. Well, I'm handing in my resignation to the Committee. This is one mink who's going to leave the sinking ship to the women and children.'

'Hello, darling, sorry I'm late, the traffic's foul. Oh hello, Stephen, sorry about your furry chum.' Iona pushed past Marle's arm and pecked Charles's cheek.

'Oh you, hello. You're on the shit list too. The lordling wants your front bottom on a plate.'

'Really? I wouldn't have thought he'd know how to eat one.'

Stephen sneered. 'You've been warned. You might get a position on the cash-only till at Asda, but I wouldn't bank on it. Must dash.'

'Silly queen. Have you talked to anyone else?'

'No. I'm not sure I really want to.'

'Come on, I'll introduce you to the author; we were at university together. He's a sweet little prat. Had a hopeless crush on one of my boyfriends, followed us round for weeks, made a lunge at me just to get close to his sperm.'

'Gordon Mac?'

'Yes, how on earth did you know? Oh, by the way, I owe you my front bottom on a plate. You were right about that horrible terracotta head: Spanish, ten to twenty pounds. You are clever. Toby, Toby. God, you look sort of, so substantial.'

'Iona, sweetheart, my favourite after-dinner streaker.' Toby was round and soft and pink, with a lot of baby-blond hair, which had been given a severe seeing to. He was dressed in the sort of suit that Conservative junior ministers favoured at the time of Suez, set off by a throttlingly knotted greasy tie and a signet ring. Charles recognized him from the Op Ed pages of Sunday newspapers, writing 'we've seen it all before' historical perspectives on the Princess of Wales, Blackpool Conferences and Primary School Education. He also recognized him as one of those very young men for whom youth is the most uncomfortable of Nature's burdens. He couldn't wait to grow into his clothes and his prejudices and a dribbling prostate.

'Toby, this is Charles Godwin.'

'Hello. Didn't I read a review of yours in the TLS? Canning, wasn't it? Or the Corn Law?'

'No, not me.'

'Sorry, mind like a sieve. Who is it you write for?'

'No-one, I teach bridge.'

'Oh right, pass.'

'Congratulations on your book. It's, um, got a very arresting cover,' said Charles.

'Rather good, isn't it? Should make a great window for Waterstone's,' Toby beamed.

'Yes, I gather it's not a straightforward military biography.'

'Charles, don't be naïve. Who'd want to read about dead fuzzy-wuzzies?' laughed Iona.

'Well, I might.'

'No, what Toby does is psychological history. The closet is far more interesting than the Cabinet.'

'I must say, I've unearthed some pretty hot stuff on the field marshal,' Toby confided. 'Of course, we've all known that he was a monumental homosexual for years, but I think I'm the first person to be able to give times, dates, names and addresses. And I've discovered all these under-age Hottentots he had affairs with, and a Seaforth who spurned him and was shot for cowardice.'

'Are you homosexual?'

'Charles!' Iona spluttered white wine.

'What an extraordinary question,' said Toby. 'No, as it happens.'

'Well, when was the last time you had sex, and do you visit prostitutes?'

'Charles.' Iona exclaimed again.

'I only asked because I think your credentials for writing a psycho-sexual biography are important. I mean, when an old-fashioned historian like A.J.P. Taylor or Trevor Roper or Trevelyan wrote history they were very upfront about their expert knowledge, you know. Listed their degrees and doctorates and theses and publications and academic chairs, all that sort of stuff, as bona fides. Well, maybe I'm being naïve, but surely you, as a psychological historian, should do the same. You know, write on the dust-jacket: Toby Sills has a small penis; lost his virginity to the Captain of Hockey at fourteen; has had an ugly girlfriend who wouldn't let him come inside her; had a pash on a chap at university. Since leaving Edinburgh, he's masturbated a lot and made three drunken passes at girls in taxis, one of whom was married to a friend; he secretly buys *Nimrod – Big Black Boys in Athletic Poses* once a month. You see, then we'd all be able to say, "Ah yes, that Toby, he's an expert in repressed psycho-sexuality, I can't wait for his David Livingstone." '

'Christ, I'm glad you're not writing reviews,' Toby smiled uncomfortably. 'Look, we're having dinner at the Caprice. Why don't you come along?'

'We'd love to,' said Iona swiftly, 'but, actually, I've got a table booked at Hankies. But let's get together soon.'

'Good luck with the book,' said Charles, as Iona pulled him towards the door.

Hankies was a small stark restaurant with a celebrity chef. He was such a celebrity that he would have had trouble finding the salt in his own kitchen, but the loyal punters, like mendicants at a defunct saint's shrine, were perfectly content to continue eating his absentee reputation. The room was painted glossy, mental-home green with occasional small gold triangles on the walls. The tables were tiny aluminium and plywood constructions that fidgeted and nudged like the queue for assembly.

A waitress showed them to one set against a banquette. She sported a tattoo of a Celtic hawk hunting a heron on the nursery slope of her large, inadequately pinnied breast. Charles vaguely thought he recognized it; the tattoo not the breast. Iona took off her large green fun-fur coat, the restaurant turned and watched like bored heifers chewing winter kale. Charles wondered if he'd ever get used to the rapt attention her beauty invariably demanded.

'So what, what, brought on that viperish burst of literary criticism?' said Iona, when they had been menued, breaded and wined.

'Sorry, I know he's a friend of yours, but I couldn't resist. I don't expect he'll take any notice of anything I said.'

'Don't be sorry. It was great. Of course he'll take notice. You were spot on. That conversation will be halfway round London by tomorrow. You wouldn't have gone for anyone like that when we first met.'

'No, I think I'm a little cocky after my confrontation with Vernon. I'm tired of holding my tongue and having exhausting *esprit de l'escalier* with the furniture.'

'Good, I'm rather proud.'

'Of me?'

'No, of me.'

'I see, you think it's down to you, my new-found waspish confidence.'

'Of course it's down to me. I'm Pygmalion, I'm Professor Higgins. I'm going to take this effete flower arranger and turn him into something wonderful. You know us girls, we just see men as raw material.'

'What am I going to turn into?'

'I haven't decided yet; I'm just blocking in the basic shape.'

'Is this going to be a long-term project?'

'I don't know. See how it goes. It's like Michelangelo with his marble, the finished masterpiece is already in there, you've just got to chip away.'

'You think I might have a giant-slaying David in me?'

'Perhaps, but perhaps I'll just leave you as a partially formed captive.'

'Pygmalion fell hopelessly in love with his creation; the creator became captive.'

Iona and Charles rather gooily and exhaustively mined this creative metaphor as they played with each other's fingers, ate pistou soup, warm oysters with a champagne sabayon, pigeon with noodles and white truffles, and braised oxtail. It was the delicious due diligence that all new lovers indulge in. Troth plighting. It kept the couple on either side riveted with an envious euphoric recall.

Over the pudding menu, Charles asked casually, 'Would you like to go away somewhere for a weekend?'

The first shared weekend is, of course, vitally important. It's the point when an affair becomes incorporated, registered, open for business, with unlimited liability.

'Yes, I think I'd love to. Where shall we go? Hot or interesting?'

'Hot and interesting, comfortable, relaxed, good food, friendly people.'

'Oh right, so it's back to your flat then.' Iona looked up and gave him the partner's smile, then her eyes focused past him and froze into a sort of glacial grin. Her eyebrows rose then fell. 'Good God, what are you doing here? What a surprise.'

Charles looked into the mirror behind Iona's head and saw a pair of fawn trousers and an expensive silver cowboy belt and a large pair of hands holding an untidy stack of papers. Charles stood up, turned, and found himself facing a tartan flannel shirt.

'Charles Godwin, Tony Neibelung,' Iona stammered. 'Who are you meeting Tony?'

'You, Pigeon, just you.' The familiar pet name was given just so much emphasis. 'Toby Sills told me you were here. I missed you at Carey's.' Tony squeezed himself next to Iona, making the woman on the other side scrunch up.

'Hi,' he said, putting down his papers on the table and holding out a hand. Charles's squeamish fingers disappeared into it and played dead. 'Hello, darling,' he turned to Iona and patted the side of her head with a huge mitt and leant to kiss her. Iona turned her face and caught Charles's eye with a glance that tried to be a conversation.

He was big. Tony was very big and clumsy; expansive. He sat with his legs wide, his chest out, his arms stretched along the back of the banquette annexing Iona's shoulders and the atmosphere.

'Oy, Tina love.'

The tattooed waitress came over and simpered, 'Hello, can't get rid of you. What can I do you for?'

'Bottle of house red and a tuna steak.'

'It's not on the menu tonight, but I'll see if Gary can do you one.'

'Thanks, love. So, here we are then. I get to meet you at last. Sorry, what were you talking about? Don't let me interrupt.'

'We were just chatting, nothing,' Charles said feebly.

'Actually, Tony, Charles and I have some business to discuss, the Mona Corinth thing. This isn't really a very good idea.'

'Oh, you're right, it's a shocking idea. Really clichéd old-hat idea. I've read this scene in so many scripts I should know it by heart. You're not at all what I expected, Charles, you know, not at all what I'd imagined. I thought someone more, more, well just someone more. If I were casting you, I'd have gone sort of Sean Bean or Jimmy Nail.'

'Sorry,' said Charles, and then winced and shifted uncomfortably in his seat. Tony was as loud as he was big.

'Wine, great. *In vino veritas*.' Tony drained a glass and filled it again. 'So, you're fucking my girlfriend then?'

'Tony, for Christ's sake.'

'Keep out of this, Pigeon. This is me and him. *Mano e mano*. You're slipping the naughty to my girlfriend, Charlie.'

'Look . . .' said Charles.

'No, you look. I can't say I blame you, she's beautiful, but,' he upended the glass again, 'that's as far as it goes.'

'Look . . .'

'Look, mate, you've been caught up in something that's between Iona and me. Let me spell it out. I made a mistake, right? I played away from home with a tart at the office, drunk, you know how it is, and this is payback time, OK? OK, I've been punished, tough on me, tough on you, Charlie boy, but then you got a look-in at a bit of skirt that is frankly way out of your league, so nice memories and bye-bye.'

Charles looked at Iona. She was staring stonily into the distance, head turned from them both. There was a terrible plausibility to Tony's voice. The Charles in the back of his head said, 'Of course, there must have been some reason.'

'Tony, I don't know about your relationship with Iona, and frankly it's none of my business. I think this . . .'

'You're damn right it's none of your business.' Tony's voice rose. He leant forward, bumping the woman on the other side's elbow into her lemon tart. 'Did she tell you this was our restaurant? This is where we had our first date, at that table?' He slapped the ply next to him. The lady with the lemon tart jumped. 'Did she tell you we had the best fucking sex of our lives last night? She came, screaming, "I love you, I love you. Tony, you fill me up." Did you tell him, Pigeon, about the blow-job you gave me in the hall because you couldn't wait?'

'No, I didn't,' Iona whispered. She turned to him, her face ironed flat, like someone in shock, like someone who's being held up by the scruff of the neck. 'Why are you doing this, Tony? Why are you making it so difficult? Why does it always have to be a scene? Tony, please?' Her voice cracked and her eyes filled with tears; the restaurant strained over their cooling plates to hear her.

'Oh Pigeon, oh darling, don't, don't.' Tony grasped the sides of her head with his hands and pressed their foreheads together. He looked round at Charles. 'See, see what you've done. Why don't you fuck off out of it? Go on, just fuck off.' He was shouting now.

'Iona?' Charles went to reach for her hand. 'What do you want?' She pulled it away and covered her eyes.

'Charlie boy, don't think you're the first. Christ, this is what she does. She goes off, picks up some sad act and then we have a ruck and make it up. Like, it's the way we are, explosive, big emotional people, but Charlie, at bottom, we're in love, we're lovers, we can't be without each other, can we, Pigeon?'

'Iona, what do you want me to do?' Charles implored. 'What do you want?'

Iona uncovered her face, her eyes glossy with tears and anger. 'I want you to be Gawain.'

'Did you really think she could choose you when it came to it?' Tony staggered ungainly to his feet and leant over Charles. 'Really? When it came to this?' He unzipped his fly. 'Did you think she'd go for a little effete spiv like you?' And with an aggressive flourish he hefted the great cock. It slithered into the light and hung over Charles's plate, swaying drunkenly. 'Can you compete with this? With this? Come on, get it out. What are you offering?'

The restaurant was silent, the forks hung in mid-air. The waitress sucked her teeth. Charles hunched his shoulders. Nothing in his life had ever been as awful as this; no early morning sweaty awakening had been as fearfully embarrassing. The confrontation with Vernon had been *Jackanory* compared with this. The Charles in the back of his head turned the light out and from under the covers screamed, 'What did you expect? What did you expect? Did you really believe this would all have a happy ending? He's right, people like Iona don't ever end up with people like us. Look at this alpha male; she's his, you fool.'

'Oh, fuck it.' Iona wiped her face with her napkin and stood up with a weary composure. 'I can't do this, I'm going. Put the bloody thing away, Tony.' She stood in the middle of the restaurant and beckoned for her coat.

'Iona, please?' said Charles, turning and looking up at her, 'What is it you want? Is this your choice?'

'What I want, what we all want,' she waved her arm, 'what

all women want is men to fight *for* them, not *over* them. You none of you ever know the difference. Look, I'll call you.'

'Yeah,' said Tony, 'we'll send you a postcard.' Picking up his sheaves of paper, he caught the neck of the bottle. It fell and chortled wine into Charles's lap.

As he reached for the napkin, Charles felt the cold blast of air as the door opened and closed. Turning he watched Iona walk fast past the window hugging her coat to herself, her eyes fixed to the pavement. Tony, like a big dog shambling behind, put two large paws on her shoulders.

'Pudding, sir?'

'Just the bill, thanks,' he told Tina's hawk.

Somewhere in the kitchen someone turned up the volume. The restaurant twittered and burbled. It sounded as if everyone was saying, 'Well, did you see that?' in slightly varying foreign accents.

The bill came with the tuna steak. Charles paid and left a craven tip, and walked out. The restaurant had doubled, tripled in length. He felt every eye welded to the back of his neck. As he pulled the door open a girl's high-pitched, nasal voice exploded in tintinnabulous laughter.

Charles walked through Soho. The streets were boisterous and vulgar. Swaying, heaving, gaping, passing-out, passing through, passing looks, passing passers. The night seemed to be full of tongues; slick shiny tongues glowing green and red in the flashing neon. Tongues in ears; tongues in mouths; tongues taking the air; laughing, glossy, wet, stringy tongues. Calling, shouting, bathed in smoke, doused in beer and froth, exploring, tasting the lust musk of the city cut loose.

He walked down Shaftesbury Avenue, weaving in and out of the loitering crowds of lost American theatre-goers and lost boys hanging around amusement arcades, practising their joy-stick skills for older men's amusement. Across Piccadilly Circus, where the fat bundles of homeless pupated, and along Piccadilly, where men in dinner-jackets waved at scarce taxis to take girls who lurked in gift-shop doorways in long dresses with cigar-smoked hair back to Fulham terraces. As Charles walked, his wet trousers wafted vinegar and sour grapes. He felt blasted, numb. Just the physical striding was enough to occupy him. Past Green Park, the people few and far, on west, west, the city elegant and vital, arteries pumping, cars smoothly running. Red, amber, green, red, amber, green. The buildings tall and dark and dozing with their lights on. Finally he came to Buchan Gardens; another world: silent, secret. A million miles and a thousand evenings out from Soho. He halted at his front door, hesitated, key in hand, and couldn't face it. Couldn't face the flat, the unblinking glow of his tongue-tied answerphone, the censorious furniture.

He turned to the garden. The soft shadows and the smell of leaves and earth welcomed him, curlicues of Nature gently waved him in. Silky sylphs whispered and rustled. The shed was locked. Charles stepped into the deep darkness of the border. The green world patted his shoulders, coolly stroked his cheek, touched his hand with delicate regret. Angel wasn't here, nor was Stendhal. They were gone, or they didn't want to be found. Charles walked slowly back to the centre of the garden, to the big plane tree. Its heavy canopy hung protectively like a cathedral's vaulted roof. Charles stood in its ancient sanctuary and touched the smooth flaking bark. It was warm; another living thing. Living so slowly, so faintly and imperceptibly, but so grandly; such a monumental life.

Charles worked his way round the trunk, and then he saw them on the east side waiting to face the rising sun. Unless he'd gone right up to the trunk he'd never have noticed them hanging from nails at head height. Two small dolls, a boy and a girl, woven from corn stalks. Their heads small posies of wheat, their bodies hollow wicker cages. The man doll with a bursting laburnum seed pod as a penis, the girl with rose-hips for breasts; they were crudely energetic. Charles gently picked her off the nail. Something rattled in the hollow stomach; he held it up to his eye. Through the plaited straw poked a thin slimy grey antenna, it waved a moment and retracted. Snails. The gravid stomach was full of snails. The man had teeth, lots of little sharp pointy teeth. Charles put them back carefully. He was too full of his own simmering thoughts to be frightened or amused. He walked home.

Turning on a dim table light in the drawing-room he put a compilation disc of great opera choruses on the gramophone, took a bottle of brandy and a glass from the cupboard, sat in the little Georgian armchair, drank and waited.

The agony came like a thunderstorm at sea: distant rumbles, flashes of lightning. The natural anaesthetic the brain uses to protect itself from itself slowly wore off and the terrible sorrow began to fall. At first in large splattering drops, then streams, stair-rods, waves of despair. He went over and over every minute detail of dinner like a pathologist, prising it apart, holding it up, measuring the humiliation, the embarrassment. He screwed his eyes shut, but the great penis hung in his retina and, behind it, Iona's face, turned away, disappointed and sad.

Charles imagined them going home; the argument, the tears, the sex. 'The best fucking sex we ever had, did she tell you? Would you like to see?' He watched her face, the damp eyes, turned down, then up, then slowly closed. The beautiful mouth parted, a little sigh, a hand guiding the massive penis, slowly, gently, her hair falling forward.

'Aaaah,' Charles shouted with pain. Nabucco's slaves shouted back. The images, the hopelessness, the loss scythed through him.

He drank but drunkenness didn't follow. He paced but he'd never felt wider awake. Every pore, every node, every electronic receptor fired and fizzed and missed nothing. The Charles in his head whined and nagged, 'What did you expect? What did you expect?' Half a bottle, a whole bottle. He was sick. The whole hateful evening gulped, rewound, acid-sour, hot and wasted. Charles knelt on the bathroom floor and laid his face on the cold ceramic and sobbed with all his heart. He howled until his breath came in ragged swatches. He got up, splashed water on his face, rinsed his mouth, spat, and stared into the mirror. The tears welled and dribbled, the thin mouth trembled and turned down. Charles was lost in his own skin. 'This is the most alive you will ever be,' her voice called clear in his head. 'This is the yearning.' The yearning.

The whispering chorus softly hummed in the drawing-room. Butterfly watched the dock all night for her Pinkerton. Charles watched Iona having sex, naked, on her knees, back bent, bottom in the air, arms hugging the pillow, the huge hands spreading her, big cocks. All night he sat and watched and listened and with the dawn he fitfully dozed, head lolling, dribbling onto his stinking shirt.

The doorbell woke Charles with a start. He looked at his watch. Six-thirty. The birds outside twittered their contrapuntal joy. Madame Butterfly was still waiting.

He opened the door. Iona stood, chalk-white, dark-eyed, dressed as he had last seen her. Beside her a large suitcase. The horrors of the night fled, evaporated into the early sunshine.

Chapter Twelve

Dr Spindle ate his breakfast out of a tin: pineapple chunks speared one at a time with a pickle fork. He liked pineapple chunks, they were neat, uniform and they stuck on the fork. He'd tried peach slices but they had slid off; deficient in the tensile strength department, lacking moral fibre. They were an awkward size. Lychees had been a possibility, but there was a hole that dribbled, and they hadn't got the ratio of fruit to syrup right. No, pineapple chunks were best. He thought briefly of the greatness of human ingenuity that had taken an awkward, ergonomically anarchic problem like a pineapple and resolved it into bite-size cubes. He sucked a mouthful of Flintstones Mud chocolate drink from a children's carton with its clever little straw, and looked out of the dirty window at the garden.

Dr Spindle frowned. Frowned a the chaos of it, the uncontrolled waste, the do-as-you-like, wander-where-you-wish amateurism of Nature. Flattening and folding the carton, he put it in the bin and picked up his tweed jacket. It weighed nearly two stone. There was no need to check the pockets; he had worn this coat every day for twenty years and it had more pockets than a snooker hall. It contained everything a badly engineered, leaking, cracked, crumbling, seized-up world could possibly need: screwdrivers; wrenches; collapsible saw; rubber bands; bulldog clips; dexi clips; gaffer tapes; screws, crosshead and regular; fuses of all denominations; copper wire; a monkey wrench; a pencil torch; a wireless; three-in-one oil; a pressure gauge; a micrometer; one of those clever little plastic change sorters; a handkerchief; a pen which wrote in four colours; and four condoms which would never be used for the purpose for which they were designed. He left his basement flat and turned the six deadlocks.

He walked across the garden and popped a furry humbug into his green-grey mouth, and sucked ruminatively. The garden bothered Dr Spindle, the world bothered Dr Spindle. He was a man who couldn't see a bend without wanting to straighten it, an inclination without wanting to flatten it. The earth and everything on it was a series of engineering problems aching to be rationalized. Dr Spindle had beheld nothing in Nature that he couldn't have improved with half an hour's tinkering, a bit of galvanized zinc and a whack with a lump hammer.

He walked quickly towards the church, counting his steps. He didn't notice the circle of small smooth pebbles set on the edge of the lawn, in their centre the cranium of a jackdaw filled with salt. He passed Iona pulling her suitcase – he didn't notice her either – and unlocked the great double wooden door and flicked on the light switches in their regular sequence.

The vestry neon tube stuttered awake; that would have to be seen to. He went round the church opening and closing things, pushing and pulling joints and hinges. Finding a cupboard that stuck, he took out a small screwdriver from a plastic pouch and began to whistle tunelessly. Ever since taking early retirement from a prosthetics design and development board, Dr Spindle had filled his time doing odd jobs, fixing schools, community centres, surgeries, charity shops, churches. Anywhere that couldn't afford the Yellow Pages, Spindle would botch and bodge. He saw himself as a crusader against chaos, staving off Armageddon with a lump of linseed putty and a promise to see to it by Monday.

'Hi, hi, hi.' The Rev Trev panted into the apse from his early morning run. He was wearing a pair of minute shorts, running shoes without socks and a cut-off T-shirt that shouted Run to God above his cupolaed belly button. 'OK, let's hit it.' Trev jogged into the vestry to don the teenager's nightie that did service.

The doctor acted as verger, sidesman and warden for the church. Trev didn't like any of these tabs, preferring to refer to him as Worship Coordinator. Reluctantly the doctor folded away his tools and stood in the first pew, checking bulbs.

Trev cantered up the aisle and started to intone. The bishop insisted that at least one communion service a week be from the 1662 prayer-book, so at seven o'clock every Wednesday, unannounced, Trev and the doctor went through the motions, both hating it. Trev because the archaic words failed to take into account how God had grown, matured and mellowed spiritually since Trev had started counselling him, and Spindle because he was that rare thing: an innate, complete and utter atheist.

Between them they had managed to get the service down to twelve minutes. At the appropriate moment the doctor slumped to his knees and took the chalice. The wine tasted odd after the humbug, sort of like bitter blood.

'Right,' said Trev, draining the cup and looking at his watch. 'In the name of the Father, Son and Holy Ghost. How're we getting on with the wheelchair access?'

'Er . . . should be ready next Sunday. Wooden would be quicker, but concrete's better. I've been working out gradients, it's quite a knotty little problem. Now you might think . . .'

'You're a member of the Garden Committee, aren't you?' interrupted Trev, pulling on his tracksuit.

'Yes. My concern is brake speed on the downward journey. Now, just suppose, for the sake of argument, a twenty-stone passenger in a wheelchair started on the ramp at, say, two miles an hour; what speed would they be going, given an incline of say one-in-five? I reckon a hump of four inches at, say, three feet from the start would stop them running into the road, but then how will the hump affect momentum on the upward journey, you may ask . . .'

'You may indeed.'

'Given a twenty-stone passenger with weak arms or no arms.'

'Yes, interesting. But about the Garden Committee. I happen to know that Stephen Marle is about to resign.'

'Oh, really. Of course, if we made the ramp wider, had two-way traffic and extended the hump only halfway for the downward journey . . .'

'I've been thinking that the Church should be represented.'

'Oh right. That would cut down the width of the step though. You'd probably only get single file traffic for the able, but then they're nippier, better brakes.'

'Sounds great. I think that, considering the Church's vital role in the life of the square, it should have a positive say in the garden, so . . .'

'So?'

'So, will you nominate me for the Committee?'

'You?'

'Yes me.'

'OK, right you are Vicar.' Dr Spindle briefly wondered what on earth the vicar had to do with anything as godless as a garden.

Stephen Marle came back to bed carrying the weak Earl Grey; no sugar and just a cloud for Vernon, no sugar and just a cloud for himself, three sugars and just a dash for the rent-boy. Vernon still had his Concorde eye patch and earplugs in. The ferret-faced, margarine-skinned and lumpy-chested Donny lay smoking.

'Euugh,' winced Marle. 'Don't move, I'll get an ashtray.'

Vernon turned over heavily. A worm-cast of hot ash fell into his open mouth. 'Euugh, euugh,' he sat up spitting. Lifting the eye patch he looked at Donny, who smiled with as many teeth as he could muster, which weren't many. 'How can anyone expect the youth of today to become responsible contributors to society when there is no sanction on their taking up ghastly anti-social vices first thing.'

'Want a blow-job, chief?' said Donny in a whining Glasgow accent, reaching for Vernon's stubby morning erection. 'Fifteen quid.'

'Tea first.'

The three of them lay together sipping for a blessedly quiet minute while they contemplated the fresh day.

'Right then,' said Stephen, 'which end do you fancy, dear?'

'Neither much,' sighed Vernon. 'You have botty, I'll take gobbles.'

'That'll be an extra thirty quid,' said Donny hopefully.

'Twenty,' replied Marle.

'OK, but go gentle. I think I've got a tear from that hefting dildo you used last night, and no kissing.'

'Definitely no kissing,' sighed Vernon.

Dropping his tab into the tea, Donny shuffled round to present his pasty, abused, bony bottom to Marle, and fitted Vernon's little undershot penis into the gap where his front teeth should have been. For a few happy moments the three of them wobbled and muttered in unison. The working day starts early for rent-boys.

The ornate Louis XXXth telephone tinkled on the bedside table.

'Oh, no rest for the wicked,' Vernon leant across, knocking over the small heart-shaped photograph of Princess Michael of Kent shaking what appeared to be his nose. 'Hello, Barnstaple. Yes, no, no, at my desk. Oh yes, yes, yes, yes, really, really, yes, yes.'

'Yes, yes,' said Marle, shortening his run up.

Vernon waved at him and pulled a face. 'No, just the butler. No, I know. Are you sure that's all we need? Yes, right away, as fast as you can. Absolutely, yes.'

Donny lifted his head and squealed, 'Oh shit a brick, mind my fucking arse will you,' into the mouthpiece.

Vernon slammed the phone down. 'You uncouth little yob,' he shouted. 'Do you know who that was?' Grabbing a handful of greasy hair he pulled the head back. 'That was the Queen's sodding lawyer, you wretch. Hurry up, Stephen, we've got work to do.' He took himself in hand and deposited a sticky gob of goo into Donny's ear.

'All done, darling.' Marle extracted himself. 'What did Jarndyce and Jarndyce have to say? Good news?'

Donny rolled off the bed and stood, pathetically, looking like a medically excused soldier at a 1914 call up, one finger raddling his ear, the other hand massaging his tender sphincter.

'Excellent news, Stephen, the best. I've got them, I've got them. The Committee is finished, done, dead and buried. Now I want you to get on the blower and get Peshware to deliver her pile of scrap as soon as possible. And ring the chief constable again. I want to know what's taking him so long to shoot Melbourne's murderer and lock up that vile Tenby.'

'Excuse me, chief. Could I have a bath?' asked Donny.

'Can't you have a rub-down at your halfway house, or remand home, or wherever it is?' Marle looked at the lust object of a moment ago with a shimmy of disgust.

'Be a sport, chief. I'm due at the vicar's in a moment, and cleanliness is next to godliness.'

'Oh, all right. Have a quick shower and take the small towel from the loo, and no crevice work. Tip the little lad an extra quid, I feel generous, but check his pockets.' Vernon added, 'I have a feeling it's going to be a very good day.'

Iona half lay and half sat on the day bed, her head back, hand thrust into her pocket. Charles pulled the suitcase into the hall and went and sat in the small armchair beside the empty brandy bottle. Neither of them spoke.

At last Charles said, 'I can't ever have another night like this, ever.'

'Charles,' Iona looked at him, 'listen, before you shout at me, two things. First, nothing Tony said to you last night was true. I know how it sounded, I know what you've been thinking, but it simply wasn't true. I'm sorry I left with him, I'm sorry I left you. I couldn't stand it, I had to take him away to leave him, and now

I've left, finally, irrevocably. I've been up all night fighting and packing and it's over.'

'Oh, Iona, I'm so relieved but I'm sort of frightened. How can one feel utterly desolate and then incredibly elated? I'm just so pleased to see you, it's like a miracle cure. You have no idea what it's been like. How could you behave so badly?'

'Charles, for Christ's sake,' Iona got up and knelt in front of him. 'Do you really imagine you're the first person in the world to fall in love?'

Charles examined his fingers. 'Who said anything about love? What makes you think I'm in love?'

'You've been in love with me from the day you saw me on Mona's bed.'

'I have?'

'Uh huh, head over heels; but if I ever doubted it last night convinced me. Only someone in love could have sat through that. Another man would have walked out, thrown wine, argued. You just sat there. It was the bravest thing I've ever seen.'

'Well it didn't feel brave. What was the other thing you were going to say?'

'Oh that. Um, I think I've fallen in love as well, which is lucky as I'm homeless and I've just left a brilliant, rich television producer for a bridge teacher.' She got up. 'I need a shower.'

'Iona?' Charles's voice was shallow.

'No, darling, I didn't. I know what you've been seeing in the dark, but I didn't.' She had her back to him.

'It was awfully big.'

'Wasn't it just, and you never saw it excited. Such a relief not to have to wake up with that again.'

Iona stood in the shower and turned the soap over and over in her hand. She let the water wash away the night; shriving, baptizing, making new, blessing without judgement. Gently, she wiped her hand between her legs and down her thigh. Dried pleading and foaming sticky revenge spattered on the tiles and spun away into the earth. She held her head high so the jet of water washed away the tears before she'd even shed them.

*   *   *

Bon Bon took a stroll. Belman had gone fishing, gravel pits in Hampshire, might stay over in a country pub if the carp got too convivial. She'd packed his monogrammed Swaine and Adeney picnic bag with peanut butter and banana sandwiches, fun size Mars Bars and a bottle of Southern Comfort. The day stretched ahead, twinkling with the cat's eyes of minutiae that marked out the route of her life.

She didn't really want to walk much. She'd gone into the garden to see whether her new fawn, chamois leather coat with the tassels coordinated in the daylight with her new calf-length suede boots. She thought probably it didn't. It was while trying to get a sideways view of her foot, to work out if it was the boots that didn't go with the coat, or the coat that jarred with the boots, that she noticed the arrangement of petals on an empty square of packed earth under a rhododendron. On closer inspection the circle of torn flowers and fresh green leaves made a mosaic, an intricate picture of a man's face. An ancient young man; rosebud eyes staring; magnolia mouth shouting; daisy-petal teeth; peony cheeks ruddy; wild ivy and hornbeam hair; oak-leaf beard; trailing coils of convolvulus wound out of his nostrils and ears.

Bon Bon looked, amazed and unaccountably annoyed. It didn't belong here, this wasn't its place. A light breeze passed a *frisson* across the old new face. It must have just been made, it was too delicate to last long. Something stirred in the open mouth, the dark curling vegetation moved. She bent down. A large stag beetle, its heavy prehistoric ecto-skeleton rocking back and forth, tried to move out of her shadow. Its legs paddled but it wasn't going anywhere. It had been tied down by a thin web of gold and purple thread, across its shiny brooch-black back. Bon Bon stood up and shuddered. She put out her foot to stamp but didn't – new boots.

She turned on her heel and trotted back to buff the brass finger-plates, hugging the soft calf.

Iona walked into the bedroom rubbing her hair with a towel. Charles was on the telephone, his fingers played elaborate cat's cradle with the flex. 'No, no, no, you can't say that. I never said that. No, that's not what I meant; what I meant was what I said. Yes, here. No you can't, she's in the shower. Yes I will. Goodbye.'

'Who was that?'

'Are you living with me?'

'Charles, do you know you have this habit of making every decision a question?'

'I don't, do I?'

'Ha ha, very funny.'

'So, are you staying,' said Charles, 'seriously?'

'Seriously, are you asking me to?'

'Yes.'

'Then yes, I'd be delighted.'

'Good, because that's just what I told Birthright.'

'Birthright, the journalist? Birthright, the gossip columnist? Birthright, the foulest titbit-monger in the whole whispering midden of Fleet Street?'

'Yes, that's the chap. That was him. He called about last night.'

'About last night?'

'Yes, he'd heard about my conversation with Toby Sills. Oddly enough from Toby Sills, and someone had told him about the restaurant.'

'About Tony, and shouting that you weren't to fuck his girl any more, and getting his dick out?'

'Yes, that sort of thing.'

'Charles, what did you tell him?' Iona sat heavily on the end of the bed.

'Oh, nothing much really.'

'Really, what really?'

'Well I said that Toby's book was obviously autobio-graphical, a thinly disguised but sensitively written piece of auto-erotica.'

'You didn't, oh God. What about Hankies?'

'Ah well, I thought it was probably best to draw a veil over that.' Charles smiled broadly and tugged at a cuff. 'I said it was all a misunderstanding; that Tony was a dear old friend and that he had been showing us the results of his Californian penis enlargement surgery, and that he'd drunk too much and started shouting because it had burst, or a nerve had been cut, or something had gone wrong, and now he needed a splint to make it work, and we were all terribly sympathetic, and you were living here.'

'You didn't say that, Charles? You didn't?' Iona grabbed his lapels.

'Something along those lines, yes.' Charles was beaming.

'Oh my God, he'll never print that will he?'

'Probably not, but he will tell ever so many people.'

'Charles, what have you done? You're rather pleased with yourself aren't you?' She shook him. 'Aren't you? You look unpleasantly smug. There's a nasty, calculating, ruthless streak in you.'

'Yes, I'm rather enjoying it. I can't think what got into me.'

'I'm creating a monster.'

'I need a shower and a shave; you make breakfast. I've unpacked your case; you've got the bottom two drawers of the linen press and half the *armoire,* and I've thrown away that hideous backgammon set made of common bits of Arab stone.'

'Charles, it was a present, it cost a fortune.'

'I don't care, we couldn't possibly have it in the house, the furniture would never stand for it.'

Celeste Kotzen put the last of the bags for the long country weekend into the boot of her BMW. She stared at the neat leather cases, trying to remember what it was she had forgotten. She looked at her watch; time to get going. She needed to stop at Sainsbury's; two dinner parties, three lunches, breakfast, booze, biscuits for bedrooms, loo paper. Sighing, she slammed the boot. The noise thudded across the square like a distant howitzer and the pigeons gang-banging in the plane tree took off in a dense squadron. Celeste watched them clatter and climb, then turn in a tight arc over the roofs.

Her eye was caught by something small and dark high up in the tree. Something hadn't been alarmed in the branches. She looked at it swaying gently for a moment. Odd. She climbed into the car and put the key into the ignition and then stopped, opened the glove compartment and took out her husband's small German binoculars. Leaning her elbows on the window she looked again. It took a moment to find the place with the magnification. Slowly moving down a branch a body turned into focus. It was a squirrel, its front paws bent begging. She could make out its little yellow teeth. It was hanged by the neck with a piece of flex. 'Oh, how horrid.' She pulled the glasses down, then looked again. Further along, partially obscured by leaves, another small corpse trapezed. She panned across the top of the tree; there were more squirrels and a crow and a tawny owl, looking as though it was sleeping in mid-air. 'Who would do such a thing?' she said out loud. The air felt chill. The bodies hidden in the top of the tree were silently grotesque.

Wicked, or warning of wickedness. They were reminiscent of other flame-lit after-dark trees in other places. In a sepia flash, Celeste re-saw the tatty overcoated figures lynched from lampposts in Budapest, smelt the cordite and burning rubber.

Her knuckles were white as she gripped the glasses, her throat tight. For a second a child's face was clearly visible, then hidden again. 'Oh Mother of God.' The foliage parted and she was looking into two Venetian blue eyes and a small heart-shaped mouth, parted as if cooing. It rocked on the wire noose somnambulantly. It was a long moment before Celeste realized, with heart-pounding relief, that it was a child's doll, pink and plastic, naked bowed limbs.

She threw the glasses on the seat beside her, turned the key and yanked the wheel. 'Nothing, say nothing, see nothing, keep your eyes in front of your feet. This country, these damn people, so smooth on the surface, so tepidly poisonous beneath. Oh what a thing.'

Lily let herself into Charles's flat and sauntered into the dining-room. Charles and Iona were kissing.

'Hi, Joe.'

'Oh, Lily, you're early, good,' he said nervously. 'Before you start on the cleaning,' he emphasized the word, 'this is Iona Wallace, she'll be living here now, with me.'

Lily put one hand on her hip, cocked her visored head and stuck out her bottom lip. 'If you say so, Jo.'

Iona stepped forward and held out her hand. 'Hello, Lily.'

Lily looked at it and ruminated.

Iona frowned and picked up her coat. 'Right, I'll get out of your way. Just one thing. I'm Charles's girlfriend, I'm the only person who sleeps with him, OK? Do you understand?'

'Iona,' Charles blushed and blustered, 'you can't possibly . . .'

'Charles, your list, remember. Lily is the last name. You don't have to be Miss Marple to work it out, and you were both fucking here last week after I left.'

Lily's pose collapsed. 'Ho, sister, how you know that?'

'Your chewing gum's still stuck on the bedpost. Don't forget to clean it off. So, dear heart,' she kissed Charles on the cheek, 'if I ever find out that you've been having a little take-away, you'll regret it. And you, missie,' Iona stood facing Lily, she was a good foot taller, 'if you ever fuck him again I'll take your Ray-Bans and shove them so far up your tight little twat that you'll be pissing in the dark.' Iona smiled broadly and gently lifted Lily's chin and took off her spectacles. 'Unless I'm present, of course.'

'Man, you go for some of that girl-on-girl action, put on hot show for Joe?'

Iona laughed. 'I'll think about it, but I'm not sure he deserves it.' She walked to the door.

Charles chokingly followed. 'I'm sorry, darling, I meant to tell you but . . .'

'Shut up, Charles, don't grovel. And save your apologies for when they're needed; I'm not angry. I told you, I don't have your chronic need to own the past, and anyway she's cute. Will you be in at about six?'

'Here,' Charles put his hand into his pocket and pulled out a set of keys.

Iona took them gingerly. 'You're a real boy scout; prepared for anything. This is it then, the keys make it sort of official; keys, toothbrush and Camus. Call me at work.' She walked off and then turned. 'I love you.'

'I love you,' Lily mimicked as the door closed. 'Sweet, nice lady, shitty foul mouth though.' She pinched Charles's bottom.

'Lily.'

'I know, I know.'

Bryony passed Iona on the garden side of the street and they waved. Bryony was going to the newsagents, twenty Senior Service and the *National Geographic*. She didn't feel well, she was feeling old; her joints ached and she was short of breath. She wasn't up to being ill. All her hearty robust life she had caught every disease going and beaten it to a pulp. Malaria, dengue fever, pneumonia, ptomaine poisoning, gonorrhoea, syphilis, tape worm; she'd gone to the mat with them all and risen triumphant. Most of the bones in her body had been broken at least once; two horses had died under her; she'd had an engine stall at a thousand feet and had walked away from the wreck; she'd written off two cars, one lorry and a bicycle rickshaw; she'd been bitten by a cobra, a lemur, a rhesus monkey, a goat, four dogs and a deranged witch-doctor; she'd been stabbed with a bread knife, a compass, a stiletto; she'd been shot by a twelve-bore, a catapult and a two-bob rocket, and they'd left no more than scars; but now, for the first time, she felt frail. She was no longer getting old, she had finally arrived. Stopping to catch her breath, she leant against the railings.

The garden; how beautiful it was, how tranquil and safe, how much she valued this place being just as it was. Bryony thought of all the other views of her life: the humid lines of tea bushes stretching up the hillside of her farm; the red veld, crevassed, stunted, home to more thorns than anywhere else on earth; the dusty redan and the squat tin-roofed barracks; her sickly vegetable garden marked with whitewashed stones. And she remembered how often, in all the years of following flags, cattle, rain and men, she had looked at the flat shimmering horizons and dreamt of a garden just like this, with its changing light and its greenness. Only travellers know what a deep, lush, luxury living with cool greenness is; to be surrounded by green, the million subtle shades of green. Who knows England, who only England knows? The softness of it never failed to enchant her. She would die here, soon, the long journey over, the circle complete, happily home.

Bryony noticed that beside her hand on the railing someone had left a shoe, a child's shoe. It was old-fashioned. She picked it off the spike. It was ancient, no-one had worn a shoe like this for four generations. Black with a tapering toe and a canvas top, buttons up the ankle – you'd need a buttonhook. Lord, when had she last seen a buttonhook? There was something stuffed into the toe; she put in her fingers and pulled out a small fold of calico. Inside was an old cracked photograph, not much bigger than a Christmas postage stamp. It had been cut from a bigger picture. The fuzzy face of a man in uniform, with a soft cap and a full moustache, his eyes shaded. It must have been from the First World War. The man was smiling. Under the picture were two frail pressed flowers; their petals had come away from the stalk, the frangible tissue-thin fairy wings, like the picture, faded to sepia. Bryony recognized a poppy and a pansy; poppies for remembrance, pansies for 'in my thoughts'. She stared at the secret package. The calico was fraying and there was a brown stain on it where it had been folded. It reminded her of bandages. She was stroked with a warm sadness. She thought of her father, her brother, her husband and her dear, dear sons. Carefully she folded the things again and replaced the shoe on its spike. The pleasure of the warm melancholy passed; she felt better, her breathing sweeter. 'Fuck the *Geographic*. *Playgirl* and a Monte Cristo.'

Charles left Lily to the dishes and the soundtrack of *Full Metal Jacket* and sauntered over to the garden. There was really no other way of describing how he got there. It was a particularly disgusting, self-satisfied saunter. He sauntered onto the lawn, took a deep breath, hands in pockets, and crossed over to the great plane tree, noticing, without any real interest, that the dolls had gone.

Charles needed to talk to Angel. He needed to talk in the way that people who have just declared love need to tell people who haven't. There is, outside of an alcoholic's rehabilitation clinic, no proselytizing bore like a shy man who's just exposed his heart for the first time. The world was a bright, shiny, newly minted place, chock-a-block with day-to-day sentiment and *aperçu* philosophy. He was bursting with the need to rub someone else's nose in the armpit of his good fortune. The door of the hut was ajar. Charles pushed it open. 'Angel, you'll never guess . . .' He stopped in mid-sentence.

The hut had changed. The gardener wasn't there and neither were any of his things. The room was neatly clean; the cot had gone, the rafters were bare, only the garden equipment stood fastidiously, the mower and the barrow in the centre of the room. For a moment Charles thought he must be in the wrong place; there was no trace of the clutter that had seemed so organically permanent. Seed boxes and pots stacked along the wall, the tortoise stove coldly slumped. Charles considered the transformation for all of ten seconds, then, like a compass needle, his thoughts swung back to the true north of his own good fortune. 'Spring cleaning, of course,' he said to himself by way of explanation, and, turning back into the sunlight, he failed to notice the mildewed copy of *Puck of Pook's Hill* with an oak, ash and elm posy marking the 'Song of the English' lying on the earth floor behind the door.

He sauntered again, slowly this time, taking in the perfection of the grand sweep of Nature. Charles was so replete with hormones, lust and great explanations that this square of greenery seemed ripe for a metaphor or two on life, time, civilization, striving, achievement, hope, spirituality and everything. He trod in a little revelation; not so much the road to Damascus, more the path to lunch experience. For a fragile, sun-drenched moment all the jumbled chips in the kaleidoscope of life came together to make a glorious recognizable pattern, before turning again into

227

bright chaos. 'Love' the crystals spelt out. Yes, thought Charles, with what passes for profundity amongst the terminally besotted, love is the answer and Nature is the outward and visible symbol of that love. He shook his head in humility at the awesomeness of his discovery.

Charles then went and did what most Englishmen of his ilk do when they come to profound junctions of their lives. He went to see his tailor.

Constable Spry was also looking for Angel and answers in the garden. He entered at the bottom as Charles was leaving at the top. He didn't saunter, he proceeded in an appropriately plodding manner, taking time to admire the flowers. The potting shed didn't come as a surprise to him, its emptiness was a silent relief. He proceeded on and at the farther gate picked a sprig of myrtle and carefully put it into the envelope with the warrant where the shiny leaves curled round Angel's name.

That evening Charles and Iona went to the opening of an exhibition of paintings by an Australian Aborigine who traced his sherry-induced Dreamtime on pillowcases with a Biro. Ralph Pistol raised a languorous glass towards Charles across the room and then returned to the group he was in conversation with. One after the other they looked over at Charles. Iona stayed by his side, resting a light proprietorial hand on his shoulder. Next they rushed to the Donmar Warehouse in Covent Garden and watched a play about people racked, stuffed, tortured and finally beaten to a pulp by love. They giggled inappropriately and held hands in the dark. Then they had supper at the Ivy, shared a truffled black-leg hen, and willed, stroked and cheered each other to brilliance, wit and anecdotal derring-do. The rich and the famous, the talented and the powerful watched them and were envious. They were gilded lovers, they glowed with something money, fame, power and talent can buy but nothing can keep.

A taxi dropped them at Buchan Gardens. 'Good evening, squire?'

'Magic,' sighed Charles.

'Change for a twenty, squire? No problem.'

'Unbelievably magic. Good night.'

Iona was about to open the door and had her key in the latch when Charles suggested they walk round the garden. 'I'm a bit worried, I haven't seen Angel, and it's a wonderful night.' It was a wonderful night, indeed, a magical night. The moon was full and high; there seemed to be twice as many stars in the sky as usual, they shone and glistered with a theatrical *élan*. Hand in hand they stepped through the gate into a still-scented scene that you only come across once or twice in a lifetime and only when you're deeply in love, or drowning in despair.

The garden was formless, endless. The square receded, the railings, buildings, bricks and gravel, all the man-made things vanished and Nature, polished silver and black, stretched over the curve of the earth. It was not a real place, but the great night-cloak of ancient England. A land that dwells beneath the surface of sight and soul in dreams and snatches and rounds and half-remembered verse and the trill of distant, drifting music. The garden had thrown off the prosaic, daylight order and become the Forest of Arden, Puck's sacred glade, Herne's great glen without end.

They walked in silence, maybe for hours, on the down-soft grass. Iona squeezed Charles's arm and pointed. In a bright splash of moonlight under the giant plane tree, a figure stood dancing very slowly, swaying like a rowan on the scree or hawthorn in a salt squall on a chalk down. At his feet a familiar beast lightly stepped, jinked in and out of his shadow and then, rising on two hind legs, turned in fitful little circles, its forepaws held high and crossed above the great grey muzzle that bayed silently at the moon.

The lovers moved closer. Angel and Stendhal danced on oblivious, caught in an irresistible beat. Charles felt it in his chest and it came tapping through Iona's touch like the thrumming of tiny cloven hooves, the beating of a muffled drum.

Angel was naked. His skin, like mossy bark, was smeared with ochre and green, and in his hair he wore the velvet antlers of a young stag and garlands and circlets of plaited flowers. Fern and ivy swagged his shoulders and arms, tangles of heather and hip and haw clung to his dripping filigreed body, bindweed and mandrake climbed his legs and coiled round his shiny curved penis, suckers and tendrils grew from his mouth and nostrils.

Angel began to chant. First very softly, with a singsong whisper like the wind racing through a stand of pines or the rustle of frosted rushes, and then louder, coarse and deep, then ethereal and keening. He sung the Song of the Earth; the chant of the mud and the seed that grew the man who covered the woman who suckled the nation that ploughed the earth; of the son who moved across the earth who ate the seed and sank to the ground; of the men who scarred, who moulded, who mined, who dug, who built, who scythed, who threshed and burnt. He sung of the clay and of the blood, of bone and bronze, sinew and iron, skin and gold, the seed in the hand, its brilliant bow, the fruit in the scrape, the sapling child, the man that stood and fought, the man that ran and hid, the black blood and backsweat that drained to the soil that formed the brick that made the lime that crumbled and endlessly turned to stalk and harvest and husk, turning the earth to the earth to the earth. Angel sang. Charles and Iona didn't understand but they knew. At times the song was like a child's rhyme, sometimes a blank dirge. It rose and fell, stuttered and whispered, clear as night, muted as shadow. Snatches of runes, chants in Latin, hoarse rhythmic Norman, whining Celtic incantation and the vowel-formed grunts and aspirations of the words before language all mixed together, heard at once, turning and turning and turning. The grass writhing, caressing his feet; the green things throbbing and pulsing to the rhythm of the sap rising. There was no knowing how long it went on for, there was no beginning and no end.

Slowly the sky greyed and the false dawn darkened the stars and flattened the shadows. Iona and Charles found that they were standing alone under the great plane tree. The street lights shone sickly yellow and the great cliff of the square slid blankly back. Arms around each other they walked to bed. They made love like the sickle and the sheaf, seed time and harvest. They lay together chest to chest, hip to hip, thigh to thigh, one breath, the rhythm of the garden gently beating retreat.

Iona whispered, 'I want to go away, now, today. I need to go home.'

'But you are home.'

'No, my real home. I need to show you.'

'Where?'

'Scotland.'

They lay silently listening to the morning, lips just touching.

Chapter Thirteen

And then the rains came. Charles packed jerseys; the sky packed clouds. Winceyette mauve, Toshiba grey, coley white. It piled them, like a late maid stripping hotel beds. The sky bowed and sagged, squeezing the air into the square. When it couldn't fit any more in, when the dirty laundry hung in tendrils that touched the trees, it let go. First one or two splatting suicide drops and then an incontinent stream, that pished and sighed across the garden. The leaves and branches bobbed and jerked, drive-by bystanders. The pavements bubbled and shivered, skating leaves and fag-ends and parking tickets down glossy drains. The rain waved and blew into the borders, beating the soil and then pocking it into streams of gritty viscous gore onto the dashed pebbles. The rain beat the petals from the last flowers. All the bunting and colour leaving the square, cold and steely, stripped for action. After the first bladder-straining, the clouds settled into a solid, windy, skittling fusillade.

*   *   *

Edinburgh, as ever losing no opportunity to show itself a capital of an altogether different mettle, was clear warm and bright. Iona and Charles travelled up on the sleeper. In the early morning the steward had banged open the door of their tiny cabin and had been wafted by the humid nidor of coitus and waxed cotton. He noted with dour politeness the luggage-strap burns on the naked arm that sleepily took the tea and biscuits. Rolling down the corridor he muttered, 'A bloody knocking shop, I'm just a pimp in a mobile brothel. What is it with these Sassenachs and trains?' He imagined Iona's splayed legs in the blue night-light, back arched over the bunk, wrists twisted in the nylon belts, breasts reflected in the mirror, buttocks rocking over the points. 'Oh well, there are worse jobs. Only twelve more to go.'

Iona was out on the platform hopping from foot to foot, banging on the windows with exasperation whilst Charles was still trying to shave in the tiny foldaway sink. She ran ahead down the platform as he stoically humped the bags. Waverley Station opens right into the centre of the city. It is an untypical gesture towards the traveller. Edinburgh is not by nature a demonstrative place, but its terminus shows its best side to the visitor. In London if you step out of King's Cross or Waterloo or Paddington your heart sinks, but in Waverley, weather permitting, the Athens of the North leaves you in no doubt that if anyone tried to refer to the Greek capital as the Edinburgh of the South it would take it as a serious insult.

Iona flung her arms round, from the castle, past the Scott Monument, towards Calton Hill and shouted, 'Isn't it wonderful?'

'Yes, dear.'

It was an exchange that Charles was to get used to in the coming days. It wasn't enough for a place to be wonderful, it had to be seen to be wonderful, its wonder ticked off. Iona's excitement and bubbling happiness was infectious.

They ate a solid breakfast of lumpy porridge, eggs, sausage, bacon, fried bread and daunting millstones of black pudding, each vying with the other for durability and resilience. Iona bought the *Scotsman*, the *Herald* and the *Dundee Courier*, and awarded little flurries of 'wonderfuls' to the plates, the waiters, the view and the literacy of Scots journalists.

They hired a car and pointed north. As they crossed the deeply wonderful Forth Road Bridge, Charles asked, 'Exactly where are we going?'

'North, then east, and there's no point in telling you. Just head for the A9.'

He'd only been to Scotland twice before, once as a student to the Festival, of which he remembered very little other than a nude wheelchair production of *The Aspern Papers*, vicious hangovers and rain, and once as a child on holiday with his mother; a trip that had been memorable for a huge cold bathroom with brown water, a ferocious old dog and more rain.

The House of Shaws was a long, white granite two-storey manse with a heart-stopping view, but Presbyterianly small windows. It sat shrouded in rhododendrons and Scots pines at the head of a short blind glen. A rattling river and a thin loch ran away to the south. Behind it a humpbacked mountain slept.

They arrived at sunset. Iona leapt from the car and rushed to the door. Her cousin, his wife, two nieces and four dogs rushed out. Charles was folded easily into the general excitement. Like most remote country people the Wallaces were incredibly grateful and a little perplexed by visitors who'd travelled more than two miles to see them. They chided Iona for staying away for so long and congratulated Charles on getting there at all.

It was an easy, comfortable, smelly, rather dim household of wet shoes, hairy sofas, smouldering fires, dirty plates and endless lists. The estate was small and shambolic; a few cattle, some forestry, a bit of shooting and the sort of fishing that suits those with arthritic fingers or the squeamish who don't like wriggly, slimy, fishy things on barbed hooks.

Iona was breathless with the joy of being there, of being bound into a family, of belonging, and they in turn treated her with the sort of disbelieving admiration that's reserved for the incredibly brave, or the mad. The pair of red-haired nieces were happy just to watch her, as if she were a favourite cartoon programme. Donald, big and woolly, who had served on three continents with the Black Watch, shook his head at her simply being able to walk down a London street. There was a joshing hard edge to Catherine's 'Now tell us all the news.' With the meagre resources Providence had endowed her, she had managed to catch a husband, a family, make her home; and Iona, for all her state-of-the-art sophistication and ergonomic beauty, was still seeking.

Charles stood back, saying little, smiling a lot, picking up plates, scratching dogs. He was both envious and pleased; envious because this couldn't have been more different from his own solitary, singular family, and pleased because Iona had wanted to include him in it.

After dinner the first night, Catherine said, 'Well you'll be wanting your bed. I expect that's what you came up here for.'

'We've very thoughtfully put you next to the girls,' added Donald.

Catherine went over and sat on her husband's knee. They were both flushed, florid, rotund, dishevelled. Having caught each other, they had let themselves go.

'So you'd better make as much noise as possible, they'll be terribly disappointed if they don't hear something. Sex mad, both of them.'

The bedroom was warm and spare, with a peat fire, a huge wardrobe full of coats and kilts, and a big iron bed with goose-down pillows, a horsehair mattress and heavy, rough blankets.

The next day was taken up with Iona pinning wonderfuls on things, a lot of digging out of old photograph albums, much to the hysterical joy of the girls, and walks. They visited neighbours who wore bald smoking-jackets and ate grouse that were hung longer than they'd lived and cooked for longer than they'd been hung. They rowed in the loch and fished for tiny brown trout. The long weekend unwound into a week.

Charles watched Iona in her woolly jumpers and tweed jackets, her hair pushed up into an old cap. She was a million miles from the woman who had embarrassed him at Vernon's party less than a month before. Charles was perfectly aware that

235

this bucolic persona was in part a performance for his benefit, not that she didn't really love it and not that she didn't naturally fit, but the local pronunciation of 'kirk' for church, 'messages' for shopping, the 'ayes' for yes, the faintly rising intonation, were just too enthusiastically embraced. The effect was damply, warmly, stirringly stunning, not least because she so obviously cared enough to turn it on for him.

On their fourth night, after the inevitable cotton-wool salmon, Donald asked, 'Would you like to go stalking? I know Archie wants to take you; he's already asked me a dozen times to send you his best.'

'Love to, wouldn't we,' replied Iona. 'You'll love Archie, darling.'

After the plates were thrown at the sink, the girls thoroughly overexcited themselves kitting out Charles in Donald's old plus-twos, shirts, stockings, boots. There was much hilarity over the choice of a hat.

At seven in the morning, trying to get to grips with a horn-handled crummock, Charles followed Archie and Iona up the hill. The old stalker was prematurely bent and appeared to be made out of dun tweed and rusty leather. He'd obviously been overjoyed to see her, but had managed to keep his exuberance to a terse, 'Morning, Miss Iona. You're looking bonny.' Archie took a rifle out of its sleeve and passed it to Iona. 'There's two in the chamber, take your time.' Iona lay down, squirmed for a moment, and then pulled the trigger. The report was shocking. It was immediately followed by another. Charles couldn't make out what she was firing at, and then, what seemed like half a mile away, he saw a life-size stag cut out of iron leaning against the hillside. 'That's a killing shot,' Archie looked through binoculars. 'First was a bit high but fair enough. Is the gentleman taking a shot?'

'No, no just watching.'

'Oh go on, Charles, have a go.'

Charles felt foolish enough in his voluminous trousers and coat and the absurd hat. He really had no desire.

'Come on, darling, you're not going to wound it.'

He sighed and lay down beside the sandbag. Archie squatted beside him.

'OK, it couldn't be simpler. Americans do it all the time. Look through the sight, aim for the front of the body, just above the foreleg, rest your hand on the bag, let out half a breath and squeeze the trigger gently. Take your time, hold it firm.'

Charles pulled the trigger; there was a click. Archie inserted two bullets. Warily, Charles curled the smooth tine in the crook of his squeamish finger. The stock punched his shoulder, the barrel jerked up; the noise was surprisingly deep: a round boom. The second shot was easier.

'Well done, brilliant,' shouted Iona, as he got up.

'Aye, both spot on, couldn't get a fifty pence piece between them.'

They carried on in silence, zigzagging up the hill. Round one corner there was a boy lying beside a grey garron pony, both chewing grass. With a nod he tagged along behind. Up, up to the spying place. At first Charles thought the stalk was going to be just an uncomfortable, gruelling, two thousand feet. The hike ached his knees and razored his lungs and threatened to resurrect his breakfast, but slowly the ancient throb of the hunt stole up on him. When Archie finally crouched and flapped his hand for them to kneel in the heather, he was breathlessly excited.

'There's a likely looking beast in the corrie there. We'll crawl from here,' the stalker whispered. 'Who's taking the shot?'

Iona mouthed 'Charles' and she looked directly into his eyes with an expression Charles hadn't seen before: part love, part gift, part dare and part something that only lived here on the hill in the heather with the deer. There was no space, no time for argument. Charles crawled after Archie. They stopped just under the lip of the corrie. Very slowly the stalker peered over and then dropped back.

'There's a shootable stag straight ahead. He's got three hinds with him. They're quite alert, moving about. Wait, he's facing us at the moment. When he turns broadside and you get a clear shot, take him.'

Charles nodded. He'd never killed anything before; he'd never believed he could kill something bigger than he was. Slowly he snaked to the edge and looked, his throat tight and parched. His head felt light, eyes darting, looking but not seeing. Never in his life had he felt so close to the edge of his senses. It took a moment; there was the stag. It was far further than Charles had expected. He saw two hinds. Archie slid the binoculars' case in front of him and then the rifle. 'There's one in the chamber, the safety's there.' Through the scope the stag was wildly entrancing, familiar but unique, a thing seen clearly for the first time. Charles stared hard. The cross-hairs intensified the image, stripping away the clutter of association: the scenery, the context, the varnish, the artful soft lyricism. A razor-etched crucifix fixed the animal, not as a symbol or an ornament or romance, but put this beast precisely in the moment, at exactly this distance. Hunter and hunted synchronized and were meshed by the closing of two converging paths. The cross of the horizon cut by vertical aspiration; the point where they meet destiny. The nervous hissing fear subsided and focused down to that point: the access. Charles's single eye dilated, ravenous for light, bleaching colour. He caught the third hind. She was lying much closer to them, just her elegant leaf-like ears turning. An eddy of breeze behind the knoll, no more than a sigh, brushed his neck and she was on her feet nuzzling the air. The other two hinds started, and trotted off with exquisite grace. The stag looked, half turned, thick-bearded head lunging forward, heavy antlers laid across his back, and he roared. If any noise in the world is the call of the wild, the rutting red stag's challenge is; a vibrating, thick, rasping yell, it curled and ricocheted round the natural amphitheatre. He waited for the last hind to pass him and, turning, took quick, boxer's steps down the corrie and then, in a heart-stop, turned his head and looked straight at Charles. The horizontal line of life ran along his flank, the perpendicular hair of time stretched from earth to sky across his shoulder. The crucifix crashed. Charles didn't hear the double crump thump of the report, didn't feel the jar in the hollow of his shoulder. When he looked over the barrel the hinds had gone. In the distance, now a long way off, in a Landseer landscape, a romantic stag stood, head forward. He took two steps and fell out of sight.

Archie economically set about the gralloch and called for the pony. Iona bounded over the heather.

'Well done, well done. Where did you hit him? How do you feel? Right this moment, how do you feel?'

Charles blinked and stared at the head with the unblinking, marble eye, the lolling tongue, still with the half-chewed grass, and tried to fit the pieces back together coherently, but couldn't.

'I don't know, sort of elated, relieved. No, more. I feel terribly happy to be alive.'

Iona hugged him.

'Well, he's a good animal. A good shot, through the lungs. That's pretty instant. About eighteen stone, ten years, I should say.' The stalker got up. Cupping his hands, he turned to Charles and wiped a palmful of gore across his face. Charles gasped, Archie smiled.

'Your first stag; the blooding.'

The hot, complicated, delicious, repellent smell of the beast filled his head. He felt the thump of his own blood and another faint rhythm, heard a keening chant.

'You go on ahead,' said Iona.

'Aye, if you say so.' Archie didn't look up from tying the antlers back to the leg. 'You know the way.' He took his coat off the garron's head and rolled down his sleeve. 'I'll see you in the game room for a dram, sir. Well done.'

Iona pulled Charles to the heather and kissed him as if life hung on it. The taste of iron and musk. Afterwards, panting, they lay and listened to the stags roar. Above them a pair of hawks turned. The air was thick with a sweet, dusty scent: heather and the sour, mulchy hum of the stag's pluck. Charles leant on his elbow and looked down at her, smeared with blood, her face, breasts and thighs streaked and crusted with life and death. The rise and fall of her echoed out over the hills. The oldest things in the world. This landscape was like seeing granite dinosaurs. Over a hundred thousand years this view had tentatively, remorselessly, organically evolved into Buchan Gardens. It hadn't just been Iona's roots he had been brought here to admire. She rolled over and ferreted in pockets for the whisky flask.

'Are you contemplating your harem and considering, perhaps, roughly taking her again from behind while bellowing your challenge as you shaft the imperative of the victorious hunter's genes?'

'Funnily enough I wasn't. I was just thinking I'm suffering from a surfeit of metaphors.'

'Where the suppurating fuck have you been?' Bryony answered her door with a face like a postponed second front. Charles stood dripping on the step; it was still raining.

Iona had gone straight from the station to work, ostentatiously still wearing her tweed and a sprig of heather in her bonnet. Charles had got to Buchan Gardens and found his answerphone blinking furiously.

'Charles, Bryony. Call me.' Click.

'Charles, Bryony. We need a meeting. Man the sodding ramparts.' Click.

'Charles, Bryony. The centre cannot hold, send reinforcements.' Click.

'Bastard boy – Bryony (drunk). All is lost. Fuck, I did my best, but fuck it, where the fuck were you? That's what I want to know. Oh fuck, the bath's still running.' There was the sound of the telephone being put down on a table and then the distant smudged noises of Bryony moving around, snatches of rugby songs, the clink of glass and then sonorous snoring. The tape ran out.

'Come in, come in. Where have you been?'

'Scotland.'

'Shagging Scotland, how nice. Well, you were needed here, Charles. All hell broke loose; we've been buggered, well and truly caught with our pants down, bent over and sneakily pronged in the back passage.'

She led the way into the kitchen, which smelt like a garage.

The table was full of rum bottles. On the floor a milk crate held more with strips of torn sheets stuffed into their necks. Bryony put a metal funnel into the neck of one and picked up a heavy, khaki jerrycan, and slopped petrol into the bottle.

'What on earth are you doing?'

'What's it fucking look like? Haven't you ever seen anyone making Molotov cocktails before?'

'No, as a matter of fact I've led a rather sheltered life, and I haven't.'

'Our houseboy at Huutsbrut taught me. We used to ambush the Yaapies on the way to church on Sundays. Happy days.' She paused for a moment, turning the memory over. She looked splendid, dressed in the uniform of a colonel of the Natal Native Levy, with chain-mail epaulettes, black buttons, wideawake hat and a silver leaping leopard insignia with a black cockade.

'Well, don't just stand there. Pour an inch of washing-up liquid into the empties.'

'Washing-up liquid, Bryony?'

'Makes the fuckers stick.'

'Look, why don't you just stop for a minute and tell me what's happened.'

'Yes, let's have a drink.' She started picking up bottles, examining them. Finally she found one that smelt mildly less fiery than the rest and took a swig. 'Last Monday I got a call from that dung-tongued quisling, Marle. Vernon, may wild asses shit on his unmarked grave, wanted to meet the Committee because he had something important to say. Well, I tried to get you, but you were away, so,' Byrony unbuttoned her ribboned, breast pocket and pulled out a pack of Senior Service and a Zippo, 'I took command and mustered the rest of the troops.'

'Bryony, no!' Charles screamed, suddenly realizing what he was looking at.

'What?'

'The petrol.'

'Oh right, well spotted. Let's go and sit soft.'

She stood four-square in the fireplace, glossy brown riding

boots apart, cigarette and rum in one hand, zebra-hair fly-whisk in the other. Charles sat in a chair made up of bits of animal, under a giraffe's-foot lamp stand. The room croaked, growled, mewed and grunted like the opening credits of a Tarzan film.

'So where was I? I could tell something big was afoot, that the niggers were massing for a major shindig. We had to face them in Bon Bon's chintzatorium, seeing as you weren't here.'

'Sorry.'

'Couldn't be helped. You can't choose the ground; just turn up and rummage their bowels before they rummage yours. Anyway I got our lot there an hour early. Oh Charles, you'd have been bloody proud of us, lined up in the cold grey morning, not showy, not blustering, no martial pomp, just steady and true, the flower of the forest. Bon Bon took the left flank, Celeste the right and I was arrayed in the centre, with the doctor in the rear as reserve. He brought the first set-back. Did you know that snivelling vicar has been co-opted on to the Committee?'

'No.'

'Well, Spindle, bless his trusting heart, brought him. I didn't like the look of him, that twisting fuckwit – you never know with co-opted natives, they melt away when the gut juice hits the punkah. I gave them the talk, you know the sort of thing. Screw your courage to the sticking post; great deeds to be done today; some of us may not survive, but the memory will live for as long as . . . etc., etc. I asked the vicar to give us a prayer, Lord of Battles, we trust the rightness of our cause, sort of thing, and he came out with some liberal cock-cheese about forgiveness and mediation, and then it was just fucking waiting. You know Charles, I think that was the worst bit, the waiting.'

'Yes, I can imagine.'

'So it was with a sort of relief that we heard them approach; a noise like a locomotive far off: Vernon's breathing. And then, suddenly, they were there, the enemy host, the old charging buffalo formation: Marle the right horn, a murderous-looking lawyer the left, and Vernon himself the loins. Seen it a thousand times before, classic Kaffir impi. We let them come, the line silent, everyone with his own last-minute private thoughts of home. They pranced and puffed and capered with their mumbo jumbo. There was a pause,' Bryony lifted the fly-whisk, 'and Vernon swept his hands and the horns charged.' She took a mouthful of rum and chain-lit a cigarette, blowing a long billow of smoke up the wide nostrils of a hartebeest.

'Yes,' said Charles, 'yes?' perched on the edge of his seat. 'What then?' He'd never heard the minutes of the previous recounted as if they'd been taken by G. A. Henty.

'Well, for as long as I live, I never want to go through anything like the next hour again. Marle came first, testing our defences. "The Committee was unrepresentative, old-fashioned and oligarchical." Bon Bon stood her ground, wavered a bit over oligarchical but saw him off. Then the lawyer, moving fast and low, closed with Celeste, "Legal position tricky, no standing in law, Committee not properly constituted, undemocratic, no proper accounts." The jargon flew so thick that our front line disappeared, but as the legal smoke cleared, there she was still standing firm, firing volleys of "It's worked perfectly well so far, why change it?" And then Vernon marched – teeth glinting in the sunlight in perfect order, the finest heavy committee man in the world – straight at me. He lined up three deep as close as I am to you now and fired. Fuck, Charles, it was ring-looseningly awful. He's been to court, you know. Taken the Committee to some chamber and had us set aside. We're illegal.' Bryony cut with her whisk and took another swig. 'Apparently, we have no right to levy a subscription. The lawyer sniped more legalese. He's collected signatures from the square people and says a majority of them would rather not pay a levy but have the garden finance itself. He said that he would form a new committee with commercial sponsorship, without a subscription, paid for by the Mona Corinth Trust. Well, you could see our front line crumble. Bon Bon wavered, Celeste faltered, but I might have been able to hold him, except that we were stabbed in the back. The vicar, God swell his testicles, came from behind and fell upon the baggage train. He said that we should embrace change, and that he thought Lord Vernon's plans sounded the best of all possible worlds and, twisting the knife, he proposed a vote.

Well it was three against, one for and one abstention – you. It wasn't enough; divided we fell.'

'Bryony, I am sorry.' Charles saw the battlefield littered with bodies, heard the groans of the wounded, smelt the black powder smoke. 'This is terrible, he's bought the garden with Mona's money. Isn't there anything we can do?'

'Well, we disengaged in the best order we could, retreated by column. We've got thirty days to appeal, but honestly, Charles, I don't hold out much hope. We've no money.'

'I can hardly believe it. It's not just the memorial, we've lost the whole garden. Christ, has anyone spoken to Angel?'

'Angel's disappeared. There's been neither hide nor hair of him or the dog for a week and the police are after him; Vernon's got them wiping up after him. But never say die; while there's breath there's hope.'

'But Bryony, what can we possibly do?'

'Go underground, that's what I'm doing. A guerrilla campaign, lightning strikes, in and out, chaos and disorder; think long term.'

'The petrol bombs? You can't be serious; they'll send you to prison.'

'Got to fucking catch me first. They'll never take me alive.'

'Bryony!'

'I'm serious, Charles. I'm an old woman, I've come to this garden to die, and if I've got to go with Vernon's throat in my fist, then all the better.' She burped loudly to add emphasis, and then with a quiet intensity, 'I won't see the things that I've loved and dreamt of all my life rubbished by the sort of man my father would have thrashed for not using the tradesman's entrance.' She slumped into a water-buck-skin armchair, the rum and the emotion catching up. The wideawake hat slipped over to one side; she looked frail and drained.

'Bryony, promise me you won't do anything immediately. Give me some time to come up with a plan.'

'Charles, you're a sweet man, but frankly you're not a man of action. We're all amazed you managed to come up with Iona. I remember when we asked you to be President. "There's a chap who won't do anything," we said, "just perfect." You're a peacetime leader, dear boy.'

'That's what they said about Churchill.'

'No, Charles, that's not what they said about Churchill, I was there.'

'A week, give me a week?'

'OK, but then it's direct action.'

'Can I help you put the bombs away? You shouldn't have them in the kitchen.'

'You would have been proud of us you know.'

'I'm sure. I am sorry I wasn't there.'

'Well, you've got a week to be here now.'

Charles went home and lay in the bath, thinking. Walking back into the bedroom, he bumped into a bottom sticking out of the wardrobe.

'Ah, Joe, you give me fright. I thought you still away.' Lily was holding one of Iona's frocks. 'No no, Joe. You put your pecker away, I don't want your girlfriend whipping my butt.'

'Lily, I've just had a bath. What are you doing with that dress?'

'I borrow it for disco. You don't tell, please, Joe, please? I look a million dollars.'

'Fine, I won't tell her, but go and hoover next door, I need to use the telephone.' Charles lay on the bed and thought that once you had slept with home help it rather took care of having to be discreet and modest round the house. He rehearsed conversations. 'Now look here, Vernon . . .' 'Vernon, you shit . . .' 'Now, Vernon, we're both reasonable men . . .' 'Here, you, Vernon, outside now . . .' He dialled. 'Hello, Vernon?'

'No, it's Stephen Marle. Who's calling please?'

'Oh, Stephen, hello. It's Charles. Could I speak to Vernon?'

'Can you tell me what it's about?'

'Well the Garden Committee, of course.'

'Of course. Hold on.'

There was a pause, then a muttered conversation.

'I'm afraid His Lordship's busy. He says there is no Garden Committee. If you have any questions about the Mona Corinth Memorial Garden, please put it in writing.'

'For Christ's sake, Stephen, stop being so pompous. I need to . . .'

'Get that tarty bit of smelly fish twat to look after your needs, duckie. Don't call again.'

Charles just heard Vernon's high-pitched giggle in the background before the line went dead.

'Damn, damn, damn.' The white anger of injustice started to bubble like ignored milk. It foamed and boiled inside him. Charles had probably only been truly angry half a dozen times in his life, and certainly not more than twice since his balls had dropped. He jumped off the bed and hit the wardrobe with the flat of his hand. 'Damn, damn, damn them. Vernon and his catamite.' They had stolen the garden, sent Angel into hiding, reduced Bryony to the brink of terrorism, traduced a dead neighbour's memory, insulted the woman he loved. Vernon had remorselessly manipulated the goodwill and manners of everyone who came into contact with him, and he was laughing, smug and self-satisfied. How foolish, how pathetic Charles must have seemed, how amateur and lightweight. 'Well, fuck it.' There was a time when a man had to walk into the street and stand up for what was right. Charles stood in front of the mirror, narrowed his eyes, flexed his fingers. He felt like the gunfighter who had given it all up to work on the farm, who put up with the taunting and indignity until they finally messed with his woman.

Lily put her head round the door. 'What you banging for, Joe?'

'Get the tin trunk from under the bed, Lily. I'm strapping on my pistols. Don't try and stop me.'

'What you talking about, Joe? You gone shell-shock?'

'Never mind, pass me the phone.'

'Here you are. You one loony tune soldier.'

Charles set his jaw and drilled a number like bottles on a fence, faster than the eye could follow.

*　　*　　*

246

'You know the way.' The girl with the cheese-grater voice didn't look up from her magazine. Charles took the steps up to Jocelyn Draper's office two at a time. He had dressed with care, in the late twentieth-century equivalent of a gunslinger's duds. Grey, bird's-eye eighteen-ounce worsted, single-breasted; cream shirt; plain gold links; a thin steel watch with a leather strap; navy-blue silk madder tie and guardsman-polished black calf shoes. He'd stopped off on the way at his barber's for a general tidy-up: head, neck, nostrils, ears, eyebrows, nails, no smells.

Charles meant business and he looked it. All the matt drabness an Englishman can muster when he wants to be really impressive was on show for those with the eyes to notice. Josh noticed, but didn't show it.

'Hello, Charles, nice to see you. How are you? Well? Good. Take a seat. Now, the Mona Corinth bequest, how's it going?' Josh surreptitiously had the file hidden under a copy of *GQ*.

'It's not exactly about that that I'm here, Josh, although it is related.'

'Aah.' The lawyer raised a riveted eyebrow and steepled his fingers.

'You know I am, was, the President of the Buchan Gardens Garden Committee?'

'Yuh, vaguely.'

'Yes, well, we've come rather unstuck.'

Charles told the saga as economically and as matter-of-factly as possible. Even so, he realized that the doings down on the square sounded remarkably trivial. Josh's attention never quavered, his fingers remained perpendicular, his eyebrows quizzical.

'So,' said Charles, 'I want you to act for us, to find some way of putting everything back the way it was.'

'Right, Charles. That's quite a story, a veritable hotbed of rape and pillage hidden beneath the petunias.'

'Will you take it on?'

'Well, Charles, from where I'm sitting, there are a number of problems. Speaking purely professionally, which is after all what you've come to hear, it's not really this firm's area of expertise. Let me put it another way. You did point out that there is no money involved, and from this side of the desk, I'm afraid, that's a pretty fatal drawback. There is no up side, we are looking at hours of work, possibly years in court, with no-one who can be handed a bill at the end. That isn't by any means to belittle the merit of your case, just that it's not our sort of case.'

'I had a fair inkling your answer might be along those lines.'

'Yes, you struck me as a perceptive man.'

'There is another aspect that I didn't mention.'

'Fire away.' Josh fleetingly perused his watch.

'Well, you remember Bon Bon Velute introduced us at Mona's funeral?'

'Yes.'

'She introduced you as Belman's solicitor.'

'As I am. You know I act for a lot of people in the entertainment business.'

'Yes. You may also recall that the first time we met here you told me an amusing anecdote', the steeple gently folded into a dome, 'about an old rock star who had a second family of whom his wife was blissfully unaware. Now, call it coincidence, call it fate, call it putting two and two together, but I have come close to passing that anecdote on to Bon Bon, attributing it to you, of course. Now, without confirming or denying any of the facts, would that put my original request in a new light?'

Josh's aspect never faltered, his face remained an open but blank book. 'It may well.'

'Before you answer let me put yet another point to you. This is to do with Mona's bequest. Her personal papers, which were locked in her safe and only I have access to, are libellous; not just libellous, they're scurrilous, pornographic and lavishly illustrated. Their contents will highly embarrass three-quarters of Hollywood, ruin reputations and spread a Chernobyl of gossip and scandal that will keep the tabloid press and European glossy magazines on exclusives for a decade. Now, if they were to become public, there would be an enormous amount of work for lawyers. Carefully handled, the papers could generate millions of pounds. Of course, I might just do the decent thing and burn them.'

'Charles, as you rightly surmise, all this puts an entirely different perspective on the very interesting case of Buchan Gardens. I think I can guarantee that this firm will be delighted to look into it. I will, in fact, personally devote my full attention to it.'

'Good, I am very grateful, and, oh, you've got a week to sort it all out.'

Josh took a deep breath. 'Fine.'

Charles stood up and shamefully offered his hand. It was grasped, squeezed and pumped with alacrity. 'Sorry I had to resort to blackmail and bribery.'

'Charles, Charles,' laughed Josh, walking down the stairs behind him. 'I'm a lawyer, ninety per cent of law is blackmail and bribery. If it weren't for blackmail and bribery my children would be dropping their "h"s in a State school. You very sensibly offered me a number of options in full and frank discussion.'

'I'm glad you see it that way.'

They reached the door.

'I must say, Miss Corinth certainly knew what she was about when she appointed you as her executor.'

'She didn't, appoint me I mean, you did.'

'You've moved the ibis.'

'The what?'

'The ibis, the mummified ibis, second dynasty, you've moved it.'

'That pass-the-parcel parrot, I haven't done anything with it. It's on the side-table beside the sofa where it's always been.'

'Yes, it is on the Davenport beside the day bed, but it's been moved. It should face three o'clock, now it's at six.'

'You tell her,' growled a Danish ship's decanter.

Charles stood in his drawing-room fidgeting with his objects and shouting. Iona sat on the loo reading the *Evening Standard*.

'Who gives a fuck?'

'I do, it does. And the Meissen shepherdess, she's got her back to the shepherd.'

'Lucky her.'

'Iona, why can't you put anything back in its place?' Charles began to arrange a collection of antique coins. 'You've got Diocletian next to Pompeii and after Trajan; it's so annoying.'

'Christ, now I'm responsible for the fall of the fucking Roman Empire.'

'While we're talking about it, I found a J. R. Ackerley with a corner of a page turned down; it's a first edition you know.'

'If anyone would appreciate a dog-ear, I expect Ackerley would.'

'And we can't possibly have these flowers here, they're the most evil colour, they clash with everything.'

'Stop it,' Iona said quietly, standing behind him.

Charles turned. 'They're hideous, they're just dropped into a pot, they look like you got them from Brompton Cemetery.'

'Do you really want a row? Because if you do I'll give you Tony's phone number and you can go and get your head kicked in. Don't take it out on me. Do you like living with me?'

'Yes, of course.'

'Don't you think I'm the best thing that ever walked into your life?'

'Iona, you know I adore you.'

'Well, don't pick fights with me, and certainly not about all this junk. I have to deal with this shit all day.'

'I'm sorry.' He stroked a bronze jockey. 'It's just that I really mind about these little things. I don't have many skills; I can read cards – which bores me to death – and I've got nice manners and perfect taste. I can't help it, I just know when things are right. It's like perfect pitch, a crooked picture clamours like a flat oboe. It's not much in the way of talents.'

'Well, at least if you do hide them under a bushel, it'll be a really beautiful bushel, and anyway, darling, you're a good kisser and drop-dead brilliant at oral genital stimulation.'

'Thanks.'

'Don't knock it, mate, that trumps a double first and a black belt in anything.'

'I'm just so bloody angry. You're right, it's not about you or the things, it's Vernon and Mona and the garden. I got so furious when I saw Bryony. I thought the anger would go away, but it doesn't, it sits like a tight little gutta-percha ball in the back of my throat. The bloody injustice and the unfairness and the sadness.'

'Darling, just let it go. Move on. You had a shot and Vernon pissed higher. Don't give him the added victory of sodding up your life. Move on, fuck him. There are more important things to care about, like what are you going to make me for dinner?'

'You started this. You said, "Care; be Gawain; kill the dragon." '

'I know, but that was then. And you won the fair maid. Vernon got the field, you got the bird; who really won? Leave the dragon to his bad breath and his scorched earth.'

'No, I can't.'

'OK. By the way, talking of arguing with Tony . . .'

'Which we weren't.'

'Your little chat to Birthright has borne fruit.' She handed him a copy of the *Evening Standard* open at Londoner's Diary. At the bottom of the page in Cheesecake Corner, a spot usually reserved for pictures of barely working actresses, was a smiling Iona, resplendent under the headline AUCTIONEER GOES FOR SMALLEST BID: 'As if getting a table weren't enough, Tony Neibelung, television hotshot (*Jude the Obscure, A Bit of Baudelaire, Hotel Babylon*) has lost out in the ratings war. Tony, famous at his Alma Mater, Monkton Combe, for being excused shorts for games, has lost his girlfriend, Gandolfs gorgeous gavelette, Iona Wallace, known as "The Hammer of the Lots", to another, less well-endowed by Nature. There was, I'm told, a heated altercation in laid-back diner Hankies last week, when Tony confronted Iona and her new acquisition having a quiet tête-à-tête. Eye-bulging witnesses swear he rudely took out his own lunch box at the table, much to the astonishment of the ladies present and the discomfort of the men. The new man in Iona's life, millionaire epicurean, Charles Godwin, slyly declared, "It was all a misunderstanding". In a high-pitched voice he told Londoner's Diary, "Tony has had an operation that's gone wrong. He was just showing us his scars. Iona is now living with me." A Hankies waitress sighed, "It was by far and away the largest portion I've ever seen served here." Whatever can she mean?'

Charles laughed. 'He really is a terrible shyster, Birthright. He's managed to make us all sound hideous.'

'Good picture of me though.'

'Yes, you look wonderful.'

'Is it true?'

'What? You were there, you know as well as I do. It's not lies, but it's a long way from being the truth.'

'No, the bit about you?'

'What, about having a squeaky voice and being an epicurean?'

'No, don't be obtuse. About being a millionaire with a small willy?'

'Oh, that bit. Well, yes and no.'

'Yes and no how?'

'Yes, I'm a millionaire. No, I don't have a small willy. It falls into that quadrant that is considered average, according to my GP, Dr Gulliver.'

'Just how much of a millionaire?'

'Oh, it's difficult to say.' Charles's hand stroked a tapestry coyly. 'Most of it's tied up in cash, a pretty run-of-the-mill millionaire, I expect. Well, multi, there being more than one of them.'

'Charles, why didn't you ever tell me?'

'It's not the sort of thing you go round saying – bad form. I don't use my title either.'

'You've got a title?'

'Oh yes, the proudest title an Englishman can bear: Mister. But I don't go round saying, "Hello, I'm Mister Charles Godwin" or "It's Mister Godwin to you." '

'Charles, I don't know what to say. I see you in a whole new light.' Iona pouted, pulled up her skirt and put her arms round his neck.

'Does it really make a difference to you, seriously?'

'Does my having perfect tits and a face that could launch a thousand shipping forecasts make a difference to you?'

'You bet.'

'Precisely.'

'Good. Mummy always said it would come in useful. By the way, we're going to see the vicar tomorrow.'

'Not that big a damn difference,' laughed Iona, pushing him away and pulling down her frock.

Chapter Fourteen

'Bright and happy, full of the joys of salvation, or muted and respectful for His Infinite Majesty?' Iona stood in her underwear, looking like one of those cut-out-and-dress dolls in pre-teen comics. She held alternate hangers up to her neck.

'I don't know.' Charles sat on the end of the bed in a Savile Row tweed coat, grey flannel trousers, suede shoes and a knitted silk tie. 'Neither. Haven't you got something sort of ethereal, floaty, spiritually yearning?'

'Old hippy? No I haven't. It'll have to be sensible-girl-about-town with just a touch of devil-may-care exuberance.'

'Fine, but make that God-may-care exuberance.'

She flicked through the cupboards. 'You still haven't told me why we're going to see the ghastly vicar, and why my clothes are so important.'

'You don't need to know. Just keep quiet and look supportive.'

'That's what I like about you, Charles, you're so modern.'

'I need you there because the Church has an unnatural reverence for couples. Couples are the gold nuggets of organized religion. And clothes are important; how you look is vital, particularly in Church. They are obsessed with clothes. Christians have more uniforms than any other group in history. Come on, I don't want to be late.' Charles picked up a manila folder.

'Make-up?'

'Just a touch; pale and slightly sickly.'

The Rev Trev was up a ladder trying to nail banners into roof beams. In a dusty heap on the floor lay the regimental colours of Princess Beatrix's Artists' Rifles and the Second Battalion of Hyde Park Yeomanry. The flags were fretted and faded, their union stripes pale pink, watery blue and filthy cream. In many places their netting was showing through, but the battle honours were still ghostly legible: Spion Kop, Alexandria, Palestine, Loos, Cambrai, Passchendaele. They'd been brought into the church with ineffable solemnity in 1921. A royal duke and a brass band were in attendance. The church had been full of black-feathered widows holding the hands of solemnly shocked sons and daughters. A battalion of tears had fallen as the band had played Thomas Tallis and two cadets had marched the colours to the altar. The vicar, the Rev Trev's distant antecedent, had given the sermon that a stoical generation of widows got to know by heart. A trumpet had sounded, bells knelled, and the flags had been hung like heavy shrouds *in memoriam ad infinitum*.

As it happens *infinitum* added up to barely two generations. Now Trev struggled with polyester-mix sheets celebrating the far more pressing and relevant crusades against intolerance, sadness and being generally under the weather. The colours were as bright as the sentiments were simple. They'd been made by a battered mothers' collective in Purley and a special needs junior school in Nuneaton. Tap, tap, tap, Trev banged nails for God. 'Colour me Christian' shouted the sheet that hung crookedly, obscuring the simple marble plaque commemorating Paul Timothy ffoulkes, RN, HMS *Antigone*, died Battle of

Jutland, aged 17, beloved son and brother, 'He has no grave but the sea, sleep on the further shore.'

'Hello Jacob.' Charles and Iona stood hand in hand at the top of the aisle.

The Rev Trev peered myopically. 'Aah, Charles, Iona, Iona, Charles. What?'

'Jacob. The ladder.'

'Oh yes, right, great. Hold on.' Trev descended carefully. 'Come into my sharing space.' He tripped on the flags and, with an irritated sigh, kicked at them and then led the way into the vestry which was now happily kitted out in non-confrontational beige with posters of kittens, Swiss mountains and foetuses. The floor was mined with children's toys; a large television sat in a corner. Trev deposited himself on a moulded plastic chair and motioned Charles and Iona to a Swedish-style settee.

'Good, great, wonderful,' he beamed, lavishing even amounts of non-judgemental eye contact on them both. 'Now, there's no prizes for guessing why you're here.'

'Well . . .' the prospective happy couple said together.

'OK, before we go any further,' Trev held his palms out, 'let me give you a little homily. I say this to all couples who sit on that sofa. Love is a wonderful thing, and physical love its most wonderful manifestation. The twinning of naked glowing bodies in the full vigour of youthful health. The hot passion of quivering limbs and the yielding sweat-scented flesh. The probing and surrendering of mutual fulfilment. There really is no more joyous sight in the eyes of Jesus, but, and this is a big but, the physical joy of sex should only be expressed through the framework of a sanctioned marriage. Now, I know this sounds old-fashioned and you might be surprised to hear it from me, a vicar, but we in the modern Church are quite clear about pre-marital sex. The word is No, the word is Stop, Don't.'

Iona had her mouth open, Charles held his forehead as if taking his own temperature.

'Iona, my dear, I understand your guilt and sense of shame at your loss of a squandered virginity, really I do. I know the regret and the emptiness that giving in to sensual peer pressure presses down on you, but joy, I bring great joy. Christ can give you back your virginity.'

Iona gasped.

'Yes,' Rev Trev clapped with excitement, 'I know, I know. I always find that's the reaction when I drop the good news. We can have a re-virginizing service. Isn't that miraculous? Christ is boundlessly loving and forgiving, the Holy Ghost can, and will, if humbly asked, implant a born-again, clean, new wholesome virginity in you. What I suggest is that on the morning of your nuptials you have a simple and moving ceremony witnessed by your family and friends. It's very beautiful. You kneel at the altar rail and, with me, you ask for forgiveness for all the pre-marital lovers you have had, by name. We ask the Holy Ghost to fill the hole in your life. I give you a symbolic balloon of joy and in turn you give it to Charles and tell him, and the congregation, that you come to your marriage in purity. I can guarantee that your wedding night will be as the first time. There now, how about that?' Trev hugged himself.

Iona struggled for words. 'I rather wanted to spend my wedding night in bed, not in a park. And does Charles get a balloon as well?' She leant forward and was about to tell the Rev what he could do with her bloody hymen when Charles cut in smoothly.

'There has been a misunderstanding, Vicar. Miss Wallace and I are not here to get married.'

'Oh, well I assumed . . .' Trev looked rather deflated.

'Yes, you did. But we've come here about the Mona Corinth Trust and the plans for the garden.'

'Ah, yes, yes, very exciting. Did Bryony tell you about the open-air healings, the prayathons? So exciting.'

'Yes, we're very excited. Now, as this is all being done under the auspices of the Mona Corinth bequest, and as I am her trustee and Iona is handling the sale for Gandolfs, there were one or two things I just wanted to run past you, to get your input, seeing as the Church is going to be a direct beneficiary.'

'Of course.'

'Since Mona's name will be so closely associated with the

church, I wondered if you wouldn't mind writing a short piece, just setting out your plans for the money, etc. Perhaps we'll use a photograph of the church and the garden in the auction catalogue.'

'Charles.' Iona squeezed his hand hard.

'I'll get to that in a minute, darling. Just let me put the vicar in the picture.'

'But . . .'

'Now, let me show you the sort of thing we're proposing.' Charles opened the manila folder. 'This is the picture that will be on the front of the catalogue, and it's the one we'll be circulating to the press.' He took out a glossy 8 x 10 of Mona standing on a table in a café, lifting her skirt like a flamenco dancer. She had forgotten to wear underpants. A group of men sat grinning, looking up at her. A stilettoed foot rested on a bald head.

'Oh, my word.'

'Yes, full of life, isn't it? So typical of her, I think. And on the inside page we'll have your letter and a photograph and then facing it probably . . . this,' another 8 x 10, this time of Mona with a very black penis in her mouth, her chin was tilted up and her eyes contemplatively closed.

'Oh heavens, no.'

'No, maybe you're right. Maybe this one of her dressed in a nun's wimple, masturbating with a crucifix would be more appropriate. What do you think? I wanted to save this one of her on her hands and knees with the cowboys for a double page.'

'Stop. What is this filth?' Trev shouted.

'This is the Mona Corinth legacy,' Charles said innocently, carefully laying out photographs on the floor, until the Rev Trev was marooned in a sea of gaping vaginas, elevated cocks and statuesque bosoms.

'But this is pornography, this is . . . this is hellish.'

'Do you think so? Iona here assures me it's cultural gold. It's an important insight into a contemporary icon. That is what you said, isn't it, dear?'

'Yes, and worth a huge amount of money. There'll be a good deal of publicity. I'm sure you'll have lots of girls wanting their virginities back. You'll be able to sell them off the peg.' She pulled the hem of her skirt over her knees and smiled silkily. 'Do you think we should ask the Bishop to add something?'

'The Bishop?' Trev squeaked. 'Stop. The Church simply can't, simply mustn't be associated with these things.' He kicked out at a picture of Mona peeing on the upturned face of an androgynous girl. 'It's out of the question. I had no idea. I'm horrified to the quick. There can be absolutely no mention of St Bertha's in connection with Mona Corinth.'

'Please be careful, these are worth a great deal of money. I am sorry you feel that way. I see that it puts you in a rather difficult position; I mean the Mona Corinth Memorial will benefit the garden and all your exciting plans, and then, of course, there's the diary, and the letters, the detailed descriptions of all her lovers.'

'You see, there's always a silver lining,' added Iona, picking up a photograph of Mona kissing an anonymous bottom. 'You could say that this is just the sort of area in which the Church would be most needed. Isn't sin rather your line of business?'

'Stop it. Stop it now. Take these things away. This is evil, evil.'

'I'll do what I can, of course,' Charles carefully packed the photographs, 'but really it's out of my hands. It's really Vernon you need to talk to, he's the one who's actually running the bequest.'

'I'll speak to him immediately.'

Iona and Charles stood up.

'Gandolfs have to make a decision about the catalogue posters and press releases today,' Iona said, examining a picture of a twenty-four-week-old foetus that had 'Unwanted for Murder' written in bloody letters under it. 'So odd, what some people think of as pornography.'

'Are you absolutely sure you want nothing to do with the Mona Corinth bequest?' asked Charles.

'Absolutely nothing, nothing whatsoever, and don't think I don't know what the pair of you have done. This is on purpose. You're steeped in sin, both of you. Get out of my church.' Trev followed them down the aisle, shouting, 'Pray for forgiveness, fornicators, pedlars of filth.' The yeomans' fallen colours, motto 'With God and a Long Arm', wrapped itself round Trev's toe. He took two unbalanced steps and fell headlong onto the ladder, hitting the third rung hard with the bridge of his nose. It slid down the wall. Charles and Iona heard a slow ripping as the mixed media Good News fluttered to the floor.

Iona lay on the sofa and held her sides as the cackles of laughter subsided. 'That was heavenly. I'd have worn a tiara and a wet suit to see that little hypocrite's face when you showed him that photograph of Mona with a cock in her gob.'

Charles opened a bottle of wine. 'Yes, it was very gratifying. But it doesn't actually fix anything. Vernon's still got control. Not having the Church's support may annoy him but it won't stop him.'

'No, I suppose not.' Iona kicked off her shoes and started taking off the business suit. 'But I did notice, in passing, that you've agreed to sell Mona's papers.'

'Yes, I thought you'd notice that. I've decided that you can put some of them in the sale, some of the less personal photographs and one or two of the letters, but not the diaries or the really filthy stuff.'

'Fair enough. But can we decide on which together?'

'I want something from you in return.'

'I don't make deals, Charles. What do you want that you haven't already had?'

'A balloon.'

'Fuck off.'

Bryony looked out at the grey garden; soggy, blanched, empty. She just had that feeling. The night before the invasion feeling, the one you get in the dark when you've bought a ticket for a film about the Normandy landings but you pretend it comes as a surprise. All those little things that seemed innocent, in retrospect it was really the Maquis doing their prep. The man with the onions on the bike, is he really just an extra? Or does he get a credit for cutting the telephone lines? There was nothing, it was all quiet, too quiet. Just a traffic warden putting yellow, parking suspended, firing-squad bags on the weeping meters' heads.

She turned from the window in search of a bottle. The wireless droned *Gardeners' Question Time* topical tips. 'Now's the time to dig trenches.' Bryony's thoughts wandered back through the gloom, bumping into memories.

'This is London calling, London calling. Boom-boom-di-boom. The violins weep with a mournful languor, the violins weep with a mournful languor.'

'Sod it.'

She picked up a copy of *Nimrod – Big Black Boys in Athletic Poses* and took it to bed. The evening held its breath; bided its time.

Dawn wasn't best pleased to be woken this early. It was a shitty day; the rain had long since given up any attempt to impress with fancy footwork or syncopated beat, nobody cared, nobody was watching. It fell straight down like greasy hair. Bryony woke; her head ached and her pubic bone was bruised. She shrugged on a greatcoat and shuffled to a shivering pee, put on the kettle and noticed the shaft of flashing yellow light winking through a gap in the curtains. She nudged them aside and peered into the street.

'Fuck, fuck.'

A long, low flat-bed lorry blocked the road. On its articulated back lay a bulky figure shrouded in polythene, tied down with rope. In front of it a police van idled. A small dinosaur-like digger on Caterpillar tracks dozed on the pavement. A knot of half a dozen men and one crop-haired, muscular woman huddled under umbrellas beside the railings. Bryony recognized the policeman who had been looking for Angel, Marle, and, in a cream trench coat, the bulk of Vernon, holding a bright golf umbrella with Glyndebourne written on it. They were watching a squatting figure in a heavy face mask, the bright white-and-blue lance of oxyacetylene flickered on their slick faces and danced in their shifty eyes, making them look ghoulish. Smoke puffed and eddied through the flame-flecked rain.

'The Visigoths are at the gate.' Bryony reached for the telephone. Engaged. 'Fuck.'

Iona and Charles were still in bed. Iona had taken the day off to make the selection for the sale. The bed was littered with photographs, letters, scripts, notebooks, plates of pastries and figs.

'This one. You've got to let me have Gary Cooper. Please, he'll go for a pouf's fortune.'

'OK, you can have Gary, but I'm not sure about Yul Brynner.'

'Oh, yes. I wonder if they really did dance all night like that.'

'This one of Carmen Miranda with the fruit. That goes with the love-letters, you can sell them together.'

'Can you imagine them doing it? Carmen and Mona, with the blindfolded mariachi band under Sugar Loaf Mountain?'

'Hi, Joe; hi, ma'am.' Lily walked in, dripping.

'Hi, Lily.'

'You no going to work, ma'am?'

'No.'

'Oh.'

'That's a pretty dress, you look really great. I've got one just like it. Isn't it a bit sophisticated for the hoovering?'

Charles silently smiled.

'Don't be mad, ma'am. Joe, you tell her not be mad. It is your dress. Sorry, but this your dress. You should be at work, never notice. Sorry, no damage, just wet. I iron it, you never notice.'

'Lily, just put it back,' Charles said conciliatorily.

'OK Joe,' Lily pulled the thin shift over her head and reached for a hanger. She stood at the end of the bed, naked and gawky, goose-pimples pricked her flat tummy, the long nipples stared hard at the ceiling.

Iona frowned. 'Lily, you're wicked,' and then she laughed. 'No, of course I'm not angry, but ask next time.'

'Oh, ma'am, thanks. You've got such beautiful things.'

'Here, come and get into bed, we're looking at filthy pictures.'

'Iona!'

'She's freezing.'

Lily scampered across the ocelot counterpane like an agile monkey. She slid down between them, smooth and cold. Iona put an arm round the slight shoulder; she lay on her side, Lily's brown body pressed into her. She picked up a picture.

'This is Mona Corinth.'

'Ah, you know Mona? Joe sometimes calls you Mona.'

'Does he now?'

'No, Lily, you just misunderstood.' Charles felt deeply uncomfortable. He shifted and looked at the two women. Iona: pale, elegant, curved. Lily: all angles and joints. It was like a dusty bicycle leaning against a polished cream Bugatti.

'She pretty woman, big tits, big eyes, big everything. Fuck me, you ever do this, Joe?'

'No, Lily, I can't say I have.'

'Oh I have,' Iona cocked her head.

'You didn't? When?' asked Charles.

'Oh, once in Italy, in a hammock. It's not as much fun as it looks.'

Lily shuffled through the photographs, giggling and exclaiming, 'Oh what a stupid hat.'

'It's not a hat, it belongs to the man standing behind her.'

'Oh yeah, what an ugly one. Ma'am, you mind if I ask something?'

'Anything.' Iona's face hovered above Lily's, her breast resting on her forearm.

'Well, when you do blow-job, like here,' she pointed, 'do you use your teeth like that?'

'I don't know.'

'But ma'am, it's a big worry. I always wonder if I do it right, you know. Don't you ever think?'

'Yes, I suppose I've wondered if I do it the same as everyone else. Mind you, I've never had any complaints.'

'No, but Joes never complain. Joes will do it with mud or meat. They'd do it any time, never complain, but I just like to know for me.'

'You're absolutely right, I'd like to know too. Show me what you do.'

'OK. Joe, lie back.' Lily tugged at the sheet.

'No, absolutely not, Lily, no.'

'Oh come on, Charles.' Iona leant over and slapped his hand. 'You've been waggling a lonesome, pining stiffy all morning. This is research, it's a girl thing.'

'Yeah, Joe. Get with it, it's a girl thing.'

Charles sank back onto the pillows. 'I'm reduced to being a sex toy, a marital aid.'

'God, Charles, you're the only man in the whole world who could find something to complain about in this situation. Go on, Lily.'

Lily grabbed Charles's cock. 'He has got a pretty one, hasn't he? I mean compare with those snaps.'

'Yes, it's very elegant, I like it.'

Lily pushed her hair behind her ears and bobbed her head.

'Oh now, you see, that is interesting. I don't do that, I never start that fast. I do a lot more licking and fiddling. Like this. Move over to the other side.'

Charles groaned.

'That look very complicated. Joe, you like that?'

'Yes, Charles, which do you prefer?'

'Oh God, I don't know, I don't know. This is so humiliating.'

'No, Joe, it's all your Christmas and birthday in one go. Oh, Joe, concentrate, you going soft. Here, I know you like this.'

'You use your whole hand, I just use two fingers and a thumb. Under here. This thingy, what's it called, darling?'

'A frenum.'

'Yes. Now close your eyes and see if you can tell who's who.' Iona settled down on her tummy. Lily opposite giggled. The cock, like a microphone between them, listened alertly.

264

'Let make this a contest, missus. Hold on, if he prefer me I get off ironing.'

'You're on. No ironing and I make his life miserable, and if he prefers me you wash the windows.'

Charles covered his face with his hands, crossed his fingers and concentrated. The first round was pretty evenly matched, nip and tuck. The room was riveted. The only noise was the occasional stifled giggle and gasp and a sound like fish snoring.

Just as the contest was coming to a climax, there was a splintering bang, the bedroom door flung open and thudded against the wall.

'Fuckers, fuckers; to the barricades. Man the . . .'

A fabulous vision lurched itself into the room and came to a panting halt at the end of the bed. Everybody stared at everybody in a stunned silence for a moment.

'Fuck, Charles. There must be more to you than meets the eye. What an elegant little penis. Now that's interesting, Iona dear, you use two fingers, I always give it a fist.'

'Bryony, you look, um, extraordinary.'

And she did. Dressed in an ancient, cracked, leather rocker's motor-bike jacket with a dented, rusty, Life Guards' breastplate tied over it with a pair of Wykehamist ties. Stout corduroy land-army jodhpurs were tucked into heavy paratroopers' boots. Around her neck was the flag of the old Southern Rhodesia, tied as a bandana, and a pair of Afrika Korps goggles. On her head was an ostentatious Cossack's wolfskin hat with a black enamel skull-and-crossbones insignia. To complete the ensemble, Bryony had striped her face with bootblack and she carried a pair of driving gauntlets, a plastic Harrods bag and a tartan umbrella. It was a spectacle.

'Sorry about barging in, the door was open, and there's no sodding time to lose. Charles, the week of appeasement has ripped its sphincter sitting on the fence. No more Mr Chamberlain. The Goths have caught us with our cocks in our mouths, the tanks are rolling.'

'What? Who?'

'The Mona Corinth Memorial, man. It's here, they've crossed the border.'

'Good Lord.'

The odd group dressed hurriedly and ran through the rain to the garden. Lily, barefoot, wearing Charles's billowing mackintosh; Bryony, galumphing and clanking, a little way behind in her huge boots. Charles reached the hole in the fence first and gawped in disbelief. Water streamed down his face.

The square was a dark battleship grey, lit by the lazily turning yellow-and-blue lights of the lorry and the police van. The prehistoric Caterpillar digger had ploughed through the hole and across the herbaceous border, churning up plants and crumbling the brickwork, scattering gravel. Its heavy tread cut ragged, slimy lumps out of the lawn. Already the forked bucket was gouging mouthfuls of earth, snorting and shuffling, digging a hole in the middle of the garden. Two men in hard hats with picks were loosening the top soil, ripping turf.

The Mona Corinth Memorial itself had been manhandled and dragged, cutting a long curl of wet grass. Now standing upright, it was twenty feet high, swathed in plastic sheet. Underneath it Vernon, Marle and Peshware, the artist, talked to an official-looking man in an anorak. Marle was handing round cups of beef tea from a Thermos; Vernon was expansively laughing, waving his hand. Constable Spry was slowly busying himself redirecting traffic.

'Christ, it's huge,' said Charles. 'Far bigger than I'd imagined.'

Iona wiped the rain out of her eyes. Charles's shirt hung wetly over her cold bosom. 'Bryony's disappeared.'

'Officer, officer?' Vernon strode across the lawn towards them. 'Constable, keep an eye on these people, they're troublemakers.'

'Morning, Mr Godwin.' The policeman touched his hat.

Charles felt the ball of fury expand in his throat. Choking, he could taste the bitter aloe of injustice, eyes pricking with the bloody unfairness of it. He clenched his fists and shouted,

'Vernon, look what you're doing. Look at the garden, for Christ's sake. Stop it. Stop it now. This is awful.'

'Keep on the pavement, little man. You're trespassing on my influence and good nature.' Vernon threw back his head and laughed. 'Peshware, my dear, this is the little middle-class philistine I was telling you about. Pathetic. But then art has always had to rise above the little people.'

'His girlfriend's got nice tits though,' the artist said in a bass Australian accent, winking at Iona. She was a large girl and stood with her calloused hands on her bulbous, denim-clad hips. She looked like she had been bred to pull gun-carriages.

They turned away and slithered back to the meagre shelter of the statue. The digger was making good progress, its bucket trawling deeper into the guts of the garden.

'You wouldn't happen to know where Mr Tenby is, would you sir?' asked Constable Spry wearily.

'No, I'm sorry, I don't.'

'I know, and you wouldn't tell me if you did. I don't like this job, Mr Godwin, if that's any consolation; I don't like it at all. It was a beautiful garden and Tenby's a good man. It's not what I joined up for, to do the bidding of men like him.' He jerked a thumb at Vernon. 'Arresting blokes like Tenby, but . . .'

'No, Constable, you're right, it's no consolation.'

They both watched the heavy angle-poised neck spastically scoop earth and drop it like a spoilt child in a melting heap on the ground. The pronged bucket punched back into the hole and stuck. The engine throttled and gurgled like a diesel dog with a bone. The cab shook and rattled, blue plumes of stinking smoke coughed. The digger strained, the men with hard hats looked into the hole. One of them cupped his mouth and shouted, 'Roots.' The ancient plane tree's arteries, thick as an arm, wound and twisted in the slime around cold steel teeth. The hundreds of thousands of thin blind veins and capillaries that had darkly burrowed for nourishment since before the square was built shredded. The raw mechanical strained and puffed, whining and farting. The root cables frayed and tore, yet gripped with a desperate, bleak tenacity. Imperceptibly, a hiss eddied across the lawn. The garden let out a long sobbing sigh; leaves quivered and shook. The oldest thing amongst them was fighting for its life.

What happened next must have occurred very fast, but Charles always remembered it as being in slow motion.

A long clear howl rang out above the rain and the diesel chug like Rowland's horn. A bright voice shouted a long 'No'. Over at the far end of the garden a dense curtain of vegetation parted and a figure leapt onto the lawn, behind him a wolf-like dog. Angel ran with an almost ethereal lightness across the greasy grass, each brief footfall sending up a haze of water that hung in the air. His naked body was shiny with mud, the long hair matted and flailing. The rain coursed bright cat stripes across his shoulders and back. He sprinted, hunched and low, a small axe held lightly like a tomahawk. Stendhal jackknifed in the spray beside him, villainous teeth glinting.

Without breaking stride, Angel leapt into the open cab and flew out of the other side, carrying the driver before him. They rolled in the piled mud. One clubbing blow and the man was flung to his feet like a thing of rag and straw. He teetered and then tipped headlong into the hole. Angel turned and, with vicious chops, hacked at the exposed guts of the metal beast. The axe bites rang and the monster squealed, shuddered, bled, belched and died. The cantilevered neck, still buried in the earth, quivered insensibly.

Stendhal had jinked sideways and, baying, aimed himself at the two workmen. The first, seeing what was coming, took a step back and swung the heavy pick in a scything blow. The flat blade grazed the twisting dog's hackles. Its momentum pulled the man round, booted feet skidded in mud and the shaft caught his mate a cracking blow on the shin. They both fell in a heap of curses. With a clatter of foaming jaws, Stendhal hurdled them and raced for the group standing under the statue. They, in turn, took a brief look at the hound and ran in pointless little circles. The dog's genetic memory of sheep herding singled out the marked ram and separated him from the rest. Vernon shrieked in a paroxysm of fear. To the others this was an anonymous horror, simply a genus to be avoided, but for him it was personal. He had seen what this animal was capable of, and the knowledge winged his feet, expanded his lungs, clutched at his pumping black heart. Vernon fled with gay abandon.

As the ripping fangs closed on his coat's flapping tail another figure burst from the undergrowth. So bizarre, so extraordinarily unlikely, that even the dog skidded to stare. Bryony, in all her mad Ruritanian glory, pounded onto the lawn bellowing, 'No prisoners. Take no prisoners,' indistinctly, through the bandana that was tied, terrorist fashion, over her mouth. Straining to see through the fogged goggles, she galloped like a very slow cart-horse towards the statue. At arm's length she held a rum bottle, flames spurting from its neck. Barely gaining speed, but with trance-like remorselessness, she trundled on. 'No quarter, no quarter.' Then, assuming the 1911 infantry manual's recommended stance, she bowled. The bomb flared, guttered and rose into the air, every eye fixed on its parabola. Up, up, up, then turning lazily a moment, down, down, down, crashing with a whoosh at the feet of the Mona Corinth Memorial. Even from twenty feet, Charles felt the warm gust on his face as the petrol exploded. A flame shot out and the kitchen-sink napalm bubbled and stuck. A black hole, like a cigarette burn in a pair of tights, opened and spread. The plastic sheeting, recognizing a distant relative in the petrol, melted into its flailing arms and foul, sticky smoke gushed from folds and creases. The embrace quickened and in an instant the whole totem was a running, dribbling, sticky pall of sickly flame and foul putrid fog.

The fire cast dancing lights over the mud-spattered figures, the rain strobed like dashing fireflies and, slowly, the Mona Corinth Memorial stripped. No shaman of idolatrous Baal, no false prophet of Gath could ever conceivably have constructed a more awesomely hideous graven image. As the nylon rope writhed and unwound, and the sheet lifted and disintegrated, immemorial Mona brazenly flaunted herself. A pair of arms wielded a psycho's kitchen knife and an Oscar. On her shoulders, in place of a head, was a jutting movie camera. Beneath that a second pair of arms were bent, fists closed, middle finger erect, pointing at the sky. Her broad chest sported three pairs of

269

huge drooping breasts with lactating nipples; her stumpy legs, teetering on stiletto heels, were bent outward at the knee like an Indian dancer's. A final pair of hands were holding back the fleshy labia of a gaping vagina, which was gushing a solid fountain of bubbling pee. Or it might have been popcorn. It was difficult to be precise because the whole thing appeared to have been originally sculpted in margarine with a spoon and a trowel. The flames subsided and the monument stood hissing, black treacly chemicals dripping from its dugs. The pall of smoke drifted across the garden into the monotone sky.

'Ah Kali, Mummy, Destroyer, Mona,' the mortified sculptress wailed. The Australian voice jerked everyone back to the here and now. Peshware, crazed beyond creation, aimed a huge power-driving blow at her sternest critic. Bryony took it on the breastplate. There was a clanging crunch and both women fell back to the mud; Bryony wheezing, the sculptor yelping, holding twenty-four cracked carpals.

'That's a blow struck for art,' said Iona.

'Mr Tenby, Mr Tenby,' shouted the policeman. 'You are wanted for questioning, do not move,' and started to proceed, none too purposefully, towards Angel.

Marle, who now found himself next to Iona, turned and slapped her hard, a long swinging blow with the back of his hand. 'Stinking fish bitch, laugh at that,' he hissed as she doubled over silently holding her face.

Charles's anger vanished, the hard choking ball at the back of his throat melted into icy resolution. He saw the girl he loved kneeling in the mire, saw the vulnerable white nape of her neck bent at his feet. He felt nothing cerebral, all the fretting and the either or-ing were slammed shut. He became simply, coolly, purposefully murderous. The first blow caught Marle just under the diaphragm. Behind it were all the years of smiling irritation; a lifetime's unmeant pleasantries. It was delivered with such force that it exploded every sip of air from Marle's lungs, out through his gaping mouth and doubled him over like a folded newspaper. The second and third punches irretrievably smashed £3,000 worth of bridge work and a neat nose with delicate sinuses. Marle straightened, pirouetted on one foot and collapsed face down.

Charles and Lily gently lifted Iona. She was crying, her lip cut and bloody. 'Kill the fuckers.'

'Whatever you say, darling.' Charles kissed her cheek.

The tall man in the anorak now stood in front of them with an expression that managed to be both disapproving and supercilious. 'You people,' he began, as if addressing a meeting. Passing him, one on each side, Charles jabbed two stiff fingers into his astonished eye sockets as Iona chopped with her heel at the side of his knee. His leg gave way. He put his hands to his eyes and so, unfortunately, was unable to guard against Lily's little ironing fist as it bit into his groin. All of this wasn't altogether entirely fair, the poor chap was really only peripherally involved, having come along as an interested observer. But as he was a member of the Arts Council Board, he probably deserved it for something else.

The three of them ran to where Angel was coming to grips with the two hard hats on the mound of slippery mud. Constable Spry got there first, a pickaxe handle skittled his helmet.

'Now you three.'

An elbow caught his temple; his feet shot from under him. Angel tripped and pulled down the workmen. The four of them squirmed and clawed. Charles, Iona and Lily leapt on and tried to pull out Angel.

Within minutes they were a mass of mauling viscous bodies, occasional gasps and screams emanated from the medieval morass. Occasionally a pink mouth would gasp, a white eyeball would roll, as fleshy bits were pulverized, thumbs hooked into lips, boots twisted on fingers. Slithering and butting and clawing, it became difficult to tell where one person finished and another started. Lily yelped as she viciously bit her own hand. The exertions got slower and slower, until they rolled and kicked and flopped like drowning fish in a muddy bucket.

Vernon wasn't having such a good time of it. Stendhal had pulled him to the ground and chewed and ripped off most of the clothes below his waist with hellish intent. One sock and a shredded shirt tail was all the fat lordling could muster for modesty's sake. His thighs and buttocks were a mass of contusions and teeth marks. Vernon lay on his tummy kicking, holding his shrivelled penis and scrotum in one protective palm, whilst trying to bat away the fiendish hound with the other. He was exhausted and stupid with terror.

'Mam, oh Mam. Help Mam,' he whined in a broad Welsh accent.

Stendhal went about his business.

Raggedly regaining control of her breath, Bryony found that she couldn't get to her feet. The weight of her armour and her waterlogged breeches was too great. She did manage to pile-drive the heel of her boot heavily down onto the knuckles of the sculptor's remaining hand, and then, with a lot of puffing and swearing, she achieved the halfway house of all fours. Setting her sights, blowing like a stranded porpoise, she shuffled, like the wheels of justice, towards Vernon, who, glancing over his shoulder, saw what appeared to be the last survivor from Bergman's version of *The Student Prince*'s grim advance.

He also saw something far worse. Shining obscenely pink in the matted haunches, Stendhal had unwrapped the monstrous bitch prong. 'Aah, Mother of God, no.' The shriek whistled across the garden. Vernon tried to scrabble to his feet. Disembowelling, emasculation were eminently preferable to canine rape, but he was too weak and too late. The heavy forepaws pounded on his shoulders, the gin-trap jaws closed on his neck, pinning him to the ground he'd worked so deviously to control. Vernon felt the wet tendrils of hair brush his thigh and the unspeakable thing squirm its nose into his clenched buttocks with a loathsome appetite. It breached the fleshy walls and slid into the moistly, mucused trench, nuzzling for a manhole. Vernon blubbed, he blubbed with a pathetic childlike misery.

Turning his tear and snot-slavered jowls, he found himself staring at the flag of Southern Rhodesia and Mr Toad's goggles. A spark, the merest pinprick of hope; a fellow human being. 'Mercy,' he whispered, 'I'll give you anything. Mercy. Help!' Bryony's gimlet eye regarded the sad man for a long puffing moment, drinking in the full delicious, glorious rightness of it all.

'Fuck you, arse-hole,' she grunted between gritted teeth, and crawled on, until her vast corduroy bottom blotted out his horizon. It began to rock, building momentum.

The mêlée on the muddy hill floundered to a standstill, transfixed by the tableau. The digger driver, who had been lying insensible at the bottom of the hole, stood unsteadily, tugged at a leg and wheezed, 'Hawomb, hawomb.'

With a guttural sigh and a muscular shove, Stendhal sunk up to the nuts into Her Majesty's Privy Councillor. Vernon's eyes bulged. Bryony pulled back her leg, and, with a kick like a hornet-stung mule, powered the steel-capped paratrooper's boot into his face. Unconsciousness came as a blessing. A whispered, 'Thank you,' slithered over his bloody gums.

'Hawomb, hawomb,' the driver hoarsely repeated, then coughed and spat and shouted, 'A bomb, a fucking great bomb.' And there, clearly visible in the pool of ochre water at the bottom of the hole, cradled in the web of roots like the leviathan, was the rusted, steel black tail-fin of a sizeable piece of ordnance all the way from the Ruhr.

'Right, evacuate, evacuate.' Constable Spry staggered to his feet. 'Go quickly to an exit.'

Bodies skidded, picked each other up and ran.

'Not you, Tenby, I want you.' The policeman caught Angel in an arm lock. 'Sorry.'

A slight figure in a muddy tent rose from the ground in front of them and kicked a little heel at the policeman's thigh. 'Run, Joe, Ho Chi Minh Trail, go, go, go.' The constable staggered, Angel slipped his wrist and, turning briefly, caught Lily's eye with a look that spoke more than words, and then he was gone into the mist.

'Right, love, you're nicked. Obstruction.' Constable Spry collared Lily, who simply dropped out of the mackintosh, rolled over and nimbly sprinted away. 'I'm getting too old for

273

this,' said the policeman, neatly folding the coat over his arm and pouring a pint of gritty slop out of his helmet before placing it on his head and proceeding over to the ravaged and supine body of Vernon. 'Come on Your Lordship, you can't lie there. Be a good little Lord and move along now. Move along.'

Birthright walked fast into the square, his photographer trotting along behind. Through the rain a small naked Vietnamese girl, her arms held out at her sides, wrists limp, ran up the camber of the road towards them. The ace reporter stopped in his tracks. 'Strike me, Dave. Quick, get a shot of that.'

The smudger sucked his teeth and shook his head. 'No mate, no point. It's been done.'

Charles, Iona and Lily sat together in the bed sipping oxtail soup and whisky through split and scabbed lips. They were pinkly clean and smelt strongly of surgical spirit and witch-hazel. They had spent an hour dabbing at each other with cotton wool and, like Beowulf's house-carls, telling expanding sagas and comparing bruises. Iona had particularly liked the vanquishing of Marle; she made Charles tell her three times and Lily twice, with illustrations. Smiling crookedly and touching the purple welt on her cheek-bone. Now tired and aching warmly, they ate in silence.

Charles thought that he couldn't remember ever feeling this relaxed; maybe he'd never been relaxed. He was filled with a sense of well-being, that whatever happened tomorrow and the day after would be sufficient unto the day. Odd, he thought, for thirty years he'd believed that the key to contentment, competence and peace of mind lay in books and manners and culture, when all along all that was needed was to punch someone really hard. Godwin's rule: if it's broke, thump it. It may not work, but you'll feel better.

'So, where were we, before we were so rudely interrupted?' Iona put down her bowl and ran her hand down Charles's stomach. 'Who was better then? Lily or me?'

'Well, I'm not sure. Um, I'd almost decided, but I think we ought to have another go.'

'Oh yeah, Joe. Surprise, surprise.'

'Sorry, darling, bust equipment,' Iona touched the side of her bruised mouth, 'and anyway, I think it's my turn. I wonder who's better, you or Lily?'

'Same deal, Joe? Ironing or windows?'

'Down you go, darling.' She stroked Charles's head. 'You'll have to be very, very good to beat him at this Lily. He's a bit of a whiz.'

'Ah, I know ma'am. You no teach grandma to suck omelette.'

Outside the night was lit brighter than day. The square was thick with the growl of army lorries and the gurgle of generators. An aviary of walkie-talkies twittered and shrilled. Heavy boots ran and stamped. The garden tried not to make any sudden movements.

Inside the furniture watched quietly and the big fish snored.

Chapter Fifteen

Charles was woken by someone trying to manoeuvre a lorry;
actually he was woken by someone trying to get someone else,
a deaf, blind, aphasic, stupid someone else to manoeuvre
a lorry.

'Turn the other way, the other way, the other way. Down
a bit, a bit. Lock, lock. Keep her coming. Straighten her up,
straighten her up. Woah, woah. Woah. Right slow, slow, slow.
Stop. Stop. Stop! Bang. Fuck! As you were.'

The reverse gear beeped insistently like a travelling alarm.
Charles lay in the early light and listened. There was something
comforting about having the Army outside in the cold dawn. It
was cold; he only had the corner of a crumpled sheet and his
leg was hanging over the edge of the bed. Beside him Iona and
Lily were wrapped up in each other and the blankets; blonde,
black and ocelot, the sleeping faces, the Prince Charmingly
kissable lips, the languid limbs and curved breasts. Charles
looked and thought that this, the emperor cliché of so many

male mono-erotic fantasies, was not quite what it was cracked up to be. Nice certainly, cosy, better than waking up next to a Welsh stevedore and an adenoidal black-faced ram, but not the pumping, growling priapic goad to lust that men imagined. What one really craved first thing was that universal morning twosome of a loo and a cup of tea. Gingerly he got up, everything ached, everything hurt. He dressed in the dark, pulled on a heavy tweed coat and quietly slipped out of the house.

The rain had finally given up, the clouds lay back exhausted, a damp wind gusted across the garden, rippling the pools of water caught in the ruts and potholes. Charles walked down the middle of the street; it was lumpy and smeared with mud and turf. Most of the army lorries had already left, just one ten-ton truck with a canvas roof was parked under the plane tree. A couple of squaddies slowly threw tarpaulins, planks and snakes of rope into the back. Bending under the plastic, striped police incident tape that was stretched across the hole in the railings, he surveyed the devastation. There was still a strong burnt-chemical smell over everything. The lawn was a thick quag; the neat paths had disappeared under a lake of mud. Most of the herbaceous border was crumpled and crushed, shrubs and bushes lay wilted and flattened, the odd frayed branch slapping drunkenly. The prize magnolia lay broken in a smatter of flowers where a truck had backed over it.

Charles picked his way slowly through the rubbish. He remembered a boy he'd been at school with who had gone on to Sandhurst telling him, with great awe, that the Army had disposed of twelve years of biology and geography prep, had ripped up the first four pages of Genesis and allocated the natural world a barked, binary simplicity. To the Army there were only two types of tree: 'fir and bushy top'. All the vast variegated diversity of the green world was segregated into 'cover sparse or cover thick'. All animals were corralled as 'threat inedible or non-threat edible'. Views were 'fields of fire', horizons notches on a range finder, harmony was 'good tank country'. Armies were like elephants, they didn't live in the world, they made the world live with them. Armies didn't make lands fit for heroes, they made lands fit for armies.

A policeman walked slowly towards him. 'Morning, Mr Godwin.'

'Good morning, Constable Spry. That's a fine black eye.'

'Quite. How are you feeling this morning, sir?'

'A bit stiff, a bit sore.'

'Quite. A terrible shame this, terrible. A beautiful garden.'

'Looks like a bomb's hit it.'

'Quite.'

'Well, of course, in a way it has.'

A young soldier strode over purposefully. He had the eager, open, confident, rather dim look of a subaltern. 'We're just about all done here, Constable. I'll hand over to you as a representative of the civilian power.' He inflected a solid portion of jolly irony into the phrase.

'Mr Godwin. Lieutenant Nick Upham, Bomb Disposal Squad.'

'Good morning, Mr Godwin.'

Charles shook a brown leather glove.

'Well, excitement's over,' smiled the soldier, in that particularly grating, matey-with-dukes-and-dustmen way that's such an intrinsic part of officer basic training in the lean, modern, make-peace-with-anyone military. 'You can all sleep safely in your beds now.'

'That's a comfort.' Charles thought about the content of his own bed. 'Was it really a bomb?'

'Very much so, Mr Godwin, very much so. Five hundred pounds of high explosive, quite tricky, dummy fuse, badly corroded, unstable. Had a devil of a job identifying it. Woke up some bod in the Imperial War Museum. We had an exciting half-hour in the wee small O-hundreds. It's harmless now. Would have made a mess of your garden if it had gone pop though.' He waved a blind hand.

'Yes, I expect it would.' Charles returned the jolly irony with seconds.

'Right, that's me back to Aldershot for breakfast then. The hole's all yours.'

'Thank you, Lieutenant.'

'Don't mention it, all in a day's work.'

Charles and the policeman walked over to the hole, which, as holes go, was impressive. It had, as is the nature with holes, grown considerably since yesterday. It would now have made a comfortable mass grave for a symphony orchestra, with instruments.

'What a mess,' said Charles.

The great spiralling roots of the plane tree were clearly visible, amputated, their white stumps sticking out of the mud. The pair stood and looked, trying to fill it in with the grass and flowers of memory.

'About yesterday,' the policeman said at last.

'Yes?'

'It never happened.'

'It didn't?'

'No, sir. I think this whole business has gone too far. I've spoken to my chief inspector and he agrees. The fracas yesterday . . .'

'That didn't happen?'

'Quite. That must be an end to it. Understand? I added up the possible years in prison if everyone present was charged and convicted, it came to over a century. There were a few cuts and bruises, a couple of lost teeth, but someone could have been killed. It's time to draw a line.'

'I suppose you're right, but it still means Vernon's won. He still controls the garden.'

'Look at it, sir. I mean look at it now. It's like the Somme. I've been to see Lord Vernon in hospital. He'll make a full recovery, you'll be pleased to hear, and Mr Marle. They won't be on solids for a bit though. I went and saw Vernon and said that we strongly suggested he dropped the allegations against Mr Tenby.'

'And he agreed?'

'Well, not immediately. Grudgingly, I'd say. But I put it to him that it had gone further than just the death of a dog;

serious charges were pending, crown court, publicity. Lord Vernon would probably have to have an internal examination, possibly by a vet; photographs for evidence, etc.; identify the dog in court; it might be embarrassing. He agreed in the end.'

'So Angel's in the clear?'

'As far as I'm concerned. Would you tell him if you see him? I don't expect he's got a job, but then there isn't much of a garden.'

'No.'

'Was it really all about this thing?' Constable Spry pointed at the Mona Corinth Memorial, which stood, black and malevolently hideous, at a sloping angle. Kali, Mother, Destroyer, Mona.

'Yes. No, not really. It started about her, but really it was about living with each other and Nature. I think maybe it was about change and progress and power and letting sleeping dogs lie, and Vernon being an arse-hole.'

'All a bit beyond me then, I live in Shepherd's Bush.'

'What's that?' Charles pointed at an object that was stuck at the bottom of the hole. It looked like a semi-submerged haggis. 'Hold on.' He slithered and then jumped down, his feet sunk into the cold mud; he walked with slow steps, crouched, and started digging with his fingers. His back was to the policeman. With an effort and a slurping noise something emerged from the ground. Charles stood and examined it.

'What have you got, sir?'

Half turning, Charles held up a muddy hand. A pair of blank eyes glared up at the sky for the first time in a long time. 'Somebody died.' Charles turned the skull to face him. It grinned, as they do.

'Right, Mr Godwin, put it back, very carefully, exactly where you found it.' The policeman spoke with that battened down, exaggerated calm tone that people use in films when there is a cobra in the children's sleeping-bag. 'Retrace your steps and get out of the hole, now, sir.'

*　　*　　*

Iona and Lily were sitting in their dressing-gowns eating breakfast. Charles kissed Iona, sat down and picked up the coffee pot.

'Guess what?'

'I know, I know, Joe. Lily clean the windows.'

Bryony sneezed with exhausted gusto. A soppet of greasy phlegm mortared across the room and hung off the nose of a gemsbok. 'Aah fuck.' She sunk back into the pillows, hacking, and reaching for a Senior Service. She had been in bed for two days with the wicked stepmother of all flus. If she looked sick, her bedroom was positively terminal. The air was fetid and thick, you could have bottled it with a spoon. It smelt like a Karachi slaughterhouse in August. The floor seethed with limp pornography, hundreds of cigarette ends, sweating tins of luncheon meat, empty rum bottles and chamber-pots slopping with odoriferous, viscous murky human goo.

Charles and Bon Bon had both phoned with offers of soup and medicine, but Bryony had said no, just sweat and sleep was what was needed. Even with her pachyderm's hide she was self-conscious about the squalor. It was time to get up; the flu was hell, but she was in danger of catching far worse from her bedroom. Wrapped in coats, scarves and a Hausa birthing blanket, Bryony opened the door and snorted the air like a coke dealer in the Hall of Mirrors.

'Fucking hell.' She stared at the piece of ragged common that had once been the garden. 'Shit a breeze-block.' The hole had grown again, neater this time, trimmed its ragged edges, straightened its sides, and grown a pseudopodia-like trench and four or five secondary, smaller holes. A handful of what appeared to be hippies or Wessex travellers squatted on the ground gently turning over the mud with trowels.

The warm balm of anger ebbed and flowed, invigorating Bryony's aching bones. She steamed in. Looking into the mother hole, she found a man standing in a grid of string tied to pegs. He was not the sort of man Bryony would have invited to share her sandwiches. He was wearing jeans and trainers, a poncho, and a tooled silver-and-turquoise bracelet. He looked to be about sixty, with a straggly beard and long grey hair, a small portion of which had been made into thin beaded plaits. He might have been a computer Identikit for a record producer who had been murdered at a Bury My Heart at Wounded Knee Native American benefit gig.

'Who the fuck are you?'

'Greetings. Professor Bill Drum. Who the fuck are you?'

'Never mind who the fuck I am, I belong here. What the fuck are you doing in that hole?'

'Excavating.'

'Well go and excavate in your own fucking garden.'

'Sister, this is an archaeological dig. It is out of bounds to the public.'

'I'm not fucking related to you and I'm not the fucking public. I live here.'

'Well, I and my colleagues are working here and what we've found is very, very exciting.'

'I was told you'd found a body. What's exciting about that? If you get excited by bodies, go and dig up fucking Brompton Cemetery.'

'It's an old body.'

'Well how old does a body have to fucking be to excite you?'

'You're being unnecessarily hostile.' Bill smiled, revealing teeth that looked as if they had been found on a previous job. 'The body isn't the exciting bit. What was exciting is where it was found.'

'It was found in our fucking garden, and that was quite exciting enough already.'

'It was found under your garden. Under the garden, on a seventeenth-century midden. Maybe a sixteenth-, fifteenth-, fourteenth- and thirteenth-century midden, yes?'

'Yes what?'

'Yes, you see, it's fascinating. Now look at this.' Bill burrowed into his poncho and produced a small clear plastic bag containing a curl of something hard and brown.

'Are you offering me drugs?'

'This is a seventeenth-century stool, now that's exciting.'

'Shit? Shit! You're digging up my beautiful garden for pieces of shit.'

'Seventeenth-century shit, maybe thirteenth-century shit, maybe Iron Age shit.'

'Anything else? Queen Elizabeth's tampons? George I's condom? The Duke of Clarence's snot-rags?'

'You're being hostile again, aren't you? Archaeologically speaking, this is winning the lottery. Shit doesn't just tell us what these people ate and what they died of, their social arrangements, feast and famine, weather conditions, migrations; we can trace DNA in shit, sift whole generations, economic systems. A shit heap is the *Coronation Street* of time. There is nothing in the world as expressive, as honest, as open, as informative as shit. Shit doesn't lie; shit has no pretensions. It boasteth not; it's not puffed up,' Bill hit a roll, caught a wave, strummed a riff. He held up his little bag, 'This is the fundamental truth of humanity. What's jewellery and ornaments? Lies, snobbery and artifice. What are buildings, temples and houses? Merely the shells and hubris. Coins, treasure? Just money. No, this is the stuff of humanity; this is life's rich tapestry.'

'You're talking utter crap.'

'Sister, I've devoted my life to this shit, I talk of little else. And I've heard every joke and every tired pun. Why people use shit as a euphemism for lies has always escaped me, shit is the ultimate truth.' He put the precious turd back in his pocket. 'Look . . .'

'No, you look, you mad squit-shifter. How many people have lived in London? Millions.' Bryony pointed a QC's finger. 'They all strangle a couple of ounces of darkie a day, don't they? For a thousand years, that's how many biggies. Must be hundreds of millions of tons of the stuff. Dig anywhere and you'd be lucky to find anything else. Enough tapestry of bloody life to cover every wall in the world with the dirty.'

'A layman's misconception, dear. Shit isn't valued. Like the truth, shit is hidden, shovelled into corners, despised, washed away. When I think of how much precious material has been flushed into the Thames, it makes me weep. What we have here may well be the most perfect, undisturbed, complete pile of dung in Britain.'

A young female delver for human clay, with a runic symbol shaved into her hair, trotted over holding a trowel. 'Bill, Bill, look at this. Almost perfect; pointed both ends and a single clockwise spiral. What do you think?'

Bill carefully took the trowel and sniffed. 'Well done, Linnet, love. I think that what we've got here is a modern reproduction.'

Linnet sagged, crestfallen.

'I would say late twentieth century, possibly April, May this year. And if you look carefully here, just underneath the anterior neck, you can see there's a maker's mark. Canine.'

'Good girl, dog shit.' Bryony slapped Linnet's back. 'Someone might have trodden in that.'

'Never mind, love, bag it anyway. We'll see what they're feeding their pets, adds to the socio-economic background. Keep digging, I'll buy you a pint later.'

Linnet gave him a look of utter devotion. If he fancied a bit of after-hours digging, she'd supply the hole.

'Let me get this fucking straight?' said Bryony. 'As far as you're concerned our garden is the cess version of Troy and King Tut's dunny rolled into one, and you plan shovelling old poo into plastic bags for the foreseeable future?'

'Not just in my opinion, Sister. This site is, as of yesterday, an officially designated Heritage dig, Grade I, protected under the act, and you're trespassing.' Bill looked at his muddy watch.

Bryony took a deep breath.

'I'd love to discuss this further,' Bill said, 'but I've got an appointment with Lord Vernon, who has kindly agreed to chair the Steering Committee. I'm sure he'll look after the interests of the local residents, I understand he's a neighbour of yours.'

Constable Spry thoughtfully tapped the cardboard box with a ball-point pen. It had once held apples, so it said, from New

Zealand. Now it contained a body. Evidence. But evidence of what? Evidence of life. A dead body, a dead end.

It was taking up a large portion of his already crowded desk, a femur poked through the folded tabs. Amazing how neatly a body folded away when it wasn't bagged in skin, full of gristle, fat, flesh, beer and oaths. He thought of the bodies he had to manoeuvre every weekend into the cells; heavy, damp, awkward, sticking in doors. Smelly loud bodies that barked his knuckles on walls, ached his back. Take away all the soft, limp, 'my rights' and 'my opinions' and you were left with these neat, hard, beautiful bones that would fit into an apple box that you could put onto a shelf or under a desk. But of course you couldn't. These were the bones of the matter. A sergeant had just dumped them onto the collapsing urgent piles of paper, pamphlets and forms and said, 'Get rid of these, Constable. It's not good for a police station to have skeletons in the closet. I've got enough lifeless sods here as it is.' And he'd laughed.

The forensic surgeon had laughed too, when he'd been shown the body in the hole in Buchan Gardens. 'Whoever did this is long gone, Constable. You'll not get a medal from the commissioner solving this one.' He'd picked up a tibia and turned it over. 'Young, not yet fully grown. Look at the joint. I'd say about fourteen, perhaps a bit older if he was malnourished. A boy, see the ribs. And over a couple of hundred years dead probably, given the depth of the hole. Dig him up, put him in a bag and send him to the lab, and call the archaeologists.'

Constable Spry had said thank you, and done just that. Carefully bagged the bits of body and called the university the Met used on occasions like this.

Their team, led by Professor Bill, had arrived, like the Bomb Squad, with expedient haste and eagerness. They'd leapt from their beaten-up Transit and within a matter of hours the garden was reassigned from amenity to heritage.

Constable Spry considered the box of bones. How quickly and efficiently the retrospective departments of the country worked. Mention the magic word 'Heritage' and its wheels spun, civil servants were pulled from their beds, doors opened.

And he considered the zebra crossing he'd been trying to have painted outside a junior school on his beat. He'd made requests in triplicate, had meetings, left messages and the blind bend was still monotone. A small body had lain there too, about the same size and age as this one, but then he'd only been dead for four years, not long enough to obtain the VIP, jump-the-queue Heritage pass.

'Don't ask questions, Spry. The first rule of police work. Don't ask questions that make things more complicated.'

He pulled the telephone round the apple box and dialled an undertaker.

Yes, of course they could inter a body, that was their job. A skeleton made no difference, except to the pallbearers. Who would pay?

The answer, Constable Spry knew, was no-one. 'No-one,' he said. 'Couldn't you just stick it in the furnace at a quiet moment, as a favour.'

No, that would be illegal. Did he have any idea how many forms were involved in dead bodies?

Actually he did, but he just said thank you for your time anyway.

The next three were the same. The best offer he got was a discount at 300 quid, no box, no headstone, no service, but plenty of decorum.

'Why', the undertaker asked, 'don't you just chuck it on a municipal skip or bury it in your own backyard? Nobody would be any the wiser.'

The constable said, 'Quite,' and thanked him for his trouble.

He looked at the brief autopsy report. Name: unknown. Sex: male. Age: 12–15. Height: 5'4". Weight: unknown. Time of death: 150–200 years. Cause of death: unknown. Remarks: All soft tissue decomposed. Skeleton intact. Three teeth missing. Twisted third anterior rib, probably inherited. Signs of fractured left ankle. Further action: none – unless carbon dating required. The sergeant had written 'No' after this, and initialled it.

Spry tried not to picture the boy, but knew that he couldn't simply chuck his remains in the Thames. He'd lain quietly, for whatever reason, under that beautiful garden for over a century, and whoever he was he deserved better.

Constable Spry tried the London Museum.

No, they weren't interested in an anonymous, two-hundred-year-old Londoner. 'We don't exhibit body parts any more.'

Thank you for your time anyway.

He stared at the telephone. One last shot.

Vernon looked out of his window at the beaten square. He would have laughed if humour hadn't been so acutely painful and risked the intricate needlework that held his face in place. Marle came into the room.

'Well, my God, I don't know how you manage it, dear. Always being so nice to the streams of appalling people we have to deal with.' He had just shown the exuberant Professor Bill and his little colostomy bag to the door.

Vernon shrugged self-deprecatingly.

'My God, what a foul character. Did you see that absurd hair? I'd spend all day in a hole in the ground if I had that on my head.' He joined Vernon at the window.

In profile the two of them might have been choruses in a repertory Greek tragedy. They sported white tape and gauze masks with little pointy beaks. Or they might have been Papageno and Papagena. Actually, what they most looked like was a couple of New York Jewish Princesses after rhinoplasty, the kosher yashmak.

'That's rather torn it, duckie, hasn't it?' Marle watched Bill walk over to Linnet.

He was laughing and miming something, pulling his nose. She started to laugh with him.

'Now, you're the Chairman of the Mona Corinth Memorial Toilet. Look at it, what a mess. And that horrible sculpture.'

'Stephen, your trouble is you lack imagination, and don't say toilet.'

'I like that. I sleep with you. Do you have any idea how much imagination that takes?'

'Things couldn't have turned out better.' Vernon surveyed the squalor below him like a victorious general regarding yesterday's field. 'Heritage. We've been awarded Heritage. That is the gold card of advancement. We're untouchable now. That dirty turd collector is only interested in what's under the garden. We can cover it with anything we like to protect his precious artefacts. I will build an amphitheatre on top of this Heritage. Stephen, we've moved on to something far greater than I'd originally envisaged. I'll get Tod von Bott to design a floating stage in the round. Oh yes, the minister adores him. The money will roll in. Heritage and culture, the unbeatable, the most prestigious twosome in the country, the couple everybody wants to be introduced to. As a garden we would have had trouble building anything, but as an archaeological site that needs protecting, well . . . Stephen, I think this might be my valedictory project, the Mona Corinth Memorial Theatre, home to the world-renowned Vernon Opera Festival.' He drew his hands out, seeing the name, picked in tasteful lights.

'Barnstaple's Ballet,' Stephen mimicked. 'Well, dear, you're a constant education. You leave me sighing with admiration.' Stephen patted Vernon's bottom. 'Woof, woof, duckie.'

'That's not funny, Stephen. You bastard.'

Marle started to laugh maliciously and then the gut popped in his gums and his septum shifted. He held a protective hand to his bloated face. 'Ooh ow.'

It was Vernon's turn to smile fleetingly.

Charles was rearranging his book shelves when the telephone rang. Shuffling books was a constant and endless source of pointless pleasure. He had perhaps five thousand ordered, idiosyncratically, by subject. The telephone rang when he was at the top of a very academic and rather stuffy set of library steps. Hovering above lyric poetry, he was holding the *Iliad* in one hand and the *Odyssey* in the other and wondering, not for the first time, if they didn't actually belong in classic history three shelves down.

'Damn. They'll have rung off by the time I get down, ignore it.'

But the siren's rhythmic call pulled him.

'Hello, Charles. I didn't get you out of the bath, did I?'

'No, down from the towers of Ilium actually.'

'What? Oh. Anyway, Josh here, from Phibbs. I've been digging into your garden problem.'

'Oh yes, well thanks. But events have superseded us, I'm afraid. It all came to a head last week. It's a bit academic now.'

'I gathered you'd had a bit of a fracas, but I think you'll be surprised at what I've uncovered. In fact, it may be unique. I'm rather chuffed. I reckon I may have set a precedent. I'll send all the papers over on a bike, with a layman's synopsis. I've taken the liberty of discussing the content with Lord Vernon's solicitor, in confidence, of course; he's in the next office actually, and he agrees with my assessment. There's not much point in going over it on the phone, but give me a ring if there's anything you don't understand. By the way, how's Bon Bon?'

'Jolly well. Healthy and wealthy and none the wiser, as far as I know,' replied Charles.

'Good, good. And any news of the Mona Corinth stuff?'

'I'll probably need to talk to you in a week or so.'

'Fine, fine. Whenever you're ready. Must dash, got a soul singer waiting outside with a platinum disc. He's given an entire Mormon choir herpes.'

'Don't tell me any more.'

'Oh Christ, no you're right. Speak soon.'

Charles had just reached the top of the ladder when the telephone sang again.

'Hello. Is that Mr Charles Godwin?'

'It is.'

'My name is Angevin. You don't know me, I am Keeper of the Home Seed at the Royal Botanical Gardens, Kew.'

'What a lovely title.' Charles pictured a small ruddy-faced, whiskery gnomic man in a richly emblazoned green tabard, sitting cross-legged on top of an ornamental rockery.

'I enjoy it. You are the President of the Buchan Gardens Garden Committee?'

'An empty title, I'm afraid. Used to be, there isn't a committee any more.'

'Ah well, no matter. You do have access to the gardens?'

'Yes. Why are you calling?'

'Just ascertaining bona fides, Mr Godwin, just ascertaining bona fides. I am in receipt of an anonymous missive that gives your name and telephone number.'

'Oh really. What does it say?'

'Your name and telephone number.'

'What else?'

'That you are the President of the Garden Committee.'

'And?'

'And what?'

'And what else does it say, Mr Angevin?'

'Nothing, Mr Godwin, nothing at all. It doesn't have to. There is an enclosure.'

'An enclosure?'

'An enclosure, Mr Godwin. I can't explain over the phone, but it is imperative I see you, right away. Might I impose on you?'

'Impose away, Mr Angevin. I shall be here all afternoon.'

'Thank you, Mr Godwin. You will be amazed.'

'Do you know, Mr Angevin, I already am.'

Constable Spry let the telephone ring. Patience, he thought, and looked at the memoranda on his desk. A breathless, irritated voice finally answered.

'Yes. St Bertha's, Trevor speaking.'

'Reverend, this is Constable Spry, Earl's Court Police Station. We met briefly.'

'Ah yes, Constable. How can I help you?'

It was a day for ladders. The Rev Trev had been up his trying to get the blessed banners to stay aloft. Now he sat in his moulded chair in the sharing space.

'I'm calling you on behalf of a parishioner who is in need of your professional assistance.'

'Oh dear, Constable. Have you locked up one of my flock? Some poor wretch who has fallen off the straight and narrow?'

'Not exactly, sir. I'm actually trying to get rid of him. He is sorely in need of a burial.'

'A burial? But you'd . . . you . . . you'd need to be dead.'

'He's managed that bit, sir. He's been dead for over a hundred years. It's the young man who was dug out of the garden.'

'Oh yes, well I suppose he was a parishioner. Do we know anything about him?'

'Not much, no, Reverend. Anonymous young male. He'd been thrown onto a rubbish heap, as I understand it.'

'A rubbish heap? Really, Constable?' This piece of information galvanized the Rev Trev. 'A young man thrown onto the rubbish heap as he approached his prime. Do you imagine he was one of the young homeless, killed by an uncaring capitalist system?'

'I couldn't say, sir.' Constable Spry caught the vicar's drift. 'But it sounds as likely as anything else.'

'What a metaphor, Constable, eh? For the degradation we see all around us today; wasted, abused, ignored youth. Don't you think it's a sign, Constable? A terrible indictment of our society?'

'If you say so, Reverend. Can I drop him round?'

'Yes, bring him home to God. I'll prepare the church. How big's the coffin?'

'Aah, he's not got a coffin, I'm afraid. I've got him in a cardboard box.'

'A cardboard box, Constable? A *cardboard* box!'

'Yes, Reverend. But if, as you say, he is one of the young 'omeless, then I'd have thought that was rather appropriate.'

Charles sat at the top of the library steps and read the file from Phibbs. The covering letter from Josh was matey and signed by his secretary. The page of synopsis was clear and profound. Charles read it again and then turned to the wadge of photocopied legal documents and letters that backed it up. Some were very old, all written in that effusively polite, opaque legalese, the blade always scabbarded in soft, weatherproof, formulaic cliché. He sat and pondered and looked out of the window.

A small purposeful man in a gabardine raincoat and a maroon

muffler walked with fast little steps up the street. He was looking at the numbers of the houses. He wore a bowler hat and carried an old-fashioned civil servant's briefcase. Charles tried to remember the last time he'd seen someone wearing a real bowler hat who wasn't trying to sell something or raise a laugh. The chap stopped immediately outside, looked at the door, then he bent, pulled off a pair of bicycle clips, and rang the bell.

'Mr Godwin. Angevin, Keeper of the Home Seed.' He held up a leather wallet with an elaborate identification card, full of stamps and seals and curly writing.

'Come in.'

'I'd rather we got straight over to the garden, if you don't mind. I can explain everything as we search.'

'Search?'

'Search, Mr Godwin. Might I suggest an overcoat? It's come over quite chilly.'

Charles went to get his tweed coat and tried to think whether Mr Angevin had a moustache or wore glasses or if his eyebrows met in the middle, and couldn't. For a man who owned the most beautiful title, he also had the most forgettable face Charles thought he'd ever seen. He might have come across a less memorable one, but then, of course, he wouldn't remember it.

It was cold. The sky was white and the air bit the back of your nose. Thin crystals of ice were growing in the corners of the rutted puddles. Mr Angevin walked quickly through the hole in the railings.

'Might I see this letter?' asked Charles, his breath pluming.

'Yes.' The Keeper of the Home Seed handed him a neatly cut envelope. Inside was a piece of notepaper with Charles's name and address and title, written in capitals, in pencil. Folded into it was a long green-grey leaf.

'This is the enclosure?'

'That's the enclosure, Mr Godwin. I see you are none the wiser. Well, all, I hope, will be revealed. We are looking for the plant that leaf came from.'

292

They were standing in the middle of what had once been the lawn.

'A bit of a mess, your garden, Mr Godwin. You weren't much of a committee, were you?'

'Yes, it is. No, we weren't. Well, we had our moments.'

The shit-diggers stood in their holes and watched the two interlopers like nervous, inquisitive chipmunks.

'Over there, I should hazard.' Mr Angevin ignored them and walked towards the plane tree, and then swiftly got down on all fours and started to crawl, saying, 'Yes, yes, perfect conditions. Very interesting,' to himself.

Charles, feeling foolish, stamped his feet.

They had got almost entirely round the trunk when Mr Angevin gave a girlish shriek.

'Oh, oh, Mr Godwin. Look, look.'

Charles knelt and looked, and there a small plant, flattened in the grass, nestled beside the plane's rocky trunk. It was as entirely unremarkable as its discoverer. Thin, etiolated, green-grey, waxy leaves growing in a small clump.

'There, there's another. Oh I never did. I never imagined I would live to see it.' Mr Angevin was transported. He sat back and looked up at Charles. There were tears in his eyes. 'You'll remember this day for as long as you live, Mr Godwin. You will tell your grandchildren about this day.'

'I'm sure you're right, Mr Angevin, but what exactly is it I shall be saying?'

'This, Mr Godwin, this is the Britannia orchid.'

'Ah, and that's important, is it?'

'Important, Mr Godwin? The Britannia is extinct. Was extinct; vanished from the land that named it. Eighty years ago was the last recorded flowering, in a churchyard in Hove. Until today.' Mr Angevin took a deep breath and blew his nose, then, composing himself, he opened his briefcase and took out a compass, a small pot and a trowel. 'South-east, yes that seems to be about right,' he said, writing in a notebook with an elastic band round it. Carefully he scraped a sample of soil into the pot and stowed it, and then took out a document, quite as imposing looking as his identification. He signed it with a crabby, perfectly legible signature and pinned it to the trunk of the plane tree.

'Can I help you gents?' Professor Bill stood behind them.

'No thank you.' The Keeper of the Home Seed didn't even turn around.

'Let me put that another way,' Bill lowered his voice an octave. 'What are you doing here? This is a site, closed to the public.'

'Indeed it is.' Angevin now turned to face the archaeologist. 'I have just put up a sign saying precisely that. Please don't come any closer.'

The two men stood ten feet apart, their respective trowels held at the ready like duellists.

'I'm not sure who you are, but let me tell you this is a National Heritage site,' said Bill.

'Quite right,' our man from Kew beamed.

Charles stood between the two, feeling uncomfortably like a second. He recognized the look on each of their faces; bad card players who believe they have an unbeatable hand.

'I am Professor Bill Drum from the University of Streatham, Department of Archaeology, and this is an official archaeological dig.'

'I am Mr Angevin, Keeper of the Home Seed, The Royal Botanical Gardens, Kew.' He really did enjoy the title. Even though he was a good six inches shorter than the digger, Angevin seemed to grow as he said it. 'And this is now an SSI.'

'An SSI?' Charles butted in.

'A Site of Scientific Interest, protected under the act. I am empowered in the national interest to claim it for Heritage. It will need to be ratified by the minister, of course, but I have no doubt.'

'The dig that I am overseeing is the most important, the finest midden in Britain. What could possibly be more important than that?'

'The Britannia orchid.' The man from Kew flourished his ace of trumps.

'An orchid? You're pulling my leg. There are dozens of flower shops within half a mile of here that will do you as many orchids as you could possibly want.'

'Not the Britannia,' Angevin said, reverently. 'The Britannia is unique.'

'Look, Mr Posy,' Bill was losing his temper, 'I don't think you're hearing me. What is under this soil is the history, the heart of this country.'

'Well, Mr Droppings,' the little seed servant wasn't going to be intimidated. He protectively stood in front of his plants. 'This orchid is the soul of the country. The Britannia is mentioned by Shakespeare: "Lay me down on banks of myrtle, bowers of maidslipper, on a dark bed where the Britannia orchid grows,"' he recited with a histrionic flourish. 'Herrick, Clare and Southey refer to it. The ploughboys who innocently left their fields in Cornwall to fight for Monmouth wore the Britannia in their caps. Sad, beautiful Lady Jane Grey carried nine flowers to the scaffold, one for every day she was Queen, and gave them to the headsman. The Duchess of Kingston, concubine to four monarchs, had herself painted wearing a garland of Britannia orchids and nothing else. There is strong evidence to show that the Britannia was the emblem of the Athelings, the first kings of a united England. Forget that nasty Arab immigrant, the rose. If any one flower should truly be our national symbol it would be the Britannia. What are your holes in the ground, compared to that? Your dung, and your rubbish?' Mr Angevin paused. 'The Britannia's also supposed to have magical properties, incite passion in the impotent, give courage to the cowardly, cure baldness, barrenness and colic in ewes. Or maybe it gives colic to ewes. No matter. This field belongs to Britannia. Put up your trowel, sir. There will be no more digging here.'

'Now look here.' Bill took a step forward.

Mr Angevin took a step to meet him.

'Gentlemen, gentlemen.' Charles interposed himself. 'Come, come. There must be a way that you can both coexist and the public can enjoy the heart and the soul of Britain.'

The men looked at him as if he were mad.

'Are you mad?' said Professor Bill.

'Insane?' said Mr Angevin. 'You couldn't possibly let the public in here.'

'Absolutely not,' agreed the archaeologist. 'They'd ruin everything.'

'Lavatories.'

'Hot-dog stands.'

'Information centres.'

'Wheelchair ramps.'

'Feet.'

'Bottoms.'

'Picnics.'

'Questions.'

'But . . .' Charles realized that this had all the makings of a stupid question, 'doesn't our heritage belong to everyone? Isn't that the point of all this?'

'Yes,' said Mr Angevin, guardedly.

'And no,' added the professor. 'There are places set aside for the public.'

'Places we've finished with,' added the Keeper of the Home Seed.

'Stonehenge, Wales, the Tower of London, the Lake District. Real heritage is too delicate, too precious, too . . .'

'Important.'

'The public can have videos and books and television.'

'They like it better that way.'

'Oh,' said Charles, lost for words.

Marle watched the confrontation from the drawing-room window. 'We might have a problem with the Vernon multiplex, duckie. Come and have a look.'

Vernon walked to the window. 'Who is that little man with Godwin, upsetting my archaeologist?'

The two men were waving their trowels at each other, breath exploding out of them like blank speech bubbles. Every so often a short thought would come from Charles.

'We'd better go and see. Get the coats, Stephen. I don't want that little git causing any more trouble.'

*　　*　　*

Constable Spry, walking back from delivering his cardboard box at the church, saw Marle and Vernon approach Charles and thought, all things being considered and deterrence being preferable to detention, he might just stand close, by way of a calming influence.

'Good afternoon, gentlemen,' Vernon called, 'and Charles. A bit cold to be taking the air.'

'My word!' Mr Angevin said, under his breath, at the sight of the pair of Venetian Pierrots in identical green Loden coats and fur hats. Professor Bill sniggered.

'Vernon, Marle,' Charles nodded. 'This is Mr Angevin, Keeper of the Home Seed, the Royal Botanical Gardens, Kew.' Mr Angerin touched the rim of his bowler.

Constable Spry proceeded across the lawn, past the shivering hippy diggers in their freezing foxholes. He watched Vernon nod from one to the other with his head cocked, and then watched the blasts of hot air arise from under his mask, like the election of so many popes. The committee man's committee man smoothly oiled and purred. He came within earshot. Vernon was gently taking control.

'Now, Mr Angevin, you know we really are very proud of the work you've done here. I can assure you that your name will be mentioned in some very august places. The Britannia orchid is safe with me. This couldn't be better. How lovely. Flowers, Stephen, do you think we might send a spray to Prince Charles? Anyway, as I am in charge of this garden, for my sins, as Chairman of the Committee, rest assured our national treasure is in safe hands.'

'Vernon, you are mistaken.' Charles spoke louder and with more vehemence than he'd intended.

'I beg your pardon? What can any of this possibly have to do with you? You have no powers here.'

'Neither do you. Neither does anyone.'

'What're you talking about?' Marle sneered.

'It has been brought to my attention that no-one owns this garden.'

'Godwin, you are a cretin and a fool. Of course someone owns the garden. Members of the square, leaseholders and freeholders jointly own it. It's in our contracts. And I run it on your behalf,' puffed Vernon.

'That's what I thought. That's what we all thought, but it's not the case. The houses and the garden were never joined together. We all assumed that they were because they are everywhere else, and because nobody ever thought to ask, but Buchan, the crooked old speculator who built the square, it turns out, never owned the field in the middle. We just all assumed it was ours, we've run it and collected dues for decades, but the leases mean nothing, never have.'

'You're talking utter rubbish.'

'Ask your solicitor, Vernon. The papers have been sent to him.'

'Excuse me,' Constable Spry broke in. 'If it's not the residents' and it's not the committee's, who's is the garden, Mr Godwin?'

'Well, it seems it counts as common land. It belongs, under ancient law, to whomever has been living on it for a year and a day. If nobody lives on it then it belongs to the Crown.'

'Ah well, if that's the case then it's as you were.' Vernon smiled at Marle. 'Belongs to the Crown, under the direction of Her Majesty's ministers, no doubt. I think we can safely assume that we are still in charge, Stephen.'

'Someone does live here.' Charles's voice was as cold as the wind.

'Ridiculous. No-one lives in the garden. Who on earth . . . ?' Slowly it dawned. 'You can't mean that criminally insane gardener. Oh no, no, no.'

'He lives in the hut there.'

'Absurd. It's a tool shed. No-one lives in a tool shed, it's got no plumbing. It would never stand up in court. You couldn't prove it.'

'Well now, Lord Vernon.' The policeman unbuttoned his tunic pocket. 'I might be able to help there.' He extracted a folded envelope. 'I have here a summons for Angel Tenby, addressed to the Potting Shed, Buchan Gardens. It's official, stamped by the court. Now I'm no expert, but I have some experience in these things and I'd imagine a legal document like this would probably prove his address. Especially as it was issued on behalf of yourself, a respected citizen, who gave me the address in the first place.' He pulled it out of its envelope. A sprig of dried leaves fluttered to the ground.

'This is outrageous, we'll see about this. You'll be hearing from me, Godwin. And, Spry, I know your chief constable, I'll have you demoted to ... to ... to ... less of a constable than you are already.' Vernon turned on his heel and, with Marle in tow, strutted off.

The first acrobatic scurry of snowflakes blew out of the north and across the garden. By the time Charles had reached his door it was falling in a steady benediction, gently wiping away the shit, the Britannia orchid, the latrined lawn, the broken border, the furious monument, laying the garden with a clean sheet.

Chapter Sixteen

There is a vale of difference between a victory and a triumph. Victory creeps up and sidles away, it doesn't tarry. Like ripeness, it is an imperceptible moment, somewhere between budding promise and blousy collapse. We recognize victory in hindsight. We look back and say, 'Then, that was the moment. That was the sweetest bite. After that it was all gravity.' Triumph is what victory ought to feel like if we were prepared for it, if someone sent us an invitation, 'Come and win. Come at eight for eight-thirty. Wear decorations.' Victory looks much the same as un-victory: drab, gaping, adrenalin sour. It wears hunched shoulders and slippery underpants. Not triumph though. Triumph looks the part; triumph wears its dress uniform, makes a speech, takes the salute.

You could understand why the Romans invented the idea of a triumph. A general stumbles away from the field, sick to his stomach, frightened to his follicles, and the politico runs out to meet him, slaps him on the back and says, 'Fan-bloody-tastic.

That's the Punic business sorted. You must feel great.' But the general doesn't, he feels like crying. He knows he ought to feel victorious. The politician says, 'We're very grateful for all the work you've done, we'd like to give you something. Anything. What do you fancy? A bit of a drink with the boys? A couple of vestal girlies?' And the general says, 'No, that's what we did to stop from weeping on campaign. You know what I'd really like? I'd like to feel what I should have been feeling when the third cohort's flank held against the odds and the legion of Phrygian mercenaries made their advance, because that was the moment of victory. After that it was all gravity, and I missed it, I was being sick behind a hedge.' 'Sure thing,' says the politician. 'I tell you what, we'll have a triumph. We'll get the third all polished and standing in line and the Phrygians can quick march, and we'll have horns and bells and drums and cheering, and you, in a new cloak, in a chariot being pulled by Carthaginians in chains. You'll feel like a million dinari.' You can see why triumph caught on, it's victory without tears.

Charles went back to the top of his ladder and slowly shuffled and blew on books, without ever noticing that victory had come and gone, its tracks covered by the snow. Years later, in the cheese-rind and leas of after-dinner anecdotage, retelling the death of Mona Corinth, he would recognize that this had been the last time he had ever spoken to Lord Vernon; that this was where the advance of the bright cohorts of plans had flagged and faltered in the first snow of winter. After this, it was all gravity. Charles never basked in the triumph, because, although the victory was complete, it didn't achieve what he'd been fighting for. You can never win back the past, all you get is a say in the future.

Charles sat and read and it grew dark. Iona came home and blew him a Parthian kiss.

'God, what a shitty day. I think it's the cold. Every mad hoarder in the city must have gone into the attic to lag the pipes and found their old Beano albums and Dinky car collections and brought them into me. I'm desperate for a bath and a cup of tea. Would you be a dear and bring me one?'

Charles sat on the edge of the basin and told her about the Britannia orchid and the garden not belonging to anyone.

'How amazing.' She ducked her head under the water and simultaneously lifted her breasts out. 'What's it look like?' She emerged and submerged simultaneously.

'Rather boring at the moment, just leaves. I looked it up. There's a portrait of Lady Kingston wearing a garland of them; little white flowers with bent heads like pixie hats. Sweet. And there's a line in Clare about them.'

Iona went under again and came up, wiping her hair back.

'What a lot of things there are to fill up a day when you don't have a job. Can we have dinner in bed and watch telly? Oh, by the way, I've got the catalogue for Mona's sale, it looks great. I think there's going to be a lot of interest.'

'Good, I'm pleased. I'll go and cook then.' Charles went to the kitchen.

He felt the dull irritation that is the acceptable face of sadness. He felt an absence, he missed Angel. Where had he gone without saying goodbye? How could he leave the garden? How could he leave their friendship? Charles wanted to talk about the day, Angel would have been thrilled by the orchid. He neatly chopped carrots, onion, celery. Iona really only cared about the square insofar as it affected him, as a test, and that was done now. They'd moved on. Damsels send young men on quests not because they want to wear dead dragons' teeth but because they want devotion. And when they're assured of that they want their swains at home, cooking veal chops, not dashing all over the country chatting up other Grails. He sweated the vegetables in a heavy pan and went to close the curtains.

The square glowed in the reflected light, every branch outlined in white. The snow ran elegant curves over the broken border and the great plane tree, vast, magical, weightlessly hovered, pristine and bedecked in the soft Jack Frost night.

Angel stood under the branches, looking up at the window, Stendhal crouched at his feet. He lifted a hand in greeting and beckoned. Charles grinned, a great, bright, white light heart, ear-to-ear grin. He was halfway out of the door, pulling on his tweed coat, when he remembered, and ran back to the drinks cabinet, bumping into Iona wrapped in a dressing-gown.

'Where are you going?'

'Angel. He's back, in the garden.'

'What about dinner?'

'Later, darling.'

'Great. We're together less than three months and already I'm dumped for a night out with the boys.'

The soft snow squeaked excitedly underfoot as Charles ran across the road.

'Where have you been? I miss . . . I was concerned.' His voice sounded muted, deadened, as if the air had turned the treble button down.

The two men stood facing each other. Angel took a step forward and clasped Charles in a great hug. Charles smelt the familiar, rank, sweet, animal scent.

'It's good to see you, Angel. Where have you been?'

'Keeping an eye on things. I had to make a trip. I'm glad the missus let you out. I've got a job for us. Come on, I'll take the whisky. Make a snowball.'

Charles laughed and bent down and scooped snow. It crunched and stuck in that way that is always surprisingly satisfying, that rushes you back to childhood, that you always forget about until you do it. The first snow remembers in a way the first sunny day of spring never does.

'Right, start rolling.'

They pushed the ball round the garden, Stendhal running in big looping circles like a wolf on the steppe. They laughed and slid and joshed each other until it stuck fast and they couldn't push any more. The childish activity, the exertion and cooperation melted the awkwardness, warmed hurt feelings.

'Right, now a head.'

They rolled another ball, and hooting and puffing, lifted it onto the first.

'I haven't made a snowman since God knows.' Charles panted. 'I'd forgotten. We need a carrot and some coal.'

'Better than that.' Angel led the way to the shed. A thin trickle of smoke wafted out of the chimney, warm yellow light flooded through the door. It was as if nothing had changed; the cot was back in its place, the rafters were laden, books and junk slouched and teetered sleepily, the tortoise stove hissed.

Charles opened his mouth but said nothing.

Angel picked up a sack. 'Right.'

Charles made a vegetable face and Angel arranged pine-bough arms and a garland of dried flowers for a scarf. They stood back, all three smiling crookedly. Angel put his hand back into the sack and pulled out a pair of stag's antlers and carefully pushed them into the icy brow. The men sat in the snow leaning against the new totem.

'There's so much I want to talk to you about.' Charles swigged the bottle and handed it to Angel. 'There was a bomb. Of course, you know that, you were here.'

'I always knew about the bomb.'

'But you didn't know about the body. They found a body.'

'The boy. I told you about him. Murdered for love.'

'That was him?'

'Charles, of course it was him, and I know about the heap of shit, and I know about the orchid.'

'How? How did you know? You never mentioned orchids before.'

'They were never here before. That's where I've been. I had to go and get them.'

'But the man from Kew said they were extinct in this country.'

Angel laughed and slapped his thigh. 'Oh, the Keeper of the Home Seed, isn't he something? They are extinct in this country, but they grow like weeds in Southern Ireland. They call them dry-nipple there, because they look like ewes' teats. I remembered them from holidays when I was a boy. You know, countries are funny about Nature. One place a bird can be an endangered species and they're spending millions building nesting boxes, habitats and breeding areas, sending people to prison for picking up cold eggs, and a hundred miles away they're putting up scarecrows to frighten them off and stuffing pillows with them. Birds don't carry passports, they don't care or know what country they're in. The Britannia isn't rare, there just aren't any here. Did you know that there are more tigers in Kent than Ceylon?'

'But I didn't think you cared. You told me that it made no odds what they did with the garden. You told me off for minding. You said that Nature was bigger than all these little schemes.'

'Yes. Well, I thought that until they cut the big tree and I heard the garden sigh. It became personal, and I'd never tell you this, but I couldn't just stand by and see them do it to you. You cared so much. It's not just plants that grow in this garden.' Angel paused. 'Well, it's a weakness, but I'm only human, I'm sorry to say.'

'There is something you don't know.' Charles laid his trump down with a quiet smugness. 'You own the garden, it's all yours.'

Angel snorted. 'You're right, I don't know that because I don't.'

'You do. I had a lawyer find out, it's all to do with the original Buchan; it's complicated. Anyway, it belongs to the person who lives here, and that's you.'

'No, Charles, I don't own it because no-one owns it. How can you own Nature? Men pass money and bits of paper over land as if it meant anything. And they say, "I own these acres, or from this river all the way to that mountain", but all they have is the right to stop other men walking over it. Saying he owns land makes a man a bouncer outside a club he can never join. If anyone owned the garden, that great tree did. It did more to keep this place free than any human. It held the bomb and the body, fought the digger.' Angel drank and wiped his mouth with the back of his hand. 'It died for the garden; it's dying now.'

'The plane tree? Our wonderful tree?'

'Tap root cut. Nothing we can do. It'll take years; trees die in their own time. It'll plant a successor and go.'

'Oh that's so sad. That's awful.'

'No, Charles, it's not sad, it's Nature. It's the way of things. It'll go back to the earth.'

The bottle passed.

'Angel, I wanted to talk to you about the dance. When Iona and I were in the garden, before all this.'

'There's nothing to say.'

'But what did it mean?'

'Nothing, Charles. It didn't mean anything that you can say or think. What does the sound of water mean? It's incoherent, but it's not nonsense. What does a mountain mean? It's silent, but silence speaks. There is a world of meaning that is beneath what you can arrange into thoughts; a whole world. What did it mean when afterwards you went to your woman?'

'That I was lustful, in love.'

'No, Charles, that was the why, and that's not the same. The why of things is not their meaning. Anyway, I know what that means.' He hooked his thumb at the window. 'Your curfew's up.'

Iona had drawn back the curtains and was standing with one hand on her hip, smoking. She was exuberantly naked.

'Oh God, I'd better go.'

'Yes, you'd better.'

'Angel, are you going to stay? Are you going to stay now there's no garden? Except for this orchid and all these holes, and there's no money.'

'Me, the plane tree and him', Angel patted the snowman, 'will stay here until we melt into the earth. By God, she's got some tits on her though.'

Charles got up and gingerly patted Stendhal. He walked back across the snow. He knew nothing would be quite as it had been. He and Angel would always be friends, but something had died in the destruction of the garden, and something else had grown. He'd fallen in love, he was moving on. It filled him with sweetly painful melancholy.

Iona leant against the wall in the hall. 'About bloody time. What have you two been doing? Building snowmen and giggling about sex? Boys!'

'Sorry, darling. I'll cook supper.'

'Too late. I had a bowl of cornflakes and a bottle of champagne. I'm drunk, take me to bed.'

The Mona Corinth sale was a great success. Gandolfs was packed with the sort of people who rarely go to sales and consequently bid far too much. There were a couple of film crews and half a dozen reporters and photographers. Mona had made full pages in all of the papers. The broadsheet press in particular had managed to run pictures of her on three or four consecutive days over thinner and thinner stories. It's a rare treat for the quality press to find a pair of white woman's bosoms that they can print without obvious prurience.

A blown-up studio portrait of Mona's face hung over the lectern where Iona stood arranging papers and giving instructions to the porters. The huge black-lashed eyes looked out across the audience, her final sell-out performance, standing-room only. She didn't appear surprised, or pleased. She was a star. Her broad lips turned down, not so much in a sneer or disapproval, but in an expression of expressionlessness. A face that defied interpretation or understanding. She glassily refused to focus on the sad remnants of a lonely life, the chipped and rickety furniture, the stained rugs and ugly mementos.

Charles stood at the back and thought that even though he had read and seen the most intimate moments of this woman's life, he still couldn't match them to this face. She'd have been good at bridge.

Padua Pocket came and sat, in a very short skirt, at the front with a lot of hemming and hawing. She bought Mona's make-up box with Bubba Yukon's money. When the gavel dropped she leapt to her feet and one of her nipples made a perfectly timed bid for recognition. What a trooper!

There was a tense duel over the painting of Diana and the Dobermanns between someone on the telephone and a gaunt Ralph Pistol. When the hammer fell it was Pistol who had his hand in the air, having paid three times the estimate. He sidled out immediately afterwards and passing Charles in the door, said, 'You can tell your girlfriend that that's one up to me. They thought that Corinth's name would inflate the price and they didn't do their due diligence. That hideous painting is by Christian Schad, German. I have a hunch it belonged to Goebbels. When I find out how Corinth got it, it'll be worth half a mil. Are you interested in anything? No, don't tell me. But let's have a drink soon.'

Charles hadn't planned on bidding, but he found himself raising his hand to a cardboard box of junk for a ludicrous £150. A small voice had called indistinctly across the room. When Iona marked it down to Mr Godwin, he searched the catalogue. 'A collection of miscellaneous items, including a glass globe musical box and snowstorm over Paris.'

On the same day as the sale, the Rev Trev held the memorial service for the young man's skeleton. It wasn't well attended, there were no notables, living or dead, to attract the vultures of the memorial society. The sparse congregation huddled frostily. Bryony sat at the back with Bon Bon, who had spent a miserable morning racked with indecision about which function to attend, finally leaving it so late that she just managed to run, precipitously, into the church on a pair of fuchsia stilettos that had looked sensational in *Vogue*. The organ was starting Ralph McTell's buskers' favourite, 'The Streets of London', a tune that must have made more money and paid fewer royalties than any other this century. It rather missed the ponderous echo of an underground tunnel. Constable Spry was there, smart in his dress uniform with white gloves. Dr Spindle acted as pallbearer. The Rev Trev had thought it would be a nice touch to keep the bones in their cardboard box, add emphasis to his homily on homelessness and vagrancy and the general beastliness of people with spare bedrooms.

The lad was finally laid to rest under the aisle with a brass plaque that read, 'The Unknown Dosser. In Righteous Memory of the Homeless and Poor of Kensington and Knightsbridge. While you sleep in your warm bed, think where your brother lies.' As the box was lowered the organ played a clever arrangement of 'All I Want Is A Room Somewhere' from *My Fair Lady*.

Unnoticed, beneath it, was an old lead coffin. The owner's tablet read, 'Emma Lewis, Spinster of the Parish, died 1860 aged 87. Daughter of George Lewis. She strove tirelessly for Christ and the poor.' Sad Emma, who after a blameless life devoting herself to good works, was now, at last, united in death with her only blot, her once-in-a-lifetime lover.

The bell tolled over the muffled garden and Angel dropped two small corn dolls with rattling tummies, tied face to face with stalks of grass, into a midden hole. He pushed the hard salt-and-pepper earth over them with his foot, muttering something into the wind.

Like an initially welcome guest who then starts moving his books into the spare bedroom, the snow stayed and stayed. Days whitened into weeks, weeks greyed and froze into months. The square tried to send it to Coventry, tried to shovel it away, and finally tried to poison it with grit and salt, but winter squatted with a grim determination. The weather-vane frosted hard to the north-east; the bone-snapping wind hurried on bandaged feet from a distant tundra, carrying the faint odour of cabbage soup and pepper vodka, hunching everyone into a fatalistic gulag depression. The ground changed from greeting-card splendour to chopped-hard-boiled-egg white, sootily airbrushed by choked exhausts. The cold seeped into the ground, cauterizing and dessicating the green things. Only the trees stood inert and immune. The sap fell like a thermometer. In the earth the seed and the spore dreamlessly slept, awaiting a kiss.

One Monday lunchtime, weeks after the Mona Corinth sale, Iona went shopping. She was just going to have to get a warmer coat. She'd put off buying a serious coat for as long as possible. Coats were inexplicably tied up with childhood, with nagging up warm, with immobile arms and the slimy salt stripe of unwiped snot. She'd left overcoats in the closet with flannel nighties and mutton-frill collars when she'd left home. Grown-up city girls didn't wrap up warm, they took taxis. But the thigh-length, bottle-green, fun-fur number just wasn't cutting the ice. So she hurried with short, slush-careful steps along Fulham Road towards Sloane Street for something with a bit more length, a bit more weight, a bit more Solzhenitsyn.

She passed the Tottie d'Or, a restaurant favoured by ladies who got their coats direct from Nature. She looked in the window and saw a man remarkably like Charles. Her stomach gave a little lift, she was pleased. Even after several months, the sight of a chap who looked like her boyfriend created a stir in the gut. It's reassuring for a girl to have the peristaltic parts endorse the choice of the cognitive. And then, with a chilly surprise, she realized it was Charles, sitting alone at a table for two. What on earth was he doing here, this wasn't his sort of place. He never had lunch out, or at least she assumed he never did; he never mentioned it; he never asked her. She moved away from the window, walked a few paces and stopped indecisively. 'Hell.' She went in and stood in front of Charles's table. Someone had filled the empty seat opposite. There was a handbag, expensive, conservatively fashionable. He was reading stapled sheets of typed paper. 'Thank you,' he said without looking up.

'Pudding or condoms, sir?'

He hastily got up, leaning across to kiss her. 'Darling, what a coincidence. Are you lunching here?'

Iona laser-scanned his face for guilt or discomfort, but could make out nothing beneath the usual camouflage of public unease. 'I saw you through the window. Who are you tête-à-têting with?' She immediately regretted the direct question.

'Sit down, have a drink. Are you hungry? I've got a secret, I was going to surprise you.'

'Oh, you were? Let me give you a little advice. The only surprise a girl appreciates is one that she's wrapped herself.'

'Shssh, she's coming back.'

Iona turned and watched the girl walk across the restaurant; tall, curvy, broad comfortable chest, high hips, neat ankles, lots and lots of curly reddish-blond hair. Handsome. Eyes just touching thirty. A big, meaty, chin-dribbling spare rib of a woman.

'Iona Wallace, Puss Lavia.'

The table was full of smiles, like a cannibals' pot-luck picnic.

'Iona. What a surprise. Charlie has just been telling me all about you.' Puss spoke with a voice that was Home Counties, muck and gravel. 'I'm very excited about our project.'

'Yes?'

'He's quite a catch.'

'Isn't he just.'

'Um, er, Puss. I haven't actually told Iona about anything.'

'No, Puss. Why don't you fill me in?'

'Oh heavens, what must you be thinking?' A little tinkle of cannibal laughter. 'Charles has just agreed to edit Mona Corinth's letters and diaries and write a steamy biography and, happily, he's going to let me handle him.'

'Puss is my agent,' Charles added swiftly for the sake of clarification and the crockery.

'Aaah, aaah. I thought you'd be impressed. Please. Ow, ow.' Iona twisted Charles's nipples as if she were winding a stiff grandfather clock. She was sitting on his stomach with his arms pinned under her knees. They were in bed.

' "I'm so excited to be handling Charlie, he's such a catch." ' Iona mimicked. ' "We're going to auction the book, but then you'd know all about knocking things down to the highest bidder. Aren't you in antiques?" Bitch, and you bastard. Simpering and innocent. Bastard.' She dug in her thumbnail. 'And hypocritical bastard. What was all that shit you gave me about not trawling in dead people's knicker drawers? And the hard time you handed out to Toby about Lord Kitchener? You . . .'

'Iona, please. I thought about . . . about what you said about it being important, culturally significant, and I'm intrigued by Mona, and I thought I'd see if I could do it honestly, with care. I want to know about her, I want to understand how she lived that life, went for so much excess, and then just walked away, apparently untouched. Between Mona and you, you changed my mind.'

'Bollocks. Puss waggled her bits at you and your mind turned to fudge sauce and KY jelly.' Iona let go. 'God, Puss! Who can walk around with a name like Puss? Charles, why couldn't you get a short American man with a paunch and dandruff called Dale?'

Charles heaved with his hips and turned her over. He lay between her thighs, his arms hooked behind her knees. He looked down at the perfect round breasts and the flushed face, felt the taut stomach where it pressed against his, and the elegant cock, now a creature of habit, nuzzled.

'Hey, hey, hang on. What happened to my foreplay?'

Charles leant forward to kiss her and slid inside.

'Oh, I see, that's how it is. Cat's got your tongue.'

Through the long winter the botanists and archaeologists fought over the garden. The letters and memos and minutes swam internally through the lymphatic corridors of Heritage, until, exhausted, they came to rest in quiet, nodal, cul-de-sac, pending trays. A muttered compromise was reached: the midden would remain unexhumed but protected for the light of some future day and the Britannia orchid's habitat would be preserved by rigorous inertia for posterity. Neither addition to the national coffer would be made public in case the public actually showed a passing interest.

Angel, without ever applying or filling in a form, became a civil servant. He was nominated as caretaker for all that lurked under and grew on the garden, thus neatly avoiding a tortuous examination of ownership and rights.

Burke, able fellow that he was, was wrong when he said that all that was needed for evil to triumph was for good men to do nothing. Masterly inactivity often does the best of all, and the beauty and the luck of it is that you don't have to be good or clever or even moral to practise it.

In a small village high up in a German canton in Switzerland, Lottie, Mona Corinth's dresser, housekeeper, companion and only human friend, walked the mile to the post office to collect her post. There was a letter from England. She took it to a café and sat at a corner table, sipping a hot chocolate. She turned it over and over. The paper was headed Phibbs and Co. The cheque fluttered out and lay face down. The message was short. 'Please find the enclosed payment relating to the Mona Corinth will being the proceeds of sale of goods and publishing rights. Any enquiries contact Jocelyn Draper.' She turned over the cheque and stared at it for a long time; then she quietly called the waitress and ordered a slice of sachertorte.

The Mona Corinth Memorial Garden, with or without amphitheatres, died in the snow. Vernon's scheming was no match for a small white flower. He didn't mourn long for the project. Other tempting geegaws took its place in the window that he'd spent his life pressing a fat little nose up against. All of them in the end eluded his grasp. He was a man who would go to his maker having achieved almost nothing, despised and lampooned by everyone who had ever shaken his clammy hand, and by many who hadn't. His pinkly scrubbed thick skin remained impervious. Craving advancement, he weaved plans of baroque ingenuity that invariably unwound, leaving him back where he'd started, his gaze forever fixed on the next landing.

It would be neat, right, by the conventions of fiction, to have organized a great comeuppance, a final public humiliation for Vernon, although perhaps an alfresco rape by an Alsatian went some of the way, but men like Vernon, and there are many, rarely get their just desserts in this world. If it's any consolation, then it's also true that they never get what they think they really deserve either: deference and respect. The failure to give a grateful world the Barnstaple Opera Festival did grate occasionally though, whenever he looked out of his window and saw the lopsided bronze harridan of the Mona Corinth Memorial, with its thickly gushing vagina and its mono-eyed, Ariflex head pointing up at him. A constant teasing joke at the expense of his remorseless quest for public approbation.

* * *

On the first Saturday of the new year Charles handed a hungover Iona a set of keys and led her next door. He had tried to write Mona's biography on the table in the window of his drawing-room, but the furniture kept interrupting, asking questions, gossiping. He couldn't work with them and he couldn't get rid of them.

'Surprise.' Charles kissed Iona.

'I warned you about surprises. Don't tell me, you've taken on a peroxide estate agent called Nymphet with a forty-inch Wonderbra.'

'We need somewhere bigger. I've bought the flat next door.'

'Bought it? You're bonkers. Have you been testing my bath-water with a pregnancy kit?'

'We can knock a hole through the wall. I can have a study, you can have a sewing-room.'

'Fuck off. We can both have an office. But I want to decorate. All on my own?'

'Absolutely, I won't say a word.'

'Heaven. It'll have nothing in it older than I am. Your manners will be the only bloody antique thing allowed.'

Spring fell on the garden with gusto. Early in April the weather-vane creaked round to the south. The sun shone, immature clouds did their scudding. The crusty slush finally lay back and seeped away. The ground, gutted and soggy, lay sunning itself for a week, and then like prisoners who find that the guards have left, bulbs and seeds rioted. Their tiny, hidden energetic memories stretched and pushed for the light. The earth was furzed with simple green shoots; blackened twigs sprouted clitoral nubs. The soil heaved and vibrated with the great spring offensive of Nature.

The old order was dead, a new cacophony, a free-form chaos, raced to take its place. The once neat, gaol-striped lawn swam with mugwort, sneezewort, buntweed, coltsfoot, feverfew, tansy, groundsel, burdock and clover, petty spurge, caper spurge and dog's mercury. The gravel path scattered under the new families of airborne immigrants; the thistles: meadow, woolly, musk, slender, weltered, cabbage and creeping. The dandelions and daisies: red-veined, cat's-ear, hawk-bit, mouse-eared. Primroses formed ghettos; ox-slip, yellow loosestrife and creeping Jenny, sweet dog and yellow wood violets lay claim to shady corners; nettles, knotgrass and bastard toadflax, swarmed in to reclaim ancient ground. The vast thrusting of green things pulled apart brick and mortar, wound and choked iron and wood.

By summer the garden was a wild meadow of snapdragons, foxgloves, speedwell, teasle, harebells and peach-leaved bellflowers. Saplings elbowed their way through the warm knotted undergrowth. Goat willow, bog myrtle, alder, hornbeam, witch elm, holly, oak, ash and the tree of heaven. The urban indigenous inhabitants were strangled in their beds or went native, reverting to older root stocks. Roses became simple and leggy, fuchsias crawled, carnations buttonholed their neighbours.

Angel moved amongst all the industry with whispering encouragement and his hands in his pockets. The garden tools, the cruel metal instruments of slavery and oppression, collected dust and woodworm in the shed. The roller and mower with its vicious blades rusted in darkness. The garden grew for joy and freedom and for its gardener. The green stuff adored him, showed off for him, rubbed itself against his legs, flung seeds into his hair, stuck burrs to his clothes. The only thing in the garden Angel needed to take in hand was the Britannia orchid, which didn't get on, was sickly, backward, and had to be propagated carefully in mossy pots.

The large hole that had contained the boy filled with water and made a small pond that blackly bore puselanes, duckweed, biswort, crowfoot, meadowsweet, yellow iris and willow-herb.

Ivy and hop and wild fig sucked up the Mona Corinth Memorial and hung in lazy encarpa, and, over it all, the great London plane finally went about the business of planting a successor. One half of the great span was still in winter, the knotted branches unleafed, naked and flaking like a stroke victim palsied into a demi-death. The pigeons still came to fuck in its airy wyndes and alleys.

And now other birds and beasts quietly stole into the lawless garden; flocks of tits swarmed in the bushes, thrushes and blackbirds shouted from the railings. The ground rustled with mole and mouse and vixen and vole. Grass snakes coiled in old woodlousey bark. Toads and newts played Grandmother's Footsteps on the slithy banks, a kestrel hovered, and in the dark, the weird creeping nightjar sung its half-mad rambling to the tawny owl.

One pollen-thick, dragonfly-hot day in early June, Lily sauntered along the cracked pavement on her way to clean Charles's flat. Angel and Stendhal were lying in the sun on a bank of wild flowers. She stopped and looked, regarding them darkly through her sunglasses. 'Hi Joe.'

'Come into my garden, Lily. Lie in the sun. Eat a peach.'

She looked over at the shaded side of the street and work and then back into the bright garden and the brown-chested gardener.

'Yeah, why not, Joe.'

The breakfast things congealed in the sink that day.

Lily stayed. She finally got what she had stopped looking for. She had come to the end of the refugees' trail and found a refuge, a home, in this small wild acre with this silent wild man. She grafted herself on to new roots that became hers, not borrowed. She reverted to simple peasant stock. Occasionally one might catch a glimpse of her, slim, bare-breasted, collecting apples, or plaiting garlands.

She still went and cleaned for Charles twice a week; the money was useful. He'd find her sitting in the kitchen, her hair a bird's nest of knots and leaves, laughing with Iona. The tinny, staccato, singsong voice softened and lightened. Once in a while, Bryony, taking an evening stroll, would catch Angel and Lily lying in the grass, her arms round him, slowly wanking the gnarled brown penis into a pot of Britannia orchids.

Bryony would quite often walk in the garden on warm evenings. She'd take a bottle and a couple of pornographic magazines and a shooting-stick. The stick had become a necessary part of her life after a fall in the hard winter. She looked much older now, still biltong-tough and sour-tongued but slower and more deeply lined; the ramrod back bent at the neck. Through the long summer she became curiously close to Lily. Sometimes Iona would join the two of them in the potting shed and they'd get filthy drunk and sing and laugh at photographs of naked black men. After the battle of the garden had been won, Bryony restlessly cast around for something else to aim her voluminous anger at. After unsatisfying fracas with the RSPCA, the Commission for Racial Equality and the woman three doors down who did aromatherapy, she set her big guns on God and devoted a good part of her time and astringent energy to making the Rev Trev's life a living hell. She attended every service and sat big-hatted in the first pew and bellowed from Cranmer's prayer-book contrapuntally across Trev's free-form services. When, finally, the tearful vicar had begged the bishop to ban her from the church, it was gently pointed out to him that even in the modern Church of England you couldn't really excommunicate parishioners for reading the *Book of Common Prayer* during services.

Bon Bon, whose marriage had secretly done so much to save the garden from cultural heritage, didn't remain to see the result. In the middle of the foulest week of February, Belman suffered another bout of wanderlust and bought a Victorian vicarage outside Dublin from a photograph in *Harper's and Queen*. Bon Bon sighed and packed up the Buchan Gardens house. Actually, Ireland suited her. The Irish were without snobbery or side and she finally felt at home. Belman fished and drank and was lionized and, on Josh Draper's recommendation, tore up his rock-opera will and tearfully told Bon Bon about his other family. She reacted with saintly equanimity, sighed some more and added this trial to the laden laundry basket of trials that were her lot. She insisted that they had the children to stay and then spent a nervous month decorating and redecorating rooms for them.

If you were a pigeon, and two years on you decided that, considering what a nice day it was, you might go and see how the gang were banging up at Buchan Gardens, you would still find the plane tree there, quite bald, bleached white and hollow. At its base, in the bole of smooth roots, you might notice a rush crib with a little naked baby playing with a posy of white flowers. It has a mass of black hair and the most beautiful blue slanting eyes. There'll be a large dog not far away and perhaps the mother will be sitting by the pond, laughing with a blonde lady who has taken off most of her clothes. Upwind, a couple of men fiddle with a fire and sausages and pass a bottle. You might notice that the child has round its neck an ancient gold torque with carved heads on each end; a final bequest from a dying king.

But none of this will interest you much. As you circle the square and climb up over London, you will see that there are dozens of gardens like this, each with their babies and dogs and women and chaps poking fires. And that the little patches of green are stitched together in a haphazard counterpane, much as they have always been, to make an island that stretches out over the horizon to the sea.

Starcrossed
A.A. Gill

'BRITAIN'S FUNNIEST AND LEAST POLITICALLY
CORRECT AUTHOR'
Daily Mail

Like Byron, John Dart, poet and bookshop assistant, wakes up
one morning and finds himself, if not quite famous, then the
next best thing: in bed with someone famous.

'REVERBERATES WITH LOW HUMOUR AND LURID,
EXTRAVAGANT SEX . . . EVERY PAGE EXPLODES WITH
THE GAUDY COLOURS OF EXOTIC METAPHOR'
Independent on Sunday

'HIS WRITING IS LIKE A NUDE BY LUCIEN FREUD:
UGLY, BUT HUMAN AND TRUE'
Claus von Bulow, *Mail on Sunday*

'GENUINELY ENJOYABLE, OFTEN FUNNY AND
SOMETHIMES TOUCHING'
Sunday Telegraph

'FIRING OFF HIS CAUSTIC, CYNICAL OBSERVATIONS
AND WITTY EPIGRAMS, HE COMES ACROSS AS A
MODERN DAY OSCAR WILDE, A CURIOUS MIX OF
NAKED AGGRESSION AND HIGH CAMP'
Daily Mirror

'HIGHLY RECOMMENDED'
Sunday Express

'THE WIT AND BRAVURA ARE WHAT ONE EXPECTS
FROM HIM, BUT HE HAS ADDED A BROADER
EMOTIONAL RANGE AND ENGAGING CHARACTERS'
Lynn Barber, *Observer*

'CAPTIVATING STORYTELLING PEPPERED WITH
PERCEPTIVE HUMOUR AND THE OCCASIONAL
PHILOSOPHICAL GEM. THIS IS A.A. GILL AT HIS BEST –
FUNNY AND IN FULL FLIGHT'
Sunday Business Post, Dublin

0 552 99751 X

BLACK SWAN

A SELECTED LIST OF FINE WRITING
AVAILABLE FROM BLACK SWAN

☐ 99830 3	SINGLE WHITE E-MAIL	Jessica Adams	£6.99
☐ 99946 6	THE ANATOMIST	Federico Andahazi	£6.99
☐ 99822 2	A CLASS APART	Diana Appleyard	£6.99
☐ 99842 7	EXCESS BAGGAGE	Judy Astley	£6.99
☐ 99619 X	HUMAN CROQUET	Kate Atkinson	£6.99
☐ 99832 X	SNAKE IN THE GRASS	Georgia Blain	£6.99
☐ 99824 9	THE DANDELION CLOCK	Guy Burt	£6.99
☐ 99853 2	LOVE IS A FOUR LETTER WORD	Claire Calman	£6.99
☐ 99686 6	BEACH MUSIC	Pat Conroy	£7.99
☐ 14698 6	INCONCEIVABLE	Ben Elton	£6.99
☐ 99770 6	TELLING LIDDY	Anne Fine	£6.99
☐ 99751 X	STARCROSSED	A.A. Gill	£6.99
☐ 99759 5	DOG DAYS, GLENN MILLER NIGHTS	Laurie Graham	£6.99
☐ 99609 2	FORREST GUMP	Winston Groom	£6.99
☐ 99847 8	WHAT WE DID ON OUR HOLIDAY	John Harding	£6.99
☐ 99796 X	A WIDOW FOR ONE YEAR	John Irving	£7.99
☐ 99887 7	THE SECRET DREAMWORLD OF A SHOPAHOLIC	Sophie Kinsella	£6.99
☐ 99037 X	BEING THERE	Jerzy Kosinski	£5.99
☐ 99748 X	THE BEAR WENT OVER THE MOUNTAIN	William Kotzwinkle	£6.99
☐ 99807 9	MONTENEGRO	Starling Lawrence	£6.99
☐ 99876 1	TALES OF THE CITY	Armistead Maupin	£6.99
☐ 99874 5	PAPER	John McCabe	£6.99
☐ 99762 5	THE LACK BROTHERS	Malcolm McKay	£6.99
☐ 99905 9	AUTOMATED ALICE	Jeff Noon	£6.99
☐ 99718 8	IN A LAND OF PLENTY	Tim Pears	£6.99
☐ 99667 X	GHOSTING	John Preston	£6.99
☐ 99783 8	DAY OF ATONEMENT	Jay Rayner	£6.99